Hermann of Reichenau

HERMANN OF REICHENAU

A SPIRITUAL NOVEL

MARIA CALASANZ ZIESCHE

Translated by
Brian McNeil

A Crossroad Book
The Crossroad Publishing Company
New York

The Crossroad Publishing Company
www.crossroadpublishing.com
© 2017 by The Crossroad Publishing Company

Crossroad, Herder & Herder, and the crossed C logo/colophon are
trademarks of The Crossroad Publishing Company.

Original publication: *Die letzte Freiheit. Hermann von Altshausen,
Mönch der Reichenau, Verfasser des "Salve Regina."* Rheinbach near
Bonn: Schwestern Unserer Lieben Frau, 1966. Translated from the
16th ed., Beuron: Beuroner Kunstverlag, 2012.

Library of Congress Cataloging-in-Publication Data available from
the Library of Congress.

ISBN: 978-0-8245-2084-7

Cover design by George Foster

Books published by The Crossroad Publishing Company may be
purchased at special quantity discount rates for classes and institu-
tional use. For information, please email info@crossroadpublishing.
com.

Printed in the United States of America

"I have been glad to be alive
despite my sickness."
—Hermann of Reichenau

ABOUT CROSSROAD NOVELS

CROSSROAD NOVELS capture stories of the ultimate adventure—seeking and daring to follow the spirit of life. While featuring a diversity of authors and styles, CROSSROAD NOVELS offer rich narratives from the lives of great figures of faith and how they face questions of love, suffering, redemption, death, and the last hope for eternal life. CROSSROAD NOVELS are as thrilling and enjoyable as they are meaningful.

ABOUT THE NOVEL

The story of medieval scientist, historian, Benedictine monk, and quadriplegic Hermann of Reichenau is profoundly uplifting and an encouraging example that life can be lived to its fullest despite a severe handicap.

One of the most brilliant minds of the Middle Ages, Hermann of Reichenau was a severely crippled monk who, though he was marginalized and even mistreated by his fellow monks, is celebrated for his groundbreaking scientific work and the beauty of his musical compositions, among them "Salve Regina," a song Catholics sing to this day during their official evening prayer in monasteries and churches around the world.

A quadriplegic since childhood and brought to the monastery at an early age, Hermann lived at one of the most influential and powerful medieval monasteries, situated on a small island in the Lake of Constance on the modern-day border of Austria, Switzerland, and Germany. As he grew and studied, investing his hope in the medical promises of the time to alleviate his physical ailments, his days meandered between deep despair and his growing faith. When his music was played and sung, an exhilarating joy entered the whole community, and the monks came to see the extraordinary spiritual strength, beauty, and true happiness coming from the weakest among them. A deeply encouraging book about the life of a man who overcame numerous obstacles, this work captures the grandeur of the human spirit.

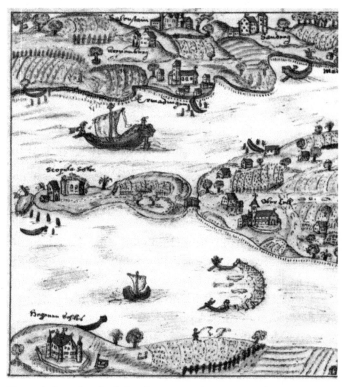

Plan of the island of Reichenau. Colored pen drawing of 1627. Heinrich Murer copy of the *Chronicle of Reichenau Monastery* by Gallus Oeheim. Thurgau Kantonsbibliothek, Frauenfeld.

Hermann "Contractus," July 18, 1013–September 24, 1054

CONTENTS

SALVE REGINA

Salve, Regina, mater misericordiae;
vita, dulcedo et spes nostra, salve.
Ad te clamamus exsules filii Hevae.
Ad te suspiramus gementes et flentes
in hac lacrimarum valle.
Eia ergo, advocata nostra,
illos tuos misericordes oculos ad nos converte.
Et Iesum, benedictum fructum ventris tui,
nobis post hoc exsilium ostende.
O clemens, o pia, o dulcis Virgo Maria.

Hail, holy Queen, Mother of mercy,
our life, our sweetness and our hope.
To thee do we cry, poor banished children of Eve.
To thee to we send up our sighs, mourning
and weeping in this valley of tears.
Turn, then, most gracious advocate,
thine eyes of mercy toward us,
and after this, our exile, show unto us
the blessed fruit of thy womb, Jesus.
O clement, O loving, O sweet Virgin Mary.

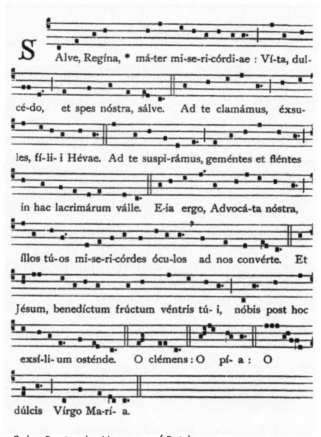

Salve Regina, by Hermann of Reichenau

TRANSLATOR'S NOTE

The footnotes in square brackets were not present in the original text. They provide brief explanations and translations from Latin.

Scriptural translations are taken from the version by Ronald Knox, who translated from the Vulgate text that Hermann and his contemporaries used.

Translations from the *Rule of Saint Benedict* are by Abbot Justin McCann OSB (London: Sheed and Ward, 1970).

View of the monastery on the island of Reichenau, on Lake Constance

B.HERMANNUSCONTRA[T]
MON.AUG.ADEVOTEMARCE
LEBRIS OB 19 Jul 1054

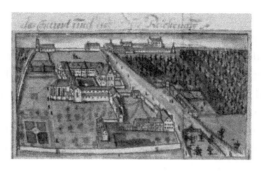

CHAPTER 1

* * *

GRANT ME ADMITTANCE

The Flame

WHEN HE LIFTS his head with great effort, all he sees is the grayness of the overcast sky—nothing else. The human wall made up of the unvarying dull black of the rough woolen habits is far too dense. But he knows that the Gnadensee[1] is not glittering today. He knows that it lies dull and motionless, dead and leaden like a blinded eye. A sluggish wind, tepid and languid, prowls through the bed of rushes that grow tall as a man. The pale brown stalks scarcely shiver. Somewhere, a gull cries, harsh and contentious, and little coots call out like wailing children.

---

1. [The Gnadensee (literally, the "Lake of Grace"), between Allensbach and the island of Reichenau, is in the western part of Lake Constance, known as the Lower Lake.]

Hermann of Altshausen does not get angry with his confreres whose thoughtless eagerness blocks his view. All he would have liked was to breathe a little more freely. In the narrow corner between the wall of human bodies and the bed of rushes, the air—disagreeably mild for the late fall—is motionless. The crippled monk is tired, and he lets his upper body, which is already bent over, sink down even farther. He takes his skinny hands from the wooden arms of his wheelchair, lets them fall into his lap, and closes his eyes. If only he had stayed in his cell!

A wave of cries surges up, sudden and exciting: "The Holy Father!" Automatically, the sick man opens his eyes, but in vain … The wall of bodies has become even thicker. The monks are pressing forward. "The Holy Father!"

And then they sing, with joyful animation and too loud, much too loud, the song of greeting for which Hermann had written the melody. *Ave, Pater et Pontifex! Augia, filia Dei et Mariae, exsulta in Domino. Benedic Christum, Insula. Lux fulgebit hodie: Fuit homo missus a Deo—Summum Pontificem Leonem quem totius Ecclesiae esse pastorem.*—"Hail, father and pontiff! Exult in the Lord, O Reichenau, daughter of God and of Mary. Bless Christ, O Island. A light will shine out today: there was a man sent by God—the Supreme Pontiff Leo, whom he has granted to be the pastor of the entire Church."

The austere, pedestrian voice of the abbot rings out. The Lord Udualrich reads out the Latin address of greeting. The Abbey of Mary on Reichenau offers Pope Leo IX its reverent homage. Hermann does not pay attention to the words that are spoken, since he himself had written the address. Abbot Udualrich strings together the sentences, monotonously and tunelessly. A slight unrest flows

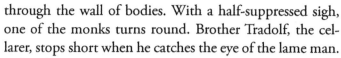

through the wall of bodies. With a half-suppressed sigh, one of the monks turns round. Brother Tradolf, the cellarer, stops short when he catches the eye of the lame man.

"Father Hermann," he muttered, with consternation all over his kindly face. "You can't see the Holy Father!"

The sick man lays a warning finger on his lips. "Speak softly, good brother. Otherwise they will hear you down at the Herrenbruck harbor."

But the cellarer does more than utter a word of regret. His right hand roughly shakes the shoulder of Master Fridebolt, who is listening, immersed in what the abbot is saying, and the old scholar looks indignantly at the one who has disturbed his peace. Tradolf whispers an emphatic instruction to him. Fridebolt moves aside, and the strong figure of the cellarer clears a wide path. Before the gap can close again, he takes hold of the wheelchair and pushes it forward with a rapid jerk. Pain slices through the sick man. He wants to cry out, to whimper like a child, but no sound comes from his firmly closed lips. Only his blue eyes darken for a little time.

When Hermann can see once again, his eyes widen in happy amazement. Pope Leo IX stands close, very close to him. The Holy Father is just replying to the abbot with a voice that is calm and deep, and yet full of life. Restrained masculine gestures accompany the steady flow of the Latin words. His speech has something vibrant about it, a melody of its own. The tall figure of the Pope seems calm, serene, and exalted; but like his voice, it is full of life. This priest radiates a restrained glow. His haggard face is dominated by the gray eyes under dark eyebrows. The steep brow, the narrow lips, and the powerful chin reveal prudence, wisdom, and solidity. Abbot Udualrich plays uneasily with the heavy gold chain of his pectoral cross. Has he not noticed the glow of kindness in the eyes of the Pope, nor the mild smile on the narrow lips? For him, Lord Leo is a faithful follower of the reform of Cluny—a thought that gives little pleasure to the abbot, with his zest for life.

Hermann of Altshausen hears the words of the Holy Father, but he does not register them. He is all eyes, all looking, an amazed, sparkling, enthusiastic looking. He pays no attention to what is going on around him. Nor does he notice the splendid entourage of the Pope.

If anyone had asked him how he was, he would not have known how to put into words what had burst into his life and caught him up into the light of an overwhelming joy. Out of the depths of his subconscious, a picture rises to the surface, the memory of a tall, shining figure before a sky overcast with gray clouds.

"Yes, I have met him once before," he murmurs, and he knows at the same time that this cannot possibly be true. "I have met him ..." Yet that cannot be the case. Against everything that reasons says, he secretly insists that he knows Leo IX. Against all reason ... It was only a couple of months since the election of Leo, the count's son from Alsace and bishop of Toul, and he had never before visited the island in Lake Constance, the *felix Augia*.[2]

"

Now he had come in order to meet Hermann of Altshausen, the lame scholar about whom he had heard marvel-

2. [Happy Reichenau.]

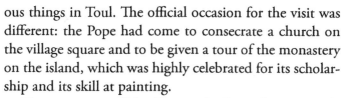

ous things in Toul. The official occasion for the visit was different: the Pope had come to consecrate a church on the village square and to be given a tour of the monastery on the island, which was highly celebrated for its scholarship and its skill at painting.

Hermann was still looking at the Pope, his eyes wide open. "I have met him once before …"

Suddenly, someone took hold of his wheelchair and steered it swiftly toward the village square. The sick man did not ask who it was. The fragile vehicle took the same detour as all those who wanted to get to the little church before the Pope, the abbot, and the cortege of the great men, in order to secure a good place. The wheelchair made its way, jolting and swaying over the bumps and stones in the rutted field-track, through hurrying monks, pupils, farm hands, and fishermen. Laughter and talk, cries and shouts swirled around him, as the churning waves swirl around a rowboat in a storm. The lame man frantically clutched the wooden arms. There was nothing to soften the blow of jolt after jolt on his poor body. His mouth remained silent; the only response was a terrible litany of pains. His cries were restrained by the strict self-discipline in which thirty years of suffering had trained him. Branches with the red-yellow leaves of autumn brushed against the sick man's face, and he could not even lift his hand to ward them off—not even the thorny branch with fiery red rose hips that whipped his forehead and slit it open. Berthold, his faithful companion, would never have driven him so carelessly along this path. That day, the young monk was one of the Holy Father's altar servers. In the midst of his pains, Hermann nodded. He shared Berthold's joy that he had been given this favor.

The wheelchair landed in a hole in the path, came to an abrupt stop, and almost toppled over. The lame man hung helplessly on the very edge, half swaying over the ground. A strong hand tugged him back onto the seat.

"Keep on!" the lame man gasped. He was unaware that tears were running down his sunken cheeks, tears that the excessive pain squeezed out of him. He wanted to see, to be able to see, to see—to see the Pope again, in the church on the village square. Seeing the Pope had given him a joy that he had not experienced since the death of Abbot Berno, so he was willing to accept the pain involved.

The wheelchair jolted violently as it made its final bump against the stone threshold of the church and rolled across it. Pearls of perspiration flowed across the forehead of the lame man as the vehicle came to a halt beside one of the gray-yellow sandstone pillars, one of those closest to the sanctuary. Hermann wanted to thank his boisterous helper, but he was no longer the master of his own voice. He laboriously gasped for breath. His heart was beating furiously, as if he had run all the way to the Herrenbruck harbor. His trembling hands fluttered over his lap as if they were looking for something. They brushed against something cold and smooth, and he looked down in shock. It was only an autumn leaf, a delicate yellow, transparent leaf. Did it not bear the sun in itself? Is not a leaf like a light?

He closed his eyes; tears and perspiration ran down his pallid face. He crouched motionless in his little wheelchair, the monk with the slight, twisted figure and a yellow autumn leaf in his lap. This was how the Pope found him, when he consecrated the church of Saint Adalbert and came to that particular pillar in order to bless the cross of

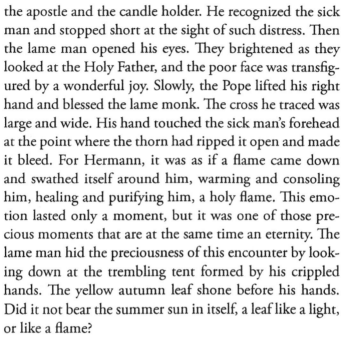

the apostle and the candle holder. He recognized the sick man and stopped short at the sight of such distress. Then the lame man opened his eyes. They brightened as they looked at the Holy Father, and the poor face was transfigured by a wonderful joy. Slowly, the Pope lifted his right hand and blessed the lame monk. The cross he traced was large and wide. His hand touched the sick man's forehead at the point where the thorn had ripped it open and made it bleed. For Hermann, it was as if a flame came down and swathed itself around him, warming and consoling him, healing and purifying him, a holy flame. This emotion lasted only a moment, but it was one of those precious moments that are at the same time an eternity. The lame man hid the preciousness of this encounter by looking down at the trembling tent formed by his crippled hands. The yellow autumn leaf shone before his hands. Did it not bear the summer sun in itself, a leaf like a light, or like a flame?

Around midday, the Pope and the monastic community met in the refectory of the abbey for a festive meal. Young brothers bore excellent dishes to the table, one after the other—fowl from the steward's farm, venison from the Hegau woods, trout, whitefish, eels from Lake Constance, vegetables and herbs, white bread, and marvelous fruits. Golden yellow wine from the island, or sweet red wine from the Italian lands of the monastery, sparkled in the richly decorated goblets. The Lord Leo ate sparingly of the fine foods, which even in the rich alluvial plain were served only seldom. His gray eyes noted carefully all that was going on around him. Sometimes they met the dark, restless eyes of Archdeacon Hildebrand in a silent agreement. The Pope already guessed something of what the severe and fiery champion of the Church's cause would tell him that evening ... The Pope engaged in an apparently relaxed conversation with the abbot on his right. The Lord Udualrich was pleased with himself, and thought that the Holy Father doubtless felt at ease in the island monastery. Once again, he had been worrying needlessly about the ability of his abbey to pass the test of the scrutiny of Leo, who was an adherent of the Cluniac reforms.

"I miss someone, Lord Udualrich. Do you know who that is?" asked Pope Leo, pensively.

"Father Abbot of Einsiedeln, who is sick, Holy Father?" asked Udualrich obsequiously.

"No, one of your own sons from Reichenau—the sick man with the wise and childlike eyes, whom I saw earlier today in Saint Adalbert's."

"You mean Hermann of Altshausen, Holy Father?" There was an unmistakable undertone of aversion and displeasure in the abbot's voice, and he pursed his full lips. "No doubt, he is in his cell. His bad health usually keeps him away from the community."

One of the brothers who served at table drew near to the Pope and asked reverently: "May I fill up Your Holiness's glass?"

The Pope declined with a smile: "Thank you, my son. This drink is good only when it is enjoyed in moderation. We do not want to get tired. The service of the Lord on Reichenau has not yet finished today. Vespers begins soon."

These words were spoken in a friendly tone, but they brooked no disagreement. They dashed the abbot's hopes. He had been certain that Leo would take a long rest after

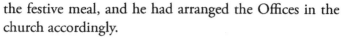

the festive meal, and he had arranged the Offices in the church accordingly.

"Vespers … ah, yes …," he murmured uncertainly. "Do you not wish to rest, Holy Father? Vespers … of course … with an especially solemn celebration in your honor …"

Leo IX understood him. Udualrich had assumed that he would not be present at Vespers. He noted that the prior, who was shocked and confused, gave the abbot a sign.

"Not Vespers … Compline will be celebrated solemnly!" whispered the prior, urgently and very audibly.

The Lord Udualrich shrugged his shoulders. What was he to do? Who could guess that the Pope intended to take part in all the Offices? Most of the high prelates in the empire who visited Reichenau were perfectly content to attend one single service. In those cases, Vespers had to be celebrated with an extraordinary solemnity.

When Udualrich believed that the Pope was deep in conversation with his neighbor to the left, the bishop of Constance, he summoned Gunter, the abbey choirmaster.

"Which Vespers have you prepared?"

"The weekday Vespers, Father Abbot," replied the monk, somewhat indignantly. "You yourself said that we should sing Compline …"

The abbot interrupted him curtly: "'I said, I said …' That no longer applies. The Holy Father is coming to Vespers. Insert something special into the order of service."

Gunter bit his lips. He checked his anger and replied: "Father Abbot, the various solemnities of this day have made, and will make, excessive demands of the choir. We have rehearsed and rehearsed, and we have really overexerted ourselves. We have nothing exceptional left, noth-

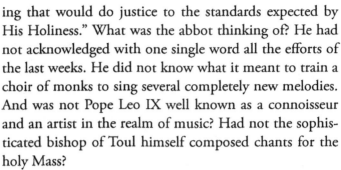

ing that would do justice to the standards expected by His Holiness." What was the abbot thinking of? He had not acknowledged with one single word all the efforts of the last weeks. He did not know what it meant to train a choir of monks to sing several completely new melodies. And was not Pope Leo IX well known as a connoisseur and an artist in the realm of music? Had not the sophisticated bishop of Toul himself composed chants for the holy Mass?

A deep cleft appeared between Lord Udualrich's brows, and his little eyes narrowed to slits. Gunter knew these warning signs and hastened to ward off the impending outbreak.

"Hermann of Altshausen once composed a solemn Magnificat, but it was never performed, and the choir does not know the melody …"

Udualrich breathed an audible sigh of relief. "Good, then let the lame man sing it. He has a pleasant voice. Go and tell him!"

The choirmaster ventured to make one last objection: "Only … it is against the custom for one monk to sing on his own, especially at the Magnificat in Vespers, Father Abbot."

The abbot leaned back with a laugh. "Oh, really? 'Against the custom'?" he said cynically. "What a lot of scruples my virtuous son has!" He suddenly leaned forward and hissed: "Once and for all, Gunter, listen to what I am telling you: On Reichenau, the 'custom' is what I make it!"

Pope Leo IX had heard these last words.

Silence

Hermann of Altshausen lived in a little corner cell in the north wing of the abbey. Its windows looked onto the Gnadensee. After the exertions of the morning, the lame man was once again entirely dependent on the help of the young monk Berthold, his companion, who had to feed him. His left arm was around the shoulders of the sick man, supporting him, while he carefully fed him spoonful after spoonful of strong soup.

"Now I am helpless like a little child again," smiled Hermann. "But today I am a happy child, a blessed child."

"We have a good and great Pope," said Berthold warmly. "I was so glad when he blessed you, Father!"

"I think we have a holy … yes, truly a Holy Father, after a long period of dishonorable conflicts about the Chair of Peter. We cannot thank God enough for giving his Church a Pope Leo. By the way, Berthold, it sounds unbelievable … I have met Pope Leo once before in my life … I met him somehow and somewhere …"

Berthold pricked up his ears in astonishment. Father Hermann never made unclear, hesitant remarks like this, spoken as if in a dream. He was shocked, and asked: "What is the matter, Father?"

Hermann's clear eyes met his concerned look. "No, no, my son, I am not dreaming. I clearly feel that I have met him once before. But I have forgotten the exact circumstances of our meeting."

The young monk put the plate aside and took the goblet with the island wine. "Father, I don't understand you. You cannot …"

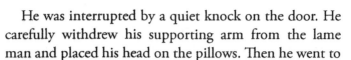

He was interrupted by a quiet knock on the door. He carefully withdrew his supporting arm from the lame man and placed his head on the pillows. Then he went to the door and opened it.

"Gunter? Do you want to see Father Hermann?"

The choirmaster looked in consternation at the recumbent figure. "Father Hermann, are you sick again? This is terrible! You ... are supposed to sing ..."

Berthold quickly tried to send him away: "You see that Father Hermann needs rest. He needs looking after. He has already overtaxed himself this morning."

Then the sick man's voice rang out, labored and distinct: "Not so fast, Berthold! Gunter, wait, please ... Who sent you to me?"

"Abbot Udualrich ..."

Berthold looked angrily at Gunter, who was drawing closer to the bed. "Then tell the Lord and Father Abbot that ..."

"Berthold!" The lame man's weak voice took on a sharp tone. "Gunter, what am I to sing?"

The monk replied almost shyly: "Your Magnificat at Vespers. The Holy Father will be present unexpectedly at Vespers, and we have only rehearsed something special for Compline, as the abbot told us to do. Your glorious Magnificat should ..." The choirmaster did not finish the sentence; he looked at the ground in embarrassment. If only he had not made the suggestion! The abbot's injunction made an unreasonable demand of the sick man, whose every spoken word had to be wrested from his pains.

Hermann of Altshausen nodded almost imperceptibly. "Good, Gunter," he replied with serene confidence and tranquility. "Tell our Lord and Father Abbot that I shall sing my Magnificat. Help me to pray that, with the help of God, I will be able to do so by the time Vesper comes."

After thanking him almost excessively, the choirmaster left the cell. Hermann would sing! *Deo gratias!*[3] Vespers will conclude solemnly.

Berthold gave the sick man his wine, feeling uneasy. Did he not deserve a rebuke for his over-hasty and dismissive words? "Father ... ah ... I ...," he began, tentatively.

The lame man did not allow him to finish. "Berthold, you will be beside me in the choir stalls. You will help me and hold me while I sing the Magnificat. I do not want to crouch while I sing Our Lady's great song."

The younger man stammered abashedly: "Father ... I ..."

Once again, Hermann interrupted him: "If I did not have you, my faithful son, I would be really poor. I realized that this morning, when you were not with me," he said kindly. "My Magnificat will therefore also be a thanksgiving to the Lord for giving me a John to stand beneath my cross."

"

At the conclusion of Vespers, the Magnificat resounded powerfully through the abbey church, which was fragrant with incense. It did not sound as if the voice came from the distorted breast of a cripple who was wracked with pains. Abbot Udualrich looked complacently from under his half-shut heavy eyelids, looking for applause. Leo IX stood immovably, taut and upright, before his

---

3. [Thanks be to God!]

faldstool with its velvet and brocade. An uncomfortable man, this Cluniac Pope ... so pious, so learned, so ascetic. The people were already calling him a saint. Abbot Udualrich secretly feared that this visit might turn into a visitation. He felt unease at the thought of the address of homage that he must read at the ceremony in the chapter room. The Latin this Hermann wrote was much too eloquent. The abbot hoped that the Lord Leo would be content when he had presented him with the sick man's *Life of Saint Adalbert,* and that he would then depart.

Oh, sometimes it was a good thing to have this lame man in the monastery—whenever it was necessary to convince an outsider of the scholarship and holiness of Reichenau. It was said that outsiders told fabulous stories of miracles in connection with the lame man.

Udualrich was surprised to hear the deep, resonant voice of the Pope.

"My dear brothers and sisters in Christ," began Leo IX. He looked around at the expectant faces of the monks and brothers, of the bishops, prelates, and priests. His eye looked kindly on the island people, the farmers, fishers, and servants, who stood in the west-work of the church, and on the fresh faces of the boy pupils. The Pope read human faces like a book. He saw the traces left by struggle and suffering, by pain and distress, by sin and luxuriousness; he noted integrity, serenity, enthusiasm, joyfulness, and piety. He met the blue eyes of the sick man with a look of profound oneness. Were not those eyes guileless like the eyes of a child, and wise like the eyes of an old man on the threshold of eternity? The Holy Father's look said: "Thank you for the Magnificat, Brother Hermann."

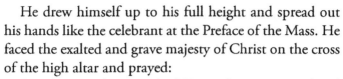
He drew himself up to his full height and spread out his hands like the celebrant at the Preface of the Mass. He faced the exalted and grave majesty of Christ on the cross of the high altar and prayed:

"Lord Jesus Christ, exalted King of eternity, Lord and judge, Almighty God,

"We bow down before you in this hour and dare to join with profound reverence in the prayer of your most holy Mother, Our Lady Mary.

"You are the only Lord and Master of this blessed Reichenau. You are the only Lord and Master of your Church. In this song of your Mother, you stand in your glory before us, you, the eternal God.

"Who are we, that we should be permitted to draw near to you, O Most High? We are all poor, sinful human beings, poor, maimed creatures. No personal prestige, no beauty, and no bodily strength counts for anything in your eyes. We all are darkness, if you do not give us a spark from the infinite glowing sea of your divinity, you who are light from God, you who are true God from true God.

"Even when we receive your grace, we are only little sparks, wretched and weak. And yet what else can we do, Lord Jesus Christ, than come to you with the faith of Simon Peter, who once confessed, on behalf of us too: 'You are the Christ, the Son of the living God'?

"We draw near to you with the shame and the confidence of the leper, and show you the ugly wounds of our souls. 'Lord, make us clean!' Stretch out your hand and heal us.

"We want to remain with you, with the fidelity of your apostle John that led him under your cross. Your love for him was greater than the human narrowness of his heart. His love for you was more powerful than his fear.

"Lord Jesus Christ, your cross ought to be the center and the dwelling place of our life. With you, we are ready to bear it over hard and painful roads; with you, we want to hold out under the cross in a fidelity that is stronger than the wretchedness of our creaturely being; with a love that is truly crucified with you, because it is consumed for the glory of the Father in a restless yearning for the coming of his kingdom.

"We will have to force ourselves to make our sacrifice every day. You know our weakness and our cowardice. But when we say our 'yes,' your grace will bear us up; and thus a secret exultation will be alive in us, a supernatural joy that we have been found worthy of your cross.

"Lord Jesus Christ, we belong to you. We are the vassals, the messengers, the bondsmen of your love and the heralds of your cross. Receive the oath we swear at this house: We are yours, O Lord. We want nothing other than your love. Lift up your holy cross high above this island and in the hearts of those who dwell here, so that all may be blessed and may become a Magnificat for you. Amen."

The Lord Leo made a deep bow before the altar and knelt down. The monks waited, spellbound. The simple island people too had felt the fiery glow of this faith and looked silently and reverently at the Pope, who was praying, lost in contemplation. Leo IX was a man of prayer! His fervor made the Lord Udualrich even more uneasy. There was something unearthly about the Pope—a man full of depths and surprises ... The abbot stared in irritation at the shining face of the lame man. It was the face of one who had received rich gifts and had been made

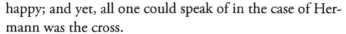

happy; and yet, all one could speak of in the case of Hermann was the cross.

Was the Pope intending to go on praying much longer? Had they not already spent far too much time in the church today? Was the festive meal to be ruined by overcooking? Abbot Udualrich noted the discontent on the faces of some monks. They were probably muttering now: "Abbot Berno would have found a better conclusion!" They were still grieving after his death. Abbot Berno ... A cold fear gripped Udualrich as he thought of the Pope's praise of the deceased abbot.

With some effort, he reined in his wandering thoughts. The Pope was still praying. But what was he to do? He could not tug the Pope's vestment and tell him it was time to stop. Perhaps Hermann of Altshausen had another chant he could sing? Then Leo would pay attention, and he could finish the service. As a matter of fact, Hermann had supplied the words for the whole day. All the hymns, chants, and verses were his work. But ... Pope Leo was still praying, and he was as deeply recollected now as if he had only just started.

"Hermann should sing ... something," murmured the abbot to the prior, who nodded and made his way silently to the sick man, who did not object to the command. After a brief pause for reflection, Berthold lifted the lame man to an upright position.

The cripple was ugly! When he saw him, the Lord Udualrich's shoulders were already wide under his cowl. But whenever he saw the cripple, he automatically made them even broader. The pale man from Altshausen, the son of one of the most powerful counts in the Swabian region, stood in the choir stall, a pitiable figure with a hideously crooked back. His narrow head sat between his high shoulders; the head was too big for the rest of his frail body. The hands on the choir screen were noble and slender, but the illness had distorted them and bent the fingers. If Berthold had not held the sick man with both hands on his leather belt, he would not have been able even to stand. Abbot Udualrich was unaware that a strange smile played on his full lips, a smile that told of arrogance, dislike, and fear.

Young Berthold seethed with anger: "They make use of the Father and despise him," he thought. "He is good enough to help them out of their predicament." He took such a firm hold of the belt that Hermann was forced to protest in a low voice: "Not so firm, Berthold, not ..."

Then the lame man sang. His face was calm, unself-conscious, recollected. His voice had found its best tone—clear, sonorous, and warm. He thanked the Holy Father for his prayer, which gave him strength. He sang for Pope Leo.

"Death cannot defeat you. For you came, O Lord Christ, to bring me your light, you who are my life.—Therefore my heart exults in you and is very glad in you. It sings in the cross and in pain and in every trouble. You are my path and my end and my homeland, O Lord Christ. I place myself in your hands, you who are my life.—Alleluia, alleluia, alleluia ..."

Had the Alleluia ever resounded so exultantly and strongly through the church of Our Lady on Reichenau, as it now resounded from the mouth of a maimed and crippled man? His strong certainty in faith that he was kept safe in the love of Christ sounded like an echo of Leo's prayer.

Christ. Did not the heavy curtain that natural thinking weaves between time and eternity part for a moment? Christ was near, with a nearness that both startled and brought joy.

"

The Lord Udualrich shook off the unwelcome spell that had fallen on him and approached the Pope impatiently. Leo IX looked up, and his clear eyes became cold and severe. Now he was the *Pontifex maximus*.[4] Udualrich blushed under his gaze and started to stammer an excuse, but the Holy Father arose, genuflected deeply before the high altar, and left the church with quick, unceremonious strides. The abbot hurried gloomily after him.

Berthold set the lame man down again in his place as soon as he had finished singing. To sit down unaided required more independent power of movement than the man from Altshausen possessed. He was exhausted, and waited with his eyes closed for Berthold to bring him to the celebration in the chapter room. He heard whispers, the rustle of monastic habits, and the scraping of feet. Then there came the voice of Brother Eginhard: "Come, Master Hermann." Where had Berthold gone? Eginhard lifted him into the wheelchair and took him into the side aisle. He murmured: "Our Lord and Father Abbot wants to spare you the exertions of the ceremony, Father. He thinks that it has all been too much for you today."

The sick man nodded and smiled his weary, knowing smile that was not wholly free of bitterness. "Yes, it was

---

4. ["Supreme Pontiff."]

too much today, far too much. Dear Brother, please take me to the west-work, to the tomb of the Lord Berno, and leave me there. The silence will do me good."

Eginhard hastened to grant this modest request, and then left, since he did not want to arrive too late. The door slammed shut behind him.

The lame man was alone in the church. The last golden rays of the sun contended with the dark shadows between the pillars, light at the end of the day ... No, the morning too had its light, a great deal of light. A broad path of light passed through the open window behind the imperial loge and fell on the gravestone of Abbot Berno, lending an almost excessive clarity to the letters of the inscription, "Berno Abbas, †1048," to the severe and alien relief of the face, and to the abbatial coat of arms. The brother stonemason had not captured the abbot's face very well, but in the end, what did that matter? There was no need of a stone portrait to tell how a man like Abbot Berno looked. His figure shone out in the pages of the gospel, and he was still alive in Christ.

As he contemplated the path of light from the imperial loge, Hermann reflected on what he had experienced when he sang the last chant.

All at once, he had felt as if he saw—though only with his mind's eye, of course—a great bright unity, a path of light, that began with the Lord and made its way to many people, taking hold of them and embracing them ... Abbot Berno, Pope Leo, his own mother, Burkhard, Arnulph of Rahnwyl, the Lady Veronica, Ruodpert, Berthold, Irmingard ...

The man in the wheelchair folded his hands. The path of light had surrounded him too—the great bright unity

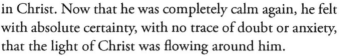

in Christ. Now that he was completely calm again, he felt with absolute certainty, with no trace of doubt or anxiety, that the light of Christ was flowing around him.

A pleasant feeling of security washed over him, like the sensation that morning when the Pope had blessed him. He wanted to pray, and he began: "Lord …" Then he fell silent. His prayer no longer needed any words. The silence held him fast and penetrated him. The silence was light and flame. There was nothing frightening in this bright, flowing silence. It lets him forget that he, a sick cripple, was crouching alone in the darkening church, while the others were celebrating the Pope with his verses and his songs, and presenting the Pope with a work that he has written. This silence was free of all bitterness. It contained neither numbers nor formulas, neither constellations of the heavens nor neums.

Nothing, nothing at all existed in this silence, not even the pain that shot through his limbs. He fell silent.

This silence knew a presence: God. The sick man no longer thought about himself. He was at rest in the living silence, in the breathing silence of the divine closeness, like a child in its mother's arms, with no wishes, safe, at home. And yet, he was completely alert, completely open, and completely ready. His alertness was an act of listening to God, whose light flowed through the open chambers of his soul, and his readiness was like a soliloquy on the part of God.

For a moment, he then felt as if all the hours of his life were rushing together like a roaring stream and flowing into the sea of a light that was not his own, into the sea of the love of the God whom he sought and loved. Was this death, the end? A creaturely fear crept out of his subconscious, but he had granted admittance to the light, the silence, the stillness of God. So now, he made no resistance, but handed himself and his will over into God's loving will.

Hermann of Altshausen did not know that this love gave itself back to him as a gift, in order that he might continue to bear witness to it among his brethren.

Oblatio

Berthold had to call the lame man's name several times before he answered, and then it was only a painfully disappointed murmur: "Not yet? Not yet?" The young man looked with concern at the sad face of his master. Hermann's eyes looked wearily at the lantern. An unfathomable pain had made them strange and dark.

"Father, what ails you?"

"A long path … Let me stay for a little while longer at the grave of our Father Berno."

"It is already late, Father. You have been alone for a long time. Compline will begin soon."

"Long, my son? No, not long. It was only a moment."

Berthold replied bitterly: "The ceremony and the festive meal without you lasted for more than three hours."

Hermann's response was mysterious: "Three hours, Berthold? But does that matter? What are three hours of eternity?"

Three hours of eternity? What did Father Hermann mean by that? Berthold was on the point of asking him, but Hermann had noted the bitterness in the voice of his faithful helper, and he reached out for his hand. "Do not

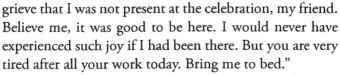
grieve that I was not present at the celebration, my friend. Believe me, it was good to be here. I would never have experienced such joy if I had been there. But you are very tired after all your work today. Bring me to bed."

Slowly, with a careful and reverent tenderness, the young monk took the light vehicle into the left side-aisle and then into the cloister courtyard. He did not need to ask which path he should take. Father Hermann loved the little detour around the inner courtyard before the narrowness of his cell enclosed him for what was usually a sleepless night.

The clatter of crockery came from the kitchen, where the monastery servants were working. A heavy odor of roast meat, fat, and vegetables hung in the cloister. Laughter and men's voices rang out, and the old linden tree rustled in the evening breeze that had suddenly sprung up.

The lame man's soul longed with an almost irrepressible yearning for the silence in the monastery church, so close to God—for the silence in which he was blessedly unaware of his own condition. Now, the pains tugged and pulled at him again, and his poor head was assailed by his thoughts. He wanted to protest and cry out to Berthold: "Why did you tear me away from this silence?"

But he answered his own question: "Because that is what the Lord wanted. Like Peter, I planned to build a tent on Mount Tabor. But then he touched me and I saw no one else but him alone, him ... in the wretched reality of my daily existence."

The wheelchair stopped with a light jolt, and Hermann was startled out of his thoughts. A group of people was drawing near, led by a man in a bright garment, the Holy Father. Berthold wasted no time on reflection. He lifted the wind-light so high that its light fell on the master, and Leo IX stopped short at once.

"Hermann of Altshausen!" he cried out, joyfully. "At last I can see you again. I have been looking for you. Could you keep me company for a little while this evening? Good, then we will forgo Compline."

Abbot Udualrich made a displeased face. After all, he had ordered that Compline be celebrated with especial solemnity! But Hildebrand, the severe archdeacon of the Roman Church, smiled at the sick man.

"It is too much of a burden for you to come to the palace, Hermann. Come with me into the library."

Berthold steered his master alongside the Pope. He felt a great joy: at last, Hermann, who had been the object of so much contempt, was receiving the kind of honor that he deserved. But then the young monk recalled the supper that was waiting for the master in his corner cell. He had eaten nothing since the midday meal.

"You are most welcome, Father Hermann!" said the Pope, when the lame man sat at table opposite him. "But I missed you earlier on, at the ceremony and at the festive meal. Where were you all the time?"

"In the church, Holy Father," replied Hermann, not without embarrassment.

At this point, Lord Leo noticed Berthold, who was lingering hesitantly. "My son, is there something you wish?"

"Yes, Your Holiness … It is this … The Father only ate a little soup at the midday meal, and he has not eaten anything since then." Berthold stammered shyly and blushed right up to the shock of dark hair about his broad brow.

The lame man was shocked and held his breath. As if *that* was so important! Why had Berthold brought this up? Was he to sit here beside the Holy Father and break the bread with his trembling hands? His fear of embarrassment made him almost angry at his eager assistant.

"Bring the food, my son," ordered Leo, who had not failed to notice the hidden distress of his visitor. "I hope that it will be to the liking of the Father in my presence."

Berthold quickly left the library. Hermann's eyes wandered uncertainly over the backs of the broad folios, until he dared to meet the Pope's gaze.

"You have a faithful companion," said the Lord Leo, appreciatively.

"Yes, Holy Father." Hermann sighed and smiled. "Sometimes I have the impression that he is too faithful."

"I noticed that," replied Leo.

The lame man warned him: "You will discover that it is not in any way edifying to be present when I eat, Holy Father."

"But what if that is what I want, Hermann, because I do not want to do without your company for the duration of your meal? It is because of you that I came to Reichenau. Is not every moment that we spend together precious?"

Berthold's entry relieved the lame man of the need to reply. The young monk placed an earthenware plate with bread and cheese and a goblet of wine on the table, and then withdrew quietly.

Hermann said grace silently and began the difficult task of his evening meal. His gaunt face had the same intentness and recollection that it had when he performed an intellectual task. His trembling hands slowly and laboriously cut up the bread and cheese and brought the small pieces to his mouth.

Pope Leo IX automatically lowered his eyelids, as if he was embarrassed to be the witness of such painful endeavors. What a terrible life this celebrated scholar of Reichenau leads, if he can scarcely manage to perform such an ordinary task! What a burden his existence must be to him, since he keeps on encountering obstacles, boundaries, and fetters where other people do things with a playful ease! A life of dependence and helplessness in everything, even in the most personal matters—surely that must make a person bitter?

The trembling, distorted fingers were trying to pick up a couple of small pieces of bread that had fallen onto the smooth surface of the table, but they kept on eluding his grasp.

We read in chapter 53 of the prophet Isaiah: "No stateliness here, no majesty, no beauty, as we gaze upon him, to win our hearts. Nay, here is one despised, left out of all human reckoning, a man of sorrows, and no stranger to weakness ..." Did not these words apply to this poor man?

Pope Leo turned his gaze from the sick man's hands and contemplated his face, which was marked by suffering. His cheeks and temples were gaunt and sunken, but the brilliant blue eyes and the clear, convex brow told the onlooker about the purity, the wisdom, and the goodness of heart of this man. Leo was once again reminded of a child's guilelessness, but at the same time of an old man's wisdom, close to eternity.

"And when are you going to drink your wine, Father Hermann?"

The lame man lifted his trembling hands in a helpless gesture. "Today I am sure I would spill it, Holy Father, and it is the wine for a feast. May Berthold give it to me later?"

The Pope declined this request gently. He rose and lifted the goblet to the mouth of the sick man. "Drink it now. The wine is good for you."

He helped him carefully until the goblet was empty. Then he pushed the plate and the goblet aside, straightened up the cushions in the sick man's armchair, and drew the candles close to him.

"I thank you, Holy Father," said Hermann simply. His embarrassment had given place to a good joy. "Today, Reichenau was truly once again a rich water meadow.[5] It has not been so rich since the death of the Lord Berno. You brought much blessing with you, Holy Father. The consecration of the church ... We ought to have sung the Vespers for the feast of the dedication! Its short reading is made just for this day: *Vidi civitatem sanctam, Jerusalem novam, descendentem de caelo a Deo, paratam sicut sponsam ornatam viro suo.*"[6]

"*Deo gratias,*"[7] replied the Lord Leo. "You are right, Hermann. I too always feel that heaven descends to our earth when we celebrate the dedication of a church. *Locus iste sanctus est.*[8] And that is really the case, is it not? Where

---

5. [The name "Reichenau" (*Augia* in Latin) literally means a "rich water meadow."]

6. ["I saw in my vision that holy city which is the new Jerusalem, being sent down by God from heaven, all clothed in readiness, like a bride who has adorned herself to meet her husband" (Revelation 21:2).]

7. ["Thanks be to God."]

8. ["This place is holy" (from the liturgy of the dedication of a church; see Genesis 28:17).]

Our Lord Jesus dwells, there is heaven. We take far too much for granted the fact that he dwells in our midst. Yet this is the most exalted, the most terrifying, and the most exhilarating mystery of our faith, that he … comes when a human mouth pronounces the words of consecration. *Mysterium fidei* …"[9]

"And Our Lord comes in other ways too. That is a great consolation for a priest who cannot celebrate the holy sacrifice," said the sick man in a low voice.

"Could you never do so, Father Hermann?"

"After my ordination to the priesthood, I have been able to do so twice, Holy Father, and I am infinitely grateful to the Lord for that. Look at this …" He showed the Pope his hands with their crooked fingers. "With these hands, I cannot even break the natural bread every day. Mostly, someone else has to do it for me. Someone else moves the spoon, the pen, and the stylus for writing on wax. There are days when I cannot even turn a page when I want to read."

"Can you not bring all this into the holy sacrifice of Christ, Hermann?" asked the Pope, who was moved by the serenity with which he bore his harsh fate. "And you yourself said that Our Lord comes to us, to you, in other ways—through his word, through his grace, through his cross. And we may be sure that his promise holds good for this moment too: 'Where two or three are gathered together in my name, I am there in the midst of them.'"

Many red-brown grains ran down in the hourglass on the bookshelf, and fat white-yellow tears of wax ran down the candles, before the Lord Leo broke the silence: "Yes,

---

9. ["The mystery of faith."]

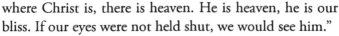

where Christ is, there is heaven. He is heaven, he is our bliss. If our eyes were not held shut, we would see him."

"Today the curtain on Reichenau was torn asunder, Holy Father. The Lord was close at hand. But his closeness must be a gift. One cannot force it. Often, he lets us wait for a long time for his coming, and then he comes suddenly, like a thief in the night ... The nights of God can have many hours. One must wait patiently, one must be sober and vigilant ... As a child, I once wanted to get heaven for myself through sheer obstinacy." The lame man laughed at the thought, and all at once, his face became young, lit up by the memory from his childhood days.

"Tell me about it," the Pope requested. It was clear that Hermann regarded dwelling in a happy memory as a gift, and Leo IX wanted to give him a very great gift.

"Holy Father, you will be disappointed. It is a small event from my childhood."

"Tell me about it, Hermann, if you would like to do so. The simple stories are always the most beautiful."

The sick man did not wonder why the Pope from Rome wanted to hear a story from him. The express wish was enough for him, since he was always ready to accommodate other people's wishes. He did not reflect on the reason for this wish, but told the following story:

"My lady mother and the castle chaplain had described heaven to me in the most glorious colors, when I was inconsolable at the death of two of my brothers. But they did not give any real answer when I asked where this marvelous heaven was, so I made my own picture of heaven. I was convinced that heaven began at the place where the earth seems to come to an end. A huge curtain must separate the two—for I had heard in a sermon the astonishing statement that only a thin curtain separates earth and heaven, time and eternity. In death, this curtain would be lifted, so that we could look into eternal bliss. I wanted to see heaven during my lifetime. My father and mother would surely be glad if I brought back greetings from my brothers. My grandfather would probably grumble, because I had run away from home. But I would see the holy Bishop Udualrich of Augsburg, who was an uncle of my grandmother Berchta. Oh, I had long ago decided that I would become like him—a bishop who wore a knight's armor when wild hordes threatened our native land."

Hermann shook his head as he thought back to his boyhood dream. Nothing in that dream had become reality. Nothing? Pope Leo IX looked reflectively at the flame of the candles. Was there not a heroism greater than that of the warrior?

"I had no difficulty in winning my younger sister, Irmingard, for my plan, and we set out one fine summer day to slip into heaven through the thin curtain at the 'end of the world.' We ran and ran, until Irmingard got tired and started to cry, because she wanted to go back home. I was angry, and brought her back to the castle. I set out on my own several times, to look for heaven. Strangely enough, the grown-ups seemed to disapprove of this. Someone found me and brought me home.

"One gray day in the fall, I escaped for the last time. One of our servants had left the castle gate open. I ran quickly down the hill and across meadows and fields that had been harvested. I felt really lonely and uncomfortable. I was a little child, a seven-year-old boy, but despite my inner reluctance, I ventured into the wood. Bright autumn leaves rained down on me, and they rustled so wonder-

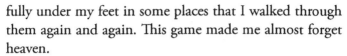

fully under my feet in some places that I walked through them again and again. This game made me almost forget heaven.

"I went back part of the way I had come. The wood was so silent, and I was tired. Finally, I came out into the open hilly landscape. I felt sad, and I crouched in the wet grass. I wanted to rest a little. An inexplicably urgent yearning filled me when I looked into the gray heaven. It seemed farther off than ever ..."

The sick man broke off his tale with an astonished cry: "Holy Father, now I have it! That is why you were so familiar to me when I saw you this morning at the Herrenbruck harbor."

The Lord Leo was puzzled. "When you saw me? Hermann, what have I to do with your childhood experience?" he asked.

"What I saw then, Holy Father—and what I remembered when I saw you today—was only a dream. Yes, it must have been a dream, woven out of my strong desire to see heaven and its radiant glory. It must have been a dream, because suddenly it seemed me to that a man was standing over against the gray clouds of the sky, a man in a bright garment, a man who was great and exalted. He was like a light, like a flame. I was not afraid, because the face of the man was also full of the light, and his eyes were kinder than those of my lady mother. Then he lifted up his hands, like rays of light that were beginning to shine. It was as if he was waving to me that I should come ... or as if he wanted to bless me. And I wanted to go to him, to the flame, to the light ...

"When the servants found me, I lay at the foot of the hill and slept.

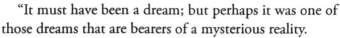

"It must have been a dream; but perhaps it was one of those dreams that are bearers of a mysterious reality.

"When I was back home, I behaved as I always did. I accepted my mother's rebuke without feeling any particular remorse. Indeed, I asked: 'Is there anything wrong about looking for heaven?' This question disarmed my lady mother.

"At the evening meal, Irmingard mocked me, because I had once again been looking in vain for heaven.

"'Perhaps I have seen something of heaven today. And I will go again!'

"'Our lady mother has forbidden you to do so.'

"Was there any objection to this? Well, I had one objection. I was not wholly sure of my theology, but I wanted Irmingard to stop talking.

"'One must look for heaven. That is what God wants.'

"I felt my first hesitations when I said my night prayers. Did not God also want children to be obedient? When my mother wished me good night, I drew her to myself and whispered in her ear: 'Please, please, lady mother, give me permission to look for heaven!'

"She caressed my hair and said: 'That is not as easy as my little boy imagines.' But she gave me permission to look for heaven. I had to promise her that I would never again try on my own. She was willing to help me in my search, and I fell asleep happily.

"My lady mother faithfully cherished these apparently unimportant little things in her memory, in her heart, including the … dream … of the figure that was like a flame. I had told her about it in a whisper. She forgot nothing of what had happened, and it was she who awakened it to new life many years later when she told me

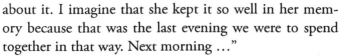

about it. I imagine that she kept it so well in her memory because that was the last evening we were to spend together in that way. Next morning ..."

Hermann suddenly paused and clenched his hands. He breathed rapidly and jerkily. Delicate pearls of perspiration appeared on his brow and his eyes flickered unsteadily.

The cross stood out sharply, black and painfully dark against the gray-white wall of the library.

After a little while, Hermann went on, calmly and collectedly: "Next morning, I was lame, unable to speak, unable to move. The Lady Hiltrud, my good mother, held me in her arms hour by hour, without complaining and without weeping. Once, she bent over me and whispered a strange word of consolation that I was to understand only much, much later, indeed years later: 'My child, now heaven has found you.'"

The Pope took the sick man's hand. "Hermann, you have a wonderful mother. With you, I thank the Lord for this grace. I am sure that, alongside Our Lady, the Lady Hiltrud will be a '*Porta caeli*'[10] for you. Thank you for allowing me to see the most painful and most blessed moments of your life."

"May I thank you for the patience with which you listened to me, Holy Father? You are giving me a lot of your time."

"And you are permitting me to share in your union with God, Father Hermann. What is the value of time, compared with that?"

---

10. ["Gate of heaven."]

"Your time, the time of the Supreme Pastor of Christendom, is an extremely valuable thing."

Pope Leo shook his head. "It is not more precious than yours, Hermann. And like your time, my time belongs to Christ. Indeed, your time is probably more precious in the eyes of the Lord, your time that is full to the brim of suffering and patient endurance."

"You suffer and endure more, Holy Father. You have the greatest share of his cross. The worldliness of the Church must cause you great distress, since you represent the Lord on earth and your task is to present the Church to him as a spotless bride. And to speak of nothing else, how heavy Byzantium must weigh upon you!"

The Lord Leo suddenly bent forward, so that his gold pectoral cross struck the table with a heavy thud. His face seemed distorted in the light of the six candles. "Byzantium," he whispered excitedly. "Hermann, you are poking around in a fresh wound. Byzantium … Must I drink the chalice, or will it pass me by? Will the separation come?" The Pope looked intensely at the flames of the candles and pressed his lips together, as if he had to suppress a cry of terrible distress. He continued, his voice breaking: "Patriarch Michael did not even reply to the reconciliatory message of greeting I sent him after my election. And what I want is peace, unity …"

Hermann looked sadly at the sorrowful face of the Holy Father. It was rare for him to see such naked pain in another person's face. "You bear the inheritance of others' guilt. The man on the Apostle's Chair was not always a *pontifex*.[11] Rome was not always willing to build

---

11. ["builder of bridges."]

bridges over the stream of contradictions, as you wish to do. Indeed, Rome not infrequently broke down through imprudence and false zeal a pillar that Byzantium had erected in the stream. Pride, impatience, pedantry and fanaticism, imperiousness and narrowness were at work on both sides. People were looking out for themselves and for what they supposed to be their rights, forgetting that they were meant to serve the one work and the one Lord."

Leo IX loved noble candor and did not resent the bold words of the lame man. "You are right, my friend. Your words are all too true. Now Patriarch Michael will break down every pillar that I attempt to erect in the stream. I have a feeling that he will not come to an accommodation with me."

The monk stretched out his hand to the Pope, imploring him: "Then let the barque of Peter cross over to the other side and ask in the name of the Lord for peace and forgiveness of the wrongs committed by past generations."

Pope Leo IX flew into a rage. "Do you know what you are asking, Hermann? The Patriarch is proud, so proud that my request for forgiveness would only make him more arrogant."

"Does humility become ... poorer, when it makes a request?" asked Hermann quietly.

For a moment, it seemed as if the Pope would be overwhelmed by his anger. His eyes looked at the monk with displeasure, but Hermann met his severe gaze without batting an eyelid. Leo's features became smooth again, and he replied calmly: "Humility does not become poorer, when it makes a request. And yet—in this case, humility's entreaty must be crowned by success, or nothing will be able to prevent the separation. Peter may ask.

But for the sake of the truth, for the sake of Christ, he must not relinquish his own self—and that is what the Patriarch demands."

The Lord Leo hid his face in his hands. His voice was muted, as he went on: "Hermann, if there was some means that I could use to propitiate the Patriarch, without harming the Church of Christ, without abandoning the truth, I would use it ... no matter what sacrifices and renunciations I would have to make thereby. If my person was the only obstacle to an agreement, how gladly would I lay the keys of Peter in the hands of a worthier man! But this is not about me, Hermann. It is about the ministry of Peter, and Peter cannot abandon his ministry without being unfaithful to the command of the Lord, who charged him: 'Feed my lambs, feed my sheep!'"

"Will Our Lord abandon Peter, Holy Father? Perhaps it is he who is sending the Church this division, because she needs a harsh penance in West and in East? If he wants unity, there will be unity. Then he will let you strike the rock like Moses, and waters will flow down, waters of salvation and of reconciliation. Our Lord does not abandon Peter. But he does not spare Peter in any way. He girds him and leads him where he never wanted to go ..."

The Pope still held his face in his hands and sat motionless. The sick man too fell silent, but he waited without inner unease. He was not disappointed, for when Leo removed his hands, the tension was gone from his face.

"Peter will lead the Church faithfully through the wilderness of these times, even if he is not allowed to see the promised land of reconciliation. But—you must help me in this, Hermann! I rely on you. Widen the walls of your cell in your spirit, until it encompasses Rome. Grant admittance to Rome and to the Pope. Grant me admittance! The Church needs you. Leo needs you. Christ needs you for the great *missa orbis,* for the *consecratio mundi.*"[12]

The sick man lowered his eyes, confused and perplexed by this forceful appeal. "For the *missa orbis*? Ah, Holy Father, how could I be of use there? Not even one little drop of water in the chalice of Christ the High Priest ..."

"No, Hermann of Altshausen, you cannot get out of it that easily," said the Lord Leo, urgently and impatiently. "More is demanded of one like you, one who has seen the flame!"

"More?" The lame man lifted his face, gaunt under the white hair, toward the light. "More?" The lines of pain around the narrow mouth looked like deep furrows in a plowed field. "More?" The candlelight darted over the crooked, weak hands. "More?"

A feeling of compassion made the Pope hesitate, but then he raised his voice and said: "Yes, Hermann, the Lord wants more from you. He wants you to offer the sacrifice of your suffering and your loving to him every day, every hour, unceasingly in a new, pitilessly clear consciousness. Place your suffering in the sacred sacrifice offered on Golgotha and say yes to it despite all the resistance offered by your nature; love it as a participation in the sacrifice of Jesus Christ. You are permitted to complement in your body that which is still lacking in the sacrifice of the Lord, as the Apostle Paul says. You must also love the contempt you encounter because you are a cripple ... and the even more painful compassion of those who are well.

"To be a sacrificial gift with Jesus Christ, to be for Jesus

---

12. ["The Mass of the world," "the consecration of the world."]

Christ in the *missa orbis*—let that be your great service for the world, your glorious office, my brother, that which makes your cell the house of God, when you prepare the bread for the sacrifice there in your suffering and through your suffering ... bread for his hands ... *oblatio*.[13] Our Lord breaks the bread that he blesses and distributes. Are you afraid, when you contemplate that?"

"Ought I to be afraid of Our Lord, Holy Father? He takes only in order to give," replied the lame man quietly. Sadness clouded his face. "My bread is not pure ... My gift is not worthy of being offered. I have often mixed in poor-quality corn when I baked my bread. I wanted to rest in my own condition. I looked for sympathy and human closeness. I was willing to accept only my own opinion, and my anger was quick and intense. There is much in me that is not good, much that must be displeasing to the Lord. Once again, a flame came over me."

"Then let the flame burn out all that is not good, Hermann. The flame of the Holy Spirit can burn without destroying what is whole." The Lord Leo bent down kindly to the lame man.

A smile of childlike honesty was the response he got. "I shall do that this very evening, Holy Father. May I ask some time tomorrow for your fatherly blessing on a new and conscious living, loving, and suffering for Christ and his Church, for you, for the world?"

"May I take from you that which is oppressing you, Hermann?" asked the Lord Leo with a reverent gentleness.

"You wish to do that in person, Holy Father?" The sick man's astonishment gave way to joyful thanksgiving, a silent

---

13. ["oblation."]

prayer, and serious reflection. He looked up to the Lord confidently, in repentance, and made a tranquil promise.

Pope Leo IX turned to the cross and listened, deeply moved, to the simple confession. He took up one point in Hermann's self-accusation: "You must no longer mourn for Abbot Berno, Father Hermann, as you have been doing up to now. Your grief for him would become a sin against the love for God and for human beings, if you were to continue to bury your talent. God wants you to sing. From now on, write down all the canticles and hymns that the Spirit of God gives you. Let your penance be to compose a prayer for Us that accompanies Us on the paths We take and that continually reminds Us of your promise to assist Us through your loving and suffering."

The Pope was still holding out his hands in blessing over the white hair of the lame man, when they heard an imperious loud knocking at the door. Before the Lord Leo could speak, the door was flung open and Abbot Udualrich appeared, broad-shouldered and full of his own importance.

"Oh ... excuse me, Your Holiness! I didn't know ... that is to say ... I thought you had called out." He looked at the sick man with displeasure and with curiosity.

The Pope rebuked him sharply: "We did not call. You gave Us no time to do so, Abbot Udualrich! But come in, come in. There is something We wanted to say to you in any case."

The abbot hesitated, then knelt down before the stern figure. Pope Leo IX was no longer the kind father, no longer the fraternal friend who was close to him in Christ. His voice was grave, and his eyes looked sternly at the Abbot of Reichenau.

"We have decided that We will not yet leave, Abbot Udualrich. We want first to look at the intellectual, spiritual, and economic situation of the abbey. We would be truly pleased if that would permit Us to act against the negative rumors about Reichenau that have come to Our ears in far-off Rome."

The abbot bowed deeply. This was the disaster that he had feared with such trembling and apprehension—the papal visitation.

"As you know, We have an outstanding knowledge of the rules and customs of the holy founder of your order. We want to be sure that these are observed to the letter in your abbey, in the spirit of the reform of Cluny. We would find it very ... painful, if these had been interpreted or even changed in accordance with your own ideas. We will eat breakfast alone. After that, We await the entire monastic community in the chapter room, where We will make Our decision known. We want no one to be informed about this beforehand. We order and command that everything be left in the state in which it is at present. See to it that your monks assemble punctually, Abbot Udualrich. We have a lot to do, and only a few days to do it. Thank you ..." A movement of the Pope's hand indicated that the abbot should leave. The Pope did not stretch out his hand for the abbot to kiss his ring. Udualrich left the library with noticeable haste.

Pope Leo IX rubbed his forehead. He was tired. His face and his voice lost their sternness when he turned again to the sick man: "Tell me honestly, Hermann, whether Reichenau still is as it was in the days of the Lord Berno."

"Is that at all possible, Holy Father?" Hermann asked

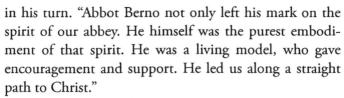

in his turn. "Abbot Berno not only left his mark on the spirit of our abbey. He himself was the purest embodiment of that spirit. He was a living model, who gave encouragement and support. He led us along a straight path to Christ."

"And Abbot Udualrich?"

"He too was given to Reichenau by the Lord, Holy Father. God wants to tell us through the Lord Udualrich that we must go along his path unshaken and unshakable, when his light can no longer be seen clearly in the words and teaching, the action and attitude of a religious superior. God is with us … in the nights without stars. Blessed are those who do not see, and yet believe." The lame man smiled at the Pope, as if he wanted to say: "You understand my meaning …" He added aloud: "God has great trust in us, and he expects that we will have great trust in him."

"And he gave you a special task through me today, Hermann. And that concerns the abbey of Mary in Reichenau too. He demands a great deal of you."

After saying this, the Pope rose and went to the door. He summoned the monk Berthold, who had been waiting and praying in the cloister all the time.

"May the Lord watch over your sleep, Father Hermann."

Stars burned like pure flames above the Gnadensee and the island of Reichenau. The sick man felt no fear of what was to come. He experienced a profound joy, a good peace, and a rich thankfulness. When God makes demands, this is always an expression of his love.

CHAPTER 2

* * *

TOWARD THE OTHER SIDE

Red Thorns

A BREATHLESS TENSION lay over the group of monks who had assembled in the chapter room. Abbot Udualrich could not conceal his inner unease. His eyes roved here and there, until they came to rest on the still, recollected face of the lame man. It was all very well for him to pray—the friend of the Pope!

The Lord Udualrich could not guess that Hermann of Altshausen was in the heart of a mountain torrent, so to speak. A stream of melodies, images, and verses wanted to take form within him, and demanded to be shaped. A profusion of thoughts and ideas assailed him. The words of the Holy Father, admonishing him and at the same time setting him free, had torn down the dam of grief behind which the stream of an entire year had piled up. Now Hermann was delivered up to the floodwaters.

In the midst of this onslaught, Hermann did not lose control. The roaring waves propelled the ship of his heart and spirit in one direction only, toward the Lord. The sick man had always experienced, whenever something new was born in him, that it came from the Lord and led back to him—grace, gift, present and burden. Often, indeed all too often, the poor vessel of his fragile body was too narrow to contain the gifts; his mouth and hands were too weak to exploit the full potential. The suffering of the spirit that was fettered by the powerlessness of the body knew hardships that wounded him more deeply than external pain. Yet even the unused abundance of gifts did not turn into insipid, stale water. A humble act of thanksgiving directed the stream back to the Lord. There was no standstill in this life. And there would no longer be any standstill, now that the spell cast by grief had been broken, the spell that had restricted the creativity of the sick man to the barren, narrow path of the explicit obligations that were laid upon him. He could give more, and he had to give more, if God gave it to him.

In the course of his reflections, he remembered something Abbot Berno had said in chapter about Saint Augustine:

"He cannot resist the Holy Spirit when he comes over him. He comes over him like dew and rain on thirsty ground. Can the earth fend off these gifts of heaven? Augustine is the earth of the Holy Spirit, and he surrenders willingly to the heavenly dew. So it is not he who writes, although it is he who wields the pen. The Holy Spirit writes out of him. And the earth bears rich, immensely rich fruit for the holy Church."

Pope Leo IX entered. His face appeared kind and fatherly in the mild morning light. His voice did not lack warmth when, after a brief prayer, he told the monks that he did not intend to hold an official visitation, since time was too short. During the night, a courier had brought him important news that meant he had to leave soon.

"But We insist, like a careful father of the family, on having a closer look at the abbey of Saint Mary on Reichenau, which We love. As the shepherd of the herd that Christ has entrusted to Us, We want to gather anew the sheep and lambs of this island around the highest Lord and Shepherd by means of admonitions, encouragement, and salutary instructions. Perhaps a careless, naughty little sheep has got entangled in thorns here and there, and We must free it from these thorns. We want to do this with gentleness and love, and to take great pains to act according to the model we have in the Lord Jesus Christ, who has left us the command: 'Learn from me; I am gentle and humble of heart!'"

The Lord Leo looked kindly at the flock of black habits at his feet. A noticeable relief rippled through their ranks as they heard his friendly words.

"Let us do the one work together, beloved brothers and sons in the Lord. Let us together prepare a dwelling place for him in our hearts; let us together prepare a dwelling place for him in this world, so that he may prepare a dwelling place for us with his Father. Let us pray, as Our Lord has taught us to pray ..." The Pope and the monks of Reichenau prayed the Lord's Prayer.

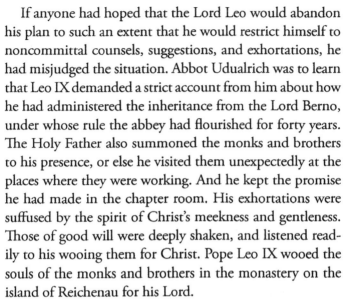

If anyone had hoped that the Lord Leo would abandon his plan to such an extent that he would restrict himself to noncommittal counsels, suggestions, and exhortations, he had misjudged the situation. Abbot Udualrich was to learn that Leo IX demanded a strict account from him about how he had administered the inheritance from the Lord Berno, under whose rule the abbey had flourished for forty years. The Holy Father also summoned the monks and brothers to his presence, or else he visited them unexpectedly at the places where they were working. And he kept the promise he had made in the chapter room. His exhortations were suffused by the spirit of Christ's meekness and gentleness. Those of good will were deeply shaken, and listened readily to his wooing them for Christ. Pope Leo IX wooed the souls of the monks and brothers in the monastery on the island of Reichenau for his Lord.

More than ever, Christ needed faithful people who lived uncompromisingly for him. And were not these to be found in the monasteries, the fortresses of the faith, the houses of God?

The Pope encountered both wheat and chaff in the community. He asked himself whether he might allow both to grow alongside each other until the time of the harvest. Could he allow an Udualrich to stay in office? He had not yet found an answer by the time he came to the cell of the lame man. He had postponed this visit to the final day, saving this joy to the last.

Hermann sat in the armchair at his desk between the two windows, one of which looked to the north, and the other to the east, onto the Gnadensee. His twisted upper body was firmly supported in a recess in the table that had been made especially for him. His left hand rested on a parchment, while his right hand slowly and very laboriously moved the goose quill. He did not stand up when the door opened. He could not turn round to see who was coming; and he supposed that it was Berthold, who wanted to carry out a service of love in his usual quiet way.

Pope Leo IX sat on the stool beside the sick man's chair and looked at the austere poverty of the whitewashed cell and the concentration on Hermann's face as he wrote. What joy there was on the emaciated face of the richest poor man whom Leo had ever seen!

Joy and peace—it was here that they dwelt, here more than anywhere else. How joyless, by comparison, was the Lord Udualrich, how devoid of peace in his desperate anxiety to get hold of the goods of this world and enjoy them! The Pope was seized with a tremendous pity for the abbot. "For he had great possessions ..." That is what we read about the rich young man in the Gospel; many goods, but not the one good thing.

A monk who did not love out of the love of Christ, and for the love of Christ, was terribly poor, since he had deprived his life of that which could give it its one and only meaning.

"I will admonish him seriously and leave him in office, so that he may have the time to become poor in goods and rich in Christ. And I charge you, my friend Hermann, with the true care of souls on Reichenau, with bringing down grace into the souls of the brothers. Your task is to ensure that this grace flows out into the Church, into the world. I am asking a great deal of you, my beloved son, and yet I am asking only that you should love the one thing that you are already doing ..."

The Pope's silent inner soliloquy was interrupted by a cheerful joking voice from the window: "You have given me a feather from a goose that is pulling up the grass out there. It must be a very stubborn bird, because the feather is still alive in my hand. The black scrawl that I have produced with this feather looks as if a goose had waded through my inkwell and then run across the parchment. Come here, Berthold, and see for yourself!" Hermann laughed lightly, and then sighed as he gave up the effort. The Pope took his place behind the lame man. "Have a look for yourself, my friend! The letters I have written stagger so much from side to side that anyone who saw them might speak of trees, of branches in an autumn storm—provided that he had a lot of good will. I am sorry, Berthold, but you will have to copy it all out again. I would have dearly loved to do it myself this once, but I cannot possibly offer the Holy Father my scribblings. I hope there is still time to do it again."

At this point, the Lord Leo drew up the stool in front of the desk and sat down opposite the lame man. "No, Father Hermann, I do not permit that. Berthold will not write one single line anew."

"You, Holy Father!" The blue eyes lighted up. "Berthold, why did you not tell me that the Holy Father had come?"

"Our good Berthold could not do that, Hermann, because he is not here with you. You have had to put up with me as a substitute all this time."

"And did I tell *you* about the living goose feather?" asked Hermann, somewhat shocked. But then he joined in the Pope's heartfelt laughter.

Leo IX nodded emphatically. "Yes, that is what you

did, and now I know that the goose first waded through the inkwell and then ran across your parchment."

With a trembling right hand, the lame man offered him what he had written. "Please take it, Holy Father. You can see with your own eyes that it really looks like that."

The Lord Leo took the piece of writing. The black army of letters stumbled and trembled, staggered and tottered. Scarcely one letter displayed any abiding tendency to remain in the same row as its neighbor. One letter wanted to get higher up, while another tried to position itself under the others; one letter thought it had to go straight upward; one wanted to go left, while its neighbor wanted to go right. But the text was legible. Before the Pope could study the words, Hermann gave him a second parchment, a carefully executed painting.

"Berthold has painted this coat of arms."

The Holy Father looked at the picture, somewhat puzzled. It depicted three red branches of a thorn bush, arranged in ascending order, beginning with the smallest. They were vigorous branches with strong pointed thorns, red thorns on a gold ground.

"May I explain it to you? This is almost the coat of arms of our dynasty, the Counts of Altshausen: three red stag's antlers on a gold ground, symbols of strength and power and courage. But it has been slightly altered, and now we have three thorn branches, symbols of powerlessness, of suffering, and of being abandoned. It is the coat of arms of those who prepare themselves for the *missa orbis*, for the *consecratio mundi*.[1] Would you like to read

---

1. ["Mass of the world," "consecration of the world."]

my verses now, Holy Father? The prayer is also an interpretation of the meaning of the red thorn branches. Or may I read it aloud to you? You will no doubt find it very difficult to read my letters."

Leo gave him back the parchment. "Read, Father Hermann, but not because of the difficulty I might have in reading your text. Such a prayer takes on its deepest life only when it is spoken by the one who has prayed it beforehand."

The Holy Father looked out onto the Gnadensee, onto the quiet, sparkling surface of the water under the cloudless, clear autumn sky.

"You who are the Lord of my life, Jesus Christ!

"You are my beginning, my blessing, my path, my joy, my hope, my only goal. I adore you and I beseech you: Let blossoms bud on the dry branch of my thorns, blossoms from the bright golden ground of grace. You yourself have bound them around my forehead, around my forehead and around my heart. You gave them to me as a seal and a pledge of divine love.

"Lord Jesus Christ, I beseech you: Let them bloom and become fruitful like the crown of thorns that you wore on the path of your pains under the cross. Let them bloom and become fruitful.

"Grant life, from the golden ground of grace, to the smallest of my bitter branches, to the thorn branch of torment, of sickness, of pains. Once you gave the thorn branch to a child, who understood the gift only when he was a man. Let it bloom and become fruitful.

"Grant life to the branch with the bigger thorns, with the thorns of inner distress and repentance, with the keen anguishes of the spirit that struggles, with the burning

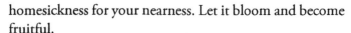
homesickness for your nearness. Let it bloom and become fruitful.

"Grant abundance, superabundance of life to the largest of my bitter branches, to the branch with the thorns of the futile endeavor to find you in the souls of the beloved brothers; the thorns of the sufferings over those who do not know you; the thorns of the tears shed because of those who do not want you; the thorns of the lamentations when your love is disregarded, and your grace is unrecognized and betrayed; the thorns of the terrible distress I feel for the sake of your holy kingdom, and of the world for which you died on the cross and that you want to bring home, Lord Jesus Christ, so that it may become a sacrifice of praise to the Father's glory.

"Lord Jesus Christ, I beseech you: let blossoms bud on the dry branch of my thorns. Let them bloom and become fruitful."

"I shall wear them in homage of her who is the purest blossom, who opened herself to the Spirit as his bride and who gave us you, the holiest fruit of blessed virginity.

"Lord, I wish to bring my blossoms to your most blessed Mother, the Virgin Mary, the mild light that shines in the hours of tribulation, the helper and consoler, the mistress and Mother of merciful love.

"Leave the thorns with me ... as the seal and pledge of divine love."

"

After the lame man finished the prayer, a long time passed before Pope Leo IX turned to him. A still light shone in his bright eyes. He laid his right hand, which had been given the authority to bind and to loose in the name of Christ, his consecrated right hand, on the slender hand of the cripple.

"Thank you, brother," said the Holy Father. He repeated his words: "Thank you!"

The monk did not reply. For what should he say? He waited calmly, with his trembling hand sheltered under the right hand of the Pope. As he took his leave, Pope Leo IX looked at the gaunt face, marked by suffering and yet so free, so relaxed and noble.

"Any more words between us would be superfluous, my brother in Christ. We have told each other what truly matters. You will give Reichenau what you can give it, because you share my concern for it. If God's plan should mean that this once radiant star of his Church should be extinguished, a new star will arise somewhere else. God becomes man again and again in those who open up the chambers of their soul to him. In them and through them, he goes on his way into the world, the way of redemption, the way of the cross. Your thorn branches bloom. God is faithful."

The Pope detached his right hand slowly from the lame man's hand and blessed him. Then he took the two parchment leaves, the painting and the prayer, with the red thorns on a gold ground ...

"

"We leave today!"

Pope Leo IX gave the command, and Archdeacon Hildebrand was the only one to show no sign of surprise.

"Your Holiness, it will take some time before everything is ready," complained the papal private secretary. "The day is already late, and we will be obliged to cross the Gnadensee in the dusk."

Leo's answer was slightly sarcastic: "Aha, you are afraid that the barque of Peter would capsize on the Gnadensee?" But he suddenly became serious, and continued: "Monsignor, we are traveling today *because* the day is already late, and night is about to fall. It is high time. The Lord calls Us. Our work here is done. We must make use for Christ of every hour that he still gives Us. Blossoms must bud from the thorn branches everywhere—everywhere, not only on Reichenau."

The Pope's white ship sailed across the Gnadensee. Only a few monks stood at the bank; the Lord Leo had given word that his departure was not to be made known. From the window of his cell, Hermann followed the calm gliding of the ship through the silver water. Soon, the lake would shine in red-gold light, when the sun sank in the west …

Berthold was with him. He had just brought him the Holy Father's greetings and told him of the task with which the Pope had charged him.

"Write down the *Vita Hermani,* Berthold.[2] Have him tell you the story of his life. Do not force him, just ask him in my name to tell you as much and as far as is compatible with the delicate shyness he feels about speaking of his suffering. Begin soon, Berthold, begin soon … if possible, begin already today. I will leave appropriate instructions for the abbot," the Lord Leo had told the young monk. "Hermann must not be forgotten. His life makes us rich

2. ["Life of Hermann."]

through his poverty, and poor through his riches. His cross makes us happier and his greatness makes us humbler. We want many people to enjoy these gifts."

Berthold did not quote the literal words of the Pope, when he told his master of the charge that he had been given. He presented Leo's request to him almost shyly, and then waited eagerly for the answer. He began to feel anxious when Hermann remained silent for a long time.

Would the father speak to him? Would he entrust to him, his pupil, secrets of his life that Abbot Berno had taken with him into eternity? All at once, the young man understood how much the Holy Father was asking of the lame man here. If only he could fetch the white ship back to Herrenbuck harbor! He would then fall to his knees and ask Pope Leo IX to excuse the father and Berthold from this charge. Is *he* to penetrate into the hidden and silent realm of this life, he who took his first steps in learning Latin as a boy at the feet of the master? He is a monk with little experience, and the father is constantly obliged to show forbearance with his boisterousness ...

"Father," he croaked. "The Pope only asked you. It was not a command. If you do not want to ..."

The Pope's ship had just docked at the far shore, and Hermann turned away from the Gnadensee. His great eyes were full of astonishment at the last words of his faithful companion. He gently rebuked him:

"But who told you that I do not want to do it, foolish young man?"

"You ... you were silent for such a long time."

The lame man sighed. "Forgive me, my son! I did not realize that you were in a hurry. I was bidding farewell to our Holy Father. Of course I will do what he asks,

Berthold. That is a smaller sacrifice for me than you suppose. Why should I not respond to your fidelity by trusting you? I will attempt to sketch a picture of my life for you. The will of our Holy Father is sufficient justification for the work that we shall do together. I do not need any other justification. And I do not know why it would be worth relating my life."

"In order to praise the mercies of Our Lord Jesus Christ, father, that have become visible in your life."

The sick man eagerly agreed. "Yes, my son, yes! Now you have put me to shame. Thank you for this lesson. Let us begin at once. I will tell you the story as if it was about someone else. That will make it easier for us both, surely. You will listen to me, and then write down afterward what you think is worth writing down.

"Where shall we go first? To Altshausen? No, we shall go to the Gnadensee, to my beloved Gnadensee, which has been a faithful companion to me, although I almost broke faith with it once and for all. You look shocked, Berthold? Well, that too happened in my life. I voluntarily parted company with Reichenau.

"Come, we will go together in our minds down to the shore of the Gnadensee. Imagine the atmosphere of a beautiful day in early spring. It was one day in March of 1030 ..."

The lame man made the sign of the cross. Then he laid his hands in his lap and began the story, looking down toward the peaceful lake that now shone with a red-gold glow.

"In March of 1030 ..."

"

The Little Bird Wants to Fly

The Gnadensee gleamed like soft mother-of-pearl. The pointed lances of the reeds stood brown against the pale blue sky, shivering from time to time when a soft breeze of early spring caressed them and wooed them. A youth crouched motionless in the yellow grass from last winter on the shore. His narrow curved back was turned to the abbey of Saint Mary of Reichenau. His fellow pupils had brought him secretly from the abbey to the shore, because he had worn them down by his asking and begging. His cousin from Dillingen had brought him some little daisies with a frayed crown of gray-white petals around the dirty yellow corona. But then he had sensed their pity, their pity for his wretched, crooked body, and suddenly he had shouted to them: "Go away! Go away! Leave me alone!"

The pupils shrugged their shoulders tolerantly and left. They were familiar with his sudden outbursts, and they did not resent them. A sick person has his moods, and these have to be forgiven.

Now the short and cheerful peals of a bell rang out from the abbey, the fortress of God with its protecting walls and towers. The youth paid no attention to the ringing. His big eyes, which shone with an uncommon blue light, tried anxiously to make out the far shore between the stalks, but they had set him down too close to the reeds! His mouth tautened with an unchildlike hardness, and his thin hands clasped each other. A bird swept out of the rustling reeds with a wooing cry, and Hermann of Altshausen followed it with his gaze. It was flying over to the other side, over to the other side, into freedom …

On the other side ... that was where life was ... cities and villages, knights and their squires, merchants and peasants, men and women in cheerful, bright-colored garments ... life. He thought of the solitary cell, of the silent monks, of his fellow pupils who were sometimes rough and thoughtless in their healthy high spirits, of the days and nights of tormenting pains ... He wanted to get over to the other side, to fly away, to escape. He needed the wings of a bird!

He brushed his hand over his brow, like one awaking from sleep. He looked at his dark pupil's garment, and at his weak feet that were in continuous pain. He let himself fall laboriously onto his side, because he could no longer endure the crouching position. The grass on the shore was wet and cool, the earth smelled bitter. A gnarled old willow tree stood a few steps away from him. If he could reach it and pull himself up on its branches and look at the far shore, without the distraction of the tangle of reeds ... But how was he to get to the willow? Only a few steps along the gently ascending shoreline ... Only a few steps ... He could not take one single step. He could not even stand up on his feet without a special support, without crutches or helping hands.

So he lay in the grass on the shore, and gave way gloomily to the bitter sense of his impotence. But the gnarled old willow and, even more, the clear view over to the far shore were too much of a temptation. Only a few steps ... He resisted no longer. One who cannot walk must crawl. No doubt, the sight would delight the other pupils. The boy from Altshausen with the extraordinarily intelligent mind, who tackled the Latin and mathematical formulas better than many a boy tackled his spoon when he ate soup, crawled across the earth like a worm. Hermann crawled. He pushed himself forward with his hands and arms over grass, gravel, and stones. With each movement, he covered only a very little bit of the way; then he rested, panting, with his face in the grass. As he crawled laboriously onward, he scraped his hands, which he dug heedlessly into the ground, and he dirtied his dark garment with soil and crushed grass.

Only a few steps … How far they were for him! Then, finally, he reached the willow, embraced the barky trunk, and pulled himself closer and closer to it. Good—now he had to get higher up. He forgot that he must not take both his arms away from the tree at the same time, and he crashed into the gnarled roots, striking his forehead. The pain spurred him on to try again. Gritting his teach angrily, he did his best. His right hand reached the lowest branch, and he tugged and pulled until his left hand managed to grasp another branch … And with an almost superhuman effort, he finished what he had begun. Supported by the branches, he succeeded after several attempts to turn his body around. The boy stood upright, with two strong branches under his armpits, and gazed with a bitter triumph on his dirty, scratched face across to the far shore. He had paid a high price for this view. He felt faint and battered. His pains stabbed through him, and he trembled as the wind grew stronger.

Toward evening, Ekkehard, the infirmarian, found him. He looked grimly at the strange picture, at the youth who hung on the tree. He freed him reluctantly from the branches and took the light body in his arms, as if it were that of a little child. "We have nothing but trouble with you!" he grumbled on the way to the abbey.

Hermann pressed his lips together and said nothing. Ekkehard brought him to the abbot. The youth was not afraid of a rebuke, but he was uneasy about meeting the Lord Berno, because he revered and loved the abbot. Ekkehard put him down in front of the abbot's cell, then picked him up under his arms and bundled him into the room. A blush burned on the gaunt cheeks of the lame youth. A scion of Altshausen had his pride, even if he was a helpless cripple.

Abbot Berno studied the picture with obvious disconcertment. Why was Ekkehard bringing him the embarrassed pupil who was covered in scratches? He turned to the youth and asked calmly: "Well, Hermann, what does this mean?"

The lame youth avoided his inquiring gaze and gasped: "I got them to bring me to the shore of the Gnadensee without asking Master Burkhard for permission." The blush on his face deepened to one single flame. Would he have to admit in the presence of the infirmarian that he had crawled over the earth like a worm?

The Lord Berno noticed his distress, and gave the order: "Put him in the armchair, Ekkehard." He nodded to the disappointed monk that he should leave the room.

Hermann breathed more easily, and the defiance left his scratched face. His scraped hands fiddled restlessly with his garment.

"And what did you do at the Gnadensee, my son?"

The pupil told his story hesitantly: "First, I sat on the shore, but the reeds blocked my view. They had set me down too close to the reeds. Then ... then ... I crawled ... to an old willow ... and pulled myself up. Then I was

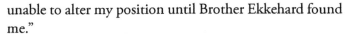

unable to alter my position until Brother Ekkehard found me."

The Lord Berno looked kindly at the slumped figure in the wide armchair. The poor cripple had in fact achieved something great this afternoon. If only he would not keep on employing his uncommonly strong will for such meaningless acts of defiance! Or might there be something more behind this than a boyish experiment to see what he could force his sick body to do?

Hermann waited for a word from the abbot. The pain compelled him to bend his shoulders farther down. He would have liked to apologize to the abbot, the father who was his great benefactor; but could he cause him pain by telling him the truth and saying: "I want to go away, Father Abbot. My family brought me here as a lame child of seven years, but the abbey of Saint Mary on Reichenau has become too narrow for me. I cannot bear it any longer, not even out of gratitude"?

If any human being was dear to him on this earth, apart from his lady mother, it was Abbot Berno, his spiritual father, his teacher, his guide and friend. He besought him silently: "Help me, father! Help me! You have always understood my distress, every other time." He bent down even deeper when the pains attacked him, as if he could bury them in himself.

"Hermann, do you now want to leave Reichenau?" The abbot asked his question gently, but the boy winced as if he had been struck, and he stared at the monk with eyes widened by fear. His lips moved soundlessly.

"Do you want to go back to Altshausen after ten years with us?"

"No, no," said the lame young man quickly. In his mind, he saw the threatening face of Count Wolfrad, his father. "Not home, not home, Father Abbot ... I want ..." He lost his courage and fell silent.

Understanding and sympathy shone in the dark eyes of the Lord Berno, as he asked quietly: "But you want to go away, don't you?"

Hermann raised his skinny hands helplessly, in a touching gesture of perplexity. "Yes, Father Abbot, I want to go away, and at the same time I want to stay. I love our abbey, and yet I want to go away. Sometimes I love it and hate it simultaneously. I don't know how to put it—being shut in, the walls, the quiet, the silence, and ... also the prayer and the study ... all of it, all of it can disgust me so much that I feel a real aversion to it, and yet I keep on loving it ..."

It became too difficult for the youth to speak. He felt confused, like a little child that had gotten lost. Abbot Berno did not even seem startled. Had he seen this coming?

"What do you want, my child? You bear some specific longing within you."

When the sick youth replied, he almost shouted. Perhaps the simple question of his spiritual father had broken down the final dam. "Life! Life! I don't want to know just from books what life is. I want to encounter it. The poor fisherman down at the lake is richer than I am, because he is alive."

The Lord Berno looked into the passionate face of the lame youth. He could rebuke him and accuse him of a terrible ingratitude. Did the celebrated Reichenau need to offer a home to a handicapped cripple? Was it not a great privilege that he had been permitted to stay there, when Count Wolfrad II brought him there in 1020 with the words: "About all he's good for is to become a monk"? Was not hard work needed over many years to bring the completely lame boy to the point where he could speak again and use his limbs to a limited extent? The abbot could have pointed out that Burkhard, Tatto, and he himself had taken care of him and trained his alert mind. Even more than that, the abbot could have reminded him of the tough struggle he had fought for the soul of the lame boy, who was inclined to shut himself up in loneliness and bitterness. He could have charged Hermann with ingratitude, and almost with a betrayal of him, his spiritual father. The Lord Berno did none of this. He spoke no words of admonition or of consolation, nor did he point to the great wealth of intellectual gifts that the Lord had given Hermann.

The young man's demand was justified. He had been specially chosen by the Lord and certainly called by him, and he must experience what life is. Abbot Berno believed, even now, that his world later on would be a monastic cell. In that cell, his heart and his eye must remain wide open for the world and for life.

A man like Hermann of Altshausen ought to give the Church and the world more than this or that academic treatise. He must not become like so many monks, who circle in a narrow radius around themselves, obsessed with their own affairs, their own work, their prayer, their asceticism, their problems and difficulties—which were often so small—without any knowledge of the total picture. His sickness made Hermann more exposed to this danger, since his lameness kept on throwing him back on his own self. The fetters were often tight around him. This was why his soul must become wide, very wide, and free for others, for Christ. The abbot thought: I will take the risk. He must go out into the world.

After a lengthy silence, the Lord Berno said, almost cheerfully: "Our little bird wants to fly."

Hermann was surprised, and lifted his head, which had sunk lower and lower during the long silence. Once again, his cheeks blushed red. Was the Lord Berno playing a practical joke on the wretched state of a cripple? The horror in his eyes was so eloquent that the monk hastened to add: "Hermann, the habit of our order should be worn only by one who desires it with all his heart. You know what I say to the novices at the hour of decision, when I show them the Rule: 'See, this is the law under which you will serve as a soldier from now on. If you can observe it, enter. If you cannot do so, go freely hence.'"

The young man murmured bitterly: "Have I any choice? What would be the use of a cripple out there? The bird in the reeds, the worm ..." He broke off at this word, and then repeated it emphatically, as he thought of his crawling to the willow on the shore of the lake. "Yes, the worm that feeds on the earth. They are freer than me, since I am tied down by the pain in my limbs. Do I have any choice, since my parents handed me over to the abbey as a gift to God?"

"I dispense you from the obligation of the oblation, Hermann. What God wants is the free consent of a free heart. You were much too young to take a decision ... I have been reflecting just now on how we can arrange for you to get to know the world, and I believe that I have already found the solution. As you know, I come from the land west of the Rhine, and I was a monk in Prüm, before the emperor's will brought me to Reichenau as its abbot. I have relatives who live in the old imperial city of Aachen, my cousin Arnulph of Rahnwyl and his wife, the noble Lady Veronica. When you stay with them, you will have contacts with the world of the court, with scholars, preachers, clergymen, and cathedral canons. You will no doubt object that you could not let yourself be a burden on strangers. But for the Lady Veronica, you would be a consolation in her grief over her son and heir, who passed away recently. The Lord Arnulph will help you to penetrate further into the world of the spirit. He is a man with an exceptionally fine education. In order that you will not feel dependent in any way, the abbey will give the income from the manor at Isny for your maintenance in Aachen. Your lady mother will surely send one of your servants from Altshausen to look after you. The sulphurous water of the famous hot springs in Aachen may perhaps have a therapeutic effect on your body." (The abbot added, in his own mind, "And the bitter tears of homesickness for Reichenau may have a therapeutic effect on your soul.")

Hermann followed with amazement the tranquil unfolding of the plan. A wealth of new possibilities was opening up for him—for the cripple who had just crawled across the earth like a worm, in order to get at least a clear view over to the far shore. He looked incredulously at the well-known face: "Do you really want to send me to Aachen, Father Abbot?"

The Lord Berno laid his hand on his shoulder. "Yes, Hermann, I am sending you out into the world, into the life that is in vigorous motion in the old imperial city. You must choose freely and decide in complete freedom

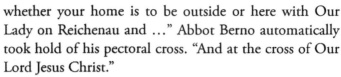

whether your home is to be outside or here with Our Lady on Reichenau and ..." Abbot Berno automatically took hold of his pectoral cross. "And at the cross of Our Lord Jesus Christ."

The lame man did not register the last words. Waves of gratitude and of expectancy threatened to sweep him away in their flood. Then it occurred to him that he still had to make atonement. In view of the generosity of his spiritual father, he was ashamed of his childish defiance and disobedience.

"Lord and Father Abbot, may I ask you for forgiveness for acting without authorization this afternoon, and also for inducing other pupils to act contrary to obedience?"

"Forgiveness is granted to you ... to you and to the others. You have prepared your penance for yourself."

Hermann was surprised and relieved, and thought: What penance is that? Abbot Berno rose, went into an adjacent room, and came back with some cloths. "Give me your hands!"

The sick man stretched out his hands obediently, without understanding what the father wanted of him.

"Turn them over!" the Lord Berno commanded.

The abbot looked at the palms, which were scratched and far from clean. He placed them on his knees and cleaned them thoroughly of dirt and blood. While the abbot performed this humble service, Hermann felt like the apostle Peter on Holy Thursday. Like him, he wanted to cry out: "I will never let you wash me!" Now, he understood what the Lord Berno had meant when he spoke of the penance that Hermann had prepared for himself.

The abbot also cleaned the lame man's face thoroughly, and even his garment. The sick man bore this help with

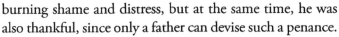
burning shame and distress, but at the same time, he was also thankful, since only a father can devise such a penance.

"So, Hermann, now come with me to Our Lady …"

With the help of another monk, the abbot brought him through the cloister to the monastery church. They set him down before the stone image of the Mother of God.

The sick man was silent within himself for a long time. Ought he not to exult in his soul? He had been given permission to go out into the world. Outside, there awaited him the life for which he had yearned ever since the terrible illness befell him. For a long time, he had not known how to define the unquenchable pain in his heart, until it became ever clearer. It was an imperious voice that he must now follow. He wanted to say this to Mary, the Lady of Reichenau, his beloved heavenly Mother.

"Mother, most beloved Mother Mary, I am allowed …," he began, but then stopped short. Would she approve of his leaving the place that was dedicated to her?

"Mother, there is nothing else I can do. And you understand me, don't you?"

As if he had found the happy solution that would bring joy to the Mother, he prayed: "Mother, I am going, because I must go. Help me to come back home."

The chanting of the monks somehow made its way into his consciousness. They were singing Compline. "*Te lucis ante terminum* …"[3] The sick man joined in the chant, without guessing that the wide path of his return home to Reichenau had already begun.

---

3. ["(We beseech) you before the ending of the light," the first words of the hymn sung at Compline.]

CHAPTER 3

* * *

DETOUR

Oil in the Jug

THE MAN LIFTED HIS HANDS slowly from the bowl. His movements betrayed a clear hesitation. Drops of water, clear as glass, formed pearls on his smooth brown skin, ran over his short fingers, slid over the pointed fingertips, and fell back into the bowl. Each drop that landed made a new circle on the surface of the water, so that a confused interlacing of little circles shivered there.

Had Master Theophilos, the Greek physician, who was known to the citizens of the imperial city of Aachen only by his family name, Cheirisophos, nothing more important to do than to look idly at the play of the drops of water?

His weak red mouth was pursed in indignation, and his heavy dark brows were furrowed. Suddenly impatient, he shook the last drops from his hands and dried them with the white linen cloth. He strode quickly through the big living room with its heavy wood-beamed ceiling. His steps were inaudible, supple and nimble. His small, graceful figure seemed strangely delicate in the rich and yet austere furnishings of the room. The massive tables and chairs, cupboards and chests of dark oak were overpowering and crushing. A stranger was creeping quietly through the room in the house of the noble Rahnwyls in Aachen, and he ran his right hand restlessly through his shining black hair. Were they coming already? He sighed impatiently.

What was he to tell the young man as the final result of his examination? What, indeed? Was he to tell him the truth, the entire and full and terrible truth? Was he to fling this truth into the very heart of the hope that had newly sprouted? Was the only answer he had for the sick man's extraordinarily strong hunger for life: "You are a cripple, and you will remain a cripple"?

Master Cheirisophos resumed his roaming through the room. Without noticing what he was doing, he went round the oak table again and again. Had he not already begun to deceive the lame man? When he saw the poor emaciated limbs, he had concealed his shock behind meaningless, noncommittal words, and the pleasant expression on his face had betrayed nothing of the shock he had felt on seeing this pitiable figure.

The servant's movements were unutterably gentle, and in such a big-boned giant, that was almost amusing ... but the doctor had felt as if the servant was uncovering the body of one who had died. It was translucent, transparent—not a "bodily" body at all, yet tied to the earth through its infirmity. Its paleness reminded him of the wax of noble candles.

But how much life spoke, indeed dazzled forth, from the eyes, from those blue, wise, and incredibly alert eyes! They had followed his movements with a tense attentiveness, as he carefully examined the slender joints and palpated the muscles. Distrust and hope struggled with each other for supremacy in this questing, piercing gaze; and on the deepest level, there lurked a terrible anxiety, a harrowing fear that the doctor would pronounce a verdict that dashed all hope.

Cheirisophos sighed and went to the window, where he stared with unseeing eyes at the narrow, dirty street. "Yes—and I put on a show like an impostor and a charlatan. I did what I have always deeply despised in the members of my guild. I used words that must inevitably kindle hope in the poor man. I made brief remarks, as if I was talking to myself. 'Ah ... so that is still all right. Better than I thought ...' And the fear departed more and more from his eyes. But I ought to have said to him: 'My friend, do not let yourself be seduced by any hope. Look at the stiff joints, which have been hard for years! The leg muscles are dead, and the backbone is severely buckled. That is irreversible. And besides, I do not even know how to define your illness properly, although we physicians give it the generic name 'gout,' and the pious ones go so far as to speak of the working of the demons. You are a cripple, and you will remain a cripple. At most, I hope I can promise you with reasonable certainty that your pains

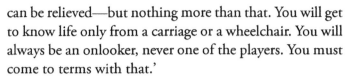

can be relieved—but nothing more than that. You will get to know life only from a carriage or a wheelchair. You will always be an onlooker, never one of the players. You must come to terms with that.'

"Why did I not have the courage to say that? Why do I still lack the courage? Why I am too cowardly to speak these firm and honest words? The men of old in Sparta were right to refuse to bring up such a human being. They extinguished a meaningless existence in good time, and as painlessly as possible. Meaningless? Yes, it is meaningless! What could give meaning to the life of a cripple who is constantly racked with pain? Can one speak of 'life' at all, in such a case? Would it not be more humane simply to extinguish this existence? Would not the night of death be the greatest act of mercy that one could perform for such a man?"

The doctor sensed that this idea became an enticing temptation. Should he help the other man in this way? He thought of a white powder that worked quickly and almost painlessly. Ought he to show the sick man this "mercy"? He walked around the oak table once again, his hands clasped behind his back, as if one hand had to hold the other fast in order to prevent it from doing something imprudent.

Then he heard another voice within him, contradicting his natural feelings, contradicting his healthy paganism, by admitting that the wretched existence of the son of the count of Altshausen had a value. And this lame man wanted to live, with a desire stronger than that of the doctor, who was bored by life in its stale monotony. Cheirisophos no longer understood himself. Why did this case affect him more than the everyday cases of his many patients? He had long become accustomed to treat the sick in general with an impersonal kindness, without any inner sympathy. Sometimes, he found it hard to suppress a yawn when they described at great length the sufferings they had endured. This cripple, who did not complain, made him uneasy.

Walter, the servant, bore the lame man into the living room. The broad-shouldered farmer's son from Swabia held the light, crooked figure in his arms as a mother holds her child. With clumsy carefulness, he set Hermann down in the soft cushions of the armchair. Now, the dark garment once again concealed the tortured body. Only the gaunt face with the lofty brow under the blond hair and the slender hands were exposed to view. The big eyes were even more demanding and inescapable. An imperious power went forth from them, and the sick man's question sounded almost mocking:

"Tell me, Master Cheirisophos, does not my good Walter treat me far too carefully? He handles me as if I was a precious vessel that he does not want to break."

A fragile and precious vessel? The doctor winced involuntarily as he heard these words. Did not this body, marked by sickness, recall one of those fragile alabaster vases, of translucent, veined alabaster, that he knew from Corinth? At home, there had been sealed alabaster jars with a precious content that was a mystery to the boy, and alabaster bowls where wicks swam in oil. A strange comparison …

"Please sit down, Master." The lame man accompanied his words with a gesture of invitation. "Sit beside me and tell me your severe verdict."

The blue eyes inspected him and put a question. The

farmer's boy behind the chair likewise stared at the doctor, as if he wanted to warn him and to protect his master.

"To protect him from my lies," thought Master Cheirisophos bitterly. Should he ... could he tell the truth? He hesitated and chewed his lower lip. The lame man stretched out his hand. The trembling, crooked hand asked for an answer. The physician smiled the confident and soothing smile of the experienced and superior expert in medicine. Had he not studied the laws of nature, and was he not capable of improving on them? Might he not think himself equal to the task, even if the chances of success were slight? Was there not often a surprising and unforeseen transformation in the process of an illness?

"My verdict?" His voice was gentle and smooth as the voice of a woman. "Well, it was good that you came to Aachen, Count Hermann. I expect much, very much indeed for you from daily baths in the hot sulphurous springs. After the baths, we will regularly massage your muscles and joints."

The tension in the blue eyes was unbearable! Did the man from Altshausen see through his imposture? Did he sense that this was nothing more than a rather crude attempt to reassure him?

The sick man asked, in a cracking voice: "You expect much, Master? But ... what do you call 'much'?"

The doctor laid his beautiful hands on his breast, as he declared: "Your pains will lessen ..."

Hermann made a contemptuous movement, as if that was unimportant. "And what else can be achieved?"

The Greek Master felt a secret disgust for himself as he gasped: "In the long term, your limbs will certainly gain a greater mobility. But that will take a long time. You must be patient, because the process of healing can take place only very slowly. Your limbs were stiff for a decade, and the muscles in the legs are completely flaccid. You can certainly not count on a quick healing. We will begin with the treatment tomorrow morning."

The doctor got up quickly, in order to put an end to the unpleasant conversation. He wanted to get away from the spell cast by his kindly lies, and out of the field of vision of those penetrating eyes. But before he could escape, the hoarse voice of the lame man reached him, the words tumbling over one another in his excitement.

"Will … will … I learn how to walk … again?" Trembling, his breath wheezing, Hermann of Altshausen waited for the answer. His crooked hands clawed at his garment.

Cheirisophos would have loved to scream: "No, you fool, no! Am I a magician? Can I work miracles?" But he skillfully evaded the question by posing one of his own: "Why should that not be possible after a lengthy treatment, Count Hermann? Naturally, you will have to give me your unwavering support, and you must practice unwearyingly. Then our combined forces will reach the goal. And you must also practice with your hands, again and again, so that the strength comes back into your muscles and the joints will become flexible again."

The doctor laid his right hand on the table surface, crooked like the hand of the lame man. His left hand pressed it down, up and down, up and down, up and down …

Hermann watched this attentively. How simple it seemed!

"And now please excuse me for today. Other patients

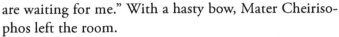

are waiting for me." With a hasty bow, Mater Cheirisophos left the room.

Hermann sat there like one under a spell. Of all the words the doctor had spoken, he had taken in only one sentence … "I am going to learn to walk again," he murmured over and over. "To walk! Then—yes, then life will begin. I will be able to walk again …"

And it was as if he already felt the solid ground, the crunching stones, and the soft grass under his feet, as he had felt them more than a decade ago.

"I will be able to walk again," he babbled, drunk with joy. "I will no longer be dependent on other people's help … to walk again, to walk again …"

He did not notice that Walter responded to this outbreak of joy with an angry sigh. The servant stretched out his hand clumsily to the doctor's washbasin, and water splashed over. He was a fine liar, this Cheirisophos!

The simple and honest mind of the farmer's son had sensed the untruthfulness of his words, and he felt pain on behalf of the young man who was taken in by them. But he could not express what he was feeling. Gloomily, he cleaned up the pool of water, while his master stammered joyfully, over and over:

"I will be able to walk … to walk. Then life will begin …"

Arnulph of Rahnwyl entered. The elderly nobleman remained standing in the doorframe, listening somberly to the murmurs of the sick man. He saw Hermann's right hand on the table surface and the left hand that kept on trying to press the crooked fingers downward—an effort that was both unwearying and useless. The hard arc of the right hand did not yield.

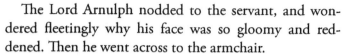
The Lord Arnulph nodded to the servant, and wondered fleetingly why his face was so gloomy and reddened. Then he went across to the armchair.

"Hermann?"

The lame man lifted his eyes joyfully to his aged host. "It's you, Lord Arnulph? Have you already heard the news?"

What a radiant and overwhelming joy shone out of those eyes and resonated exultantly in that voice!

"I'm going to be able to walk again. Just imagine … after ten years, after ten long years. The doctor has just told me."

The old man was taken aback and said nothing. He sat down beside his guest, while Walter left the room. Hermann was incapable of quelling the exultation in his heart. Tears of joy ran down his gaunt cheeks.

"Only someone who has had the same fate can realize what that means for me. It is more than a decade since I was able to stand upright on my feet. I have not been able to take one single step. I was always dependent on other people's help. I always had to wait for that help and to ask for it. And it was not always given promptly and gladly. How often have I been ashamed of my helplessness! How often have I wept because of my terrible poverty. Now, my fetters will be loosened … Lord Arnulph, can you imagine the joy I feel?"

The man with the white beard nodded gravely. "I can imagine what this hope may mean for you, Hermann, but are you not being too …"

The lame man interrupted him, without noticing what he was doing. "I feel as if I was wakening to new life out of a dark grave. That is what Lazarus must have felt, when the Lord called him: 'Come out, Lazarus!,' and when he gave him back life—life." Hermann uttered the last word reverently. He put all his hope, all his expectation, all his joy into this one little word.

He did not see the signs of grief and consternation on the face of his host. Arnulph had come in order to take away from him the hope that Master Cheirisophos had wrongly kindled in him. The Greek had admitted to the master of the house that he had been too cowardly to tell the sick man the truth.

"I have acted like a swindler. Hermann of Altshausen will remain a cripple."

But now the happiness of the young man sealed the nobleman's lips. He simply could not bring himself to thrust him down into the deep night of hopelessness, after so radiant and overpowering a joy had erupted, and Hermann's expectations had risen to such heights.

Perhaps it would be better to break the news to him slowly, bit by bit. This was assuredly not the right moment to do so. And if Hermann did in fact go to the hot springs, perhaps he might get better—even if that seemed unlikely. And if not, well, there would still be plenty of time to intervene. This was how Lord Arnulph justified his silence to himself; but his clear feeling of guilt told him that he did not believe Hermann's condition would improve. His hidden perplexity led him to change the subject.

"Hermann, you wanted to see my books and texts, did you not? You must not compare my modest collection with the well-stocked library on Reichenau. And yet, I am proud of it. Would you like to inspect my little 'treasure chamber'?"

The lame man enthusiastically accepted the kindly invitation. Walter carried him into the wood-paneled room that the Lord Arnulph called the "chamber of books." Arnulph presented his treasures one by one to the sick man, and was delighted to see how the crooked fingers caressed a book with a shy tenderness. This young man was certainly well acquainted with the marvelous world of the spirit!

The Lord of Rahnwyl took one particular parchment and handed it to his guest with an emphatic ceremoniousness, since he knew that it would give Hermann the greatest joy.

"Abbot Berno wrote this for us ..."

Abbot Berno ... Suddenly, the expression of the narrow face, of the blue eyes, altered. The sparkle of joy died out, extinguished all at once like the flame of a candle in a heavy gale. Abbot Berno ... It was as if a mask had fallen away, and the old man saw naked pain, loneliness, homesickness, in the frozen face of the lame man. Abbot Berno ... The hand shook, unable to manage a gesture of timid gentleness as it took hold of the parchment, which was beautifully written and adorned with fine initial letters. Hermann's hand was no longer something that transmitted inner joy to him. It lay feebly on the yellow parchment leaf, as if it were handed over to suffering and pain.

"Abbot Berno wrote this for us ..."

The Lord Arnulph had to ask Hermann twice if he wanted to take any texts away with him to study them. The sick man distractedly indicated one or other book, without realizing that he had also pointed to the Lord Berno's parchment. He found it with a shock on his table, later on. Then he read the sentence that began with the

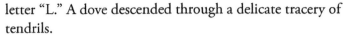
letter "L." A dove descended through a delicate tracery of tendrils.

"Love is the vital principle of the Most Holy Trinity ..."

"

He stared at the dove, he stared at the letters. He read the words without grasping their meaning. Like a blind man, he sat before the text and could not fend off the storm of feelings that swooped down upon him.

"Abbot Berno wrote this for us ..."

To live? To learn to walk? Are those real possibilities? Why is he here? Everything that he had learned and experienced in Aachen seemed to him meaningless, remote, and unreal.

Reichenau and Abbot Berno: they had regained their power and their reality. He almost thought he could see the waters of the Gnadensee shining, and hear the roar of the waves as they rolled onto the gravelly shore ...

The air he had breathed on Reichenau was pure and mild ... How well he had been able to pray in the broad nave of the abbey church! Everything there was familiar to him. It was home, and a savage homesickness took hold of him ... Home ...

Abbot Berno ...

"Was I a fool, to take the road to Aachen? What do I really want here? Why did I leave my home, the abbey, the security? Why did I run away from Abbot Berno's fatherly guidance? Why?"

He no longer understood himself.

He read the words a second time: "Love is the vital

principle of the Most Holy Trinity ..." Ought he to go home to Reichenau ... home?

Then he caught sight of his crooked right hand on the table surface. Go home? No, he wanted to live. "Love is ..." No, he must exercise! Exercise again and again!

"Love ..."

No, exercise! Exercise! He pushed Abbot Berno's parchment aside. He would not go home. He would stay on in Aachen. He wanted to live.

"

As they carried him through the sunny streets of the city of Aachen, he was dead tired after the bath in the hot springs and the therapy. The repulsive sulphurous vapors always caused him nausea. But he kept his eyes wide open and took in the view of the streets almost greedily, although he had been seeing it for months now.

There were wagons from Flanders with grain, wagons from the Rhine and Burgundy with barrels full of wine, wagons from the distant Romandy with spices and bales of cloth. Wagoners in their blue working clothes whistled, cursed, and swung their whips. Elegant horsemen in gaudy garments and knights in shining armor galloped past. Priests and monks in their dark robes walked serenely through the colorful crowd. Women and girls walked modestly by, keeping a surreptitious eye on the dignified men and the youths. Children played and cried to one another, they ran and laughed. For the lame man, borne in his chair, all this was music—the calling and laughing, the shouting and whistling, all came together to form a powerful, thrilling melody in his ears. It was not always beautiful and harmonious, but it was vigorous and intoxicating—life.

A woman's shocked eyes swept over him, and he heard the words: "The poor man in the chair!"

Hermann did not admit to himself that the woman's eyes revealed shock, and her words compassion—compassion with his distorted figure. Surely, she was reacting to the sight of his wide, dark garment. A monk in a carrying chair—that was what had startled the woman ...

"They ought to stop thinking I am a monk!"

A feeling of shame crept up on him. Ultimately, was he telling himself a lie?

"No, I am not a monk. I have never been a monk. My lord father was wrong when he said that all I was good enough for was to become a monk."

But this did not disperse his inner unease, so he gave a gruff command: "Walter, take me to the cloth merchant!"

The servant turned around in surprise. "My Lord, Vespers is about to begin in the cathedral."

The sick man was annoyed. "Did you not understand me? I said: to the cloth merchant's shop!"

The bells for Vespers rang out from the cathedral, loud and powerful. Normally, he delighted in their vibrant sound, which was itself a sublime praise of God. Were they not calling out *his* name today, the name of the traitor?

"What nonsense! I am not a monk, and I will not become a monk."

The bells rang on and on. They ought to be silent! But he was obliged to hear them until he arrived at the cloth merchant's, and the carrying chair stood under the cool vault.

The burly merchant skillfully hid his astonishment at the crippled figure of his customer. His knowledgeable eyes had told him at once that this sick young man came from a noble family. "How may I be of service, my Lord?"

"A cloth for a garment, or two," replied Hermann. He was curt and impolite, because he felt unsure of himself.

At a nod from the merchant, his assistant brought out cloths, linen and wool, finely and roughly spun in snowy white, blood-red, a light and a darker blue, lush green, cheerful yellow, autumnal brown, and various shadings. The lame man's eyes, almost drunk with joy, plunged into the sea of colors—those eyes that for an entire decade had seen nothing other than the uniform black of the monastic habits and the mild colors of the landscape around Lake Constance; those eyes that were hungry for beauty, and were so receptive to it.

Hermann was intoxicated by the sight of the many colors. Was not each color like a note of music that echoed in his heart? Each color was a tone, and the many tones united to form a melody, a soaring and thrilling melody. Here too, the lame man felt life. Was there not a life in the ecstasy of the colors, a life that was set in motion and that caught him up in its movement? He almost let himself be carried away by the wave of emotions, by the melody that he heard (but that resounded only within himself), out into the whole breadth of the sea. Was not this life?

The merchant's businesslike voice recalled him to the barren shores of reality. "How do you like this cloth from Flanders, my Lord?"

Busy hands spread out a light woolen cloth before him, finely spun, woven without a single flaw, in the gentle red-brown of the beech trees in the fall.

"An exquisite, beautiful cloth …"

Hermann was reminded of the slender beech trees in the wood on Reichenau, with their smooth silver trunks that rose straight up to the sky. Sometimes he had spent time in the beech wood, where he delighted in the light green of springtime and the warm red-brown of the leaves in the fall. How strange, that he could not forget Reichenau …

"I like the cloth," he murmured absent-mindedly. "Measure plenty for a garment and for a cloak of the same cloth. The tailor will need an extra quantity in my case."

His hands caressed the fluffy woolen cloth from France. The yellow shone like the sunlight, like a friendly smile. It was like a clear musical tone. This color made him happy. Did not many of the young men on the street wear a garment like this?

The merchant bent over expectantly. "Would you like to take this cloth too, my Lord?"

The lame man said: "Yes." He did not see the expression of contemptuous pity on the merchant's face. All he saw was the sunny, friendly smile, and all he perceived was the bright note of joy. He felt profoundly contented, because this purchase brought him one step further, one step closer to life. Was he not in the midst of life, even before he was able to walk?

"

Walter brought a tailor to the Rahnwyls' house, a wizened old man with very nimble movements. He scurried around the sick man, whom the servant held in an upright position, and noted his measurements under his breath.

Hermann overcame his shyness and asked: "Can you compensate for the defects of my shape?"

The old man nodded quickly. "Of course, of course, noble Lord. Some things can be compensated for. You purchased plenty of cloth, did you not? Then I can hide many things behind folds and a big collar, and high sleeves."

The sick man was happy to hear this, but at the same time, he felt a distressing embarrassment. Was it necessary for the tailor to look in such great detail at his defects, at his ugly figure?

He gave a quick command: "Walter! The cloth!"

The servant set him down in the armchair. "He always treats me too cautiously," thought Hermann, with unjustified annoyance. Walter brought the cloths, and the old man clapped his hands with glee when he saw the red-brown woolen cloth. His expert fingers tested the quality.

"What a wonderful cloth! What a color! My Lord, you could find nothing better suited to your blond hair, your blue eyes, and your light skin ..."

Hermann reacted with a boyish displeasure to this praise, and he blushed. "That was not the reason why I chose the cloth. I am not a harlot who wants to make herself beautiful."

The tailor was embarrassed, and took hold of the yellow cloth. He hesitated, though only for a moment. Then his face assumed once more its expression of an eagerness to serve.

"You too have decided for yellow. This color is very popular this year. Many of the young gentlemen are wearing yellow. In our rainy city, yellow is like a ray of sunshine that has stayed behind on gray days."

He talked and talked, but the sick man did not hear his words. He had noticed the tailor's hesitation, and his sensitive nature had shown him how to interpret it correctly. What on earth was a cripple thinking of, to choose such a striking color? It was true that he was young, like the others who can wear yellow; and he came from a rich family, like the others; but he was a cripple. He was not like the others, and never would be. He was not entitled to wear yellow, because he was a cripple ...

He forced himself to be calm, but his eyes were full of shadows as he gave the order: "I have changed my mind. Put the yellow aside for now, and make the garment and cloak from the red-brown cloth, as soon as possible."

He did not notice the old man's deep bow. He protested, when Walter wanted to put the yellow cloth in the drawer. "Leave it here, and leave me alone!" The servant withdrew reluctantly.

Hermann of Altshausen crouched in his armchair and gazed at the yellow cloth, a wondrously fluffy woolen material from France, such as many people were wearing on the streets ... But now, the yellow was no longer a smiling joy for him. It grinned at him in undisguised mockery. Instead of the light tone that rang out cheerfully, he heard an ugly discord, harsh, shrill, and so strident that it inflicted deep wounds on his sensitive spirit.

"Cripple! Nothing for you, cripple!"

A wave of bitterness washed over him. His back became even more crooked, and his trembling hands pulled and tugged at the yellow cloth in an impotent fury.

"Scissors, scissors ... I am going to rip it up, until it is a worthless rag!"

Suddenly, he paused and sat for a while without moving. Then he lifted his head slowly, very slowly, and gazed at the great crucifix that stood out against the gray wall, dark and severe.

"So this is the life that you have meant me to lead. A fine life, a glorious life, truly worth living, is it not? Always being different from the others, always set apart, always marked out and despised, a cripple."

His eyes grew wild and nasty, his speech became a scream. "It must give you an infinity of joy, O God, when I twist and turn here and struggle like a worm people trample upon! Or else, why did you permit this? Like a worm … like a worm."

In his mind, he crawled once more over the sand on the shore, gasping and dirty, with his hands scraped. He crawled, crawled like a worm.

"We have nothing but trouble with you," the infirmarian Ekkehard had grumbled, when he found him hanging in the tree, helpless like Christ on the cross. "Nothing but trouble? I am nothing but a burden … nothing but a burden in Altshausen, nothing but a burden on Reichenau, nothing but a burden for the Rahnwyls here, nothing but a burden … and I am the greatest burden of all for my own self. And why? What is the point? What do you get out of it, O God, when I am a worm? Does it entertain you to look at me like this?"

With a great sob, he pressed his head into the fluffy woolen cloth, into the shining yellow that was like the sun.

"

The old Lady Veronica of Rahnwyl was shocked when she visited him a couple of hours later. He crouched before the cloth like an evil gnome. Harsh old lines marked deep furrows around his mouth, lines of bitterness and almost of hate. He bowed his head in greeting, but the only words his mouth found were bitter.

"What do you think, Lady Veronica? If I wore this cloth, would I not play the part of a splendid juggler, a comedy actor who would make everyone laugh? Would not my existence then be meaningful, and … a joy … to God and to human beings?"

The Lady Veronica bent down in concern to the lame man. "Hermann, what has happened to you? Tell me."

His blue eyes looked with a cold rejection at her kind old face. He curled his thin lips in scorn.

"You ask what has happened, noble Lady? Not very much; not more than usual. All that has happened was that I have been permitted once again to feel myself to be what I truly am—a cripple, an outcast, a worm …" With furious mockery, he dwelt on the last word. "Yes, a worm. But do not let that disturb you, Lady Veronica. Do not regard it as important in any way. My fellow pupils recognized that a sick boy like me has his moods."

The lady of the house looked sadly at the agitated face. She would have loved to put her maternal arms around the poor young man.

"Hermann, you are full of sorrow because you are … different?" she asked in a low voice.

"You have guessed it correctly, Lady Veronica. Just imagine: I would like to be one of many," he jeered.

She did not get angry with him, but replied in a firm tone: "You will always have to be Hermann of Altshausen. You will never become just one of the crowd, not you— not even if your frailties were to be taken away from you."

Did he understand her? Did he want to understand her? Something strange and nasty lurked in his look, when he laughed an unmelodious laugh and asked: "What do you mean? Does that mean that you regard me as someone specially chosen?"

"God has called you," she said simply.

He balled his impotent fists, and his face was disfigured by a furious resistance. "Oh? God has called me? Do you really mean that? Called me for what? And what if I voluntarily renounce his call? I just want to be a human being, a human being, a human being—nothing else, nothing at all. I want to live like all the others. Understand me, Lady Veronica: to live like all the others ... to live, to live!" His lips twitched, as if his anger, his pain, and his bitterness would force a new sob out of his body.

The Lady Veronica wanted to console him, as a mother consoles her child. But she suppressed this emotion. She had to help him in another way. She must appear to be harsh. Her answer surprised him and affected him, although it was spoken in a low and gentle voice.

"You will live, Hermann, as soon as you submit to his will, and you will thank him for your life."

His eyes widened, and for a moment, the Lady Veronica saw clearly that her words had affected him. Then his eyelids fell and his lips were pressed even more tightly together, so tightly that his mouth was now merely a narrow line in the arrogantly hostile mask that was his face. Was his silence a "no"? Or did it conceal the invisible groping, the search for a turnaround? Was a child stretching out its hand behind the wall of pride, and calling to the Father to come to it?

From this moment onward, Hermann could no longer

find any word or gesture of prayer. His heart and his soul remained silent. The sight of the cross no longer moved him. The things of God did not concern him now. No bell wakened an echo in his soul, nor did any rejection. He did not deny that there was a God; but his God was distant, infinitely distant from human beings. Any attempt to reach him would be a meaningless and foolish undertaking. Hermann preserved his apparent calm, his apparent peace. God had ceased to be a question for him.

When he met Arnulph of Rahnwyl and his wife, he was polite and chivalrous, but he permitted them no glimpse into his inner world. He wanted to be completely alone, and he did not admit to himself that he was homesick. It was only his dreams that were haunted by the image of Reichenau, the image of the Gnadensee. When he was awake, this image was ruthlessly banished from his consciousness.

"

Master Cheirisophos too noticed the change in the sick man. In his concern, he murmured something about the bad weather as a cause of increased suffering: "All this rain is one of the disadvantages of the city of Aachen."

The sick man looked at him silently for so long that the Greek felt compelled to ask, in his confusion: "But what is the matter? What is wrong with you, Count Hermann?"

The answer was ungracious: "I shall tell you this once and for all, Master Cheirisophos: I do not need your compassion! All I want is your skill in healing, so that I can live at long last. I bought a yellow cloth a few days ago, because I liked the color. It looked ... cheerful. But I was told at once that it would be utterly unsuitable for me to wear such striking clothes. Well, now you know what the matter is. Tell me the truth: Will I ever be like the others?"

The question was uncomfortable, and the Greek felt a growing unease. Was this conversation turning into an interrogation? He put on a show of surprise and shook his head. "Is that your goal? Is that really what you want? Do you absolutely want to go around in yellow cloth like the dandies and popinjays on the streets?" He raised his hands in a theatrical gesture. "And if we were to admit that such a garment would suit you, with its cords and fringes, its buttons and braids and other such fripperies, is that not beneath your dignity? Are not you worth more than the other men? Or at least, could you not become more than them? Are you feeling completely well, Hermann of Altshausen?"

The lame man's gaunt, pale face twitched involuntarily. "Pray do not fob me off with your well-chosen pearls of wisdom, Master. They are powerless to make me forget my wretchedness. When will my sickness get better?"

"You must have more patience!" said Cheirisophos severely. "Did I not tell you at the very beginning of my treatment that much time would elapse before any improvement? Do you remember my words? Have more patience with your body and with your physician. And in the meantime, make use of the freedom that you possess. The Lord of Rahnwyl told me, before you came here, that you were a young man with an uncommonly animated and active mind and that you were eager to perfect your studies in the various branches of knowledge. Forgive me if I speak too openly, but you have shown me very little of that eagerness in these past months. Have you touched as much as one single book?"

Hermann's eyes had been challenging, but now he lowered them in shame. The Greek had touched him in a sensitive spot. "You are right, Master. Since I came to Aachen, I have not taken up my studies. My only thought has been how I might become the master of my illness."

The doctor looked down at the sick man with a triumphant smile. His strategy had been successful: he had distracted his attention. "Do not reproach yourself, Count Hermann. It was good and necessary for you to take time to settle down in your new surroundings. But now, spread your wings and fly into that kingdom that knows hardly any boundaries. You have certainly acquired a good foundation in the monastery school. If you wish, I will help you a little to build on that foundation. May I bring to you Greece, so that you can get to know and to love the ancient culture of my native land? Then, if your spirit desires further nourishment, we shall travel into the Near East, which is our brother-land. A new realm of magic awaits you there. Learn Greek and Arabic, study the strict science of arithmetic and geometry, of philosophy and astronomy. Take delight in the charming poetic art of the peoples and in the solemn gravity of our dramas. You will find more water in our wells than the thirsty spirit is able to draw. Tell me, what prevents you from undertaking this bold flight into the realm of the spirit? Nothing, nothing at all … You are gloriously free, and every intellectual conquest will make you increasingly, and more joyfully, conscious of this freedom. At the same time, like a good father of the household in Greece, you will accumulate oil in your jug, so that you will have rich stores, when ..." The doctor swallowed a few times before finishing the sentence: "When life begins for you."

The lame man looked gratefully up at the doctor, since the yearning for this freedom had taken hold of him. His spirit would have liked to spread its wings at once, in order to begin the ascent. His blue eyes shone expectantly.

The doctor told him about some texts that he owned. "I have copies of the Letters of Paul in Greek, as well as texts of pagan wisdom, especially Plato and Aristotle. Would you like to read them, or are you afraid of the influence of the ancient pagans?"

Hermann laughed at this question, but at the same time, he felt hurt. Was this the inner protest of a young man who was no longer willing to be treated like a child? Or was it the protest of a Christian who was condemned to be silent?

From then on, the celebrated Master Cheirisophos spent many hours with the sick man. Initially, he devoted himself to Hermann's service out of an unadmitted feeling of shame, since he had failed him so miserably as a doctor and as a human being; but soon, he was motivated by a genuine eagerness to supply fresh nourishment to the receptive and alert spirit of his pupil, and he led him further and further onward. He had the impression that Hermann's strong will and his general intelligence mastered with an almost playful ease the difficulties of the foreign language and alphabet. The lame man also displayed an exceptionally powerful memory. Even when he did not write something down or check the text in a parchment, he could quote it days later with great fidelity. He was not always able to use his hands, and his bodily

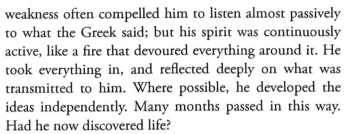

weakness often compelled him to listen almost passively to what the Greek said; but his spirit was continuously active, like a fire that devoured everything around it. He took everything in, and reflected deeply on what was transmitted to him. Where possible, he developed the ideas independently. Many months passed in this way. Had he now discovered life?

The world of the spirit took him captive. His endeavors in this field almost let him forget the wretchedness of his body, just as he forgot the one God when he was with the gods of Greece. He seemed to have a greater equilibrium and serenity, although there was no decisive improvement in his physical condition. The pains abated temporarily, and in general, he could move his fingers with less effort. He could write for a longer time, and more clearly. But there were always days when his old feebleness suddenly came over him; days when the gift of speech deserted him; days when Walter was obliged to tell the Greek, with a somber and worried expression, that his master's poor body was completely paralyzed.

Master Cheirisophos had two crutches made, so that Hermann could learn to walk with their aid. When he brought them to him, he experienced a strange surprise. The sick man ran his fingertips over the smooth wood and asked: "Beech?" This was the only word he uttered, and the doctor too said nothing, as he put down the crutches in a corner. He dreaded the first exercise and the inevitable disappointment. But why did Hermann have no other question? Did he suspect something? Months passed.

"

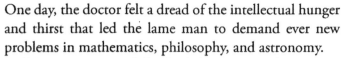

One day, the doctor felt a dread of the intellectual hunger and thirst that led the lame man to demand ever new problems in mathematics, philosophy, and astronomy.

"How many jugs full of oil do you now have, Hermann, instead of the one jug that I recommended you to collect?"

Hermann thought that this was a joke, and replied, with a laugh: "I am gathering together a huge store, Master. I want to become a rich man."

"Do not gather it so quickly. The olives have to ripen after they are picked. You want to harvest, but the blossom is still on the trees."

The sick man dropped his wax tablet in astonishment. "Not so quickly? But why should we not go on, if I am ready? Let me use your own image: you need not wait for a new harvest, because you have nothing but ripe olives."

When they were on their travels through the world of Arabic culture, the doctor sighed and confessed to the Lord Arnulph: "My wisdom will soon be exhausted. Your young guest is so restless and eager that he snatches one trump card after another out of my hand. Today, *he* explained to *me* something that I wanted to explain to him tomorrow! I fear that the wells of my wisdom are running dry."

The aged nobleman looked critically at the Greek. "Your wells are running dry? Are there not inexhaustible wells of wisdom, Master Cheirisophos, that are able to quench even a thirst like this?"

The doctor said nothing. He knew what the Lord of Rahnwyl was alluding to, but a Master Cheirisophos did not go to that well to draw.

I Am Made for God

When guests stayed in the Rahnwyls' house and gathered around their cultivated host for serious conversation, the lame man sat as a silent participant in the circle of scholars, monks, and cathedral canons. Some of the visitors looked thoughtfully at the narrow, expressive face of the young man. His brow and his eyes revealed an alert mind and undivided attentiveness. Hermann crouched in his armchair and listened spellbound, when the gentlemen talked about happenings in the empire, about the emperor, about the dealings and the problems of the mighty, and about the sufferings, the victories, and the scandals in the Church. The conversation often turned to the last things, to eternal matters. When they spoke about this—about God—Hermann only listened. He did not answer; nor did he put up any resistance. He simply registered what was said.

The men around Arnulph of Rahnwyl reached for the stars with reverent hands. In some way, they were at home in eternity. They had more substance than Master Cheirisophos; they were purer, and more lacking in ulterior motives. But although the sick man sensed this, he could not yet identify the root of this otherness. He felt more and more attracted to this circle. Soon, he spent the entire day waiting for the evening hours.

After one evening conversation about grace as the effective power of the good in the human person, and as a free gift of the Almighty to his creature, which has no right or claim to it, Hermann ventured for the first time to stammer a prayer to God. He trembled at his audacity, but he tried it again and again. His stammering became a sentence, and his sentence became a prayer.

"Lord, let me see you once more. I know that I have no right to that. Nevertheless, I ask you: show yourself to me. Manifest yourself to me, so that I can know you. Lord, give me a share in your grace, which I can never merit. You know my poverty and my blindness. Lord, teach me yourself! I want to know about you, as those men know about you."

A new and imperious yearning had awakened in the sick man a new thirst. Could Master Cheirisophos quench it?

Next day, Hermann listened with only one ear to the Master's words, until he suddenly interrupted him and cried out with urgent impatience: "Master Cheirisophos, Plato wants to get out of his cave!"

The doctor was shocked, and sat back in his chair. Was this a joke? No, there was no smile on the gaunt face of his pupil.

"Do you wish to give me a sample of your humor, Count Hermann?" he asked sarcastically.

"No, not at all, Master. I do not feel like making jokes. I have meditated a little this past night, looking back on what I have learned from you. Or, if you prefer to hear it put in this way, I have counted my jugs of oil."

"And what conclusion did you reach?"

The sick man sighed and lifted his bony shoulders in perplexity. "Well, my jugs are full of the best Greek oil. I am profoundly grateful to you, Master Cheirisophos. And yet …"

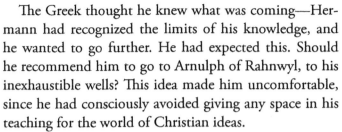

The Greek thought he knew what was coming—Hermann had recognized the limits of his knowledge, and he wanted to go further. He had expected this. Should he recommend him to go to Arnulph of Rahnwyl, to his inexhaustible wells? This idea made him uncomfortable, since he had consciously avoided giving any space in his teaching for the world of Christian ideas.

"Master, you know better than anyone else that I am hungering for life in its fullness, but all you gave me was a symbol of life. You gave me a few single stones, well formed, beautiful, colored stones, such as one might give to a good child, and then you told me: 'Put these together, then you will have life!'"

The doctor sprang up in anger. "Beautiful colored stones? Hermann, are you comparing the immense breadth of our culture with children's toys?"

"Do not be angry at my comparison. It may not be perfect. But I ask you, is the culture of Greece … life, Master? Is life itself the best interpretation of life? No, no, you cannot block my path, and you cannot convince me. Plato wants to get out of his cave. He no longer wants to see only the shadows, the inexact images on the wall of the cave. He wants life."

Cheirisophos paced up and down in a rage. The young man's wish sounded in his ears like a mockery of his own worldview. Then he stood in front of the armchair and bent down. His black eyes flashed with malice at the lame man, but they encountered only a tranquil serenity.

"For Plato—whose venerable name you frivolously choose to apply to yourself—the images, the ideas, are the highest expression of reality and of all that exists …"

Hermann pointed to the chair. "Pray sit down again, Master, and try for once to listen to me calmly. I have assimilated Plato's great notion, and I admire this towering spirit. 'All that exists, exists only to the extent that the ideas of the true, the beautiful, and the good are realized in it.' The more I assimilated Plato's teaching, the more I grasped, first with the heart and then with the mind, that the ideas are not life."

The Greek replied automatically, in a contemptuous mutter: "And who consults his heart, where ideas are concerned? And what, in your opinion, belongs inalienably to life?"

The sick man replied at once: "Happiness!—Are you happy, Master Cheirisophos?"

A strange word, a strange question from the lips from a maimed cripple. But it touched the doctor at the point that he had consciously avoided hitherto. Happiness? How did that occur to Hermann? He was a ruminator, odd and dangerous. Cheirisophos had no idea that Manegold, the cathedral canon, had spoken of eternal happiness, of eternal joy, in the circle that gathered around Arnulph of Rahnwyl the previous evening ...

The Master laughed an unfree, forced laugh. "Happiness? And what is that? You are no philosopher. It is true that the men of old also knew the word 'happiness.' But have you not grasped what they basically meant by it? Happiness is a product of the human mind, like the whole pantheon of Olympus. Happiness? No, only intoxication and disgust. Accepting things as they are, soldiering on with decency, broadening the boundaries, making the best out of a miserable existence—that is what human dignity and freedom are. If the concept of happiness is important to you, you could see a kind of happiness in the fact that we can develop our personality to the highest degree possible. That gives us a kind of satisfaction. If you like, you can call that 'happiness.'"

The sick man's eyes shone. "When our personality develops, what is its goal? The bud develops into a blossom, in order to become a fruit. What about the bud of our mind and of our heart?"

"It ripens towards the primal ideas of the good, the beautiful, and the true. It wants to come as close to these as possible. But a human being is never really perfected. He is, and remains, a torso."

Hermann bent forward, as if a great tension were taking hold of him. Oblivious of his surroundings, his hand plucked at the silk sleeve of the doctor. "Do you believe that? Do you really believe that, Master? The human being is the one creature on this earth who may not attain perfection, because he is not only matter, but also spirit—soul? No, no, that is nonsensical, and it contradicts the logic of your own system of thought. The creation allows the creatures to come to perfection, and then takes them back into its bosom as ripe fruit. And only the human being is to remain a torso? How absurd, how horribly meaningless human life would then be!"

The Master shook off the sick man's hand, but he did not notice, and continued, almost fiercely: "No, Cheirisophos, no! You gave me no answer to my question about the ultimate meaning of existence. Nor did Plato or Aristotle. Life is more. Life is …"

He struggled to find the right expression, and then he avowed: "Life is also a mystery. Life cannot be confined to the excessively narrow framework that you stake out for it. Life is something great, unique, and wonderful. And did you not also forget that life is a receiving and giving?"

The doctor felt as if the poor crooked body had grown. The blue eyes shone with a strange, victorious glow. The spirit of the cripple had outgrown the doctor, and he could no longer guide it and shape it. He smoothed the folds of his expensive garment and played with the buckle on his belt, while he made a confession:

"I did not speak specifically of that point. One can, of course, occasionally give other people something of one's own riches, within prudent bounds, as a form of self-affirmation. But do not do so too zealously, for other people are always ready to take."

"When should I give something?"

"When you feel like doing so."

Had the doctor enriched him with his knowledge only out of a passing whim? "To whom should I give?"

"Only to one who is worthy. Assess cautiously whether the other person deserves your gift. Never waste even the slightest amount on someone who does not know how to thank you and does not know how to prize your gift. Guard your heart against an excessive compassion for the neediness of others, for otherwise you will be plundered of everything. My impression is that you have a soft heart."

"But am I not always obliged to give, Master? And am I not obliged to give to everyone? Does a river flow only sometimes, and only for those who know how to appreciate its strength and its beauty?"

"You are a dreamer, Hermann! To give all the time, to give to everyone—what folly! You would exhaust your resources far too soon ..."

The lame man struck the table angrily, and cried: "No!

You do not understand me! One who wants to live must direct the river forward, so that new water can flow into its bed. One who does not give is incapable of receiving, and his heart and mind remain unfruitful."

Master Cheirisophos breathed a sigh of relief and leaned back. "So that is what you mean! *Panta rhei,* 'Everything flows.' Being is eternal motion."

Hermann did not accept this, and his voice clearly betrayed his impatience. "No, that is not what I mean. One must give. If one wants to live, one must not shut oneself away in self-absorption and close one's mind to life … life … and what I mean by that word is the realm that is incomprehensible and immeasurable, and yet is real …"

He faltered, and bowed his head. Embarrassment closed his mouth—how could he speak to a man like Master Cheirisophos about grace, about the circulation of the divine grace?

The Greek looked at the silent man. He was perplexed—if only he knew what was going on in his mind! He no longer understood him.

After a pause, Hermann lifted his head and continued in an emphatic tone: "A life like yours, a life for science, is not enough for me, Master Cheirisophos. I have examined myself seriously to discover which field could satisfy me, but I found none. All that I saw were individual pieces, but no finished mosaic, no all-encompassing life."

This annoyed the doctor. "You are insatiable, Hermann, and you are almost unbearable in your hunger for the whole of life—for something that does not exist. You will no doubt learn how to scale back your demands, since the human being is a torso and remains a torso. Accept

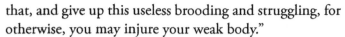

that, and give up this useless brooding and struggling, for otherwise, you may injure your weak body."

He laid a parchment on the table, yellowed and dingy.

"Here you can read a copy of the Letter that John the Son of Thunder wrote. He too was a passionate man, and he is related to you in a way, because he was a man of absolutes. He wanted to call down fire on those who did not believe in his Master ... who did not believe in what he supposed to be life. I found this text for you in the ghetto. A Jew gave it to me, after a great deal of haggling. Read it, see how good your knowledge of Greek is, and find tranquility by playing with this ... beautiful colored stone."

The doctor departed. Hermann looked at the closed door and listened to the short receding steps. The doctor had been his companion for many hours and had guided him through Greece and the Arab world, but Hermann found him very strange that afternoon, strange and cold as the world of Plato's ideas.

When the Lady Veronica paid him her daily visit, he asked her shyly, but not without feeling a certain tension: "Pray, tell me, Lady Veronica: Is there such a thing as happiness?"

Unlike Cheirisophos, she did not dismiss his question as nonsense. A good light played over her features, which had retained a noble dignity even in her old age.

"Yes, Hermann," she declared in a calm and firm voice, "there is such a thing as happiness. I have experienced it, and I still experience it."

"Are you happy?"

She smiled at his disbelief. "I am happy. You doubt that, because my son died, do you not? Hermann, I know, as far as one person can know such a thing about another person ... and a mother knows a lot about her beloved child ... that my son accomplished the task that God had given him. He was a sincere man, and he believed in God. Now he is at home. Ought his mother to begrudge him the happiness of being perfected at a young age? Ought I not rather to rejoice with him?"

Hermann replied, as if he had not understood her words: "Lady Veronica, what is happiness? Happiness in the truest sense of the word ... while still here on earth?"

"Being loved, Hermann, and being permitted to love. We experience the deepest, truest, and most lasting happiness in being loved by God. And often, we receive that gift when we stand under the cross. When we love human beings and are loved by them, that is a small portion of the immense happiness that is to be found only in God."

"Under the cross?" The lame man was astonished, and turned his big childlike eyes on the Lady Veronica. "Then I ought in fact to be happy?"

"Yes, Hermann, you ought to be happy. I hope, indeed, I pray that you may recognize your happiness ..."

She rose to her feet, but the sick man's voice held her fast.

"My lady mother ...," he stammered agitatedly. "Could my lady mother be happy with such a son?"

"You could do a great deal for her happiness, Hermann. She will be sad now, when she thinks of you. But I am convinced that you will soon make her happy."

"

Hermann called his servant, as soon as Veronica of Rahnwyl had left the room. "Tell me, Walter, was the Lady Hiltrud sad when I wanted to go to Aachen?" He looked with apprehension and tension at the man's broad face, as if his reply would be important, and even decisive.

The farmer's son from Altshausen rubbed his broad hands thoughtfully together, and then he nodded: "Yes, my Lord, yes, that is how it was. Your lord father, Count Wolfrad, was very pleased with your decision, but the Lady Hiltrud sighed. She was sad. When we were alone, she charged me ... excuse me, my Lord, but that is how it was ... to take good care of you. You were on the point of taking a very dangerous and toilsome detour, before you would find the path back home to your own self. I did not understand what the countess meant by those words ..."

Did the sick man understand the words of his mother? He was silent for a long time, before he murmured: "Do you want to go out? You are free until the evening meal."

"May I remain with you, my Lord? I feel like a foreigner in this city."

"After all this time, Walter?"

The servant scowled and looked almost guilty. "My Lord, I can't change that. There are many lanes here where you can scarcely see the sky, and I am used to our open land with its hills, its fields and woods."

"You are right, Walter. That is how things must be. We must remain foreigners here."

Walter was happy that his master too was still a foreigner in Aachen, although he did not know why that was important. He remained in the room; and with him, there remained the Lady Hiltrud's words about the dangerous and toilsome detour before the return home to his own self.

To go home? How was that possible? And where did the path lead? What "detour" was the Lady Hiltrud speaking of? How was Hermann to make her happy? She could not have meant a return home to Altshausen, because that would never be accepted by his father. To go home? A detour? What on earth had his lady mother meant?

But he did not want to brood. It would be better to read the parchment that Cheirisophos had given him, the Letter of John. He was familiar with it, and he was almost bored as he skimmed through the text in the melodious language that he had come to know so well. He was not really paying attention as he read the well-known passages, the well-known sentences, all too well-known … Would it not be better to read the Arabic poem?

"God is love."

He stopped short, and read the sentence a second time.

"God is love."

What an extraordinary affirmation this John made! "God is love." He had often read this sentence, but now it gripped him for the first time.

"God is love." If that was true … God, the Almighty, the Omniscient, the Most High, the Lord, the Judge, Creator, and Sustainer, is love. Could the being of God be held fast in such a simple sentence?

The lame man did not think through to the end what this insight might mean for himself and for his sickness. He did not reflect on the meaning it could give his wretched, fettered existence. "God is love." He stood dazzled and helpless before the bright light of this decisively important affirmation about God, and he groped around like a blind man. Now he needed a hand to hold him and guide him, and he remembered … Had not Abbot Berno written about the love of God on the parchment that Arnulph of Rahnwyl had given him so long ago?

"Walter, come here quickly! Where is the Lord Berno's parchment? Do you remember it? The Lord Arnulph gave it to me years ago, at the beginning of our time in Aachen."

After a lengthy search, the servant found the parchment, forgotten and covered in dust. Hermann removed the film of dust with careful fingers. "How could I have forgotten it?"

Abbot Berno had written about the love of God. The sick man read with reverence the words of his spiritual father, which he had once despised, and it was as if he was hearing the voice he knew so well.

"Love is the vital principle of the Most Holy Trinity. Love is also the one and only meaning of human existence, because the human person is made for God. God's love for us is the Father's 'yes' to his child, taking us up into the communion of his life, which we call 'heaven.' The human person's love for God is a humble and confident openness to the grace, the light, the love, and the life of God. It is a reverent act of carrying home the divine gift; and it is often a lonely and hard path of faith, through the night and through trials, leading to the morning of light.—I am made for God, and God is love."

The lame man's breath came quickly, and his eyes shone. "'I am made for God, and God is love.' Thank you for these words, Father Berno, thank you!"

To go home? A detour? Was this what his lady mother had meant? He sensed that he would soon understand her. Already, he knew: "I am made for God, and God is love."

Was there not still one stone, one piece of the mosaic, missing from the picture that Hermann was putting together in his mind, as he trembled with joy and with fear? Only one more stone, and the whole picture would shine out, the picture that was life.

"Thank you for the Letter of John, Master Cheirisophos! If only you had known what a service you were doing for me with this 'beautiful, colored little stone'!"

The bright splendor of the learned physician faded, and he saw him as a poor man, as a wanderer without a true home. "Greece is a lie, my friend, a shimmering lie, no doubt, but without God, only a lie. Art and science are dead, if one makes them idols, as you do. It is only their relatedness to God that breathes the spirit of life into things—even into the boldest ventures of the human spirit. 'I am made for God, and God is love.'"

"

That evening, Hermann was once more in the circle that gathered around the noble lord of Rahnwyl. Usually, when his elders spoke, he was a silent and reserved listener, but today he was transformed. His gaunt face had lost much of its severity. A relaxed smile played around his mouth, and his eyes shone like those of a man who had had an exhilarating encounter with something new and beautiful.

Manegold, the aged cathedral canon, observed the change with a keen interest. He surprised Hermann by asking him: "Something good has happened to you today, has it not? You are cheerful, if I am not mistaken?"

The sick man breathed deeply and turned his face to

him. "No, reverend sir, you are not mistaken. I have discovered a glorious ... doctrine today."

A new joy and a new seriousness made his face appear more mature and masculine. Could it be that Hermann had encountered love in the realm of the mind, which was his own true realm? The canon smiled to himself. He noticed how everything in Hermann wanted to make a statement, and he realized that he must free an overflowing heart of its burden. At the same time, he could give Hermann the gift of sharing in his joy.

"A new doctrine? Who gave it to you? Tell me, was it Plato, Euripides, Aristotle, Pythagoras, Euclid, Tertullian, Paul, Augustine ...?"

The young man laughed heartily at this arbitrary stringing together of the great names in the realm of the spirit. If only Master Cheirisophos had been there to hear it!

"You have not guessed correctly. One of the givers is the apostle John, and ..."

The other men were looking at him now, and delighting in the shining of his face.

"Tell us now who the other giver is, Hermann," demanded the Lord of Rahnwyl.

Hermann met his gaze directly and said: "The other giver is our father abbot."

It was only with difficulty that Arnulph succeeded in concealing his joyful surprise. Our father abbot ... Only yesterday, he had received a message from Abbot Berno: "When will the imperial city of Aachen give us back our beloved son in Christ? In our opinion, he has lived for far too long away from the home that Reichenau is for him, in Christ Jesus ..."

Canon Manegold seemed not to have understood the

answer. "Your father abbot? Whom do you mean?"

The lame man now grasped what he had just said, but he repeated it courageously and finished the sentence: "I owe my new doctrine to the apostle John and to our father Abbot Berno of Reichenau."

He could not prevent his voice from wavering uncertainly, when he said the name of the island. It was the first time in months that he had spoken this word.

"May we be permitted to hear your new doctrine? You have awakened our curiosity."

All at once, he found it difficult to talk about the newly discovered treasure. Would that not take away something of its value? But he had already begun, and he gasped from between clenched teeth, gruff and harsh in his embarrassment: "I am made for God, and God is love."

His cheeks burned, as though he had said something vulgar, and had simply blurted out an unutterably tender mystery. He was ashamed of himself.

The aged canon nodded. His supposition had been correct: this young man had met love in its highest form in the realm of the spirit. The words of John had somehow become a living reality for him—a presentiment as yet, but already much more than that. "And it will become even more than that, Hermann. I am happy that you have found the beginning. One who suffers so much as you is capable of great love, if he suffers in love."

The voice of the lame man broke the men's pensive silence: "Permit me to withdraw, Lord Arnulph!"

The head of the house cordially granted him his request, and Hermann bowed politely as he took his leave from the guests of the house of Rahnwyl. A servant lifted him out of the armchair and pushed the crutches under his armpits. His hands trembled as they clutched the smooth crossbars. He hesitated. Although he had been using the crutches for some days now, his body still shrank from exposing itself to the torment of "walking." He pushed the crutch cautiously a little way forward, and dragged his leg after it—he was unable to bend the knee. Then he pushed the other crutch forward … No, this was not walking. The crutches were walking. All he did was to drag and shove the powerless, stiff legs and feet behind them. The wood of the crutches cut painfully into his armpits. The entire weight of his body rested on them. Was not the floor treacherously smooth? The crutches that supported him did not give him any sensation of security.

Were the men looking at him? It was very quiet in the room; no one spoke a word. The silence caused him an additional pain. He thought that he could feel the observant eyes on his back.

The servant drew back the curtain on the door. Hermann went as far as the door and rested, leaning on the door panel. The curtain had closed again behind him. The corridor beyond it was so long that he needed fresh strength and new courage for the long path to his rooms. Trembling with weakness, he stood in the darkness, in the narrow enclosed space between the door and the curtain. The wood brought him the rich, resinous smell of the forests, and the curtain smelled like dry grass, like hay on the summer meadows. The lame man had learned from his childhood, to a greater degree than healthy persons, how to become familiar with things.

Now he heard the voice of canon Manegold, the voice of the friendly old man, in which all the kindness of the priest resonated: "Lord Arnulph, your young protégé is still Hermann of Reichenau."

The lame man pricked up his ears. What would the Lord of Rahnwyl reply? Would he agree? The dark voice of the head of the house sounded joyful, when he answered: "Thanks be to God! Hermann will once again become what he was … and in fact has always remained."

The man in the dark corner pressed his brow against the cool wood. He was not aware that he was smiling. "Hermann of Reichenau? Hermann of Reichenau? I will once again become what I was, and what I have in fact always remained … Hermann of Reichenau. Not Aachen, not Greece, not even Altshausen—Reichenau. Is that true?"

And he wished, with all the unspent strength of his young heart, with a great and pure yearning, that it might indeed be true.

He pushed himself along the corridor, laboriously and cautiously. He scarcely noticed the effort and the pains now.

"Hermann of Reichenau? The lame man, that is who I am, Hermann the Lame."

He stood still in the middle of the corridor, hanging heavily on the crutches that supported him. "I will become Hermann the Lame. The border has been reached."

He had long fought against this knowledge, and had expected and demanded more, much more, from the hot sulphurous springs and the healing arts of Master Cheirisophos. Now, he knew that the lameness would remain.

"Am I Hermann of Reichenau?" That was the question that exercised him. "Have I not lost that happiness once and for all? Did I not squander it and cast it aside through my departure for Aachen?" The question became a piercing torment. Only one voice spoke within him to deny that happiness was a thing of the past. But did that voice give an answer to the question?

"I am made for God, and God is love."

Was it possible that the love of God was giving him the bitter chalice of an unquenchable homesickness for the happiness he had thrown away? The unresolved question numbed his tender spirit and his excessively alert mind. That night, sleep fled from his eyes, which looked unwaveringly into the darkness. The silence solidified into the one question:

"Am I Hermann of Reichenau?"

Lumen Christi

Master Cheirisophos's brows creased when he look at the sick man. "Why did you not come to the bath this morning?" he asked, blowing into his hands. Coming from the warmth of Greece, he felt the coldness of the wet day in early spring more keenly than the people of Aachen. "I waited for you in vain. And you look terrible, like a ghost!"

Dark rings made the lame man's eyes seem larger. In the harsh midday light, his gaunt face was pale like a ghost. His lips were bloodless, and his hands trembled more violently than usual. But his voice was calm, firm, and almost cheerful.

"You need never again wait for me at the bath, Master. You know, better than anyone, that no healing is possible. What could be done for me, has been done. As for the rest, I am, and I remain lame."

Cheirisophos turned pale. He had not expected this so soon, and he wanted to reassure him with promises, but Hermann raised his trembling right hand in a gesture free of all reproach or hostility.

"That will do, Master. Do not talk about healing. It was wonderful to be allowed to hope for a time, and I am not angry with you for giving me too much hope. You did what was humanly possible to soothe my pains and to loosen my narrow fetters, and I am deeply grateful to you for that. Please do not say anything! I bear no grudge against you for withholding the truth from me so long ago. I would probably have been unable to bear it then. That was how things had to be. It was necessary to take that course ... a detour ..."

The young man's face revealed his inner cheerfulness. "But there is another reproach that I cannot spare you."

Another reproach? Was it not his fault that he had made Hermann hope for healing, although only all he could do was to assuage the pain, and that he had spoken of walking, although all that was possible was an agonizing crawling with the help of crutches?

"You have deceived me, Master Theophilos!"

The doctor flinched, as if he had been struck. Theophilos! Why was Hermann using for the first time his half-forgotten baptismal name, his consciously forgotten Christian name? And how had he deceived him, if not by pretending that a healing was possible? He looked uncertainly at the lame man, who met him with the mature, open gaze of an adult. This was no longer the boy who was amenable to persuasion and whom, with some craftiness, he could lead in the right direction.

On the path to his own self, Hermann of Altshausen

had taken his fate into his own hands. He had formed his judgment with the clarity of his penetrating understanding. What did he mean now?—The uncertainty made the doctor uncomfortable.

"You were my physician, Master Theophilos, but at the same time, you had my mind and my soul in your power, more than is commonly the case with a physician. I was surrendered to your influence for a long time—handed over to you, defenseless, through my confidence in you, especially since I had to do without my spiritual guide here in Aachen. You never spoke to me about God."

He spoke dispassionately, but his words were a terrible accusation.

"Am I a priest?" protested Cheirisophos, in a pointless attempt to defend himself.

"No, you are not a priest, Master Theophilos," said Hermann serenely.—Once again, he used that name! Was it not unbearably hot in the room? The doctor wanted to open the windows, but he remained seated, crouching down, surrendered to the young man's voice with its inexorable calm.

"But you usurped the rights of a priest. You showed me a new cult of the veneration of new gods ... science and art. You showed them to me, detached from the Eternal, as absolute values, and you painted a seemingly intact and shining world without God. Such a picture of the world is a lie and a terrible deception. There is a great risk that a young, inexperienced person who hungers and thirsts for life may be content with this illusory world without God, and may believe in this mirage, for then he will perish miserably in the waterless, barren wilderness of a world without God. A deception, Master, or a dream?

The dream of a proud man, of a spirit that succumbed to the temptation of the dark angel, because it refuses to bow down and adore in humility? *Non serviam!*[1] Master Theophilos, tell me one thing: Do you believe in an intact and shining world without God?

"Your silence says everything. But you want to believe in it. You talk yourself into believing in it—this illusory world, this ideal begotten by your pride. You make yourself homeless, because you pursue something that does not really exist. You cheat your life of the one and only meaning and value, and you suffer because of the unfruitful loneliness that you yourself have chosen. You wander around in the pathless desert, because you have despised the path."

The Greek shook off his torpor. Hermann had seen him as he was, and his words had hit home. Now, he fought back vigorously, without realizing that it was precisely his protest that confirmed the truth of what the lame man had said. He was no longer a friend talking to a friend. His black eyes blazed with hostility as he shouted at the sick man: "And what if that were the case, Count of Altshausen? What business is that of yours? Why should you worry about my interior life? Pray spare yourself this concern about my 'soul'—and I doubt whether such a 'soul' exists. My world is enough for me. I do not need your world, and I do not wish—let me make myself clear—I do not wish you to make me any offer out of an 'apostolic disposition.' For all I care, you can love the ropes with which the Church binds you. I love my freedom, the freedom of the one who does not bow down before any god."

---

1. ["I will not serve!"]

He stopped and gasped for air. Hermann quickly interposed: "At any rate, please understand that I dare to speak so openly only because of my gratitude and affection, Master Theophilos ..." The lame man's voice was full of suppressed sadness. "What other reason could I have? I am infinitely sad that you are not free. Your soul is withering away, caught fast in the close-meshed net of your pride. And it must hunger and thirst for freedom in God, just as my soul did, when it believed it was at home only in the world of science. You bring many things to your soul, both trumpery and things of value, but you refuse it the one thing necessary ... You are made for God, and God is love ... When this relationship is lacking, everything—even the science and art that you love—is folly, a shard, a torso, a fragment. Our life would be a wretched meaninglessness and not worth living, if it did not point out beyond earthly existence, and so come to perfection. Even my existence, the life of a maimed cripple, has a meaning, if (and only if) it is lived for God."

A request, wooing and beseeching, resounded in the final words, but the doctor refused to open the door to it. His face remained shuttered, and his voice was dismissive. He got up and said:

"My Lord Count, we are speaking two different languages. That is a pity! I take it that you no longer need me."

He bowed slightly and went to the door, without giving the sick man his hand and without even turning round. His departure resembled a flight. Hermann called after him:

"I no longer need you, but I remain your friend." When the door closed behind the Greek, Hermann knew that one period of his life had ended. Would the next period be in Reichenau, for a second time? Would he be permitted to dwell once again in the place that had nourished him for a decade, and where he was still rooted? He did not have an answer to this question, but he sensed that the problem would soon be resolved. And he yearned for this with all the power and purity of his love.

The breach with Master Cheirisophos was painful. It was not easy for him to detach himself from a teacher who had guided and inspired him for many years. In the ensuing weeks, he had several good conversations with Arnulph of Rahnwyl, but he did not yet dare to take the final step. On several occasions, he spread out a parchment and took the goose quill in his hand. He wanted to write to Abbot Berno and ask for permission to come home. But he did not write. He felt that something essential was missing, and that the time had not yet come to make the request.

"Pray for me, Lady Veronica," he said on Good Friday before the church service. "Without a special grace of God, I do not know what step to take. I want to do his will, but my eyes are bound at present."

"You no longer yearn for healing, Hermann?"

"No, Lady Veronica. Now, all I ask for is to know what God wants of me. I have said my 'yes' to being different and being set apart."

She laid her withered hands kindly on his hands. "You will know that, Hermann. And God's love will sustain you, because you no longer yearn for healing."

"

Had the Lady Veronica erred in her prediction? The sick man was tired and discontented as he took part in the service. Not one of the words in the apostle John's narrative of the Passion pierced through to his heart. All he felt was his pains. He was feeble and peevish. The moving account gave him as little as if it had been the story of some completely unknown person. He was profoundly shocked at his coldness and his listless torpor. What had become of the hoping and yearning of the last few weeks, as he struggled and kept watch for the Lord?

An insurmountable wall towered between God and him. He felt nothing and saw nothing. He was sheer powerlessness. And then, a prayer like a cry detached itself from his weakness and the congestion of his spirit. It surged up, out of the depths of his new distress, with all the momentum of his inner turmoil: "Lord, have mercy on me!"

And the wall collapsed. A man, bowed deep in all the wretchedness of human misery, besought the Lord for mercy. His soul descended into the dust before the greatness of God and his own unworthiness and powerlessness.

"Lord, have mercy on me!"

He found no other words for his prayer.

"

Then the choir began to chant the "Reproaches": *Popule meus, quid feci tibi?*—"My people, what have I done to you?" ... The Savior's laments rang out, full of pain, through the imperial cathedral in Aachen. The faithful listened, deeply moved, but no one was affected to the same degree as Hermann of Altshausen. There was no longer any wall to protect him from the coming of God ...

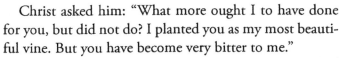

Christ asked him: "What more ought I to have done for you, but did not do? I planted you as my most beautiful vine. But you have become very bitter to me."

As if in a vision, Hermann grasped the grace that had been bestowed on his life, the gifts of God to him, the fullness of God's gifts. If the son of the count of Altshausen had not been lame, would a monastery door ever have opened to him? Even lameness is a gift.

"Lord, you always gave me everything, everything, but I wrangled with you. You gave me Reichenau, and I wanted to get away. I was bitter to you, I rebelled against you, I wanted to forget you, I fled from you. I was bitter to you. Lord, have mercy on me!"

"

And the choir took up the cry for mercy and sang in Greek and Latin: "Holy God, Holy Mighty One, Holy Immortal One, have mercy on us."

Then the lament rang out through the church: "In my thirst, you gave me vinegar to drink, and you pierced the side of your Redeemer with the lance …"

And Hermann heard the words of this lament as if the Lord had addressed them to him personally: "Yes, Lord, my complaints and accusations were the vinegar for your thirst—my moods and hardnesses, my narrowness and my touchiness. The lance that pierced your heart was my lack of trust, my lack of faith, my doubt about your love. Lord, have mercy on me!"

The choir sang. But it was Christ who stood before Hermann's soul, and the words: "Answer me!" were addressed by Christ to him …

Suddenly, the lame man received an insight, incisive in its clarity and stunning in its impetus:

"My suffering, my sickness, is a share in the cross of the Lord."

No further thought was possible—nothing more, nothing at all. All he could do was to wait in silence, blinded by the new, excessively bright light that brought both pain and joy, shame and consolation ... and that was pure grace.

"

He said nothing on the way to the house of the Rahnwyls. He was paler and more introverted than usual. When he arrived, he dismissed the servant, after telling him that he would not go to rest on this Good Friday evening. Walter would have preferred to remain beside him, but his protest died away when he saw the faraway look in the eyes that did not focus on him. Walter lit a candle and tiptoed away.

As soon as the door had closed behind him, the lame man braced himself, and then he reached for his crutches. It was only after repeated attempts that he succeeded in getting up, and the effort brought perspiration to his brow, although he scarcely noticed this. Slowly, he pushed himself forward to the cross. Years ago, he had gazed at this cross, with a piece of yellow cloth in his hands, and he had cried out bitter words of accusation. Could he now kneel down? He took his position before the cross, wobbling and trembling on his crutches. He faced the cross.

God is love. On this Good Friday evening, before the cross, he understood (as far as a human being can be allowed to understand) what the love of God meant. He understood the merciful redemptive love for him, Hermann of Altshausen. And the Lord showed him that his lameness, his torment, his pains, and his separateness, were more than a burden. They were a share in his cross, and thus both a grace and an offer. In that hour, he heard God's question in his suffering:

"Hermann, son of Wolfrad, do you love me, and are you ready to fetch the world home into the love of the Father through your loving suffering?"

The final ice in his soul burst at that moment. The river flowed freely, with nothing more to hold it back.

"Yes, Lord, yes! I want to love you …"

New life, becoming new in Christ … the last stone had found its place in the mosaic. The picture showed Christ the Lord. Christ was life, all-encompassing life.

"Christ is my life!"

The joy within him threatened to burst the poor shell of the sick body. Hermann raised his trembling hands.

"

On the following morning, Walter found the lame man lying on the cold stone slabs, right under the great cross. He lifted him up with care and bore him to his bed. Hermann opened his eyes with an effort.

"My Lord, are your pains severe?"

The bloodless lips attempted a smile. "Do not worry, good Walter," he whispered. "The pains will not last, and then we shall go home." The servant could not decipher the expression on his face. But then, how was he to understand the peace that the world cannot give, and the joy that fills the heart with exultation in the very midst of tribulation? The bodily torments were terrible, but Hermann was happy and felt secure in the joy and the peace of Christ.

The Lady Veronica looked with concern at the waxy paleness of his face. He tried to reassure her, but she sent the servant to fetch Cheirisophos, and waited at the bed of the sick man, who lay motionless, with his eyes closed. The twitching of his lips betrayed the intensity of his pains.

Once he whispered, and she bent down to him. "My lady mother … my lady mother need no longer be sad … Thank you for praying for me."

She understood then, and knew that he had completely found God and his own special vocation.

Toward evening, Walter brought the Master to the house. He had had to look for him everywhere in the city, and a great deal of persuasion had been required before he was willing to come to the house of the Rahnwyls. "No, your master does not need me," he had said dismissively. But finally, he had yielded to the inflexible insistence of the faithful servant, and had reluctantly gone with him.

He examined the sick man by the light of many candles. "How could this happen?" he asked in irritation, when he saw the bruises and swellings that disfigured the poor body in many places. In addition, the right ankle was broken.

The only explanation came from the weak voice of the sick man, who breathed: "It had to happen."

The doctor, who was bandaging him, paused and said, indignantly: "You are speaking in riddles, Count Hermann. But at any rate, you will pay for this 'had to happen' with a lengthy and painful spell in bed. Is that not much too high a price?"

"No … much too low a price, Master … Theophilos. Much too low. I … have … found … life, the … final stone … for the mosaic."

That was why the eyes of the sufferer shone with that unbearable light, so full of joy! The Master felt jealous. A happiness that could triumph over these bodily torments must be enormous. He sensed instinctively that this foreign happiness could be a danger to him.

"Oh, really?" he replied, with hurtful mockery. "And what was the glorious picture that unfolded before your eyes?"

The sick man looked into his dark, troubled eyes without speaking. Finally, his mouth bore witness, although only in a gasping whisper, light as a breath. The Greek was obliged to bend down, and he did so with a haste that he himself found incomprehensible.

"My friend …"

This address both disarmed the doctor and frightened him.

"My friend, I am … happy … secure … rich. Life … Our Lord Jesus Christ … He is … life … my life."

The Greek looked at the lame man, appalled. He had given his testimony with joy, in a state of utter weakness. But did that mean that this testimony was true? Did not Hermann of Altshausen have a marvelous freedom? His spirit had won the victory over his poor body. The lame limbs bore narrow fetters, but his spirit rose up in freedom over distress and pain, over weakness and failure.

Cheirisophos felt that his mockery was turning into reverence, into reverence before the unique meaning that

Hermann's existence possessed. He stood before the bed for a long time, strangely puzzled and disturbed. Finally, he murmured: "I cannot understand you, Hermann. But I am happy for you, that you have found a home."

The sufferer opened his eyelids, which the pain had forced him to close, and smiled.

"Home ... yes, home ... mine and ... yours, my friend. You do not ... understand me ... not yet. I ... know. But I will pursue ... you, I will not ... give you up. Until you open ... want to be ... only a bowl ... a bowl ... for the oil ... from the jug ... He is light ... he gives ... you light. You are ... made for ... God. That ... that ... is your happiness ... too. Happiness ... does exist ... Christ ... your freedom ... your home ... Theophilos."

The doctor bowed in silence before the pale face that shone from within, before the joy and bliss that he could not comprehend. He took the trembling right hand that groped weakly for his hand, but he was unable to say anything. What could he still give this Hermann of Altshausen? The lame man was the victor now. Should Cheirisophos, the defeated man, allow the victor to give him something? He was unsure whether he wanted to receive any gift.

Walter brought him to the door of the house. "Will the master live?" he asked anxiously.

"Your master will live. He is just now beginning to live, Walter," replied the Greek, and went out into the night.

Master Theophilos Cheirisophos went out into the darkness of the Easter night that was descending upon the imperial city of Aachen, a night of deep, dark velvet without stars. He walked through the night.

Soon, a light would brighten this night. "*Lumen*

Christi." And the deacon would proclaim in the "Exsultet" the praise of this truly holy night, the night in which death was compelled to give way before life; the night in which the victorious light of Christ triumphed over the darkness.

"*Lumen Christi!*"—"*Deo gratias!*"[2]

Master Theophilos Cheirisophos walked through the night.

---

2. ["The light of Christ!"—"Thanks be to God!"]

CHAPTER 4

* * *

THE CANTICLE

Homecoming

THE WAGON JOLTED HEAVILY over the rutted road, while the coachman grumbled discontentedly in a low voice. Why did he have to take such a detour through the fishing village of Allensbach? Why did His Lordship insist on taking the boat for the island of Reichenau from that place? And what was the point of setting out at this unearthly hour, before the sun had risen?

Despite his resentment, however, the man knew that nothing could be done against the will of the young nobleman. The crooked figure in the loose black garment might present a wretched and pitiful appearance, but his blue eyes had a clear and imperious look.

Hermann refused the comfortable bed that Walter had prepared for him in the wagon. He crouched on the hard bench, held fast by his servant. He wanted to see the land, and he looked around with wide eyes that were burning from the sleepless night in a bad inn. He said nothing; but that had ceased to surprise Walter. Hermann had said little after their departure from Aachen. But although he had endured the discomforts of the journey with a calm serenity, he was not so relaxed in his mind. An increasing tension had taken hold of him.

How would Abbot Berno receive him? He had been unfaithful, but God, in his incomprehensible mercy, had said his "yes" to him. Was the Lord Berno obliged to do the same? It was indeed Berno who had sent the boy out into the world, into life, years ago. But surely, the only reason for that had been that the urgency of the young man's request made it impossible for him to stay in the abbey any longer?

"How will Abbot Berno receive me?" he had asked Arnulph of Rahnwyl, after the messenger had left for Reichenau with the letter in which he requested permission to return.

The old man had replied kindly: "Like a father."

Like a father? In the decade he had spent on Reichenau, Abbot Berno had been a father to him. His kindliness was never in doubt, but he had never lacked the strictness and openness that were able to utter painful truths and serious rebukes, without ever ceasing to be love.

When he was about to set out for Reichenau, and he thanked the Lady Veronica for her help, she had sent him on his way with the following words: "One who wants to help another person must tell him the truth, even when it is bitter, so that he may come to himself. I had the impression once that you strongly resented my words, Hermann. Am I right?"

"At that time, I did not want to understand you, Lady Veronica. But your words lived on secretly within me, they continued to work in me, and they were there when God's hour struck. I owe you a great debt of gratitude ..."

Hermann's thoughts turned from the motherly woman to Master Cheirisophos. As soon as he was on the road to recovery, the doctor had stopped visiting him. Hermann sensed that he was running away from him—and, in him, from the Lord. This led him to pray intensely and often for Cheirisophos. "There is a rumor that Cheirisophos wants to leave Aachen," the Lord Arnulph had told him, before his departure. Whatever the truth of that might be, he asked God to be gracious to Master Theophilos Cheirisophos, so that he might abandon his false world-view and bow his knees in adoration, thereby doing justice to his own true being ...

"I am made for God, and God is love." Was it not the Abbot of Reichenau who had written these words that had raised Hermann up and made him happy? Father Abbot ... Father? "He will receive me like a father?" With his mind's eye, the sick man saw his father, Count Wolfrad II of Altshausen. Father? He remembered the horror in his father's eyes when he looked at the little cripple; his impatience with his son's disability and slowness; his lack of understanding of his son's sensitive character. In his father's eyes, the lameness had made him a completely useless creature, who was fit only to become a monk.

Father Abbot? Like a father? He would accept the verdict pronounced by the Lord Berno, no matter how it turned out. He would tell him the whole story of his laborious and dangerous detour, of his foolish and culpable attempt to take hold of life; and he would keep nothing back.

Hermann was not one for somber brooding. He had found peace. But he knew that he had broken with the Abbey of Our Lady of Reichenau when he bought the yellow cloth. He would confess everything to the Father Abbot. On the deepest level, he had known about his vocation, even when he brashly called out to the Lady Veronica that he renounced God's choice of him. He had denied the Lord.

He shivered in the cool of the early morning, and Walter carefully drew the cloak more tightly around his shoulders. The master was very pale again today, and his eyes were terribly big, blazing with fever.

"Do you not feel well, my Lord? Should we have a rest?"

The sick man reassured him with a smile. "No, good Walter. And we have no time for a rest. You know, the prodigal son's heart beats strongly when he returns home at last."

His lips twitched a little, when he made this confession. If such an action had been fitting, Walter would have consoled his master and laid his broad right hand soothingly on the slender hands that trembled and ran hither and thither on Hermann's lap.

The trees bordered the bumpy road like gray shadows. The morning air had a clean coolness reminiscent of a drink of fresh water from a spring. The hoofs of the two horses clomped dully, and the wheels creaked morosely. Birds, still half asleep, twittered in a low voice in the branches.

"And to think I once believed that life existed only in noise. How much life there is in silence!"

Hermann wished that he could have been lifted out of the wagon, so that he could have touched the smooth stem of a beech tree, breathing in the scent of the wood, and so assure himself that he had returned home. He had always loved the trees, and had missed them in the city. They grew upward, strong and stable, rich and beautiful in the green abundance of their foliage in the summer. In the fall, their colors shone out like flames; there was the tender filigree of the branches in winter, and soft buds in the spring. The lame boy had spent solitary hours studying in the inner courtyard of the abbey, under the old linden tree with its wide branches. He had followed the wavy lines of sunlight on the ground, as they wavered and danced in keeping with the fluttering of the leaves. He had listened to the polyphonic singing of the birds and the humming of the insects. When they fell silent, the tree sang its own melody. It rustled, swished, whispered, and breathed in the leaves. Was the old linden tree still standing? Would he see the beech wood in the western part of the island once again? And the old knotty willow down on the shore?

"I want to go to the willow. That is where my path to the other shore began, my path into the world, my detour. I hung in its branches like a crucified man, but I did not want cross and sacrifice. My heart was full of pride and thoughts of escape."

"

The wagon jolted out of the wood, and the coachman pointed forward with the shaft of his whip. "Allensbach," he snarled, without parting his teeth. Low houses crouched on the shore of the lake.

Hermann raised his hands to his breast in joyful excitement. The Gnadensee shimmered before him in the soft light of morning. In the years of his absence, he had been homesick for this lake, yearning to see the shining sheet of water that lay between the shores as if in a vessel that was open to the sky and reflected it. The sick man's eyes glided over the water to the other shore, to Reichenau.

The early morning veil of mist was still weaving mysteriously around the island of Reichenau, around its walls and pinnacles, around its roofs and towers. One last star hung in the sky, shining and large.

"They, when they saw the star, were glad beyond measure ..."

The star above Reichenau, the star above the abbey.

"And in there, I shall find the Child and his Mother."

The lame man's joy threatened to overwhelm his weak body. Walter felt him trembling and held him more tightly, but Hermann did not understand why the servant did so—he simply looked and looked. The sun gilded the familiar picture of his beloved home, which he had missed for so long. The lake shone, and the buildings and the trees and bushes on the island could now be seen clearly. In the distance, at the end of the island in the direction of Constance, he saw the severe Carolingian building that was Saint George's church, the cell of Hatto.* At the farthest point of the island to

---

* Hatto I (c. 850 – 15 May 913) was archbishop of Mainz (Mayence) from 891 until his death. He belonged to a Swabian family and was probably educated at the monastery of Reichenau, of which be became abbot in 888.

the northwest, the church of Saints Peter and Paul, the church of Bishop Egino of Verona, rose up toward the sky. The sick man's gaze lingered on the abbey church and the monastic buildings in the center of the island. These had been founded by Saint Pirmin, an itinerant bishop, and they lay so close to the Gnadensee that they were reflected in the water. The pleasant interplay of the forms and shapes in the gentle twilight of the early morning gave way to a severe and gray seriousness, and the abbey now appeared to Hermann like a summons addressed to him, like a demand from which there was no escape. His heart throbbed with rapid, irregular beats. But he would not run away from the demand, which would take hold of him totally and irrevocably. His hands became damp, and pearls of sweat formed on his forehead. His nature was afraid of what was in store for it, although his will said "yes" to it. Once again, he felt tempted to avoid exposing himself to the risk of being humiliated, if Abbot Berno were to refuse to welcome him. Perhaps he should go away at once to Altshausen, or to his sister Irmingard and her husband ...

"No!" Hermann cried out suddenly, his voice so loud that the horses pricked up their ears. "No!" He made the sign of the cross on his brow, his mouth, and his breast. Over on the island, the bells began to ring.

"*Adjutorium nostrum in nomine Domini, qui fecit caelum et terram ...*"[1]

The wagon stopped on the shore of the lake, where some fishermen were casting their nets. They looked

---

1. ["Our help is in the name of the Lord, who made heaven and earth ..."]

calmly at the wagon and at the crooked man in the arms of the servant.

"Can one of you bring us over to Reichenau?" asked Hermann politely.

An elderly man rose wordlessly and went ahead to his simple boat. The sick man remained in the wagon, while Walter and the coachman carried the bundles to the boat. Hermann could not tear his eyes away from the abbey. Slowly, his gaze moved over the buildings, registering every ledge, every windowsill, and every window, as one would contemplate the traits of a beloved face. The annex of the church of Our Lady, the west-work, had grown larger. The blunt cube of the tower rose up majestically, flanked by twin two-storied vestibules. Hermann knew that the Lord Berno loved this building, which one day would be a new church dedicated to Saint Mark.

"My Lord, everything is in the boat. May I bring you on board?"

Hermann nodded to his servant. "Let the coachman wait here. We might perhaps still need him."

The boat tilted to one side when Walter stepped in, carrying Hermann. He set him down carefully on a rough wooden bench and held him fast in his strong arms. The lame man's right hand clenched the side of the boat, and his head bent forward. The muscles in his gaunt face were tensed. Now, there was no longer any turning back.

The fisherman pushed off from the shore. A couple of reeds moved aside with a hiss, and the journey across the Gnadensee began.

The oars struck the waters with a steady rhythm, and the clumsy boat slid slowly across the smooth surface. The Gnadensee was clear and deep.

"I would like to touch the water," asked the lame man in a low voice. Walter immediately bent him down to the right, so that he could dip his fingers into the cool water. "Thank you, Walter!" Hermann blessed himself with his wet hand. "Water from the Gnadensee," he murmured apologetically, by way of an explanation.[2] The lake, this uniquely still and peaceful body of water, must mean a great deal to the Lord.

The island drew nearer. The abbey grew larger as they approached it. Was there not something threatening and overwhelmingly powerful in its walls and towers? The sick man automatically huddled against the supporting arm of his companion.

"I wonder what my master is afraid of?" thought Walter in concern. He was not sure how he could help him.

Many years ago, as a little boy, Hermann had been afraid when he saw the abbey for the first time. Astonishment and fear and a shy joy had filled the heart of the lame child who huddled in the arms of the Lady Hiltrud; and even then, he had also felt a timid love. His love for Reichenau had remained, but it had changed, brought to maturity in suffering and pain. He would be Hermann of Reichenau, even if they no longer wanted to have him in the abbey.

The blunt prow of the boat bored with a creak into the gravel that bordered the shore. The lame man had himself set down in the grass on the shore. The stalks were green, but the trees were beginning to clothe themselves in bright colors. His sickness had detained him in Aachen for a long time. His broken ankle took a long time to

---

2. [The "Gnadensee" means literally the "lake of grace."]

heal, and it was fall before their laborious journey had brought them to their destination. He wondered if the grapes in the vineyards of Reichenau were already ripe.

Hermann watched the men unloading the travelers' bundles. Walter addressed a question to him: "Should we bring you to the monastery first, my Lord?"

He firmly rejected this idea. "No, I have other plans. Help me to get up, and give me the crutches."

"Do you want to walk, my Lord? The path is too long for you. And it becomes a little steep …"

"You are probably right, Walter. But this is how it must be. I must use the crutches one last time … for my homecoming. The man who left in pride must come home in humility. Come, good friend, help me up! Bring the bundles to the monastery with the fisherman, give him a generous payment, and wait at the porter's lodge for me. And do not look so worried. I know the path I have to take."

Walter carried out these instructions gloomily. He was familiar with the firm undertone in his master's voice, which meant that he brooked no opposition.

While the two men went with the bundles to the monastery, the sick man stood on the shore, supporting himself heavily on his crutches. Today, he did not look even once across to the far shore. He made his way painfully to the old willow tree, often stopping, exhausted, for a break.

"Do you call this 'walking,' Master Cheirisophos? It is only the wood that brings me forward. From now on, I will no longer have even the wood of the crutches to give me support."

Hermann sensed that these were the last "steps" he would take by himself. More than ever, other people's hands would have to assist him. Finally, he reached the willow, which had changed greatly since the last time he was there. He felt no feelings of triumph or defiance, no restive rebellion against the bonds of his sickness, no hunger for life, no bitterness. In the true sense of the word, he was at home. He was safe.

He leaned for a little while against the gnarled trunk and rested, and then the last part of his homecoming began. He made his way painfully and laboriously to the path, scarcely able to drag his legs after the crutches. His ankle, which had healed poorly, was very painful, and he felt an increasing trembling in his hands and arms. He had to keep his eyes on the ground, since he had to take care to avoid stones and rough places. Hermann of Altshausen's solitary progress resembled a penitential pilgrimage.

Again and again, he was forced to pause in order to relieve the pressure on his heart and to get his breath back. He did not notice that a monk was standing in one of the vineyards, looking at him in astonishment. Tradolf the cellarer broke off his inspection of the grapes. Were his eyes deceiving him? Surely that was the man from Altshausen, Hermann! Ought he to help him? One look at the perspiring face persuaded him to abandon this idea. He had to take his path alone, because that was what he wanted. Tradolf turned back to the grapes, which promised a good harvest ...

Hermann lifted his crutches and set them down ever more slowly, ever more tentatively. The porter's lodge in the monastery seemed unattainably distant! He lifted his head. The walls were near, but for him, they were far away. Would he manage the last part of the way? He went slowly upward. A large stone was dislodged by the pressure from his crutches and sprang to one side. The sick man almost fell, but he preserved his balance with a great effort.

Now, he could go no farther. How was he to get the tip of the crutch out of the hole? He had too little strength. Could he not sit down for a moment to rest by the side of the road? His upper body was a heavy weight on the crutches, and his head sank deeper and deeper, as if under the pressure of an invisible burden. As he stood bent over, facing the abbey, he looked like a priest praying the *Confiteor* at Mass,[3] like the tax collector in the Temple, who did not dare to look up, but who went home justified.

The stonemasons who were working on the construction of the church tower began their hammering and pounding. The lame man staggered, as if it was on him that the blows were raining down. How long would he be able to stand?

His keen ear heard footsteps coming quickly toward him, almost running. Thank God, Walter was coming to fetch him! He would smile bashfully and ask the faithful servant to give him now the help that he had declined earlier.

"As you can see, I did not manage it," he said, and lifted his head with a great effort.

A golden cross shone and gleamed on a black habit.

"Abbot Berno, Father!" he stammered, his blue eyes fixed on the tall figure, with a child's happy amazement. His fear and hesitation were forgotten. "Father! Father!"

With the same love as once in the past, the abbot enclosed the cripple's crooked shoulders in his hands. "Hermann, my dear son in Christ!"

---

3. ["I confess to Almighty God …"]

In his joy at coming home, Hermann forgot the crutches and let go of them, because his hands were seeking the abbot's right hand. But he did not fall. The Lord Berno's left hand supported him more securely than the two beech-wood staffs of Master Cheirisophos.

"Come home, Hermann."

Home? Was he permitted to stay?

"Did you receive my ... my letter, Father Abbot?"

"Your letter arrived at exactly the right time, Hermann," replied the abbot with a smile. "I was beginning to grow impatient, because I had to be on the lookout for you for a long time."

"You were on the lookout for me? For me?"

"But of course. Do you think that Reichenau would have forgotten you even for one single day, my son?"

The sick man felt that his emotions were about to overwhelm him, but before he could reply, Tradolf came up and greeted him. The two monks brought him to the monastery church, where Berno knelt on the floor tiles beside the lame man's chair. Hermann's prayer was a silent thanksgiving and exultation. He found no words, but God knew, in any case, what he wanted to say to him.

A little later, they brought him into the abbot's cell and set him in the same armchair in which he had crouched years before, confused and covered in scratches, on that evening when Abbot Berno had decided that he should go to Aachen. "Why on earth did I ever leave Reichenau?"

Nothing in the room had changed. An oil lamp burned before the stone image of Our Lady, just as it had done then. A little earthenware jug with oil to replenish the lamp stood by the abbot's prie-dieu. Oil in the jug ... Hermann smiled fleetingly. "Theophilos, I am at home. I hope that you too may experience a homecoming."

For a time, both men were silent. Abbot Berno wanted to give the sick man time to compose himself. He turned his attentive gaze with a calm benevolence on the gaunt, matured features, on which boyish defiance had given way to manly seriousness. Hermann returned his gaze with candor and modesty. The old openness was there, together with a new readiness.

"It is good that you are home again, my son," said the abbot, reflectively. The passing of the years had left no traces on his face, but he felt an increased weariness.

"May I thank you for your prayer, Father Abbot? I am sure that I must attribute my ... homecoming to it. I would also like to thank you for welcoming the prodigal son with such love."

"The prodigal son?" The Lord Berno shook his head. "No, you were never a prodigal son in my eyes. I counted on your homecoming."

The lame man looked down at his hands. Had they not wanted to use force to take hold of life—or what he took to be life? How foolish he had been, when he started out on his journey!

A brother brought a goblet of the island wine, but while his trembling hand was still setting down the goblet after a brief sip, Hermann asked: "Father Abbot, may I tell you what happened? I took a dangerous and toilsome detour, as my lady mother had suspected."

"Tell me what you would like to tell me, my son."

"I would like to tell you everything, Father Abbot." Without sparing himself, he told the story of the years in Aachen. The abbot already knew some of this through letters from the Lord of Rahnwyl, who was his relative; but it was only now that he learned how difficult and dangerous that time had been for the young man. He heard about his restless search for life, about the foolishness with the yellow cloth, the hunger for healing, the bitterness and the hardening of the heart against God, the striving for knowledge, and finally, the slow awakening to true life out of the false dream of life.

The lame man omitted nothing. With uncompromising openness, he admitted his guilt, and with childlike humility, he told of his pardon. He laid in the Lord Berno's hand what had happened through him and to him.

The abbot was deeply distressed as he heard of the boy's hard struggle that had made him a man, and he was greatly relieved to hear of the breakthrough of the grace that allowed Hermann to see his sickness in a new light, to understand it and say "yes" to it.

"It was in fact words of yours that brought the decision, Father Abbot: 'I am made for God, and God is love.'"

"And … what is to happen now, Hermann?"

"Would you show me the path, Father Abbot?"

"Do you wish to remain with us?"

"Father, I cannot imagine or wish anything more beautiful!"

The Lord Berno's face grew severe. "But I require that you send your servant home to Altshausen, Hermann. You must become wholly dependent again, wholly reliant upon the compassion of others. You are aware that it will not always be shown you willingly. On Reichenau, you are not the rich count of Altshausen who has the right to make demands."

"Here, I am the last of the poor ones of Christ," replied the lame man quietly. He was not exaggerating, for he was always dependent on other people's benevolence, and if he no longer had a servant to whom he could give commands, he possessed less than the least beggar.

The abbot took up the phrase he had used, and repeated it emphatically: "Yes, here, you are the last of the poor ones of Christ ... nothing more than that. Do you want to remain, Hermann of Altshausen?"

"That is what I ask of you, Father Abbot, if the abbey can bear the burden of my sickness."

"If you remain here, all the obligations of your oblation will be revived. You no longer belong to yourself. You are a gift to God. In his name, I receive this gift. You may remain." The abbot's face lost its severity. "Since I received your letter, a special cell has been waiting for you in the north wing. From its windows, you can look out onto the Gnadensee. You will live there alone, even though the Rule does not envisage such a case. A few days ago, the cell received a new cross, a big cross from the castle chapel in Altshausen. The noble Lady Hiltrud sent it to us."

"My lady mother! I did not tell her that I would return to Reichenau. How did she know that?"

"Mothers sense more than their sons know, Hermann. Your servant will bring her a letter from you. And may the cross from the chapel of Saint Ulrich in Altshausen give you consolation in hours of distress. In this world, our peace is always at risk."

The traveler's bundles awaited the lame man in the cell. He wasted no time in looking around the little room, but began joyfully to fumble with the laces. Abbot Berno had to help him. He showed the abbot his texts, his drafts and notes, the parchments that Master Cheirisophos had given him, and the parchment of Abbot Berno. The abbot looked with a secret joy at the Latin, Greek, and Arabic texts, at the mathematical and astronomical notes, the sketches and the neums. There was even an astrolabe, the attempt to project the orbit of heavenly bodies onto a plane, with a movable horizon above it.

"You must explain the astrolabe to me sometime," said Abbot Berno, taking up an artistically decorated pair of compasses.

"That is a present from the Lord Arnulph for you, Father Abbot. He gave me a great quantity of good parchment too."

The sick man had no idea of the wealth with which he had come home. He drew a piece of yellow cloth from the last bundle. "The evidence of my foolishness."

"It will become an act of thanksgiving for the grace that you were permitted to discover life. Why should there not be a bright yellow curtain behind the statue of Our Lady in the abbey church?"

Hermann agreed enthusiastically. Now the yellow smiled again and became the radiant note of joy. Everything would fall into place. He was at home.

"

"Master Hermann"—that was what the young pupils in the external school and the boarding school of the abbey and the monks called him. For the students, there was soon only one master. But Hermann of Altshausen did not even wear the religious habit of Saint Benedict. Years passed, and he was still an oblate.

How could he, with his sickness, express the wish to be received into the community of the monks? Was it not a great privilege to be allowed to live in a cell of his own in a wing of the monastery? His days were spent in a stable harmony of prayer and work.

Christopher

Hermann had dismissed the students. He was tired, as he crouched in his armchair by the window and waited for his midday meal. A wax tablet lay within reach on the table beside him. He was dissatisfied with the little historical chronicle that he had written. It covered too short a period, and was inexact. He wanted to compose a great chronicle of the world, beginning with the year of the birth of the Lord. Would he ever succeed in this task? Surely such a work demanded years of preparatory study? Encouraged by the Lord Berno, he had made excerpts from some thick folio volumes. Sometimes, he had dictated these to his brother Werinher.

"It is a confusing hodgepodge," the young student had sighed, shaking his blond head in irritation. "I would lose my courage and my patience if I had to do all this detailed work."

The sick man laughed quietly to himself. Werinher and patience—two things that seldom went together! Werinher, full of the joys of life, had inherited too much of their father to allow him to wait patiently for a long time, to see how something slowly came into existence and matured. The monks of Reichenau were constantly astonished at the difference between the two brothers. Werinher was a big man, strong and healthy. He had a round and kindly face, with rough features and quick gray eyes. He was perpetually looking for something to do, something to experience, some conquest to make. He flared up easily, and was just as quick to seek reconciliation. His piety was straightforward and genuine, but somewhat too austere and sober.

When he pushed the lame man's wheelchair across the courtyard, an onlooker would never have guessed that the two were brothers. The little cripple with the gaunt and spirited face did not resemble him at all.

While Hermann was eating his vegetable soup, Werinher rushed in, without waiting for an answer to his knock. His round face glowed with excitement.

"Hermann!" he called impetuously, "Hermann, I am so happy! You must be the first to hear the news. I have been admitted to the novitiate." In his high spirits, he pivoted around, so that his broad garment flew wide. "I have been admitted! I have been admitted!"

The lame man put his wooden spoon down, because his hand suddenly shook too much. "I wish you happiness with all my heart, and God's blessing, Werinher." But a secret sadness resonated in his words.

"Are you happy with me, my brother?"

Hermann's reply drew a fine distinction: "I am happy for you." He pushed his bowl to one side.

Werinher sat on the stool for a few moments. "No longer a student ... At last I am moving on, at last!"

The sick man thought: "But who are you telling this to, Werinher? Should you not realize that your joy must wound a man who may not and cannot 'move on'?" But he bit his lips, to prevent any rash word from escaping them. At last, Werinher was moving on, and he, Hermann, was the last of the poor ones of Christ—here too, in this respect too.

"Don't you have a choir practice, Werinher?"

The younger man sprang up. "I had forgotten the practice. Thank goodness I have you ..." He hastened off with a laugh. Hermann listened to the steps that quickly ebbed away, and drew his plate nearer again. But he did not eat. He was disturbed as he noted the bitterness that welled up in him. Was he jealous of his brother, whose sacrifice God had accepted?

"No, I am not like Cain. My sacrifice was accepted too, a different sacrifice. But ... what do I have, that I can give the Lord? Werinher is bringing him all his freedom and his young strength ..."

He tried in vain to ward off the bitterness, which felt like a physical discomfort. He turned to his cold soup and began to eat.

"

When Abbot Berno entered his cell that afternoon, he found Hermann humming quietly to himself as he bent over his wax tablet.

"You are very cheerful, my son?"

"I ought to be cheerful, Father Abbot," replied Hermann, openly, "but I am not. I have been obliged to fight since noon today against a very ugly feeling. When I heard that Werinher is to be admitted to the novitiate, I have been a prey to bitterness, perhaps indeed to jealousy."

"Are you not judging yourself too strictly, Hermann?"

The lame man looked at him calmly. "You know that I must be very alert, Father Abbot, since I am not gentle and patient by nature. My nature often wages a hard fight against my will."

"God is with you. You are waging a good fight. Blessed

are those who fight for his sake—not those who do not need to fight."

"Yes, Father Abbot," Hermann admitted reflectively. "I am continually astonished at the kindness and condescension with which God aids me in the struggle. Usually, I see this aright, and I want to sing him my Magnificat, but sometimes the wretchedness of my body numbs me. Here, I have tried in my own way to sing of the Lord and of his love." He pointed to his wax tablet.

The Lord Berno took it from the table and read what the sick man had written in shaky letters.

"I am made for God, and God is love."

"Your words were the medicine I needed for my bitterness."

"My words? Hermann, it is only through you that I came to realize the profundity of this affirmation. It is through you that I learned once again how to be astonished. With the passing of time, we can come to take everything for granted, even the love of God. Ah, I see that you have written a melody to the words ... What do the letters between the neums mean?"

"I must go into some detail, if I am to explain my modest endeavor to you, Father Abbot. My sickness obliges me to stay in silence in the place to which someone else has brought me. That may be my cell, or under the linden tree in the inner courtyard, or on the shore of the Gnadensee, or in the monastery church. I have learned how to wait and to look and to listen. I must simply wait, and I am grateful for this gift of the Lord too. As you know, I spend my nights waiting for the sleep that seldom comes. In the dark, it is only the eyes of the spirit that can see, and many images disclose themselves to those eyes.

"I also listen in the nights, for they have their own melody.

"Father, it is not easy to put into words that I want to tell you ... I feel that the whole of creation wants to sing its song in praise of the Creator. This song rises up out of the life and activity of the animals, and out of the being of the inanimate creation. But only the human being has received the privilege of consciously knowing the Lord and praising him. Should we not therefore be permitted to take up the song of the creation into our praise of God? We sing many tunes in praise of the Lord. But are they not poor and monotonous, when we listen to the wealth and variety of the notes that his creation sings to him? If we were to take up their melodies into our conscious praise of God, would not that mean fetching the creatures home into the redemption?"

"But it would not be enough to take up those melodies and sing them, Hermann. We would need to record them better and more exactly, and to communicate them to other persons and ages, just as we transmit our thoughts by means of language."

"Yes, Father Abbot, music needs its own language. It requires a precisely thought-out system. But this system must not be imposed on it forcibly and artificially. It must grow out of the order of the music. I have ventured to attempt to study more deeply and to grasp the regularity of the sequence of notes. I do not know whether my system can be put into practice, of course. It would be necessary to test whether it is suitable for practical application. If my insights are of any value, we would have a simple way of noting down songs. The letters between the neums, which attracted your attention, depict the steps from one note to the next. The euphony of a melody lies in the way in which the intervals follow one another. If we write these down, the melody is unambiguously defined. This is why I have designated the various intervals by means of letters. A point under a letter means that an interval is to be sung downward. The neums and letters written down here give the following melody …"

In a dulcet voice, the lame man sang a simple tune that accorded with the words: "I am made for God, and God is love."

Abbot Berno nodded his approval. "As far as I know, similar attempts are being made in Italy and Byzantium too, Hermann. Keep up your efforts. I would be happy if you surpassed my own endeavors in the field of music. You are not only a musician of the head—your music comes from the heart." His own compositions and writings on musical theory were known and famous in the monasteries of the Benedictine order. "What you are doing, my dear son, serves one single goal: it is the conscious practice of the praise of God. But I wonder why you do not include the most melodious sound of all in the song that is your life."

Hermann looked at him in perplexity. What did the father mean by these words? What was he guilty of? Had he omitted or forgotten something essential? He asked, in a reverent tone: "Would you please show me what I lack, Father Abbot?"

"You do not know what I mean?"

"No, Father Abbot."

Abbot Berno drew himself up to his full height. The ruler of Reichenau stood before the crooked little cripple.

"Hermann of Altshausen, in the name of Our Lord

Jesus Christ, we ask you: Are you willing to give absolutely everything to the Lord? Are you willing to serve him as a monk from now on, according to the Rule of our holy Father Benedict and in the spirit of the renewal of Cluny, in poverty, chastity, and obedience, and no longer to know and acknowledge any other will than that of the Lord Jesus Christ, which is made known to you through the mouth of the abbot who is in office at that time? Is that what you will, Hermann of Altshausen?"

The sick man wanted to reply, but his voice refused to serve him. Was he, the cripple, to be admitted? The years when he did not dare to make the request, because of his sickness, were now past. It was the abbot who was asking him. Christ was asking him. Hermann suspected nothing of the hard battle the abbot had fought in the community, until the monks had given their assent to the admission of the sick man. Christ wanted him. That was joy—an inconceivably great joy.

Finally, he stammered: "You ask me what I will? Father, I have had no greater wish since I came back. I did not dare to speak of it, because an invalid is out of place in a community of the healthy. I will! I will! Father, what a tremendous gift you have given me!"

The abbot was taken aback, and bent down to him. "It is Christ who gives you the gift, my son. From now on, you belong to him, and you can sing to him alone the song that is your life ... ever more strongly, ever more beautifully, ever more purely. Create space in your soul, Hermann, space for the Lord alone. Few dare to do so. They assign a miserable little chamber to him, while they themselves inhabit the entire house. Allow the Lord to come ever further into your house, and do not fear when he comes to you under the sign of the cross. There is joy even in the cross ... Despite your sickness, I will have you ordained to the priesthood. Then the Lord will certainly give you the strength to offer the sacrifice of his cross. But sing to the Lord every day the song of praise that is your crucified life."

That same evening, Hermann wrote down a canticle, a glorious setting of the Magnificat.

"He who is mighty has wrought for me his wonders ..."

High above the earth, the stars circle in exalted orbits. And the God who created these huge heavenly bodies loved him, the little cripple on Reichenau. Could there be any greater joy for a human heart? God had said his "yes" to him.

"

Hermann joined his brother in the time of preparation. After he had received the religious habit, Abbot Berno himself assumed the spiritual direction of the exceptional novice, since Christ was the real master of this soul, and a misunderstanding on the part of a novice master could wreak destruction. Carefully and reverently, the Lord Berno created the space where grace could work.

He also looked after the physical well-being of the over-zealous scholar who was now his novice. Brother Wigbertus, the carpenter, skillfully made a light wheelchair for the lame man, an almost rickety conveyance of wood and willow rods. This meant that he was no longer dependent on a carrying chair; one monk on his own could bring Hermann out into the fresh air. Ekkehard was given the task of bringing him to the Gnadensee every day—a charge that displeased the infirmarian, since he was one of those who had voted against the admission of the sick man to the monastic community. Just as in the past, so now he regarded this Hermann of Altshausen as an unwelcome burden that he shouldered only with reluctance. And he let Hermann feel this, every time he rendered him some service—not with words, but by the manner in which he helped him. The lame man had had much to endure in these years, but he had never spoken about it. Mercy without love is an alms that is flung down before the feet of the one who receives it. The sick man experienced day by day that he was indeed the last of the poor ones of Christ, and he often had to take his heart in his hands, so to speak, to prevent the bitter words from erupting. But he said nothing. Not even to the Lord Berno did he disclose this suffering.

At the Gnadensee, the infirmarian practiced his own method of interpreting the abbot's instructions. He brought the lame man down to the lake and left him there alone for an hour, instead of trundling him over the island. In the meantime, he talked with the steward, the fishermen, or the servants, and enjoyed an hour of leisure.

Hermann liked to be alone. He loved the quiet hour at the Gnadensee. The little waves rolled onto the shore with a regular gurgle. Grebes, little coots, and gulls animated the surface of the water. Sometimes a fishing boat went past, or the white sail of a larger boat shone in the sunlight. Each day had its own little surprises in store for him. One day, a beetle landed on his hand and gave him time to admire the green sheen of its armor, before it flew off. Another time, a curly-headed fisherman's son looked in astonishment at the man in the wheelchair and played unself-consciously near him. He even gave him the red, green, and brown stones that he was playing with, and Hermann took them in his hand, recalling the beautiful, colored stones of Master Theophilos Cheirisophos. Where would the doctor be now? Had he had the courage to choose those stones that alter the picture of a life?

"

One day in summer, the infirmarian was in a particularly bad mood, and grumbled: "It is completely impossible for me to take you for a walk today!" He pushed the wheelchair with a jerky movement under the willow tree on the shore and left the sick man alone, as usual. He had told Heimot the fisherman to get him herbs from the Alpine region, and Heimot lived on the western shore of the lake—a long way in this heat … It did not occur to Ekkehard that it was not the lame man's fault that he found the long walk burdensome. He felt that it was perfectly appropriate to vent his displeasure on the sufferer.

Hermann found the lake changed. There was something threatening in the silence. The willow scarcely gave him any protection from the glaring sun that scorched him. The water had turned a yellowy gray. Not even the slightest breeze stirred. A wall crept silently and inexorably over the lake, gray with a poisonous yellow undertone. The sick man felt weak and broken. Breathing cost an effort in the oppressive heat. His eyes hurt, and he closed them. He fell into an exhausted sleep.

Suddenly, a gust of wind startled him. A storm was whipping the branches of the old willow, driving dust and clouds of sand before it, and shaking the light wheel-chair. The sun had disappeared. A wan twilight lay over the landscape, and the sky was heavy with black clouds.

Where was Ekkehard? Why did the infirmarian not come to fetch him? The storm raged ever more furiously, and the waters of the Gnadensee seethed. White spume crowned the high waves, wild and yellow-black, that rolled onto the brink of the shore. The willow branches clacked against each other and whipped the creaking trunk. The storm howled, whined and whistled, hissed and splut-tered. Where was Ekkehard? If only he would come!

For one moment, there was a total silence, oppres-sive and uncanny. Then all hell broke loose. A mighty storm gust drew near with furious speed and tremendous power. It collided hard with the little vehicle at the edge of the shore, and propelled it down the incline toward the Gnadensee. Before the lame man had the time to cry out in terror, the wheels stuck fast in the mud, so deep that the vehicle did not go any farther into the water.

The first heavy raindrops fell. There were lurid light-ning flashes and long growls of thunder from the moun-tains. The lame man's wheelchair stood in the shallow water, stood in the Gnadensee. If the mud had not given way, he would be lying in the water by now ... The white spume, cold and agitated, washed around his feet, and the waves rolled against his legs.

The rain was now torrential, and Hermann was soaked to the skin in no time. The white spume crept higher and higher, and the lightning flashes came closer. The thunder sounded ever more threatening. But all at once, the sick man became calm and serene. He was not alone.

Ekkehard had just reached the western shore when the

storm began. He rushed into Heimot's hut, but the fisherman was not at home. The infirmarian looked grimly at the rain. Should he run and fetch the lame man? But if he did so, he would not have a dry thread on his body by the time he reached him. It would be better to wait until the worst of the rain was past. Then he could set out. Besides, he was sure that Hermann would not complain to the abbot ...

"

Berthold, one of the students, was walking through the abbey cloister. He was scowling, because he had not understood the mechanism of the water clock that Master Hermann had so carefully explained. Now he would have to request the kindly master to give him a little extra tuition.

Berthold knocked at the door of the cell and listened. Had the master answered? Most likely, the storm had drowned out his words. After some hesitation, the student entered. The cell was empty; rain whipped through the window and soaked the parchments on the work table. The elaborate table showing the computation of time among the Greeks and the Romans, the Arabs, Jews, and Christians, on which the master had spent so much time, would be lost! Berthold made up his mind quickly. He hurried to the window, intending to stretch the thin animal skin, which was fastened on one side of the window, across the opening.

His hand froze in its movement, as his eyes fell on the raging Gnadensee and he saw the wheelchair with the lame man, standing in the water. The animal skin fell from his hand. He ran out of the cell, without closing the door—that task was carried out by the loud blows of the storm.

"Master Hermann!" he shouted, as he ran like one bewitched through the twilight cloister to the monastery gateway. "Master Hermann!"

The porter saw the wild look on the student's face, and cried out: "What do you want? Has somebody given you permission?"

Berthold simply pushed him aside. "Master Hermann in the lake!" he shouted, and ran off. The brother stared after him as if he was mad. A dazzling flash of lightning came, and he quickly shut the two wings of the door. He crossed himself. "Lord, have mercy!" The thunder growled …

Hailstones pelted down, and the lame man grew more and more stiff from the cold and the wetness. He lost all track of time. The lightning came closer, and the waves rose up to his knees. He was almost deafened by the din as he crouched in his little chair, defenseless and abandoned. And yet …

"*In manus tuas, Domine, commendo spiritum meum …*"[4]

Suddenly, he heard a gasping cry: "Master … Master Hermann!" Someone sprang into the water beside him, a young man wearing the garment of a student, Berthold. He used all his strength in the attempt to push the wheelchair back, but the wheels had buried themselves deep in the mud, which continued to yield. A dazzling blaze of lightning came near to them, very near. Berthold cried out and pressed his head against the lame man's breast.

---

4. ["Into your hands, O Lord, I commend my spirit."]

The knotty old willow at the edge of the shore burst into flames.

The lame man found the strength to lay his two hands around the head of the student, protecting him and consoling him. Berthold's trembling and fear gave Hermann an unsuspected strength. It was up to him to help.

"Lord Jesus Christ!" he cried in a loud voice, speaking into the heart of the raging elements. "You once issued commands to the wind and the waves. Have mercy on us and show now that you are the Lord of the unchained forces of nature."

Berthold did not know how long he had pressed his face against the damp monastic habit. When he finally dared to look up, the lakeside had become quieter; the thunder growled far off. The rain fell into the lake with a gentle regularity, and the waters had withdrawn, as if they were ashamed. Must not he be ashamed of his fear? He looked at the master in confusion, and Hermann smiled at him, his numb lips blue with the cold. "We have survived, Berthold."

The student looked with horror at the smoldering stump of the willow tree. Once again, he attempted to push the wheelchair to the shore, but this time too, the wheels buried themselves deeper, despite all his efforts.

"May I carry you, Master Hermann? There is no alternative."

"Get help, Berthold," replied Hermann, although he was so cold and weak that he shivered. "I can wait."

"No, you cannot wait," cried Berthold. He bent down and took the lame man in his arms, lifting him out of the wheelchair with a considerable effort. Stumbling and staggering, gasping and feeling his way blindly, he reached the path with his burden. It was indeed a strange sight—the tall and slender student, whose soaking garment flapped against his legs, with his crippled teacher in his arms.

They did not notice that a monk was approaching the Gnadensee from the western part of the island. When Ekkehard the infirmarian saw them, he stopped short in shock. At the monastery gateway, Berthold asked where the infirmarian was, but the master seemed not to have heard the question. Instead, he murmured with a weak smile: "Berthold as Christopher. But it is not the Child Jesus that you have in your arms."

The porter stared at the strange pair, as though they were an apparition from beyond the grave. So that was why the student had behaved like that ... But before he could open his mouth, Berthold staggered past him and stumbled hastily through the cloister, still haunted by the terrible image of the master in the wheelchair in the lake.

"Thank God that I did not understand the mechanism of the water clock!"

Finally, he reached the cell. He opened the door with his elbow, and laid the lame man down on his bed. Then he sank to his knees and crouched on the floor, breathing heavily.

"Berthold, you have overexerted yourself," stammered Hermann, anxiously. His lips were so numb that it was difficult for him to speak clearly. "You should have let me wait ..."

At these words, the student came to himself. "I will fetch help, Master. You need dry clothes." Berthold stood up laboriously and stiffly, like an old man. He made his way out of the cell.

A cold wind whistled through the open window. Hermann alternated between chills and heat rashes. Was the cross on the wall moving? It oscillated and came closer and closer to him ... His trembling increased. Where had the other man gone—Christopher? He could not remember the correct name of the student.

He tried to say aloud: "Christopher is a beautiful name," and he was astonished to hear how throaty and slurred his voice was. Had he said these words, or was there someone else there?

He heard the door opening. Who was coming into the cell? Surely he knew him? Of course ... it was Master Cheirisophos, Theophilos Cheirisophos, the Greek doctor from Corinth. The little man, who was suddenly very tall, gave him a nasty stare.

"What are you doing here, Master Cheirisophos?" he croaked and babbled feverishly. "Did you have a storm like this in Greece? Do not look at me so angrily. I have just got out of the bath. A fine bath, Master, a curative bath, but a little cool. Go now, I pray you, go! I am tired ... terribly tired, after your fine bath."

Ekkehard the infirmarian had listened with horror to the lame man's stammering. He approached the bed quietly, but Hermann raised his head with unexpected strength and stared at him, his eyes wide and threatening. He cried out, like one warding off a danger:

"Go, go, Master Cheirisophos! Your world is a lie. God is love, mercy. You do not even love your own self, and you are unmerciful. Go, go ..."

His shout became an indecipherable babbling. The infirmarian was shocked and retreated a few paces.

Abbot Berno entered the cell and rushed to the bed, without so much as a glance at Ekkehard. He bent over the sick man and asked anxiously: "Hermann, Hermann, what is the matter with you?"

A trembling hand groped for the abbot's habit and clutched the pectoral cross. "My Lord, I ask you, do not let him come nearer—no nearer! He is darkness without mercy," he babbled in fear. "You are merciful light, my Lord, good light ... light ..."

Abbot Berno laid his hand on the fevered brow, and the tense features immediately relaxed. "Be calm, my son, very calm. I am here with you."

"You ... are with me ... always, always. Christopher too should ... remain."

When the infirmarian once again attempted to approach the bed and asked, "Father Abbot, should I ...," the sick man reared up under the abbot's hand and shouted in horror: "No, no ... not Cheirisophos, my Lord, no!"

"Go," said the abbot to Ekkehard. "You will give me an exact account later on of what has happened."

Berthold brought dry garments and underclothing.

"When Master Hermann speaks of 'Christopher,' to whom is he referring?"

"To me, Father Abbot," the student admitted bashfully.

"I will put him to bed. Change your clothes, and then come back."

Outside, the evening sun broke through the splendid towers of the storm clouds, and the landscape shone, fresh and peaceful. In the corner cell, the Right Reverend Lord Abbot Berno, an Imperial Prelate, performed all the services of a nurse for his lame novice, and Hermann accepted this willingly. He also drank from the medicinal herbal broth that the Lord Berno gave him. The abbot listened anxiously to the rattling and whistling breaths. When Berthold came back, he required a precise account of where and how he had found the lame man.

"Ekkehard left him alone!" cried the abbot, enraged. "What suitable punishment can I find for him?"

Hermann opened his eyes, which shone with fever. "Do not extinguish the smoldering wick, my Lord … not extinguish. I will look for … him … Not extinguish."

Did he mean Ekkehard, or Master Cheirisophos?

"Would you like something more to drink, Hermann?"

"Drink, my Lord? Must I … drink the … cup, my Lord? It is so … bitter, but … as you will … as you will."

The trembling hands made a movement as if they were lifting a chalice. "I shall … take … the chalice of salvation …" In his fevered dream, the sick man stood at the altar as a priest and offered the holy sacrifice of the Mass.

Was the sacrifice of the life of Hermann of Altshausen about to be accomplished? He became weaker and weaker. His fevered dreams were about God, about Christ. He became calm when the abbot was present. Lord Berno stayed awake for many nights by his bed. He did not want Hermann to reveal the innermost reality of his soul to other ears.

He sat by him, hour after hour, and looked at Hermann's face. The nose stood out, pointed and narrow. His cheekbones were curved, and were a striking contrast to the yellow, sunken cheeks.

On several occasions, the abbot summoned the monastic community and intoned the prayers for the dying, but each time, the sick man recovered from his state of uttermost weakness. What had God still in store for him? Did this means that his journey into the Gnadensee was not the beginning of his homecoming into the eternal grace?[5]

Puer Natus Est

Abbot Berno sent his messenger to Altshausen, to bring Count Wolfrad and his wife Hiltrud the sad news that, in all probability, Hermann was on his deathbed.

Count Wolfrad II looked gloomily at the monastery servant, and declined to summon his wife, since the Lady Hiltrud too was keeping watch at a deathbed. All hope was gone for the life of Luipold, one of the later-born children.

"Tell your abbot that I thank him. Let him take care of the one whom we entrusted to Reichenau. We will not be coming to the island. Our son Luipold is sick, and will soon die. See that you get some food, and then make haste back to the monastery."

On the stairs, Walter met the monastery servant from Reichenau, and recognized him. "Frowin, you are here? How is my master, Count Hermann?"

Frowin gave a detailed account, and criticized the hardness of heart of the Lord of Altshausen.

Walter replied: "His mother must be told. I will speak with her, even if Count Wolfrad punishes me for doing so. She has a right to know. He is her favorite son."

---

5. [Once again, there is a play on words: "Gnadensee" ("Lake of Grace") and "Gnade" ("grace").]

"Your count makes exactly the opposite impression on me ...," muttered the servant from Reichenau.

Walter brought him into the servants' quarters and gave him something to eat. Then he asked a maid to fetch the mistress. The matter was very important.

"What could you have that was 'important'?" sneered the maid, but she went to the Lady Hiltrud, and the countess came.

When she emerged from the darkened sickroom, pale as a shadow, gaunt and exhausted, she looked so much like her son Hermann that Walter shrank back in shock.

"What do you want, Walter?" she asked kindly. Her blue eyes looked wearily at him—the eyes of Hermann. At this moment, he would have preferred to say nothing ...

"A messenger has brought news from Reichenau, noble Lady. Our Count Hermann is sick, and will shortly die."

The Lady Hiltrud staggered, but she soon regain control of herself. "His life is in God's hand, Walter. Let us trust God, and pray for him."

"Yes, my Lady ..."

The Lady Hiltrud turned in the doorway. "You must trust God, you who are the faithful servant of my son Hermann. Do you hear what I am saying? He will not leave us yet. He has a long and toilsome path before him." She smiled at him, her smile wrested from her exhaustion. He had often seen a smile like that on the face of his master in Aachen. Hermann was truly the Lady Hiltrud's son!

"

His mother's trust was repaid. The condition of the sick man on Reichenau slowly improved. On the precise day when Luipold of Altshausen was buried, Hermann took up his stylus and his wax tablet for the first time.

"You are working again, my son?" asked Abbot Berno.

"After I have caused you so much work, I would like to make myself useful again. If only I was able once again to do something!"

"Have patience with yourself, Hermann. If you are able, and if you wish to do so, you may dictate to the student Berthold. What would you say if he were to assume the responsibility for your well-being? Your Christopher has proved faithful and reliable."

"Thank you, Father Abbot. I would not have dared to ask for that ... May Werinher come to visit me again?"

"Certainly, Hermann, when he is back on Reichenau. I have sent him to Altshausen," said the abbot in a low voice, and turned to leave. But the sick man felt fear, and asked urgently:

"To ... Altshausen? What has happened ... at home?"

Abbot Berno paused before replying. He had wanted to wait until Hermann was stronger.

"Your brother Luipold has died ..."

"Luipold? He cannot have been more than twelve years old. I never met him ... My poor lady mother ..."

"Would you like to write a word of consolation for your mother, Hermann? Give me your wax tablet and dictate to me. Berthold can make a fine copy later."

Luipold was now the eighth child whom the Lady Hiltrud had buried. Was there a consolation for such suffering? The sick man knew how deep his mother's faith was, and so he dictated:

Death cannot constrain me.
For you came, O Lord Christ,
to bring me your light,
you who are my life.
Therefore my heart exults in you
and is very glad in you.
It sings in the cross and in pain
and in every trouble.
You are my path and my end
and my homeland, O Lord Christ.
I place myself in your hands,
you who are my life.
Alleluia, alleluia, alleluia.

"These words occurred to me a few days ago," said Hermann. He then made a request: "I should like you to add: 'I am made for God, and God is love.'"

The Lord Berno was full of admiration: "Your lady mother must have a strong faith, if she can bear to hear such words so soon after the death of a child."

"My dear mother is close to God," murmured the lame man, and fell unresistingly into a slumber that was the fruit of his weakness, yet also brought healing.

"

Several weeks later, Berthold brought the same verses to the abbot. Hermann had set them to music for him. "*Christus—vita mea ...*"[6]

As soon as he was restored to health, he was allowed

6. ["Christ—my life."]

to take his perpetual vows, and the Lord Berno had him ordained to the priesthood. Hermann was more sacrifice than priest; he was able only once to offer the holy sacrifice. Abbot Berno was happy to serve the Mass and help him.

The weeks turned into months. The last leaves yielded to the heavy mists of the fall. Storms howled around the abbey, and the lake and the mountains were hid from sight for days on end. It was winter, and the feast of the birth of the Lord was drawing near.

Hermann had composed an exultant "*Puer natus est nobis ... alleluia*"[7] for the choir, and he conducted the rehearsals in person, so that the monks would get accustomed to the letters he used in his notation.

While the monks were getting ready to go into the church on Christmas Eve, Berthold rushed into the lame man's cell.

"Help me get dressed and set me down by the fire," asked Hermann quietly. "I cannot come to the sacred liturgy."

The student was on the point of offering consolation, but he checked himself, since the sick man had no use for consolation. He performed his services quickly, and resolved to tell the abbot about the sick man's solitary Christmas. He crept out on tiptoe.

With eyes that were both tired and wide-awake, Hermann looked into the flames as they flickered and danced, flared up and died down, reddish-yellow, bright gold, bluish and greenish tongues of fire. From time to time, a log burst with a short, crisp explosion. And the fire sang

---

7. ["A Child is born for us, alleluia."]

its unvaried humming melody. Otherwise, all was still, totally still.

Heavy snowflakes had been falling for days outside, before the windows that were hung with double animal skins. Reichenau was swimming like a white ship on the black waters of the lake.

The heavy white covering of snow hid everything. Under it, the silence grew. Was there not something suffocating, something threatening, about it? He held his breath and listened, but all he heard was the sing-song of the fire.

In the monastery church, the brethren were singing Matins ... "Today, a sweet dew has fallen from heaven upon all the earth ..." But the covering of snow meant that the sound did not reach his cell. It had been a great consolation in the summer days to listen, when his sickness had prevented him from taking part in the worship of the monks—as it did now, on Christmas Eve!

Now, all he had was the growing silence, the wall of soft white snow that grew ever higher and cut him off from all that lived. He felt as if the snow was falling on his breast, noiseless and gentle, yet relentless and dangerous. If only he could leap up and run away, breaking the spell cast by the burdensome silence ...

But he crouched in the armchair, terribly crooked and wracked by pain, wrapped in layers of clothing despite the fire, tucked up like a little child. His hands lay on his lap, powerless. His palms were two open vessels, turned upward. His eyes moved from the darting flames to the great cross, to the feet of the Crucified. He could not see any farther, because it was impossible for him to lift his head that day.

"*Filius meus es tu ...,*"[8] he said aloud, looking intensely at the feet of the crucified Lord, at the slender, pierced feet of brown wood. He was startled by the sound of his own voice. The silence around him was too great, the growing, noiseless silence. It would be better if he too were silent.

He attempted with difficulty to collect his thoughts. The sacred night ... the birth of the Lord ... the night when the grace of God appeared ...

"Do not be afraid; behold, I bring you good news of a great rejoicing for the whole people. This day, in the city of David, a Savior has been born for you, the Lord Christ himself. Glory to God in high heaven, and peace on earth to those that are God's friends."

Hermann went through the sacred texts conscientiously—conscientiously, exactly, and soberly, as if he were studying some mathematical formula. But his meditation failed to banish the oppressive silence.

Outside, the white flakes fell continually. The snow weighed down the branches of the trees, and the white mass grew. The silence became even more oppressive.

Hermann stared into the fire again. The persistent sing-song annoyed him now. He breathed quickly, gaspingly, as if he was about to weep. He felt utterly alone. He could not go to Bethlehem. He did not envy the other monks the joy and warmth of the community, but he would have liked to experience a little more shelter in the community, precisely on Christmas Eve. Once again, he forced his mind, which was usually so obedient, to think of the liturgy of that night.

---

8. ["You are my son."]

"Rejoice, you heavens; exult, O earth, before the eyes of the Lord, for he comes."

Would the Lord come to him too, into his loneliness? He listened once more, as if he could get a confirmation that the Lord would indeed visit him, but the only answer was the humming sing-song of the fire.

Silence ... loneliness ...

"

Had things ever been any different? Was not his life the story of a terrible loneliness—a wilderness, the boundless breadth of a wilderness, sand and horizon, breadth without end, silence, solitude? That was how Master Cheirisophos had described the Arabian desert to him, the experience of being alone under a bright sky.

And the encounters with other people? Were they not mere oases in this wilderness, places of a fleeting rest? They seem to give a little shelter, but then one has to get on with the journey through the desert, through the silence, through the loneliness, into the freedom of solitude.

Father Abbot had often summoned Hermann and had allowed him to rest in his understanding and his goodness. But each time, he had had to go out, back into his wilderness, into his pains, his lameness, his condition of being set apart, being different.

Alone ... and surrounded by other people. Once again, his eyes met the pierced feet of the Crucified. Who had ever been more alone than the Lord? He was a human being, with a human heart that could feel; and at the same time, he was God. Despite all the closeness of other human beings, he was alone in the manger and alone on the cross, until he finally came to the ultimate, unfathomable, incomprehensible solitude that his cry revealed: "My God, my God, why have you forsaken me?"

"

When he compared his own loneliness with the solitude of Christ, Hermann of Altshausen realized that, in spite of everything, he had a secure place in the community of the monks. He was, of course, set apart by his sickness.

Segregatus ...[9]

But do not all human beings wander through the wilderness of their solitude? Can one person understand, welcome, love another person in such a way that the other will not suddenly wake up and realize with a shock that, in the ultimate depths of his being, he is not understood—that he is alone? Every human encounter, even in the noblest love, is both a finding and a losing. It is only in God that the human being experiences what it is to be at home—for eternity.

Outside, the snow fell, noiseless and unstoppable. All that the sick man heard was the humming sing-song of the fire, but his unease had left him. What remained was his yearning, which became a homesickness for God. The silence announced God's coming and gave the assurance of his presence. Hermann had said his "yes," his renewed "yes," to his wilderness, and this "yes" transformed the peaceless silence into a silent peace.

---

9. ["Set apart."]

He began to pray again: "*Laetentur caeli et exsultet terra ante faciem Domini quoniam venit,*"[10] but this time he prayed aloud.

And then he heard steps. He could make out the quick (slightly too quick) steps of young Berthold and the calm, measured tread of the abbot.

"*Quoniam venit …*"[11]

The door of the cell opened, and the fire blazed up in the draught of cold air, to become a mute, flickering, many-colored song of praise.

Berthold knelt down beside the lame man's armchair. Abbot Berno, looking different and solemn in the heavy gold brocade of the festive chasuble, bent down to Hermann and gave him the Body of the Lord.

Silence reigned in the room once more. Once more, it was only the fire that sang its humming sing-song. Outside, the flakes fell.

He was there …

The hands of the sick man lay on his lap, powerless, crooked, an open vessel. Abbot Berno took them carefully, folded them, and kept them together.

He was there …

Above the wilderness, his star shone. The wilderness was no longer loneliness. It was Bethlehem, the encounter with God. Bethlehem had come to him, since he could not go to Bethlehem.

After a lengthy silence, the abbot said: "Hermann, I wish you, in my own name and in the name of your

---

10. ["Let the heavens rejoice and the earth be glad before the face of the Lord, because he is coming."]

11. ["Because he is coming."]

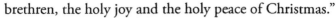

brethren, the holy joy and the holy peace of Christmas."

He removed his supportive hands, and the hands of the lame man fell apart, to form the vessel once more. In the light of the fire, they shone with a red-gold light.

The abbot went to the door of the cell and gave a sign to the monks who were waiting outside. Then they sang Hermann's canticle: *Puer natus est nobis, alleluia!*[12]

---

12. ["A Child is born for us, alleluia!"]

CHAPTER 5

* * *

ENCOUNTER

The Pilgrimage

ABBOT BERNO LOOKED at the monk in the choir stall that faced his own. Hermann sat motionless in his stall and seemed to be registering little of the prayers and chants of his brethren. His gaunt face, with its eyes closed, bore the signs of an excessive weariness. When Berthold wanted to help him get up for the Magnificat, he declined with a scarcely perceptible gesture. He did not even open his eyes.

After Vespers, the Lord Berno waited for the lame man's wheelchair in the inner courtyard. Berthold steered the little vehicle cautiously out of the side entrance to the church.

"Hermann?"

When the lame man heard the voice of his abbot, he lifted his head and opened his eyes. Despite his great weakness, he was at once alert. His eyes did not shine; their only expression was tiredness.

"Would you do something for me, my son?" asked the abbot kindly, indicating to Berthold that he should bring the wheelchair under the linden tree.

"Of course, Father Abbot," replied Hermann. He brushed his fingers automatically over his brow, as if he could thereby dissolve the thick mist of numbness that had lain over him for days.

"Bishop Radbert of Passau would like to see your new astrolabe. Have you finished it?"

"No, Father Abbot. I have been trying for days, but in vain. Once again, my hands …"—he looked down at his fingers, which trembled strongly—"are unwilling to work. Whatever I begin with them goes wrong. That is why I was discouraged and impatient. Just before Vespers, I scolded Berthold unjustly. Basically, I was very far from accepting my own failure."

"I saw this coming, Hermann. You have been doing too much. Above all, the time that was given you to write the biography of the Emperor Conrad was too short. Nevertheless, I am very grateful that you were able to finish it at the time indicated by our Lord the Emperor. He had been told that Abbot Berno and Reichenau had enjoyed the favor of his father Conrad only to a very small degree, and he was both surprised and delighted to see that the little book from Reichenau arrived on time … and to see that you treated the Lord Conrad justly. I believe that you have gained a friend for Reichenau and for its abbot in the Emperor Henry, my son."

"In that case, I am content to be tired, Father Abbot …"

"With all respect to your virtue, Hermann, that is not acceptable. You must fulfill another request: Rest for a couple of days. Do not take up a book, or a stylus, or a writing tablet. Be completely without cares, for once. You will wander through summery Reichenau with Berthold, until your cheeks have turned rosy and your eyes shine. You will spend the entire day in the open air and delight in the riches of God in his creation. And I will hear no objection!"

"I only wanted to thank you, Father Abbot, because you know how to interpret the signs correctly, and you know good remedies. The encounter with nature will be a great gift to me."

"You will find the Lord, because everything speaks about him. Every little meadow flower is a miracle of God for you, an idea that is born of his love."

Abbot Berno broke off a twig from the linden tree and gave it to the monk. "May Our Lord permit you to receive much joy."

While the lame man waited for Berthold to fetch him, he sensed that the understanding and goodness of the father had already restored his strength. He had read somewhere: "God smiles in genuine human kindness."

Hermann nodded. "Thank you for your smile, Lord."

When Berthold arrived, Hermann told him joyfully about the abbot's request—or rather, about the order that the abbot had given him, which was also a generous permission. The student could scarcely believe his luck. He was to be allowed to wander over the island for days on end with his beloved master …

"Make plans, Berthold. I leave it up to you to decide the goals of our journey over Reichenau with all its riches."

The student asked eagerly: "Do you know the little

church of Bishop Egino of Verona, Father?" Now that
Berthold was appointed to serve him full-time, and cared
for him instead of the infirmarian, the abbot had told
him to say "Father" instead of the more solemn "Master."

Hermann shook his head.

"No? Then you absolutely must see the wonderful
frescoes of Hildebertus and Ernald. Our Lord is depicted
there as ... as ..."

The lame man supplied the right words: "As your heart
pictures him." He picked up the linden twig. "Berthold,
what a blessing they are for us, the people whom God has
given a heart that can see!"

With Abbot Berno's blessing, the two "pilgrims" left on
the following day for their first journey across the island.

"In accordance with your wish, we shall begin by visiting the little church of Saints Peter and Paul."

The student slowly pushed the wheelchair past the
shore of the Gnadensee. They had all the time in the
world. The refreshing coolness of the past night still lay
over the dewy meadows. White marguerites and deep-
blue gentians bloomed in the reeds beside the path. No
boat plowed the silvery blue surface of the lake. The land
breathed the fullness and the peace of summer under
the lofty sky. The hay on the monastery meadows had a
tangy smell.

Berthold took the first break on the gravelly bank of
the shore in the shadow of a tree with wide branches. He
sat for a time, silent and contented, alongside the wheelchair, but then he felt the need to move. He wanted to
show the father how good he was at throwing flat pebbles.
Hermann watched with a kindly attentiveness as he tried
to throw the stones in such a way that they bounced two

or three times before they sank in the water. The student was as proud as a little boy when he succeeded.

Shoals of little fish played around the stones in the shallow water. Berthold fed them with tiny crumbs from his breakfast bread. Then a group of ducks, quacking excitedly, burst out of the reeds and wanted their share.

The lame man laughed heartily at the surprised expression on his student's face and at the complaining of the ducks. "Give them something. One ought always to do one's honest best never to reject anyone who makes a request."

"If they make the request, then ...," grumbled Berthold, but he obeyed. The brother cook might have been a little more generous when he gave him the bread that morning. But he could not have known that Berthold would have to share the bread with ducks. The birds greedily snapped at the chunks he reluctantly threw to them, quacking and complaining.

The student was glad when the father suggested they should move on. "I have the impression that otherwise, you will go hungry, but ... you can have my portion," said Hermann with a smile. He did not need to look at his companion—he was sure that the young face was blushing in embarrassment.

"That is not what I want, Father ...," Berthold murmured.

"But that is what I want, my son," replied Hermann, in the tone that brooked no contradiction.

After several stops, they crossed the dam that had recently been heaped up across low-lying marshy ground, and arrived toward noon at the old church that was dedicated to the two princes of the apostles.

"Do you still remember what our Father Abbot told us about the glorious basilicas of Saint Peter and Saint Paul in Rome? How great and wonderful the churches of the Eternal City are! Here, in the modest little church of Bishop Egino of Verona, one and the same praise of God is sung, and one and the same sacrifice of Christ is offered, just as in Rome. I doubt whether God attaches much importance to the building."

The monk gave his student a sign to bring him into the church. Out of the extreme brightness of the midday sun, they entered into the pleasant coolness and half-twilight of the venerable house of God. Their eyes needed some time to get used to the semi-darkness.

The lame man whispered: "Please take me forward to the altar." The wheels creaked over the worn-out flagstones, past the austere gray pillars, to the small choir. The rich colors of the fresco by the monks Hildebertus and Ernald shone out in the sanctuary. Its mandorla depicted the Lord surrounded by his apostles, the Lord in power and glory.

The face of Christ on his throne was majestic, sublime ... *Rex aeternae gloriae* ...[1] "He will come again to judge the living and the dead, and his kingdom will have no end." That was what the two monks aimed to depict, and they had succeeded beyond all expectation. Before this Christ, the prayerful heart and the contemplative mind experienced the shattering of all the criteria of earthly greatness, earthly power, and earthly dignity.

What did earthly powers mean ... pope, bishop, abbot, emperor, and king ... in comparison to the One, the only One, Christ the ruler of all?

---

1. ["King of eternal glory."]

The Emperor Henry III called himself *Imperator mundi*.[2] And yet his empire, like every human work, was doomed to decay. What name ought one to give to the King of kings? And what is a poor little invalid monk in the presence of the Son of God?

"What am I, O Lord, that you should think of me? All my petty troubles are surely not apt to give you any joy! Have I done anything that I had not previously received from your hands? I myself am a gift to myself, I am given anew to myself each moment ...

"Lord, I thank you that you are so great, so beautiful, so exalted, and so holy; that I am permitted to know this, to believe in you, and to hope in you. I thank you for yourself and for myself. I thank you for the joys and for the sufferings of my life ...

"Lord, I thank you for the prudent and pure young man who is kneeling beside me, and whom I am permitted to prepare for your service.

"I thank you for our beloved Abbot Berno, for his fatherly kindness and for his fatherly strictness.

"I thank you for your Reichenau, for your sons who are my brothers, for those who are kind and for those who are unkind, for those who are quick and for those who are slow, for our farmers and for our fishers on the lake, for the Gnadensee ...

"I thank you for the church in which I am permitted to thank you and adore you.

"I thank you for the sun, for the flowers, for the reeds; for everything that I have been able to see today ...

"Lord, I find no end to my thanks ..."

---

2. ["Emperor of the world."]

"

The student turned away from the frescoes. It was clear
that he was more strongly moved by the relaxed face of
his master at prayer, a face eloquent with the joy and the
purity of his closeness to God.

Berthold thought, self-consciously: "Was it not I
myself who made it possible for him to have this joy?" He
felt the need to give expression to his own joy, and so he
began to sing the Magnificat.

Hermann listened with a smile, and then he joined in
the singing. The great canticle of Our Lady rang out in
the little church. It was as if all those who had prayed
there down through the centuries shared in their praise.

"Lord, I thank you for your Mother, for our great Lady
Mary ..."

The "Amen" died away, and the monk told his pupil
in a quiet voice: "This church was solemnly consecrated
in 801, shortly after the coronation of Charlemagne.
Bishop Egino of Verona, who built it, was himself buried
here. You can see the gravestone in the choir. Legends,
which are always at work, wove a mystery around him,
just as they did around Charlemagne, his relative. Like
the emperor in the crypt of the cathedral in Aachen, he
too is supposed to be sitting on a throne in his tomb
and waiting for the coming of the One who is to judge
the world."

Berthold shot a timid look at the picture of Christ in
the apse. He felt suddenly cold in the crypt-like coolness
of the church.

"Do you not feel the breath of the prayers that
have been said here for more than two hundred years?

Charlemagne and his consort, the Lady Hildegard, knelt here too, when they visited our abbey."

The two "pilgrims" left the house of God, and the student breathed a secret sigh of relief. He prepared a soft bed of fragrant hay for the monk under an apple tree, and the sick man patiently allowed Berthold to lower him onto it. His pains always grew worse when he had to sit for a long time.

Berthold crouched beside him. He drew up his knees and crossed his arms around them. "Father, I have heard that the Carolingian dynasty had a special love for Reichenau and bestowed special favors on it."

"Yes, Berthold. Reichenau owes its origin to an ancestor of the dynasty, the mighty Charles Martel, who was Mayor of the Palace. He gave the itinerant Bishop Pirmin permission to settle monks on the island. They lived according to the Rule of Saint Benedict and soon made the island a 'rich meadow.'"[3]

"And Saint Pirmin's blessing expelled the snakes, the toads, and the vipers from our island? That is what you dictated to me for the year 724."

Hermann looked at the green and golden play of the leaves over his head, and chose his words carefully: "That is what I dictated, Berthold. But I understand it rather as an image of what truly happened. The poisonous serpent of sin fled from our island and from the regions around Lake Constance, thanks to the work of Saint Pirmin and his sons. The grace of God came to dwell among human beings."

---

3. ["Reichenau" (*Augia* in Latin) means "rich meadow."]

"Is that why the lake beside our monastery is called Gnadensee?" the student pondered.[4]

"Probably, Berthold. We were both in the lake of grace."

"Do not remind me of that, Father. When I think about it, my terror comes back to me in full force"

"A Christopher must know that he always rests secure in God's hand."

"But the lightning struck very close to us!" The student became excited. "And before that ... you in the lake ... when I saw you, Father, that was a terrible sight! And we were greatly distressed about you when you were sick! Were you not afraid when you stood in the water and the storm raged above you?"

Berthold obviously did not grasp that he ought not ask such a question. The monk smiled at the green and golden play of the leaves above his face. Sometimes, a little bit of the sky, the deep blue midday sky, became visible through the leaves ...

"I was afraid, until I realized that I had no reason to fear. It is always so, Berthold. If I look at myself, at my incapable person, at my limitations, my wretchedness, and my slowness, I am afraid. Can I expect anything good from myself? Am I ever secure against my own foolishness and wickedness?—If I look at human beings, at good and holy people, I feel a little more secure. But I am still aware that even the kindest and best human beings are not a reliable support. For if I were to build only on them, I would live in the perpetual fear of losing them. That is

---

4. [There is a play on words: "Gnadensee" means "Lake of grace."]

why I direct my gaze to Our Lord. The one who seeks him in love, loses fear. We can safely entrust ourselves to his mercy."

"Although we are sinners?"

"Because we are sinners! His mercy allows me to hope in his forgiveness and to trust him joyfully every day. '*In te, Domine, speravi, non confundar in aeternum ...*'[5] Sometimes, I am overwhelmed by joy at the thought that we are always on our way home to him, and that we are drawing closer to him every day ... And at the same time, my heart rejoices in all that is beautiful here on earth. You see, we must be people of this earth, Berthold, people who are always aware—joyfully aware—that they are on the way, pilgrims. 'I am made for God, and God is love.'"

He closed his eyes, as if he wanted to sleep. The student rested quietly on the grass and reflected on what he had just heard. No, he could not wholly grasp how someone could be so marvelously secure in God. But he believed the father, and he felt, with the powerful perceptiveness that pure persons have, that Hermann was free and deeply happy.

"

When the weather permitted it, the pilgrims set out and wandered over Reichenau in the days that followed. Their time passed in a companionable silence, alternating with conversations, prayers, and sometimes a song. Berthold explored new and hidden little places, which he showed to the father with the proud gesture of a ruler who displays

---

5. ["In you, O Lord, I have put my trust. Let me never be confounded."]

the glories of his kingdom to an honored guest. Hermann never failed to be appropriately astonished and to praise his zealous Christopher. The days in the open air had a restorative effect on him. His face was sunburnt, and his eyes shone. It was noticeable that his hands trembled less severely.

"

One hot and windless day, Berthold propelled him, groaning with the effort, through vine stocks up to the hill that was the highest point on the island. "There you will have a wonderful view, Father." But summer haze hid the lake and the surrounding mountains. Even the monastery was almost swallowed up by the milky whiteness.

"That's how it is," muttered the student, slashing the air with a hazel switch. "That is how it is everywhere. One does one's honest best—in the sciences too. And one is simple enough to think: when you have reached this or that higher point, you have an unobstructed view of the land. You are happy when you are up there, after toils and labors, but all you see are new puzzles and difficulties. Why does the world around us consist of nothing but puzzles, Father? Why do we know so little? Why are we so powerless?"

Hermann looked at the red face of his companion, which revealed a boyish impatience.

"Why? Well, because God is infinitely far greater than our narrow human heart and our little human understanding ... even in his own creation."

This did nothing to smooth the wrinkles on the younger man's brow. He wanted to conquer life. He wanted to read the world as one reads a book. The lame man could have said more to him on this subject, but he deliberately refrained from doing so. He knew from his own experience that a young person needs time, until he can say his honest "yes" to his existence and to being the specific person he is, to his possibilities, to his boundaries ... and to his dependence on God.

"

They returned that evening by a detour. Berthold pushed the wheelchair past the Gnadensee. A snake glided over the path and disappeared in the reeds.

"You see, Berthold, that not all the snakes fled before Saint Pirmin," murmured the sick man in a serious voice.

Gray clouds massed in the west when they reached the abbey.

"That looks like rain," said the student regretfully. "But we must go back to our work in any case, must we not?" He sighed.

"Yes, Berthold. I have recovered sufficiently. I thank you for all your efforts in these days."

"Efforts, Father? It was a great joy for me to take you over the island. I have learned a great deal in these days."

The lame man looked at the gray clouds, for which the sun was weaving a golden bordering.

"Berthold, we learn all the time, and we are continually confronted by something new ..."

The sound of voices made him stop. Strangers had arrived before the new construction of the west-work, and brightly colored garments mingled with the black of the monastic habits. Abbot Berno was taller than the oth-

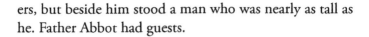
ers, but beside him stood a man who was nearly as tall as he. Father Abbot had guests.

The Lady Hiltrud

Hermann wanted to avoid meeting the visitors. He had seen all too often how his crooked figure and his name made strangers curious.

"Take me quickly through the little side gate into the inner courtyard, before they notice us."

But before Berthold could do as he wished, the Lord Berno caught sight of the wheelchair.

"Brother Hermann, here is a visitor for you." The abbot's voice did not sound particularly joyful.

A visitor? The tall stranger? A visitor for him? The sick man felt a wave of excitement washing over him. A visitor for him … His visitor. He bit his lips and clenched his hands together.

"Lord, help me!"

Before the wheelchair reached the group, he knew who this visitor was. The past years shrank into one single moment separating him from the time when this man, after throwing him a fleeting glance, turned his back on him—on the crippled little child who lay like a helpless bundle in the arms of a monk of the Abbey of Saint Mary on Reichenau.

He lifted his eyelids and looked directly at the man in the noble, colorful garment of an aristocrat. His cheeks turned red as he heard the Lord Berno speaking, once again with that strange undertone of displeasure: "Your lord father, Count Wolfrad II, and your lady mother have come to us."

His mother … at this word, the lame man's face became radiant. His mother …

Count Wolfrad looked at the crooked figure of his son with undisguised curiosity. This Hermann had not grown any more handsome. He stretched out his big hand to him, a hand made firm and hard by hunting and the exercises of chivalry. As yet, he had not spoken a word. But he twisted his lips into a sneer when he felt the slender, trembling hand of his son in his own hand.

"It has been related as far as Altshausen that you have become a famous man, Hermann."

He seemed to think little of this fact, for his eyes betrayed a verdict devoid of pity on the ugly, weak, and bowed figure of his son. This Hermann crouched in the wheelchair like a dwarf, like a gnome …

"What are you doing, then, to make people mention your name with so much reverence?"

The question sounded mocking.

Abbot Berno wrinkled his brow and answered coolly on behalf of the lame man: "Hermann is the best master of our monastery. He works in various fields of science. Shall I enumerate some of his writings for you? He has written *De mensura astrolabii* and *De utilitatibus astrolabii* about his outstanding astrolabe. In geometry, he has studied the ancient problem of the squaring of the circle. One of his writings is entitled *De geometriae arte.* As a natural scientist, he has written *De mundo et elementis.*"[6]

The Latin titles meant nothing to the nobleman, who

---

6. [Titles: "On the measurement of the astrolabe"; "On the uses of the astrolabe"; "On the art of geometry"; "On the world and the elements."]

had had the modest education typical of those of his rank. His face betrayed his perplexity, but the Lord Berno continued, unperturbed:

"In the field of mechanical science, your learned son has given us the treatises *De horologio quodam, quod chelindrum vocant* and *De alio horologio quodam.* He has also studied human beings and the life of the human spirit. He plans a treatise on the way in which the inner life finds expression in the physical sphere. It will be called *De physiognomia.* Hermann also writes history and studies the art of poetry and music. He has invented a new notation for music, which uses letters and is a valuable addition to our neums ..."[7]

Surely the count must be proud of the intellectual riches of his crippled son? But no—he was angry at the abbot, who was telling him a vast number of incomprehensible things. The sick man wanted to avoid the abbot's praises, and he was on the look-out for his mother. He nodded to his father's companions. He flinched when he heard Count Wolfrad II say in a loud voice: "Well, Lord Abbot Berno, no doubt what you have just said will compensate rich Reichenau for the loss of a modest little estate? So much noble science is surely worth a few fields and cattle in your eyes?"

The abbot's figure became tense, defensive. His face darkened. "I cannot imagine what the two things have to do with each other, Count Wolfrad. Your son Hermann belongs to the abbey as a member of the community and a professed monk. His work is the property of God. It is

---

7. [Titles: "On a certain clock, known as the *chelindrum*"; "On another clock"; "On physiognomy."]

at the disposal of the abbot alone. It cannot be measured by any other value, nor compared to any other value. It was only for the period of Hermann's stay in Aachen that we waived the income from the estate near Isny that your son brought with him as his endowment."

The count stroked his short gray beard sullenly, while his gray eyes took the measure of his adversary.

"And yet ... Lord Abbot, would it not be—shall we say—a work pleasing in God's eyes if you were to give the estate back to us? Then we could complete our pious foundation at Isny. And we are told in sacred Scripture: 'Do not lay up treasure for yourselves on earth, where there is moth and rust to consume it.'"

The abbot was enraged to hear a quotation from sacred Scripture simply tossed down in front of him in this situation.

"Is the old conflict to be repeated, Count Wolfrad of Altshausen? Are you throwing down the gauntlet to me?"

The sick man clenched his hands on the armrests of the wheelchair. What would happen now?

Years ago, the abbot and the count had fought each other bitterly for the possession of two estates. The count had challenged Reichenau's right to them, and he had not been fussy about the weapons he chose. It had been necessary for Bishop Warman of Constance to intervene, and even the emperor had become involved.

The count laughed: "Do you want a fight, Lord Abbot? Well, I am not afraid of you. But take a look now at your spiritual son. He is gawping like a wild animal caught in a trap."

Hermann met his father's eyes steadily, although his entire body shook. His blue eyes looked at the count without wavering—the eyes of the Lady Hiltrud. And these eyes silenced the count's boisterous laughter. He muttered something indistinct, and he was clearly relieved when his son Werinher came up. Werinher's unconcern turned the conversation into harmless tracks, since he did not notice the tension between the abbot and his father.

"Father Abbot, my lady mother asks permission to receive Hermann in her room today. She has heard that he has returned."

"I am happy to grant this request," replied the Lord Berno. His face remained shuttered, and his words lacked their customary cordiality. "Hermann, you are dispensed from Vespers. Remain with your lady mother until Berthold fetches you for Compline."

The sick man attempted in vain to catch the abbot's eyes. "Thank you, Father Abbot." An unspoken request resonated in his words, but Abbot Berno turned away. With the dignity of a man who ruled over large estates, he requested the count to be present at Vespers and to inspect the building work on the monastery church.

"'Father'? Ought I not to have said … 'Lord Abbot'?" thought Hermann, who felt a painful disappointment. He did not realize that Count Wolfrad's desire to have the estate near Isny had ripped open the scars of old humiliations. Count Wolfrad was responsible for a bitter injustice that the Abbot of Reichenau had suffered—and the Church and the emperor had shared in inflicting it on him.

All that the lame man noticed was the abbot's profound dislike of his father. How, then, would he look on the sons of the count of Altshausen? Would he be free in his mind in his dealings with them if they reminded him of their father—and Werinher resembled his father externally? A great disappointment threatened the peace that had long been Hermann's safe possession. As yet, he put up a resistance. Was it possible that Abbot Berno was not the man he had thought him to be? No, that was unthinkable.

"

In the guest house, the brother received him and carried him into one of the rooms on the first floor. He put him down in one of the heavily built oaken chairs, in which the delicate figure of the sick man almost disappeared. He seemed more fragile and crooked than usual, especially because he was not paying attention to his external posture. The struggle he had to fight today was internal.

The Lady Hiltrud entered, a woman with the light tread of a girl, so light that he had not heard her. No one would think that this slim woman was the mother of fifteen children. Her fine, tranquil face betrayed nothing of the burden of suffering that God had laid upon her. The Lady Hiltrud had seen eight of her children die, and one of the survivors was a cripple. Her great, clear eyes under the dark brows were full only of motherly kindness and heartfelt love, as she now looked down at her invalid son. Hermann was her child, the child of her heart. He was the only one who had inherited her nature, her religious depth, her warm-hearted openness for other persons, and her pleasant sense of humor. Like her, he had a sensitive nature that began to vibrate like a delicate string of a harp as soon as it was touched. He could sing much, and suffer much ...

The Lady Hiltrud stood for some time at the door, looking lovingly at the sunk-down figure of her son. Then she called him in a joyful voice: "Hermann!"

He looked up. "My lady mother! My lady mother!"

She knelt before him and took his head in her hands. He forgot what had just been troubling him. He was a child, nothing but the child of his mother.

They were silent for a long time, looking intently at each other.

"How white her hair has turned," he thought, and she saw the furrows in her son's gaunt face, which told her of pains and sleepless nights. Each knew the burden that the other bore, and so they smiled.

"Thank you for your canticle, Hermann," said the Lady Hiltrud.

"I was happy to sing it for you, my lady mother, and I have always prayed for you."

"It was not easy for me to part with you," she admitted, as she sat beside him. "But I have been consoled in all these years by the knowledge that you were safe here on Reichenau under the protection of the Lord Berno. Your life would not have become so fulfilled and so rich at home in Altshausen."

Did she see the shadow that scurried over his face when she mentioned the abbot's name? She had looked at him long enough to perceive the signs that something was weighing on his mind. All along the way, she had been anxious about how the encounter between her husband and Hermann would go. Count Wolfrad appreciated only rough and strong threads. It was all too easy for him to damage a fine and delicate gossamer.

She gave her son news from Altshausen, about his siblings and the people in the castle, and about the little son of his favorite sister, Irmingard, who had been given the name Manegold at baptism. She spoke and spoke, until at last he smiled at her with the relaxed face of a child who has received a present. How much there was in him still that reminded her of the little boy of long ago …

"And would you like to hear something of your own childhood, Hermann?" she asked cheerfully.

"Tell me, my lady mother!" he asked, putting his hands firmly on his knees, so that their trembling would not disturb his mother.

The Lady Hiltrud told in vivid colors the story of the little Hermann who wanted at all costs to get into heaven, and who kept on escaping from the castle, and of the gray autumnal day when the child (doubtless in a dream) saw a man like a flame.

"Ah yes, I remember now …," the lame man cried out happily.

But his mother did not omit the conclusion, the sudden lameness that befell the boy Hermann that very night, and she repeated the words that she had whispered to the lame child, acting upon an inspiration that she herself did not understand: "My child, now heaven has found you."

"Thank you, my lady mother, thank you! Now I know everything again, as if it had happened only yesterday. You spoke to Walter about my dangerous and laborious detour. After the Good Friday evening in Aachen when I ended that detour before the cross of Our Lord, the flame, the light, has been a constant presence in my life, bright, sometimes excessively bright, painfully burning and purifying, but also giving consolation and warmth …"

"You came, Lord Christ, you who are my life, in order to bring me your light," said the Lady Hiltrud, quoting lines from the prayer that he had written for her after the death of her son Luipold.

Like a reflection of the light, joy lay on the narrow face of the sick man when the monks sang Compline in the monastery church. He sang along, without thinking of the somber cloud that had gathered before his conversation with his mother. "Christ, my light ..."

After Compline, there began the period of silence, which the monks were allowed to break only in emergencies. When Berthold was about to bring him to his cell, the prior came up.

"Father Abbot would like to speak to you, Brother Hermann ..."

Berthold took him to the abbot's quarters. One solitary candle cast a flickering, unsteady light on the abbot, who sat at his desk. The sultry night air flowed through the open window. From time to time, summer lightning flashed across the starless night sky. In the scurrying interplay of light and shadow, the Lord Berno's face seemed severe and foreign.

Hermann waited for the abbot to address him. Once again, a feeling of unease threatened to overwhelm him.

"Tell me what you have done today," demanded the Lord Berno—a strange wish at the time of the great silence. Hermann willingly gave him the information and expressed his gratitude for the restorative time.

"I am sure that I can take up my work again now," he concluded.

"It is I who decide the time for that!" replied the abbot sharply. The lame man was shocked by these curt words.

Had he said something wrong? The silence stood like a heavy block between the two monks. The candle crackled. Somewhere, a nocturnal bird squawked. The oppressive sultriness felt like a hand at one's throat. Summer lightning flashed over the Gnadensee …

Finally, the abbot murmured: "And as the crowning of this glorious day, you met Count Wolfrad. It must have been an unhoped-for joy to see him again after so many years, must it not?"

Hermann stared at the abbot, incapable of uttering one single word. The Lord Berno leaned farther back in his chair, so that his face lay almost completely in darkness. His eyes were hidden in black hollows. An unknown man was sitting before Hermann and talking to him. Was it possible for so much bitterness to come forth from the mouth of an Abbot Berno?

"Answer me!" commanded the abbot impatiently. "You were happy to see your father again."

For the first time since he had known the Lord Berno, he would have preferred to refuse to answer. Tonelessly, he confessed: "No, Lord and Father Abbot, I … was not … happy."

"And why were you not happy, Hermann?"

The sick man pressed the nails of his right hand into the back of his left hand, in order not to groan. Why was the abbot asking such a cruel question?

"Because … because I am not virtuous enough to accept—and still, less to rejoice in—the contempt with which my father has regarded me since the day on which I became a cripple. Since then, my lack of virtue has made me fear the encounter with my lord father."

Had the torture now reached the zenith that satisfied Abbot Berno? Was he content with this humiliating admission by the lame man?

"I see," replied the figure in the shadows, almost derisively. "His own son fears his father. And the father of this son wants to steal a part of his endowment from us, the estate near Isny. He wants to include it in the pious foundation that he wishes to make in memory of his son Luipold. The church in Isny needs sufficient properties, and he plucks them on Reichenau. Abbot Berno had to admit defeat once before … And what does your lady mother say about this demand?"

One single tear ran down the cheek of the lame man. He did not wipe it off.

"We did not talk about Isny, Lord and Father Abbot. My lady mother spoke about things at home and about my childhood."

Was he to be allowed to go now? No, he had to tell the abbot about this too, jerkily and hesitantly. The nails of his right hand caused little wounds on the back of his left hand.

Once the lame man thought he had heard the sound of a groan from the darkness, but he was wrong. Abbot Berno said no word; he rose, went out, and summoned Berthold. Hermann did not see Abbot Berno take weary steps toward the monastery church. It was long after midnight when he returned to his room, where he knelt until daybreak before the stone image of Our Lady, with his head in his hands. The mild gleam of the oil lamp, which burned day and night in Mary's honor, fell on his bowed head.

"

The sick man waited unsleeping for the dawning of the new day, but he did not greet the daybreak with his usual willingness. His existence seemed to him more laborious than ever. He cast an indifferent glance at his books and papers, his monochord and his astrolabe. What did all this matter to him, what did it signify to him, if Abbot Berno was not the great and holy man that he had always thought him to be?

Like a puppet, like a piece of wood, he allowed Berthold to get him ready. He let himself be lifted into the chair and be brought to the church. He crouched in his choir stall, huddled and shivering. He sang and prayed without knowing what he was doing.

At the high altar, Abbot Berno offered the holy sacrifice with the dignity and devotion that were typical of him. Were his pious gestures merely an external activity, while his heart brooded angrily on the count of Altshausen and the estate near Isny? Was the Lord Berno not a holy man? Then so much that he had believed was a lie! What was Hermann to believe now? What was truth?

When the abbot drew near to give him the Body of the Lord, he shook his head silently. The Lord must not enter into a heart full of doubt and bitterness.

When he was in his cell, he immediately took up his wax tablet. "No morning meal, Berthold!" He made a few notes about the computation of time, then erased the letters and pushed the tablet aside. He turned the pages of a book and read, without understanding anything of what he had read. Finally, his meaningless and restless activity was interrupted by news:

"The Lady Hiltrud awaits you."

When the guest master brought him into her room,

Abbot Berno rose from the great armchair and greeted the sick man calmly and kindly.

"It is good that you have come, my dear son. Your lady mother was very anxious to see you."

Hermann looked up at him in surprise. This was the cordial tone that he was used to. But the abbot's face seemed tired and old. The Lord Berno bowed deferentially to the countess.

"Would you prefer to go down to the lake with your son, Lady Hiltrud? Berthold can accompany you."

Mother and son sat together at the shore of the Gnadensee. Berthold brought a stool from one of the fisher huts for the Lady Hiltrud, and then withdrew.

The Lord Berno was present all the time in the sick man's thoughts, although he wanted to talk with his mother in a natural manner. Just now, Father Abbot had been as he knew him at other times, but yesterday evening ...

Who was the Lord Berno? Lord Abbot, Father Abbot?

"Hermann, you love Reichenau, don't you?" asked the Lady Hiltrud.

He confirmed this immediately.

"And you are happy here, as Abbot Berno told me ..."

"As Abbot Berno told you, my lady mother?" he asked sharply.

"Yes, he told me. Can he not judge this and know it?" Her voice had lost nothing of its kindness and gentleness.

He replied bitterly: "Then Father Abbot ought to know that a great happiness is clouded, when ..." His feeling of dismay prevented him from completing the sentence.

"When the one who possesses happiness here below imagines that he is in heaven and would like to be surrounded by heavenly beings, people who have no sins, no limitations, no weaknesses—and then he meets real human beings."

"My lady mother, how ... do you know?" the sick man stammered, trying to look directly into her face. She moved her stool, to make this possible.

"I know about your disappointment, Hermann. Abbot Berno spoke with me. He knows you, and I know you. Even as a child, you wanted to get hold of heaven by force. You have not put aside that flaw. And besides, God has given both you and me a very delicate and sensitive nature, a strong capacity to love and to suffer. But that does not allow us to make anyone our own creature."

"What do you mean, my lady mother? Are you thinking of the desire to rule over others? That is completely foreign to me."

She took his hand. "I know, my child, I know. That is not at all what you want. But one can also make another person the creature of his own holy dreams and fancies, and clothe him in a halo that shines far too brightly. That is what happened to me with your father once, Hermann. It was only after I recognized his limitations, and came to love him with his defects, that I encountered him truly. Before that, I loved an image that I myself had created. Ultimately, in fact, I loved my own self. He had to be the person I wanted him to be. But our love must give the other person the freedom to be himself."

"Did Abbot Berno notice already yesterday evening what was going on in my mind, my lady mother, and did he tell you?" he asked in embarrassment, lowering his eyes.

"Yes, Hermann, but he also told me that your disappointment was justified. I must disagree with you, because this venerable and excellent father of Reichenau is allowed to be a human being. Indeed, he must be a human being. He is allowed to make mistakes. You demand too much of him. That is not fair on your part. If he tells you that he regrets his conduct, you must forgive him …

"We talked about the estate near Isny, which was my dowry and now is your endowment. In this matter, your Father Abbot has stuck to his principles, but he has taken the first step to propitiate the count. He has given your father a precious golden reliquary with a particle of the Holy Cross for the church in Isny, and that is a truly princely gesture. He himself received it from the Emperor Henry II, when he obeyed the emperor and left the imperial abbey of Pruem to become the Abbot of Reichenau. He gave my husband the reliquary with such cordiality and genuine goodness that the count was both propitiated and deeply moved. After all, Count Wolfrad has a good heart, and he is happy when his wishes are accommodated."

"You know human nature, my lady mother."

She stroked his furrowed face with a gentle hand. "My child, all I do is to attempt to love people in the right way. The eyes of our heart see more, and better …"

She got up and moved a little to one side. She began to pluck long-stalked blue gentians, giving her son time to come to himself. Her cheeks were red when she returned to him, more beautiful in her motherly maturity than a young bride. She bent down and laid the flowers in his lap, saying quietly: "My child, from now on, you must see people with the eyes of God. Even saints must have their mistakes and limitations. You must never again venerate a statue that you yourself have created. Instead, you must

venerate a human being—and in him, you must venerate
Our Lord Jesus Christ."

Hermann took both her hands, which she willingly left
in his. "Oh, my lady mother, what a little child you have
in this learned monk of Reichenau! But it was good to
be small before you and to receive from your hand the
medicine against self-seeking. And your words about the
dangerous and toilsome detour were a great help to me
when I was in Aachen."

"Well, I once promised that I would look for heaven
together with you, my child. Do you think I would have
forgotten that for even one single day?"

Although they both would have liked to stay longer
by the Gnadensee, they knew that people in the abbey
would be waiting for them impatiently.

"Come, Hermann, we will bring the flowers from the
Gnadensee to Our Lady."

"

Count Wolfrad was full of praise for all he had seen on
Reichenau. "Your Father Abbot is an excellent manager.
The abbey suffered a disastrous decline in the past, and
the strict Abbot Immo only made things worse. It is
astonishing that the Lord Berno has achieved so much
with the same people and on the same land."

The lame man took a deep breath and replied courageously: "That is because Abbot Berno is loved, rather
than feared. The monks, the farmers, and the fishermen
all know that he takes care of them and wants what is best
for them. At the same time, our Father Abbot is a true
ruler."

The Lady Hiltrud followed the conversation calmly. She heard her husband sigh.

"A ruler? Yes, that he is indeed, generous and brave in battle. I have experienced that myself."

Hermann ventured to put a bold question: "Should not the ruler of Eritgau[8] be pleased to honor the ruler in the Lord Berno?"

The count's gray eyes flashed. Had the question been too bold? What would he reply? He looked at his lame son with a new benevolence.

"I love it when a man is faithful to his own cause. And when a monk fights on behalf of his spiritual father, that is certainly fidelity. What do you think, Lady Hiltrud? Can we not be proud of our two sons, whom we have given to Our Lady of Reichenau?"

He paused reflectively.

"Now I see what I could do. Yes, that is a good idea! Not far from Isny, but further into the Alpine county, there is the estate of Aarwalden, which my mother, the Lady Berchta, brought as her dowry ..."

Werinher looked questioningly at Hermann. What was their father getting at? The lame man looked in turn at his mother, but she nodded reassuringly.

"Lady Hiltrud, do you too think I am a tyrant?" smiled the count, who had noticed the exchange of glances. "You, at least, must be aware that I am not as fierce as that! From now on, your bailiff shall include Aarwalden, when he draws up the list of the properties of the abbey that are liable to interest."

8. [The count of Altshausen was reponsible for collecting taxes in the county of Eritgau.]

"And whose inheritance is it to be?" asked Werinher in amazement.

"Inheritance?" Count Wolfrad looked at him, pretending to be angry. "Inheritance! Hermann is not as hungry for possessions as you, my son."

Werinher blushed because of his impertinence. He had thought that his father would sign over the estate to him, and that he could then bequeath it to the monastery. After all, his endowment was not as rich as that of the elder son.

"By handing over the estate, the Lord of Altshausen merely wishes to … honor a … ruler …"

The lame man understood his father at once, and he automatically reached out his right hand to take his father's hand. Count Wolfrad took it cautiously, held it in his own broad hand, and muttered, with a benevolent shake of his head, "Tender like a little bird. Well, you have found the right nest."

"

When Abbot Berno arrived, Count Wolfrad made a request: "Would you permit me enter the cell of my son Hermann, Lord Abbot?"

After a brief hesitation, the abbot gave him permission. He himself accompanied the guest, with Hermann and Berthold, through the cloister to the north wing of the abbey. Count Wolfrad looked in silence at the austere poverty of the cell. He contemplated the parchments, the scientific apparatus, and the writing utensils. He touched the hard bed. He stood musingly before the cross from his castle chapel.

"Thank you for this favor, Lord Abbot Berno! Do you have a little time for me now?"

They brought Hermann back to his mother. Count Wolfrad and the abbot had a long and serious conversation.

"

When the guests had taken their leave on the following day, Abbot Berno told the lame man: "Come with me, Hermann!"

He himself pushed the wheelchair into the abbot's quarters and plumped up the cushions, so that the sick man could sit more comfortably. The monk waited calmly for the words of his spiritual father. He had recovered his inner freedom after talking to the Lady Hiltrud at the Gnadensee.

"Hermann, your father has asked me to allow you to travel to Altshausen from time to time. After all her suffering, the Lady Hiltrud needs the consolation of your presence. Although this is not envisaged by the Rule, we should, and indeed we must, accept your father's request in the spirit of the love of Christ. I have seen in these days how much you are your mother's son. I have seldom seen a greater similarity or experienced a more intimate union between two persons. She understands you even without words, and it is the same with you, I imagine?"

The Lord Berno seemed not to expect any answer. His hand played with a parchment that lay before him on the table.

"You already know what this document says. Aarwalden in the Alpine county, the estate that your grandmother, the Lady Berchta, brought as her dowry, has belonged to the abbey since yesterday. Your father and I have definitively buried all that is past, and we parted from each other in peace. Only with regard to one question did we need more time to reach an agreement. Our conversation concerned you, Hermann. But I recognized that Count Wolfrad's view was correct. Your father thought that I was too hard on you. Be quiet, let me finish! He said that I must make some concessions to you, since you are a sick man wracked by pain, and you are constantly obliged to submit to the penance of pains and of helplessness. No, Hermann, do not object. It is regrettable that I allowed you to suffer want."

"Father, everything that I have received up to now was good and sufficient. I have a cell of my own, instead of sleeping in the common dormitory. You gave me Berthold as my personal assistant. Again and again, you take my weakness into account, and you never reproach me if I cannot take part in the community activities and prayers. And you have given me the greatest privilege of all by receiving me, a cripple, into the monastic community and letting me be ordained to the priesthood ..."

"But you would rest more comfortably on a softer bed. We could have a special work desk made for you, and an armchair that would give your body more support. Furs and rugs could protect your body from the cold that flows out of the stones. And better food would strengthen you ..."

The lame man had lowered his eyes. "And ... what would the brothers say if I, who already lead a separate existence, were to receive so many privileges?"

"Since when have you let other people's gossip dictate the way you live? Do you not think that they would be glad to see you have an easier life? But no matter what you think, I feel obliged in conscience to grant you these concessions."

Hermann ventured to make one last objection. "I fear that they would not be good for me, Father Abbot. What you impose on me—could it be initially only for a trial period?"

"'Impose'? I have the impression that you think I am preparing a penance for you, but that is not what I want. I grant you the trial period."

"Thank you, Father Abbot."

"For the penance?"

"Above all for the trial period," Hermann admitted honestly.

"Your openness is laudable, my son," laughed the Lord Berno. "Good! We will let time decide what is right for you."

"May I tell you about one difficulty, Father Abbot? I did not understand yesterday … or rather, the day before yesterday … when you were talking to my father about Isny … and then in the evening …"

He had begun to speak courageously and clearly, but then he became confused. He could not confess his own failure without at the same time reproaching the abbot.

"I know, my son …" The Lord Berno supported his head with both hands, as if he was very tired. "I know."

For the first time, Hermann noticed the many silver threads in the dark hair on the abbot's head.

"I disappointed you. You were looking in me for the father in Christ, and all you found at that time was a narrow and petty human being. I was unwilling to forget a wrong I had suffered, and I wanted to punish you for the pain of scars that were ripped open anew—although you trusted me. That evening, I treated you basely. I understood your pain in that night. Even today, you are looking for heaven with the pure eyes of a child, but here you find human beings, my dear son, human beings. I already understood you that night, and yet I did not have the power to utter a word of understanding to you."

"Father!" Hermann cried out.

His cry made the abbot look up, and their eyes met.

"Father, I had to experience this, in order to learn how to love more truly and selflessly. I was not in any way entitled to demand a superabundance of holiness. Hermann the Pharisee had to become a tax collector. He had to realize his own poverty. Forgive me, Father, for daring to judge! My lady mother had to open my eyes ..."

Abbot Berno nodded to the sick man, and then his eyes wandered past him to the image of Our Lady. "Hermann, how good it is that mothers exist. Our defiant maleness would so often destroy what exists, if the kindness of our mothers were not to bring about new life. The mothers catch our hard fists and fold them into the hands of men at prayer."

CHAPTER 6

* * *

THE GNADENSEE

In Order That You Too May Do What I Have Done

BERTHOLD TURNED THE SICK MAN'S wheelchair around so that he could see the students who had gathered about him in a semi-circle. Sometimes he taught in a larger room, but at other times (as today), when his weak voice did not carry and he had to drag each word out of himself, he called the young men into his cell, where they crowded together, crouched on their stools. Inquisitive young eyes looked at the furnishings in the cell, the drapes and rugs, the white coverings, the cushions and furs. Things had changed here after Count Wolfrad had asked the abbot to make things somewhat easier for his son. Hermann felt almost a stranger in the well-equipped room, and he often escaped to the Gnadensee. More than once, he had asked the abbot if the trial period would end soon.

"In any case, I have not passed the test, Father Abbot."

Each time, Abbot Berno had replied with a question of his own: "How can you know that before the time is over? Just continue to test yourself."

"

The broad black garments did not really suit the youths who sat around their master. Their heads, with brown, blond, or black manes, looked out of place alongside the religious habit. The sparkling young eyes would have looked more credibly at home between the branches of an apple tree than when they gravely examined a psalter or a Latin grammar book.

Today, it cost the lame man a considerable effort to form his sentences, and he had to pause several times. But their content was never affected in any way by his sickness; it remained just as deep and as clear as it was on "healthy" days. His facial muscles were becoming rigid, and he knew, with a certainty born of familiarity with this process, that he would soon no longer be able to speak …

"

"What did you grasp in a particular way today in this chapter from the Gospel of the holy apostle John?"

Hartmut, the easygoing young man from Unterwald, did his best to hide behind the tall Bodo from Bregenz.

"Well, Hartmut?"

The words were too clearly spoken for Hartmut to pretend not to have heard them.

"The ... the pericope was very long," stammered Hartmut.

Brother Berthold bit his lips. Hartmut had probably noted only the length of the passage—nothing else. Hermann nodded:

"The passage is long. That is right, my son, and God is patient. That too is right. He has a great deal of patience with those who take a long time, but one day he finds that it is taking them too long to convert from their slowness—or indeed, from their laziness and inertia."

The student blushed. The youths whispered and chuckled, but the sick man did not smile. His face remained serious. He himself took up the theme, without asking the students any further question.

"In the chapter about the Last Supper, the evangelist John tells us about an event that is so extraordinary that our poor human heart cannot even begin to assess its greatness."

His eyes sought the cross from the castle chapel in Altshausen. In the manner beloved of the Romanesque period, it depicted Christ as the victor on the cross, the *Rex gloriae*.[1] The lame man loved this image of the conqueror of death and of torments, who had carried out the charge given him by the Father and who was completely King and Lord of lords. Despite all the familiarity and closeness Hermann felt, Christ had remained for him the Lord before whom he bowed down in reverence.

---

1. ["King of glory."]

Closeness and distance together, both Brother and Lord ... His knowledge that he was secure in Christ was always also adoration, and his love was always also humble submission. His reverence was free of servile dread. He served the Lord with joy and with the confidence that only a pure, childlike nature could have.

Christ became more and more the theme of his life. Sometimes he saw all his activity as a game. His teaching, his writing, his compositions and his inventions were a leisure activity ... colored stones.

When his brethren talked in eager tones about the small matters of everyday life, he longed to cry out: "Dear brethren, do not speak about nonsense of that kind! Talk about Jesus Christ ..."

Would the Lord soon end the days of his life here on earth? Hermann was familiar with the ups and downs of his physical condition. Days of "well-being," on which he could at least use his hands, days on which, despite his continuous pains, he could sing and speak, were followed by days of increasing lameness. His sickness befell him silently and unexpectedly, like a cunning snake, and took possession of him. It came and went, as and when God willed. After too much effort and excitement, it arrived all the more speedily and strongly. Sometimes, it was hard for the lame man to control his temperament, although he knew that he would have to pay a bitter price for every violent excitement.

The ups and downs of his physical condition told Hermann that he would not live too long in this world. But that was no cause for grief!

His musings were interrupted when Berthold cleared his throat discreetly. Ah yes, the students were waiting for his exposition of the pericope about the washing of the feet.

"Let us begin by asking who it is that kneels down and washes the feet of his disciples, performing a slave's service … It is the Lord of heaven and earth, the Creator, who can destroy every creature with the breath of his mouth. He kneels down before the fishers of Gennesareth, who are uneducated and uncouth men. They had a good will, but they were very poor in virtue and holiness. At that time, they did not know as much as you know, and yet the Son of God knelt down on the earth before them. Perhaps it may help us to think of this, when we are proud because of our studies in this or that branch of knowledge. It is not before the learned men of his age that the Lord kneels down. He kneels down before the ignorant and the unscholarly.

"Even if it had been his own dear Mother who sat before him, the Lord would have humbled himself if he had washed her feet. The Son of God kneels down before his creature … Let us take a very close look at what we see here, when he girds himself with a linen cloth and kneels down before his disciples.

"But he who is the great God humbles himself often before us! Is not every sacramental confession much more than this washing of the feet? The Son of God must wash us through his own blood from the dirt of our sins. And what about us? Well, we all simply take that for granted. Have we ever been sufficiently ashamed of daring to offer him so much dirt and ugliness? Have we ever humbled ourselves as we should?

"And what of the holy sacrifice of the Mass? If Christ did not make himself the sacrifice on our altars, we would have to come to the heavenly Father with empty hands. Every day, the Son of God descends into our lowliness. He makes himself a sacrifice, so that we may have something to give, and so that honor may be given to the Father.

"It is only with him, and through him, and in him that what we contribute becomes valuable and pleasing to God, and that we ourselves, despite our deficiencies, become pleasing sacrifices. How humble Our Lord Jesus Christ is!

"He was not only humble in the upper room in Jerusalem, when he washed his disciples' feet. He is humble today too, when he becomes our food in Holy Communion. And that too is a service God renders us, a service that we accept much too tranquilly. If only he were entering into a house that at least was worthy of him, into a heaven! But no, mostly what we dare to offer him are huts blown askew by the wind. It is the miracle of God's love, of God's humility, that he nevertheless comes.

"He knows that we need him. Without him, we would perish on the hazardous pilgrim path of our life."

This slow and profound exposition of the biblical passage was not disturbed by any inconsiderately loud breathing or any restless movement. It was completely different from other expositions. Its center was not Peter's resistance to having his feet washed, nor the man Jesus Christ from Nazareth, but the humble God who served.

The sick man went on, speaking quietly and articulating with difficulty. Sometimes he had to take a lengthy pause.

"My friends, God is humble. He who is the greatest of all continues to bend down to our poverty, although he seldom finds modesty in us. One who is as poor as we human beings all are, one whose whole being is dependent on the merciful kindness of the Father, ought to open up willingly to receive the Lord who comes.

"But what do we actually do? Do we not make demands, although we ought to wait and to make requests?

"It is unfathomable that God nevertheless comes down to us; that he washes our feet; and that he does not simply let us proud creatures fall and perish.

"He loved those who were his own, and he loved them to the end … Neither our poor and narrow mind nor our seeking heart can understand God's serving. One who achieves a great deal begins to sense that only God's love is capable of something like that. Since his love is divine, it is also infinitely greater than our little heart.

"God's love is infinite, just as he himself is infinite. That is why it embraces us sinful creatures, despite our perversity and our ingratitude.

"The Lord Jesus Christ washes his disciples' feet." Once again, the sick man paused. And once again, there was a reverent silence. The students did not wholly understand him, but they sensed his love for Christ and they felt a deep reverence.

"He wanted to give us an example. We are to do what he did. We ought to wash one another's feet, to be ready to serve one another in humility. The rule of those who govern should from now on be a serving that benefits their subjects, a preparing of the way for the coming of Christ. Those who serve the Lamb—and that means primarily those to whom God has entrusted a sacred ministry and the great burden of a responsibility—ought to make straight the path of the Lord in the hearts of the others.

"And in doing so, they ought ever more to decrease, so that he may be able to increase. The one among you who wants to be the first, should be the servant of all.

"Read and reflect on the pericope about the washing of the feet at the Last Supper again, and then prepare the farewell discourses of the Lord ... They are very important for our life and for our suffering, and they can give joy to hearts that believe."

After a brief prayer, the master dismissed the students. Only Hartmut from Unterwalden remained behind. He approached the armchair bashfully, his big ears burning red.

Hermann put a gentle question to the contrite student: "Do you have so little love for the Lord that you have no wish to learn anything from him, Hartmut?"

Hartmut swallowed his tears and stammered: "I do love him, but I am not very bright. When I learn something, I forget it at once. If only I was half as intelligent as you, Master Hermann!"

Hermann and Berthold smiled at each other when they heard this heartfelt sigh. The lame man dealt a light blow to the student's untidy blond hair.

"You have wishes, young man, but you are not inclined to work all that hard. From now on, you must make more effort. It is true that others find it easier to study, but that should only be an encouragement to you. Every effort that we take to come closer to Our Lord is rewarded. Every life has its toil and its cross. Thank the Lord that you have healthy limbs, and thank him for your mind too, even if you are 'not very bright.' From now on, Hartmut from Unterwalden will struggle harder, will he not?"

The lame man traced a cross of blessing on the young man's sunburnt brow. Hartmut felt relieved, and sprang out of the cell.

"Are you not sometimes too kind and indulgent, Father? Master Burkhard would have given him a taste of the rod," said Berthold, as he turned the armchair back to the work desk.

"Am I to drive the love for the Lord out of him with the rod? If I was too mild, then let the Lord use the rod on me! I am a stubborn donkey, and I need it." He omitted to add: "I will get it soon, in any case."

He spent some time in silent reflection, and then he picked up his wax tablet, intending to write down some thoughts about ruling and serving. But his efforts were in vain. His right hand clenched the stylus.

"Berthold?"

But unfortunately, his companion had just left the cell. Once again, Hermann attempted to force himself to write, but in vain. He must be content with inactivity.

"Is this the rod for the donkey, Lord?"

He sat there inactive in his armchair, and waited. Before him lay the wax tablet with the strange scratchings that were meant to be letters. Then he heard someone coming. The footsteps were not Berthold's rapid paces.

Udualrich, one of the professed monks who belonged to the community, entered. After a brief greeting, he asked: "Not working, Brother?" His sharp eyes swept over the cell.

The lame man replied, with an effort: "I cannot."

"Well, at any rate, God bestows lengthy pauses for rest on you. I would like to ask for your help. I have never been particularly good at Hebrew, and there is a passage in the Old Testament that I cannot make sense of, no matter how hard I try."

How often Udualrich needed help! And it was never refused him.

"Leave the text here, Brother. As soon as I can work again, I will finish it for you."

"Good, good! May God reward you ..."

Udualrich's hand brushed the soft fur on the sick man's bed. "A number of things have changed in your life, have they not? I wouldn't mind resting on a pillow like that."

Hermann smiled painfully. "Do not wish that for yourself, dear Brother. This bed is harder than the one I had before."

Udualrich did not reply. He was busy examining in detail the food on the tray that Berthold was carrying in. White bread, baked whitefish, cheese, apples, wine ... It was well worthwhile being sick on Reichenau, if one enjoyed the abbot's favor.

"Enjoy your meal, Brother."

"If only he had meant those words sincerely," muttered Berthold, after Udualrich had gone out.

"No, Berthold," Hermann rebuked him. "You are too suspicious."

The novice would like to have said: "And you are too credulous," but he did not do so. In recent days, he had often heard the monks complaining that Hermann was given privileges by Abbot Berno. But why did they not bear in mind the suffering that tormented him?

"You must help me. My hands refuse to work."

The young monk drew up a stool, as he was accustomed to do, and fed his master, as a mother feeds her young child. Only a short time ago, the master had been expounding sacred Scripture to his students in lofty words, and now he must be fed ... Berthold was so careful and gentle that Hermann did not find this as humiliating as he once had done, when Ekkehard was charged with helping him. Nevertheless, there were also times when he would have liked to weep at his helplessness. His fetters were often a painful burden.

After the meal, Berthold cleaned the master's face and hands with a cloth. Then he guided the father's right hand to make the sign of the cross, and said a prayer of thanksgiving. He prayed alone, for Hermann had temporarily lost the power of speech.

"May I bring you to the lake, Father? The fresh air will do you good, and perhaps this attack will pass more quickly."

A slight nod signified assent, and the brother lifted the sick man into the wheelchair.

They met some monks in the cloister. "A feast-day life," murmured Brother Ekkehard.

The lame man's acute hearing had caught these words. "A feast-day life? My life is a feast day? And what feast day is it that I am celebrating all the time, brother? The Exaltation of the Holy Cross? I would not want you to have the pleasure of my feast day, Ekkehard. Indeed, I would not want anyone to have it, not even someone who is so hostile to me as you."

This kind of talk hurt him deeply, although he had hitherto believed that he was immune to the foolish remarks of stupid people.

"A feast-day life ..."

Abbot Berno came from the monastery gate with a guest from Saint Gallen.

"Brother Reginald, here you see our dear master Hermann, whose treatise on the elements I sent to Saint Gallen some little time ago."

The sick man did his best to produce a smile for the visiting brother, but his rigid face was more like a tragic mask.

Reginald looked at him with curiosity, as if he were some strange exhibit. Why did people not understand that their eyes wounded him, when they looked at a lame cripple with curiosity, astonishment, and disgust?

Berthold explained the silence of his teacher. "Forgive me, Father Abbot ... Master Hermann cannot speak. His lameness has got the better of him once again. We want to go down to the lake ..."

The Lord Berno bent down and laid his right hand, with its glittering ring, on the weak hands of the lame man. "I hope that you will soon feel better at your beloved Gnadensee, my dear son. I shall show Brother Reginald some of your works. Perhaps you yourself can give him further explanations this evening."

The lame man's eyes looked at the abbot with gratitude and trust.

Reginald had observed this scene attentively. He assumed that the sick man was a favorite of the abbot—a rumor to that effect had already reached as far as Saint Gallen, and gossip said that this had led to some discontent among the monks, although Abbot Berno had been a beloved father of his sons until then. Reginald would make his own enquiries. The monks in Saint Gallen liked to be kept informed as precisely as possible about the monastery on Reichenau, which was their neighboring community (but which they did not always love).

For a long time, Reichenau had been outshone by the mighty abbey of Saint Gallen. In the period of its decline, it had merely been an object of pity or derision for the neighboring monks, but the island monastery had prospered after Abbot Berno began to govern it. Saint Gallen was larger, but Abbot Berno had transformed Reichenau into a seat of piety and learning. The school of painting was flourishing, and the works of the abbot and of his lame Master Hermann took the name of Reichenau into many countries. Moreover, Berno was a friend of the emperor. Was he not planning to invite the emperor to the dedication of the west-work? The guest from Saint Gallen had not liked the high bell tower, modeled on a campanile south of the Alps, because there was only one tower like that north of the Alps ...

Abbot Berno knew nothing of the thoughts of his guest. He took him to the lame man's cell and showed him some of his apparatus, his instruments, and his writings, with a spiritual father's justified pride. Reginald listened to him with a divided attention, while he looked around the cell. In his own monastery, not even the abbot had such a splendid room.

When he sat with the monks of Reichenau at recreation after the midday meal, he shot an arrow at a venture. By chance, the man on his right was called Udualrich.

"Here on the island, it is worthwhile cultivating friendship with Father Abbot, is it not?"

The monk looked at him sideways. "What do you mean, Brother Reginald? Is that not worthwhile in Saint Gallen?

"It is worthwhile there too, when the sun of the abbot's favor shines on a monk. I myself am not one of the lucky, chosen ones."

"Nor am I, you can be sure of that," exclaimed Udualrich.

Reginald smiled. "It is easier for us in Saint Gallen, because we do not have a cripple in the community. You have to look on while this Hermann gets one exemption after another, while you faithfully take the path of strict penitence. I have heard that your Father Abbot is an enthusiastic adherent of the reform." The guest sighed sympathetically.

"The cripple in the community ... We always wonder why he enjoys this or that privilege that the abbot does not grant us. In the case of Hermann, the abbot doubtless forgets that he is a Cluniac monk."

Reginald skillfully changed the subject. He now knew enough.

"

The abbot sensed nothing of the discontent that was spreading like dandelion seeds in the wind. In the chapter meeting, he ingenuously praised the lame man's new work, a didactic poem of 1,722 verses, which the abbot had requested him to write for the nuns of Buchau, on Lake Feder in Upper Swabia.

"The *De octo vitiis principalibus* is in fact a very serious work, dear brothers and sons in the Lord. We should get to know this pamphlet before it leaves our Reichenau. In this text, our dear brother describes pride as the mother and the stem of all the vices. Its children, the seven branches on this stem, are vanity, envy, anger, sadness of soul, avarice, intemperance, gluttony, and unchastity."[2]

If the Lord Berno had looked at the faces of his sons, he would have noticed several things. Some monks openly displayed their contempt, while others smiled mockingly to themselves. Udualrich nudged his neighbor Dietbart, and they exchanged a look of mutual understanding: What else could one expect? Yet another hymn in praise of the cripple ... But the abbot did not look up. He read a passage from the poem aloud: "Through it, heart and ear are hardened, so that one refuses to hear the sacred teaching of Christ, which commands one to abandon the burden of the world. The true Christian ought to flee from this burden. He does not allow himself to be ensnared by it ... May the stem of pride on Reichenau be exterminated in every heart, so that there will be no possibility at all for the seven ugly branches, which can bring so much ruin and disaster to a monastic community, to grow. But let us not deceive ourselves, dear brothers! Ever since the first sin in paradise, pride has found a rich soil in the human heart. Usually, we do indeed deny that it is there, but our sins continually show the world that pride has its roots in us."

If only Abbot Berno had realized that pride was at work, gravely imperiling the monastic peace with its branches—with vanity, jealousy, and anger! The abbot had governed the abbey and guided the hearts of his monks with firmness, wisdom, and gentleness for nearly four decades. But had this very success made him relax his attentiveness?

---

2. [Title: "On the eight principal vices."]

"

That evening, the Lord Berno went to the lame man, to ask how he was. Hermann was working again.

"May God be praised that you are better, Hermann. The attack did not last long. What are you working at now?"

"I am translating a Hebrew passage from the Old Testament for Udualrich," answered the sick man, ingenuously.

The abbot's face darkened. "A passage from the Old Testament?"

"Yes. Jeremiah 13 …"

"When did Udualrich bring it to you?"

"At midday today, Father Abbot," replied Hermann, with the serenity of one who had a good conscience.

"But I have explicitly stipulated that everyone who wants to make use of your help must first have my permission."

"You knew nothing of this, Father Abbot? Forgive me for acting on my own initiative."

"Your own initiative? You acted in good faith, but Udualrich keeps on acting as he himself sees fit. Give me your notes and his! I must once again explain to him in very clear terms what obedience and dependence mean …"

The day had already been full of tribulations. An accident had occurred on the building site. The master builder had been somewhat careless, and one of the masons had fallen and been severely injured. If the worker died, four children would be left without a father. In the afternoon, a messenger had brought the certain news that three

Popes were now disputing in Rome about which of them was legitimate. Abbot Berno suffered much because of the Church.

All day long, he had had to keep his temper, but this incident with Udualrich put an end to that. He made to leave the room in anger.

"Father ..." Hermann began to make a request, because he knew that Berno could punish harshly when things went too far. Would that improve a man like Udualrich, or only make him bitter? "Father ..."

An abrupt movement of the hand told him to be silent. Abbot Berno departed.

"

Later, Udualrich came, pale and grim. He threw the wax tablet down before the sick man.

"Brother Udualrich ..."

"Oh, I just wanted to thank you, dear Brother Hermann. You got me a wonderful humiliation. You really know how to do that! Just imagine: the Lord and Father rebuked my disobedience in the presence of the entire community. Yes, you really knew how to bring that about."

"But, Brother, for the love of Christ ...," Hermann besought him.

The monk bent down, planted his elbows firmly on the table, and stared into the lame man's face.

"Spare me your pious phrases, you learned and virtuous man. You are not going to entrap *me* with them. Go on letting yourself be spoiled by our Lord and Father Abbot—at our cost. You deprive us of the love and benevolence that you receive from our common Father. He showers every gift on you. Well, no doubt you will show him your gratitude. I am sure of that."

With an ugly gesture, Udualrich indicated the cell. "Go on behaving so well and leading an indigent life, in exact accordance with the strict reform of Cluny, you who are the last of the poor ones of Christ—as you like to call yourself."

The monk went to the door, flung it open, and banged it shut behind him.

The last of the poor ones of Christ …

Hermann forced himself to be calm. "For they know not what they do."

A picture formed in his mind … the Lord on Good Friday, clothed in purple rags, crowned with thorns, a reed in his hand. Soldiers bowed their knees in mockery before the king, whom they despised, and spat in his face.

The last of the poor ones of Christ …

He wanted to protest, to weep, to cry out, to fight back.

The last of the poor ones of Christ …

And he prayed an Our Father, transcending his deeply wounded spirit.

"

From that day on, his sight and his hearing had somehow become more acute. He sensed the opposition to the abbot that was brewing up in the community, quietly and almost imperceptibly. When the Lord Berno addressed the community, Hermann saw the critical glances, pursed mouths, and contemptuous gestures in some monks. Was he the reason for the diminishing attitude of reverence for the Father Abbot? Was he (though himself innocent) guilty in this matter?

The community had lost its stable structure. A fissure had opened up, slowly but steadily widening. The Lord Berno too seemed changed. He made impatient demands; he was imperious and irritable. When he issued a command, his tone was usually harsh. If he discovered a mistake or an error, his rebuke was no longer delivered with kindly strictness and mild firmness. Now, his admonitions seemed stern and unmerciful.

Did he sense the opposition? Did he want to crush it by force? Did he not know that this only increased the number of his opponents, who were secretly working against him? Some of those who hitherto had loved and revered him now feared him. And there were only a few steps from fear to aversion.

Sometimes, Hermann felt as if even the beams and the masonry were rustling. Were rats and voles at work, bringing down the house of Saint Benedict on Reichenau with a crash? How was he to help, to protect and support?

Ought he to speak with the abbot, to warn him quite openly? But what facts could he bring before him, apart from the verbal assault by Udualrich? Had he any proofs? Could he appeal in such an important matter to presentiments and feelings?

"Lord, what do you want me to do?"

The lame man became calmer. No one knew about his inner distress, since he went about his duties tranquilly. He prayed much and intensely, and he continually offered up his sufferings for Abbot Berno.

The signs of discontent multiplied. Some monks avoided the cell of the lame man. Hermann could have endured the loneliness and the contempt, if only they had not defied the abbot.

"Am I really a wall that separates the abbot and the community?" This was the tormenting question that no longer left him any peace. Although he had nothing to reproach himself for, he automatically became shyer and more reserved in his dealings with his spiritual father.

"

Soon, the fiftieth anniversary of the day on which the Lord Berno had been ordained to the priesthood in the distant imperial abbey of Pruem came round. His thoughts often took the long path to the northwest and rested in the quiet walls of the abbey on the wild slopes of the Eifel Mountains. The young monk Berno had spent his days so free of cares then, so free of burdens. He had sung the praises of God exultantly, in the unalloyed joy of his heart. He had been a keen student, and he had been glad to let the strict abbot guide him! The same had been true of his time in the reformed abbey of Fleury …

It was easier to be led, even by such a strict man as Abbot Immo of Pruem, than to bear the burden of responsibility, which Berno now found more oppressive than ever.

"If only Emperor Henry II had not chosen me when he was looking for an abbot for Reichenau!" he thought, wearily and bitterly. "Was my predecessor here really as cruel as people say? Or was not his strictness necessary, in view of the intractability of human nature, which is always happy to deviate from the good path? Only a few men—monks like Hermann—can bear loose reins, because they love the Lord so much that they remain on his path out of love. Was I too indulgent all those years?"

Although Abbot Berno was correct in the chapter meetings, he was far too objective and impersonal. No one dared to oppose him openly, but the secret muttering took on dangerous forms. The abbot's dispassionate face seldom smiled. He went on his way, even more upright, his steps even more measured and dignified. Visitors sensed the strictness of the abbot, the ruler at Lake Constance.

Apart from the lame man, no one knew that the abbot was suffering, suffering terribly under the gulf of strangeness that had opened up between him and his sons in Christ. Hermann noticed the lines of pain around the narrow, self-controlled mouth, and he heard the hidden request behind the cool severity of his imperious voice. He saw that the white threads in the abbot's hair had become more numerous.

"

The mighty building of Saint Mark's church with its high bell tower was nearing completion. But did the lofty campanile still mean anything to the abbot? He had admired the bell towers he had seen when he accompanied Emperor Henry I on his journeys to Rome, and his keenest desire had been to build such a tower on the shore of the Gnadensee, so that the bells could bear the praise of God far and wide from its highest point … The Lord Berno looked at his life's work with indifferent eyes. Another, much more important building—the inner, divine construction of his monastic family—was being demolished. But he was not able to identify the workers, nor could he prevent the dismantling.

"

The hidden fire burst out into the open during the choir practices for the service that was to be celebrated on the golden jubilee of the abbot's priestly ordination. With great devotion, Hermann had composed solemn chants for a Mass, with melodies that expressed all his gratitude to the Lord and Creator for giving Reichenau a man like Abbot Berno. Gunter, the choirmaster, led the rehearsals very well, but something essential was always lacking in the singing. The choir sang languidly and reluctantly, since their hearts were not in what they were doing.

After repeated unsuccessful attempts, Gunter fetched the sick man from his cell into the choir. "Sing the melody to the brethren, Hermann. They need to hear how a melody can sound, when the singer sings from the heart."

Hermann sang at once. His *Gloria* praised the Lord, his *Alleluia* exulted, his *Credo* adored. His *Sanctus* was joyful expectancy, and his *Agnus Dei* bent down in blessed certainty to meet the Lord who was coming to visit him in the holy Eucharist.

Gunter cried out enthusiastically: "Yes, dear brothers, that is how you must do it! Try it one more time."

But most of the monks sang no better than before.

"Why are you making no effort? Anyone who heard you singing would have grave doubts about your good will," said the choirmaster angrily.

Then the monk Dietbert laughed nastily and cried out, without taking any account of the holiness of the place: "You should not be surprised that Hermann sings with enthusiasm when he is singing for the abbot, Gunter. After all, he must somehow show his gratitude for all the favors he receives from the Lord and Father Abbot."

The sick man started up. "What are you saying, Dietbert?"

Dietbert leant forward with a malicious grin and looked at the lame man, from his head to his crippled feet.

"I merely said something that everyone knows, Count of Altshausen. Which of us has the best and most beautiful cell in all the house? Who is permitted to use fine furs and precious rugs? Who is served the most delicious foods and the most exquisite drinks? Who is allowed to come and go to the common exercises of the spiritual life, as and when it pleases him? Who is never the object of a serious rebuke? Who is the abbot's confidant? The last of the poor ones of Christ—Count Hermann of Altshausen!"

Some of the monks loudly agreed with Dietbert's words, while others spoke bitterly against him—although they ought to have observed silence in the choir of the monastery church. The lame man looked with big eyes at Dietbert. His heart tensed up, while the voices around him quarreled ever more loudly.

He sat there, mute and rigid, and looked at Dietbert. His hands lay immobile on his lap, crossed over as if they were fettered. He stared at Dietbert, but he no longer saw him. The faces, the hands, the bodies of the disputants became indistinct before his eyes. They became a surging mass, and their words combined in his ears to form a sea of sounds that roared and whooshed.

Suddenly, the harsh voice of the abbot drowned out the commotion. "What is going on here? How dare you profane the holy place?"

A deathly silence prevailed, and the rebels looked shyly at the ground. The lame man sat there, motionless, staring with wide open eyes in the same direction, like a blind man.

The Lord Berno spoke to an older monk: "Renuald, come with me and tell me what has happened here! You others, get to your work without delay!"

The guilty and the innocent slunk out the monastery church with bowed heads. Hermann still stared in the same direction. Did he stand between the abbot and the brothers?

"Father, what disgraceful conduct by ...," whispered Berthold, but the lame man would not listen to him.

"Do not ... not speak .. about it ...," he asked, haltingly. "Bring me to the lake."

"

Salve Regina

Hermann felt unutterably tired. Little waves wrinkled the silver surface of the lake, a picture of peace. Was the Gnadensee as it had always been? Could anything in all the wide world be as it had always been? Was not all beauty somehow poisoned by envy, resentment, and hatred?

The lame monk wanted to pray, but he found no words. He was too tired and too sad. The young man by his side was silent, and doubtless shared in the father's suffering.

What would Renuald tell the Father Abbot? How Abbot Berno would suffer from the lack of confidence on the part of his own sons!

Why had his brother Werinher not defended him? Or was he one of those who had objected to Dietbert's words?

How illusory was the peace here at the Gnadensee! Over there stood the stump, the half-charred stump of the willow. It was truer and more honest. Dead wood … the wood of death … the cross.

The sick man shivered, as if he was cold. "Why always the cross, always the cross? I would like to rest just for once, just to rest, to rest … without the cross. I am tired, so tired. I cannot … bear any more. No more *via dolorosa*,[3] no more cross, Lord! No, no! Calm, quiet … nothing else. Lord, take me home. I cannot bear any more. I am too tired."

Firm, impatient steps drew near.

"Father Abbot," murmured Berthold, getting up from the grass on the shore.

The lame man felt fear. The abbot … What awaited him now? "Lord, I cannot bear any more …"

The abbot dismissed the brother with a short gesture of his hand. Then he took Berthold's place on the grass.

"Who is the abbot's confidant?" Dietbert had said. "The last of the poor ones of Christ—Count Hermann of Altshausen."

The abbot said nothing. Hermann looked down at him and saw the many white threads in his hair, and the stooped shoulders. The sick man's bitterness gave way to concern for his father in Christ. "Lord, if I can help him," he prayed, thereby giving his assent to all that would come, irrespective of his weariness.

3. [The path taken by Jesus, bearing his cross, from Pilate's praetorium to Golgotha.]

The abbot was silent for a long time. When he finally began to speak, his voice sounded brittle. It was the voice of an old man.

"Do you know why I have come, Hermann?"

"Yes, I know, Father Abbot," replied the sick man, and felt his heart beating rapidly. He prayed silently: "Lord, I am afraid, but I want what you want."

"Your lordly brethren … your noble, lordly brethren …" The abbot's voice cracked, and he swallowed once or twice. "Your lordly brethren are envious. They demand to be governed more mildly. Unlike Abbot Immo, I have given them justified pleasures and relaxations, such as richer meals on feast days. But that is not enough for them. No, they want to have white bread every day. They want a softer cloth for their habits, a warmer dormitory, better wine, and similar privileges that the strict Abbot of Reichenau has refused to give them. And they appeal here to the fact that …" The Lord Berno looked up at the lame man, who did not flinch from meeting his dark eyes.

Hermann finished the sentence: "That you have granted me all these things, Father Abbot."

"But you have never asked for one single privilege!" cried the abbot.

"No, but I have received a considerable number of privileges. Father, it was, in any case, only a trial period. So I ask you with all my heart: Clear away the offense. Give the order that my cell should take on its old appearance again, and that I should be served the same meals that I used to get …"

The Lord Berno interrupted him harshly: "No, that would be a foolish caving in to their demands. The brethren must not be envious of the gifts of mercy that are given to you—a lame man who is wracked by pain!" The abbot's hands clasped his pectoral cross so vigorously that his knuckles turned white.

"Father, forgive them, for they know not what they do," pleaded Hermann quietly. "May I not apply to the brethren the words of Our Lord on the cross?"

"No," replied Berno. "In you, they are doing it to Our Lord on the cross. It is on him that they are heaping the disgrace of their enviousness, and they know perfectly well what they are doing."

"Permit me to contradict you, Father Abbot ... They cannot know what they are doing. How are they to know the extent of my distress? They would have to have endured the pain themselves ... or to know about it in the way that only you know about it. Believe me, the brethren see only the external picture. They see the sick brother who is well cared for, the brother whom you, Father, treat with a special warmth. They know nothing of the continual pains, of the sleepless nights, of the torment when my lameness completely prevents me from using my hands and my tongue. They cannot feel in their own persons what it means when other people's hands have to do every service for me, when they wash me, put my clothes on and take them off, feed me, put me to bed ... Nor can they know that you are so kind to me in order that I may not succumb to bitterness, but may be able to try, in some small measure, to be good."

Despite the urgency of this plea, Abbot Berno was not to be shaken in his resolve. He was too deeply hurt to be able to accept and acknowledge the truth.

"They see enough of your suffering to allow them to be glad that you receive what I have given you."

The lame man's eyes were full of sadness, when he murmured: "And what if their eyes are kept from seeing, Father? I beg you, clear away the offense. The last thing I want is to be a wall separating you and ... my brethren. Take everything away from me, I beseech you, take everything away from me, Father, so that they may once again come home to you!"

The abbot shook his head angrily. "No, Hermann, that is not going to happen. I will compel them to love their neighbor. I will compel them. They will find out in the chapter meeting who is the Lord of Reichenau! They will ask you for forgiveness. If anyone is unwilling to do so, I will send him away. If I cannot do that, what is the point of my being the Lord of the Abbey of Our Lady on Reichenau?"

The sick man suddenly felt that a power outside his own self had taken hold of him. He knew that Abbot Berno was in great danger, since the only "Lord of Reichenau" was Jesus Christ ... He had to help the father. He was overwhelmed by something like a prophetic vision:

Christ was washing his disciples' feet ... And he spoke like a prophet, fearless, bold, driven from within. He could do nothing else: he had to speak.

But while he carried out the charge that he felt within him, his hands rested on his lap as if they were fettered ...

"You are the Abbot of Reichenau, Lord Berno, in order that you may serve, not in order that you may rule. In serving, you must fulfill the charge of Christ and preserve the brethren's souls for him. It is your privilege to lead the souls of the brethren to him through a humble and loving dedication to your exalted service. You must rule by serving ... and you must serve by ruling. You must not block the path of any of the weak ones to the Lord by imperious harshness. Only gentleness can open people's hearts to him … Father, love cannot be compelled. One can win it only through service in love. For the sake of Christ, Father Abbot, be gentle and kind to the brethren!"

He had spoken those terrible words. Had the Lord Berno accepted them? Hermann waited.

The abbot rose slowly. His face was pale, and he took quick, shallow breaths.

"Hermann of Altshausen, I hope that you understand that you have gone far too far. Your words were an arrogant presumption. No monk, not even you, is entitled to rebuke his abbot. It seems that I have been too indulgent with you, since you dare to do such a thing. You will answer for it at the chapter of faults."

"Father …"

The abbot paused for a moment, and then departed. If Hermann had been able to turn round and follow his movements, he would have seen that the steps he took were those of an old man.

Abbot Berno had never spoken to him like that.—But had Hermann not meant well? Indeed, what else could he have done? Was this to be the end of a spiritual fellowship in God, a fellowship grounded in God?

Had he said and dared too much? But he had no alternative, because a higher demand had been made of him. He had to speak in that way, precisely because he revered the Lord Berno and was anxious about him.

Nevertheless—as a simple monk, he had said too much. Abbot Berno could not see the matter in any other way.

And probably this was the cross of which he had been

afraid earlier on. God wanted him to go alone from now on, completely alone. In that case, he would at least atone from the heart for what had been wrong in the external form of his words ... and then, he would continue on his way alone. An unrestrained sobbing shook the poor body of the sick man. Alone? My God, was he not sufficiently alone? *Segregatus* ...[4]

"

Berthold had brought the wheelchair into the chapter room, and Hermann sat there calmly, although his face was furrowed with sorrow. In general, he was not obliged to take part in the chapter, and several monks looked at him in astonishment.

His adversaries thought: "The count of Altshausen is to be a witness in the judicial trial that awaits us."

The abbot entered. He slowed down automatically at the wheelchair. Hermann's heart beat more quickly, but he prayed his *fiat*.[5] The Lord Berno went on. He had seen the hands of the sick man, which rested on his lap as though they were fettered—and yet were marvelously free.

After the introductory prayers, the abbot spoke about the great fraternal union that linked the abbeys in Burgundy, Lorraine, and Swabia. He mentioned the death of Brother Wigbertus in Gorze; in accordance with the fraternal union, they were obliged to pray for him. One who

---

4. ["Set apart."]

5. ["Let it be," echoing Mary's words to the angel: "Let it be to me according to your word" (Luke 1:38).]

knew Abbot Berno as well as the lame man was aware that his voice lacked its old firmness.

After these general communications, the Lord Berno read a chapter from the Rule of Saint Benedict. With a severe emphasis, he read to them the section about the rights and duties of the abbot.

"'Let him not shut his eyes to the faults of offenders; but as soon as they begin to appear, let him, as he can, cut them out by the roots ...'"

Many heads were bent in the ranks of the monks. Hermann sat calmly in his chair.

Abbot Berno went on to read about the strict account that God would demand of the abbot for every soul that he had entrusted to his charge. Then, without any transition, he read a passage from the chapter about humility.

"'The third degree of humility is that a man for the love of God subject himself to his superior in all obedience, imitating the Lord, of whom the Apostle says: He was made obedient even unto death.'"

Abbot Berno omitted some lines, and then read, slowly and clearly—indeed, excessively clearly: "'The fifth degree of humility is that he humbly confess and conceal not from his abbot any evil thoughts that enter his heart, and any secret sins that he has committed ...'"

The Lord Berno put down the Rule. Many a monk now waited for the abbot to summon him to confess his guilt before the monastic community ... Udualrich, Dietbert, Ekkehard. Why was the abbot silent so long? What name would he now utter?

"Today, Brother Hermann of Altshausen is to accuse himself."

The sick man breathed a sigh of relief. Thank God! The

Lord had heard his silent prayers. He was to be allowed to atone for his error. The astonishment of his brethren was so great that they did not perceive the sign he gave several times, asking for his wheelchair to be moved into the center of the room. Finally, his brother Werinher realized that he needed this service.

Now the light vehicle with the crooked body of the monk stood in the center of the chapter room. Although the monks were not permitted to raise their heads, they gazed at him from under half-lowered eyelids.

How could they envy this poor cripple the friendship of the abbot? The distorted figure, the pale face, gaunt, furrowed, with dark rims under the eyes, the bent fingers …

They might have been inclined to gloat, but that feeling changed to one of shame.

Hermann bowed his head before the abbot, since his frailty prevented him from bending his knees. The Lord Berno clenched his hands in the sleeves of his habit. His face seemed distant and harsh. Werinher almost sobbed in his agitation. What wrong could his brother have done? Did he not look as if he had been weeping? A terrible thought … Hermann, always so self-controlled, had wept?

In a clear voice that reached the farthest corner of the great room, Hermann made his confession: "I, Hermann of Altshausen, professed monk and member of the community of the Abbey of Our Lady on Reichenau, confess to you, my Lord and Father Abbot Berno, and to all the brethren here present, before the presence of Almighty God, whom I call as my witness, and to whose mercy I recommend myself, that I have sinned against the reverence that I owe you, my Lord and Father Abbot Berno. I have dared to rebuke you in a presumptuous manner and to admonish you, although I am not in any way entitled to do so.

"For this fault, of which I accuse myself, I ask the forgiveness of you and of my brethren. I ask for your prayer, and for a penance that is in accordance with the gravity of my fault."

The unsparing self-accusation was perfectly clear. The Lord Berno waited before replying, and all the monks feared for the lame man. Would the abbot impose the most severe penance possible, or had he felt compassion when he heard this honest and uncompromising admission of guilt? The tension in the room was almost unbearable.

"Hermann of Altshausen, this will be your penance: Contrary to the wish that you have stubbornly expressed, you will receive an even better equipped cell and even richer food." The words were spoken tonelessly and impersonally. "Furthermore, you will remain completely silent in the community until I allow you to use your tongue once more. I hope that arrogant words will never again proceed from your lips."

The assembled monks shuddered, but the sick man thanked the abbot in the customary form for the penance that had been imposed on him.

The abbot ended the chapter meeting with obvious haste, without requiring even one of the rebels to accuse himself. Hermann was the only one he wanted to punish. But this gave him no satisfaction. As the Lord Berno left the chapter room, his feet faltered once again as he passed the lame man's wheelchair. He saw the "fettered" hands, then drew himself to his full height and left the room.

The lame man took part in the evening prayers as if nothing had happened. When the Magnificat was sung, he thanked the greatest of all mothers for having answered his prayer and helped him to maintain his physical strength throughout the day. The lameness could return in the night ... In every distress, the lonely man found refuge in Mary. He knew that he, as a fragile human being, as a sinner, was completely safe with her. The Mother of mercy receives everyone who finds the path to her, even a poor, lonely cripple.

When Berthold brought him into his cell, he seemed not to notice the new burden in the form of coverings, drapes, and furs. He said nothing as Berthold prepared him for his night's rest, and he said nothing as he ate his substantial meal, although that cost an effort. Did he not perceive the distress of his faithful companion? Berthold knelt down to receive the evening blessing, but Hermann declined mutely.

"You must understand me, Berthold. Before I can bless you, the Lord must bless me."

The brother was so confused that he left the candle burning. The lame man attempted to extinguish it, but he fell back, feebly.

His thoughts tortured him: "I must not bless ... I must not extinguish the light. Have I ever kindled a light for other people, or was I ultimately nothing more than a will-o'-the-wisp?"

The candle hissed and smoldered; the smoke was black and ugly. He had to cough. If only Berthold would come back! A damp cloudy air blew from the lake into the cell. The hanging would have to be fastened before the window ... If only Berthold would come ...

Hermann felt the wet coldness slowly and inexorably penetrating the fine drapes, the woolen coverings, and the thick furs. The cold rose higher and higher, until it took hold of his entire body. The lameness took him back into its terrible arms. Each time, it was like a process of dying that he experienced with his mind alert. He had expected this attack after the excitements of the day. The only good thing was that it had not come before the chapter meeting ...

Then the raging pains assailed him like waves, inundating him—like waves in which the will to live and to say "yes" threatened to drown. Were they the billows of the Gnadensee? Was this torment only a penance, or was it also grace?

He wanted to cry out, but not even that was possible; nor was he allowed to do so: "... until I allow you to use your tongue once more ..." A strangled, stertorous groaning came out of his mouth, as his teeth ground against one another. Streams of perspiration ran over the pale, distorted face.

Then ... another mountainous wave of pain. It subsided, but it came back.

Was there anything he could use to stem this assault? Should he stammer his inner *fiat,* accepting it? Would not a rebellion against his merciless fate be also a kind of liberation?

The abbot's favorite? The dead wood ... the wood of death, the cross ... "You must not block the path of any of the weak ones to the Lord ..."

Christ washed the feet of his disciples …

Presumptuous words? Alone, alone …

The pains crashed over him and receded, ceaseless like the waves of the sea, while images and fragments of words emerged from his memory and tormented him.

He did not give in. His soul struggled to find strength. He cried in his mind to Mary, entrusting his torment to her, the Mother of the Lord, the Mother of mercy.

When the pain let him breathe a little more freely, a new verse of the prayer was wrung from his heart …

"Hail, O Queen … *Salve Regina!*"

Like a star in a stormy night, Mary stood before him this night, on the stormy sea of his sufferings. "*Salve Regina!*"

But he had to get closer to the Mother. She was not only his Queen and Lady. He fled to where she was and sought shelter in her love …

"*Mater misericordiae* … Mother of mercy …" The inferno of pain threatened to confuse his mind, and his soul cried out: "*Vita, dulcedo et spes nostra* …" And once more, he could emerge from the turmoil of distress and lay at the feet of her whom he had just called "life, sweetness, and hope" his urgent plea that after this wretchedness, at the end of his exile, she would show him the blessed fruit of her womb, the Lord Jesus Christ. He knew that he was not the only pleader. With all the children of Eve, weeping and sighing, he called out from this vale of tears to her, the Mother of mercy …

Again and again, he prayed the same words, until, long after midnight, the waves of his pains diminished, until finally, all he felt was the well-known everyday torment.

With one last hiss and plumes of black fume, the

candle went out. Outside, a silver moon hung over the lake. The clouds had dispersed.

"*Mater misericordiae ...,*" the sick man thought gratefully, before he was overcome by exhaustion and fell asleep.

The thought of the Mother of God accompanied him into a dream. He saw her and was permitted to present to her the words of the prayer that he had found in his distress. She nodded graciously to him, and he felt as if she was saying: "Henceforth, all generations will call me blessed with these words too."

"

The dream made the sick man happy, and this happiness did not leave him when Berthold woke him after a brief sleep. Usually, he gave his helper all the support that he could, but today, it was impossible for him to move. When Berthold asked him to raise his right hand, it remained immobile in its position over his left hand. The narrow, crooked fingers had no strength at all.

"Father, are you completely lame again?"

The sick man's blue eyes wanted to console and calm him, but they were powerless against the young man's urgent distress and concern.

The brother did his service speedily, although it was not easy to lift the light body of the sick man when he was in this state. His anxiety about the master gave him an unsuspected strength. After he had settled him down on the bed, he rushed off.

Not long afterward, Hermann, whose lameness had led him to cultivate his acute sense of hearing, heard resolute steps, and his eyes widened. It was Abbot Berno. He examined his reactions. Was he filled with joy—or seized with fear?

The door opened and creaked on its hinges. Abbot Berno was in the room. Hermann, who was immobile, could not see him, but he knew that the Lord Berno was looking at him. Had Berthold informed the abbot? If so, he must have come immediately ...

The Lord Berno looked down at the lame man and saw the ghostly pallor of his face, which seemed to have been made of white wax. The poor arms lay crossed-over on the dark covering, as if they were fettered—and indeed, was that not the case?

The abbot approached the bed, careful to make no noise. He drew up the armchair that he had had fitted out with new cushions and furs. The Lord of Reichenau sat down beside his lame son in Christ, silent, sunk in profound reflection. His eyes met the blue eyes of the sick man, which spoke of an undiminished love and reverence.

Was it possible that a man like this, such a humble monk, had acted out of vanity and presumption when he spoke those words to him at the Gnadensee? Had he not been impelled to this daring deed by love—love for God, for the abbey, for the brethren, and for him, his abbot?

The previous evening, some monks had come to Abbot Berno. Some had confessed that they felt guilty because they had complained and been envious; and the best and most faithful monks had come to intercede for the lame man and to defend him.

Father Ruodhart, deeply shaken by what had happened, had told him: "Father Abbot, if we have a saint in our abbey, it is Hermann." And when the abbot said nothing, the old man had had the courage to add: "I do not know what words he spoke, Father Abbot. But I have known him since the day when his parents made him an *oblatio* at the altar of our monastery church. On that occasion, I was the first one whom you charged to take care of him. One who suffers as he does, and who is so patient and loving, has a share in the special grace of God and in the motherly care of Our Lady."

The abbot had spent many hours that night pondering on what he had heard, and weighing up Hermann's words in the presence of the Lord. Strangely enough, his mind's eye kept on seeing the hands that were crossed-over, hands both fettered and free. That was how his hands had been at the Gnadensee when he spoke those words that had affected the abbot so strongly, the words about ruling as a servant.

Were not the fettered hands the sign that Hermann had spoken at the behest of Another, at the behest of God? Had he not been under obligation to speak?

The novice Berthold had just told him nervously that Hermann was once again totally lame.

The abbot's heart was generous, but not without pride. His pride now put him on the defensive: "Is this supposed to be my fault?" But when he looked at the hands that lay on the dark covering, he knew that this time, it was indeed his fault.

"His words were not a presumption. They were dictated by genuine concern and by the genuine charge he had received from God. He infringed only the external form. If a man of the caliber of Hermann of Altshausen is so worried about me, there must be a lot of truth in the claim that I wanted to use harshness to make my position secure ..."

The bell rang for service in the church, but Abbot Berno disregarded it. He sat with bowed head beside the lame man's bed and examined his conscience unsparingly. Had he served? Had he ruled?

Every harshness that seeks to break other people is a sin in God's eyes. Every word that is too harsh, that wounds instead of healing and converting, leads the brethren away from God. Every facial expression and gesture of implacability and unmercifulness damages the cause of God, because people close their hearts to him ...

While these thoughts were going through the abbot's mind, the sick man prayed for his Father, as if he was aware of his inner struggle. A little strength was restored to him, and he moved his fingers quietly to and fro on the dark covering.

Finally, the abbot lifted his head and looked at him directly.

"Hermann, my son in Christ, I have acted unjustly. I have done wrong to you and to the brethren."

The lame man wanted to reply, but he could only stammer inarticulately. Nevertheless, the Lord Berno had understood him.

"No, no, you do not need to defend me. I have examined myself in the presence of the Lord, and I see my failure. What you said was correct, Hermann. The 'Father Abbot' must serve—that is all. But I was the 'Lord Abbot.' I wanted to rule, and I did rule. I wanted to extirpate evil through harshness, instead of overcoming it through patient and humble kindness. I was unwilling to wait. I was not merciful when the brethren erred. I demanded love instead of giving love. I was especially unjust toward you. You may have erred according to the letter of the law, but I ought to have known that you have never acted out of presumption, but only out of love. The worst thing is that I knew this, but I did not want to know it. I listened only to the voice of nature, and I sacrificed you to my wounded pride before the assembly of the brethren."

Hermann was moved by this confession. Abbot Berno was capable of great humility! The Lord of Reichenau bowed even more deeply before the crippled monk. He rose from the armchair and knelt down.

The sick man's lips worked hard to produce a sound. "Father! Father!"

"Hermann, you accepted everything for the love of Christ. I thank you for this, my dear son, and I ask you for his sake to forgive me what I did to you. Then, with your forgiveness and in the power of his love, I can go to your brethren and to God."

"Father!" The lame man's right hand made its trembling way across the dark covering toward the bowed head of the abbot.

"Bless me, Hermann," the Lord Berno asked, and the sick man granted this highly unusual request with a calm solemnity. But the effort was too much for him; Abbot Berno took the hand that had blessed him, and laid it back on the covering. "Pray for me, my son."

"

When Berthold returned shortly afterward, he found the master moving his stiff fingers. Hermann was not surprised to learn from the brother that he was now permitted to speak.

"We have another chapter meeting. You are to remain in your cell, Father. Should I bring you something to eat first?"

"That would not be a bad idea, Berthold. Even the most undemanding donkey cannot fast all the time." Berthold smiled at the joke.

He was soon back in the cell. Berthold was well known for his intelligence, but his face betrayed nothing of that now. He looked perplexed.

"I don't understand it, Father. The brothers in the kitchen gave me this bowl and a cup of the ordinary island wine for you ... on the abbot's instructions ..."

"I understand it perfectly well. Come, help me up."

The brother had to feed him, since he was still too weak. Berthold cast a glance of disapproval at the food.

"The brothers could really have given you something better. This is a strange penance ..."

Hermann smiled. "A penance? Your thoughts are far off the mark, my son! This is no penance, but a joyful surprise, a reward."

The lame man ate the vegetables and the oatmeal porridge with obvious pleasure.

"A reward? This porridge?" Berthold shook his head. "The wine is not the best quality, but at least one can drink it." He was so distracted that he spilled some wine.

Hermann rebuked him softly. "If the wine is the one good thing here, then one should not squander it. Did you not sleep last night?"

Berthold's reply came at once: "How could I have slept

after yesterday's chapter meeting? Why did Father Abbot not spare you all that?"

"Our Father Abbot exercised his office correctly. There are no problems between us."

"You made excessive amends, but the Lord Berno was harsh."

"That will do, Berthold! You are not entitled to judge that. But I will tell you one thing: the Lord Berno has much more love and humility than me. Our Father Abbot is a great monk, a holy and virtuous monk. He should be a model for both of us."

The brother did not reply. He was unconvinced.

"Bring me to the work desk. I want to practice while you are away, until I have so much control over my hands that I can write."

"

Hermann had to make many attempts. He needed much time and patience before he forced his shaking hands to obey him. His crooked fingers moved the sharp stylus awkwardly, as he scratched the letters on the wax tablet. He wrote down the prayer to the Mother of mercy, the words of the prayer that the torment of the night had wrung from him. He wrote it for his abbot, who was now passing through the inner torment of humiliation. Abbot Berno was kneeling before his sons, asking their pardon for his harshness, and he would emerge from this "lake of grace" cleansed and purified.

The lame man erased some letters. He had to write them two or three or even four times, before they were legible.

Salve Regina, Mater Misericordiae, vita, dulcedo, et spes
  nostra, salve.
Ad te clamamus exsules filii Hevae, ad te suspiramus
  gementes et flentes in hac lacrimarum valle.
Eja ergo, advocata nostra, illos tuos misericordes oculus
  ad nos converte,
et Jesum, benedictum fructum ventris tui, nobis post hoc
  exilium ostende.[6]

Writing down these words of prayer was a hard task for one who was so weak. More than once, he was obliged to stop and take a much-needed pause. Nevertheless, he also composed a melody to these words, and he wrote it down in the letters that were his own notation. The melody sounded solemn and stately, as he hummed it quietly to himself.

Hermann never worked with his mind alone. When he created something, the whole man was involved. He saw even the driest formula as a hidden praise of the one who had imposed order on life; in its regularity, it had a share in the order of all orders, in the law of all that existed, in God. God's greatness was not only revealed in the mighty laws that guided the constellations in their paths across the universe. It also determined the little realm of tiny living creatures in their marvelous order.

"And we human beings think we have discovered

---

6. ["Hail, O Queen, Mother of mercy, our life, our sweetness, and our hope, hail! / We, the exiled children of Eve, cry to you, we sigh to you, groaning and weeping in this vale of tears. / Oh then, our advocate, turn those merciful eyes of yours on us, / and show us, after this exile, Jesus, the blessed fruit of your womb."]

something of his ways. But we are only at the beginning. And we stand at the beginning again and again, here on earth. Even later centuries and millennia are only at a new beginning. Every insight into a mystery of God confronts us with a new puzzle. It is only in death that our seeing and guessing will become a seeing and knowing ... What a happy moment that will be, when we are allowed to see you, Lord!"

A fisher boat glided over the Gnadensee. It was caught by the evening sun and seemed to vanish into its silver gleam.

"That is how I would like to go home, Lord ... to be caught up into your light, into the pure flame of your eternal being ..."

"

The sick man had a lengthy wait. He spent the time praying and meditating in a silent and cheerful serenity. His inner peace told him that the abbot had found the path of peace, of reconciliation with the brethren and with the Lord.

"In order that you too may do what I have done ..."

Abbot Berno had performed this action in imitation of Christ. He had washed the feet of his sons, asking humbly: "Forgive me, dear brothers and sons in Christ. I have been too harsh ..."

When the monks of good will left, they were filled with shame and happiness, reflecting penitently on their own failures.

"Where goodness and love are found, the Lord is there."

"

The lame monk at the window felt happy, despite his pains. The love of God had become visible and palpable on Reichenau, and this love sheltered him too. His continuous pains and frequent attacks were irrelevant in this context, for did not the love of God outweigh them a hundredfold? If the count of Altshausen had been healthy, would he ever have received the kind of happiness that he had received as a crippled monk? Perhaps he would have been nothing more today than a knight who sought satisfaction in worldly joys, and thought rarely or never about God …

He wondered where the man who denied the existence of happiness was. Where would Master Theophilos Cheirisophos be wandering now? He had not wanted to hear the name Theophilos,[7] because he served foreign gods. But perhaps he could bear that name now? The lame man's soul sought the doctor who had no home. As yet, his soul received no answer.

"

Stars were shining in the night sky, when Hermann heard steps. Abbot Berno and Berthold were coming to him.

"I am afraid that it is late, my dear son, but this time, I wanted to accompany Berthold, so I asked him to wait until I had the time to come."

From the Lord Berno's voice, Hermann knew that he had rediscovered peace. The brother brought the sick man his evening meal.

---

7. [This name means: "the friend of God."]

"Can you eat by yourself, Father?" he asked in concern.

"Yes, there is no problem now," Hermann replied, taking up his spoon. Unlike the excessively rich meal he had been obliged to eat on the previous day, all he had now was a milk soup and a piece of black bread. But this austere meal tasted very much better.

Behind him, the abbot and the brother went out and in. Before him, the lake was a mirror that shone under the dark-blue velvet of the sky. Hermann could not turn round to see what was going on behind him, but he waited without inquisitiveness or unease.

"Have you finished your supper, Hermann? Good. We too have finished our work."

"May I first give you this canticle, Father Abbot? It was bestowed on me last night."

"A song from last night? Then I shall listen to it with particular attentiveness, Hermann … Now, you must come and see!"

The abbot lifted the sick man from the armchair, while Berthold held up a candle. In its light, Hermann saw that his cell once more presented the old picture of a clean and austere poverty. Its only decoration was the great cross from the castle chapel in Altshausen. The colorful accoutrements that had oppressed him—the drapes, coverings, rugs, and furs—had vanished.

"Your trial period is over, Hermann. You have passed the test as a son of Saint Benedict."

"Thank you, Father Abbot, thank you! Now I am at home here once again, because I am permitted to be poor."

Abbot Berno blessed him before he left. His act of blessing was like a bowing down before one who was greater.

"

With the sick man's wax tablet in his hand, he made his way slowly to his quarters. Sometimes, his age took a heavy toll on him; he was very tired. The prior spoke to him, when he was half-way there: "A courier has just brought a letter from our Lord the Emperor."

The Lord Berno thanked him, somewhat distractedly. A letter from the emperor ... it would not contain any disagreeable message. Under Emperor Conrad, a letter could bring bad news, but the Lord Henry loved the abbey on Reichenau.

In his room, Abbot Berno laid the letter aside and concentrated on the little wax tablet. How hard it must have been for the lame fingers today! He examined carefully every little stroke. How many times had Hermann had to erase what he had written, and then try to write it more clearly?

The more the abbot deciphered of the canticle, its Latin words and its melody, the more deeply he was impressed by the simplicity, the austerity, and the ardency of this prayer to the Mother of God. This canticle rose up from the soul of a man who struggled, a man who had found liberation in his prayer. It was a precious gift ...

The Lord Berno began at once to make a copy, although he knew it would take him all night. His tiredness was forgotten. From time to time, while he carefully inscribed the canticle in his regular writing on a fine parchment, he hummed the melody quietly to himself. He contemplated the content of this prayer to the Mother of mercy. Hermann was certainly right to entrust to her his petition that she would show him her Son after the distress of this present life ...

"

Morning was dawning outside when the abbot finally read the emperor's letter. The Lord Henry had accepted his invitation. He would come to the dedication of the west-work. The emperor was a good friend of the abbot; he regarded the older man as a spiritual father and a wise counselor. They had often exchanged letters.

The emperor's scribe had written the individual letters clearly and elaborately. The great imperial seal was appended to the bottom of the letter—alongside which lay the little wax tablet with the trembling letters that the lame man had scratched. What a contrast!

The emperor and the abbot were great men, each in his own sphere, while even a very light touch could erase the letters written down by Hermann of Altshausen. Would his name too be quickly forgotten by future generations? Perhaps; but was that important? Was it so important that the name of the emperor would still be known centuries later, while the name of the monk was long forgotten? Who was greater before God, the emperor or the cripple? Whose name had a brighter and purer ring to it, when God touched the strings of the soul? The one who had more love was the one who was closer to God. Abbot Berno had no doubt that the little cripple was the one with the greater measure of love in his ample soul.

Surely people would sing his canticle, the *Salve Regina,*

even when they had forgotten everything about its author? A strange and powerful charm emanated from this song.

The Lord Berno scrutinized the sky. The stars were fading everywhere, and a pallid morning twilight crept over the mountains. He felt the weight of the sleepless night, but he was not sorry that he had spent the night in contemplation. Ought he not, in fact, to devote himself much more to what was essential? Master builder Berno, your church is almost finished. Master builder God, will you not soon put a finish to the life of Berno of Pruem?

With the heaviness that came with his old age, Abbot Berno knelt down before the stone image of the Mother of God. In the gleam of the oil lamp, Our Lady's face had smiled down at the abbot for the last four decades, when he knelt before her image ... *Regina, Mater Misericordiae.*[8]

He had the parchment with the canticle in his hand, and he began to sing—at first hesitantly, then in a loud and strong voice: "*Salve Regina, Mater misericordiae, vita, dulcedo, et spes nostra salve ...*"

An old brother was scuttering through the twilight cloister, on his way to wake the brethren. He heard singing from the abbot's room, and the old man stopped to listen. "*Ad te clamamus exsules filii Hevae ...*" The aged monk nodded his approval. He liked the melody.

And soon, it could be heard again and again in the abbey. The choirmaster rehearsed it with his singers for the anniversary of the abbot's ordination and for the dedication of the west-work.

No one objected. The abbot's humble love had silenced

---

8. ["Queen, Mother of mercy."]

every resentment. The monks had begun to visit the lame man again. He seemed to have forgotten everything, for he welcomed them all with a straightforward and natural cordiality, making no distinctions. The austere poverty of his cell dispersed the last reservations. Dietbert, who had been one of his adversaries, departed from Hermann's cell as an enthusiastic supporter of the lame man. Hermann could thus have had a time of peace.

But he was worried about Werinher. He looked restless and distracted, and wandered around, disgruntled and melancholy. Finally, Hermann's concern prompted him to ask: "Dear brother, what is the matter? Tell me! I want to help you."

Werinher walked restlessly up and down. Hermann could not see him, but he could follow the ceaseless padding of his steps.

"What is the matter? I want to get away. No, I want to remain a monk, but I want to go to the Holy Land. I cannot stop thinking about it. I know that my place is there, where Our Lord lived and suffered. That is where I too must live, suffer, and die."

The lame man wanted to calm him down, although he realized that his brother's wish was meant seriously. "Werinher, you are a monk of Reichenau. As such, you have promised to stay in one place. You are entrusted to our abbey, so to speak. Your pilgrim path leads only across *this* holy land at the Gnadensee. Believe me, my brother, it is here that you find little Nazareth, the stable in Bethlehem, the toilsome footpaths taken in the search for souls and in the proclamation that the kingdom of God is near. It is here that you find the *Via dolorosa* with the cross and the thorns, with those who show compassion, with

Mother Mary, with Simon of Cyrene. It is here that you come to Golgotha and the cross ..."

"No, brother, you do not understand me. I am dying of homesickness for the places where Christ lived on earth. Do you know what homesickness is?"

"I suffered homesickness for Reichenau for three years and three months."

"Your homesickness was assuaged, but mine remains. My home is in the Holy Land. It is there that I shall be buried."

Werinher's words had a new seriousness, and his face had lost its childlike contentedness. Now, he had the face of one who suffered. What was the source of his yearning? Could this be what God wanted of him? All her life, their lady mother had longed to kneel one day at the place where the Lord had lived. Was it possible that this desire had been passed on to her son? In any case, it was up to Abbot Berno to decide whether this unusual wish might become a reality.

"Brother, dear brother, I hope that you are not being led astray by a deception of some kind. We are always at home where Christ lives; and he is in our abbey. Be careful, brother. Our path through life is short. And that is why every one of the steps we take along this path is important. Bear in mind the dangerous and laborious detour that I had to take. I would like to spare you from anything like that."

"Hermann, I am no longer the frivolous and superficial man who bent with every gust of wind. It is not for nothing that I have lived beside you. I know about the cross, and about its importance in our religious life. But there is a call that one must not fail to hear. My path in life is shorter than yours, and it must end in the Holy Land."

"You are a healthy man, eight years younger than me. You should not indulge in such somber moods! Werinher, speak with our Father Abbot, and submit to his decision."

"I will do that," replied Werinher, after some hesitation.

As Hermann had expected, the Lord Berno refused the exceptional request. But his compassionate understanding and his fatherly kindness soothed the unrest in the monk's heart for some time.

"

The abbey celebrated the anniversary of its abbot's ordination with solemnity and dignity. That evening, the choir of monks sang the *Salve Regina* in the monastery church for the first time. The guests from Einsiedeln, Fleury, Gorze, Saint Gallen, Pruem, Cluny, Constance, and Bregenz were delighted by the new melody. They asked for copies of the canticle to the Mother of mercy, and they received them before they left.

Berthold asked the lame man: "Write a dedication, or at least put your cipher under the text, Father."

"Why, my son? This is not about me. It is meant to promote the honor of Mary ... not to make people praise me. I am richly rewarded, if the *Salve* is sung in many places ... Our giving is genuine only when we are not motivated by the desire for personal recognition ..."

CHAPTER 7

* * *

ALMA REDEMPTORIS MATER

The White Dove

THE CONSTRUCTION on the west-work was making excellent progress, since the weather had turned mild and dry early on in the year. The building would be completed by the date set for its dedication.

"It is an exceptional year," thought Tradolf, the cellarer, when the buds and the green leaves began to appear as early as February, and no frost brought a setback.

"An exceptional year," thought Hermann of Altshausen, when he wrote with his own hand in his notes for his World Chronicle: "*Anno Domini* 1048."[1]

---

1. ["The Year of the Lord."]

The Emperor Henry III, the benevolent friend and patron of the abbey and of its abbot, would come to the dedication of the west-work, thereby setting a triumphant conclusion to the life-work of the Lord Berno. The sick man had an anxious premonition. Would this be the only "completion" in the year of salvation 1048? The Lord Berno's life-work comes to its conclusion … Would this be the case in another respect too?

Pilgrims brought bad news from Rome. The Holy Father was in very poor health. Until 1046, the news from Rome had meant nothing but misery and worry for the faithful sons of Mother Church. In *Anno Domini* 1045, three Popes had called themselves the "legitimate successor of Peter": Benedict IX, Silvester III, and Gregory VI. Which one of them was to be believed? This schism had inflicted great confusion on the Catholic world. In many communities, the monks or nuns disagreed about whom they ought to acknowledge as Pope.

Finally, Henry III had intervened, though in a heavy-handed manner. At the Synod of Sutri, he had compelled the three men to abdicate, and had installed Clement, a German priest with high moral standards, as Pope. But had Henry (despite his good intentions) not gone too far? Had he not made himself higher than Peter, and thereby brought the Church into a new dependency? Although Henry III had a great thirst for power, no one could dispute his genuine faith and his love for the Church. But what would things be like under an emperor whose only concern was to increase his power?

As a historian, Hermann realized that the gate had been opened onto a perilous path. And now, Pope Clement II was dying. What would happen now?

"

Berthold brought his master a book, a present for the Emperor Henry III. "Father Abbot wants you to look at the book, Father." He placed it within his reach, sat down beside him, and helped him turn the great parchment pages. The Gospel Book displayed the marvelous initials and images of the Reichenau school of painting.

Hermann gave his student a little examination: "Take a look at the majestic figure of Christ here as he heals the man born blind, Berthold. What does his sublime dignity remind you of?"

The answer came at once: "Of the frescoes in Saint George's and Saints Peter and Paul, Father. Our figures often have a tendency to the grandiose, but they do not seem frozen. They are alive. Sometimes, they are alarmingly alive. Think of the pictures of the evangelists. Is not the one who sees them caught up directly into the supernatural?"

"The light from above falls upon them, and it takes us upward. I too have experienced this strange twofold movement as I looked at these images. But our Reichenau painters are not limited to the mighty, the majestic, and the sublime. They also have a sense of humor. Think of Saint Martha at the raising of Lazarus. She is not ashamed to hold her nose, to make it clear what she means when she says: 'Lord, the air is foul by now.' And the devils in Gerasa—how comical and helpless they are on the backs of the swine! When you see them, you almost think you can see the grin on the face of the good Brother who painted them."

"Father, the little sheep in this Christmas picture seem

to possess a calm dignity, as if they were ..." He paused, and Hermann completed the sentence:

"High prelates, at the very least." They both laughed so heartily at this comparison of the little sheep to church dignitaries that they did not hear the arrival of the abbot.

"And what is causing such mirth?" asked Abbot Berno.

"The Gospel Book of Brother Theodebald," replied the sick man, ingenuously. "We noted that the little sheep in this Christmas picture have the same dignity as high prelates."

"Aha ... like me, then," smiled Abbot Berno, and was delighted to see that the famous scholar blushed like a young student. "I have the dignity of a little sheep. But that is not a bad comparison! What else am I than a little sheep in Peter's flock?"

"Father Abbot, what we meant was the dignity that our painting school gives its figures, even the little sheep. The Reichenau school was influenced by Byzantium, but it acquired a profile of its own with the passage of time."

"If only there were a continuous give and take between Rome and Byzantium ... Why do people not renounce their own little personal goals, their advantages and prejudices, in order to serve the one kingdom of Christ together?"

The Lord Berno sat down on the stool beside the work desk, and the young Brother left the cell quietly. "Turn over some more pages, Hermann." They looked at many pages of the marvelously executed Gospel Book, which was the life's work of a monk.

The sick man praised it: "A precious gift for our Lord and Emperor. No one can find any fault with it."

The abbot bent forward on the stool. His eyes were half-closed.

"Oh, Hermann, the great men who come to the dedication will find fault with any number of things, but the emperor will not be on the lookout for things like that. The Lord Henry is a just man. He is noble. But others will come and will see—indeed, they will *want* to see—things in our monastery that are not good. I could tell you even now some of the things they will object to."

The abbot passed his right hand wearily over his furrowed face. The yellow skin that covered his emaciated fingers was faded and wrinkled. His abbatial ring was loose, far too loose, and there were brown spots on the backs of his hands.

Hermann saw the many wrinkles, creases, furrows, and lines on the familiar face of the Father. He saw the hollow temples and the white hair. How he had aged recently! For many years, it had seemed that age could not affect him, but now it had suddenly overwhelmed him. The sick man was seized with an anxious presentiment.

"Let people talk as they wish, Father Abbot. Their talk does not affect the value of what we do—provided that our activity was intended to serve the Lord. Our activity always has its defects, but that is unimportant, if we have held fast to the essential point."

The Lord Berno looked past him, at the Gnadensee. "And who ... is to tell us whether our activity was intended to serve the Lord? May it not in reality have been a thirst for honor and self-importance? Perhaps the real reason I had the west-work built was an unacknowledged desire to possess the highest bell tower on German soil ... Indeed, the Imperial Prelate Abbot Berno of

Reichenau may well count for less in the eyes of Our Lord Jesus Christ than the last little sheep in Peter's flock, even if ..." The beginning of a smile played around the narrow lips of the seventy-year-old man. "Even if he puts on such a dignified show."

The lame man sensed that behind the apparently serene words there lurked a great distress, an internal distress and weariness.

"Father, you have given the Lord what you were able to give him."

"Hermann, I wish that I had your faith, your confidence, and your peace. The Lord is near to you, and you are familiar with his cross. It is a part of your life. You have said your 'yes' to him, and you have even learned to love that 'yes.' You are held fast, more firmly than any other person on earth, and at the same time, you are one of those who are most free. I am tempted to ... envy you." The abbot rose heavily to his feet.

"I cannot let him go like this," thought Hermann in consternation, and he said: "Father, it was you who led me to God. It is you to whom I owe my freedom and my peace."

The Lord Berno slumped back onto the stool and gave the lame man a piercing look. "You owe it to me that you are so close to God? To me? Well, it is of course true that you paid attention to Berno, your guide. But Berno himself must remain far away from the goal, far away from the Lord. One who preaches to others can himself be rejected."

The sick man felt a new strength in himself, in response to the Father's weakness. He had to support Abbot Berno. With the clear insight of a loving son, he recognized that the abbot's life had entered its final and decisive phase. That gave him the strength and the courage to speak openly about his insight into the abbot's state of mind. Once again, he ventured boldly to deploy all his love, although he was aware of the risk that the Father might misunderstand him.

"Father, you are close to the Lord, and the Lord is close to you. I have often experienced this. Your life has shown me the image of Christ. It was you who brought me to the Lord. Now he is allowing you to undertake a hard part of the journey. In such cases, he gives the hearts of those who belong to him a frightening unease. They must not tarry, nor be content with earthly things—and that is why he makes them homeless once again, and takes away the certainties they had had hitherto. Their only yearning is to be for him. They are to be on the watch for him, and for him alone, in this new wilderness. *Te lucis ante terminum* ... 'before the ending of the light.'"

This time, the Lord Berno did not brush him aside. Despite the boldness of Hermann's words, he understood the reverence that prompted his internal struggle, and his desire to be of service.

"*Te lucis ante terminum* ..."

He knew that the lame man was not referring to the declining day—not to the twilight that was slowly growing outside, down by the Gnadensee.

Hermann had folded his hands. He went on: "Father, night must come; but it will bring broad constellations with it. The soul will go on from clarity to clarity, from light to light, once it has passed through the night of solitude ... And then, it will encounter the light ... A radiant light arises over it, a light that will never again go out. The eternal light enfolds it in the immensely great joy of eternity, *lumen Christi* …[2] No eye has seen, no ear has heard, what God has prepared for those who love him. But it will be light, light and joy. One will be at home in Christ Jesus, Our Lord."

He spoke these words like a profession of faith. The thought of Christ's coming filled his heart with a joy that rang out in his words, victorious and overwhelming.

Christ—my life, my light!

Hermann had remained faithful to himself, ever since he had found the Lord on that Good Friday night in Aachen. He had remained faithful to the flame, to the light, to Christ, and the light in him had grown.

A marvelous warmth irradiated from him, bringing consolation and conviction. The tired face of the abbot was a mild reflection of his joy. As his strength rapidly diminished in his old age, the night was hastening to meet Berno. But even this night was grace and mercy, a beginning rather than an end.

"Sing me the *Salve Regina!*"

The lame man sang his canticle devoutly and ardently. "Thanks be to God that I have my voice today," he thought, gladly; there were more and more days now on which he was completely lame. When he finished singing, the old man laid his hand briefly on his lopsided shoulder. Then the abbot left the cell in silence.

"

On the following day, a great surprise awaited the good Brother Berthold. Apart from his written contribution,

---

2. ["the light of Christ."]

the sick man had played only a small part hitherto in the vast preparations for the reception of the emperor. He regarded it as much more important to finish his book *De physiognomia,* which he had postponed for years.[3] When the students had given him enthusiastic accounts of the preparations, his only answer had been an indulgent smile. Why were they making so much fuss about a man who, after all, was mortal like every other human being?

The uninterrupted knocking and hammering and the excessively busy activity of some of his brethren had often wrung from him a sigh that spoke of an impatience he suppressed with an effort. The chants for the Mass, which were his contribution to the festival day, were exceptionally beautiful, but he found the choir practices a time-consuming burden. He wanted to finish his book, and his tense mind saw every interruption as an unwelcome disturbance. Things had not been easy for Berthold in recent weeks.

"

Hermann was a changed man after the conversation with the Lord Berno. He laid the book aside without the least regret.

"Put it away for the time being, Berthold. I had almost forgotten something that is more important."

More important? But had not this book been very important to him? Brother Berthold was curious to know what could be more important.

The sick man asked to be helped into his wheelchair.

---

3. [Title: "On physiognomy."]

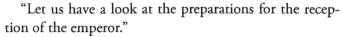

"Let us have a look at the preparations for the reception of the emperor."

Berthold was astonished. "You … you want …"

Hermann interrupted him in a kind voice: "Let us begin at the west-work, my dear son."

The craftsmen there were putting the final touches to the furnishings of the imperial loge under the apse. The prior was watching, along with some monks, and he observed, with a shrug of the shoulders, "In my opinion, the imperial loge ought to have been furnished more splendidly, but our Father Abbot holds that it is almost excessive as it is."

His companions shook their heads in regret, but they gave a start when the sick man raised his voice and called to them: "Our Father Abbot is doubtless giving the emperor what is the emperor's. We should never forget that even the Lord Henry is a mortal man who comes to the house of God in order to adore his highest Lord."

"Thank you for your instruction, Brother," replied the prior with a bow. "I do, of course, wonder whether the emperor would be happy to hear your words!"

These words sounded like a threat, and Hermann showed that he had understood them. He replied, calmly: "You will doubtless know how to find that out, Lord Prior." He then turned to Berthold, as if nothing had happened, and said: "Take me now to Herrenbruck harbor."

They looked at the wide gangplank that the abbey's carpenters had made. Monastery servants were hard at work, putting up the wooden scaffolding of a triumphal arch.

"Now they have damaged our tree. That is a pity!"

At first, Berthold did not know what the Master meant

by "our tree." But then he saw the freshly heaped-up soil in the place where the half-charred willow had stood for many years.

"Christopher," murmured the lame man.

"Father, do you really store up everything in your memory?"

"Everything that is worth giving thanks for, my son. Neither of us should ever forget that storm on the Gnadensee."

"And what do you not give thanks for? ... What are you fully entitled to forget?"

But Hermann gave him no answer to this question.

"

The lame man was a source of astonishment and turmoil for the entire community in those days. He turned up everywhere, in the cellar and in the kitchen, in the garden and in the monastery farm, in the painting school and in the carpenters' workshop, in the imperial residence, in the guesthouse, and in the steward's offices. The brethren told each other at recreation about the sick man's sudden and unexpected visits. Had the abbot told him to make these visits? The Lord Berno said nothing on this subject, and Hermann did not interfere in the work of his brethren by asking them questions. He sat silently in his wheelchair and looked with his big, friendly eyes at what the others were doing. His mere presence ensured that their hands worked more quickly and carefully. The monks unconsciously sensed that a power emanated from him.

Abbot Berno was happy whenever he saw the lame man in his place in the refectory, in the chapter room, and in the monastery church. It seemed that at present, he was able to do more, much more, than usual. His crippled hands carried his spoon and his goblet to his mouth. His voice retained its fullness when he taught or dictated, when he prayed and sang the Psalms, and at choir practice. Its pleasant sound led the abbot to instruct him to alternate with the choir in singing his new Credo.

The abbot knew the power that sustained the sick man and supported him, so that he was able to support others. Not even the wild April showers could harm the lame body. That power made him invulnerable.

"

Hermann inspected the final preparations on the eve of the emperor's visit. The flowers in the garlands shone in their full colors under the warm springtime sun that lay over Reichenau. Red carpets covered the path to Herrenbruck harbor—the same path on which the lame cripple had taken his final steps "by himself," years ago.

With his youthful high spirits, Berthold caught a white dove and brought it to the Father. Hermann carefully cradled the delicate body of the bird in his hands, and felt the quick beating of its little heart.

"A dove of peace, Father. Now all you need is the olive branch."

"And to whom should I send this messenger of peace?"

Abbot Berno spoke, before the Brother could reply: "To all those of good will." He looked with pleasure at the scene before the tower of his church: a monk with a wraithlike face, bending down with a white dove in his hands.

"Perhaps it is the dove of the Spirit. She wants to float

freely above the dark parapets of our earthiness and our heaviness." The lame man meant these words seriously. He opened the cage of his hands, but the white dove remained where she was.

"She wants to remain with you, Hermann, the dove of peace, the dove of the Spirit.

"No, white dove, you must fly up to the heights. You must be free, you must fly …"

As if she had understood him, she lifted her wings and flew up, high above the yellow-brown walls of the imposing bell tower, into the light blue of the sky. The three men stood there for a long time, following her flight with their eyes.

"Would you accompany me on my tour of inspection, Hermann?" the abbot asked.

The sick man joyfully assented, and Berthold took hold of the wheelchair.

"Remain here, Brother. Today it is I who will drive your Master across Reichenau."

And the monks and brethren, the craftsmen, farmers, and fishers saw something rare and remarkable: the Lord and Father Abbot, the Most Reverend Lord Imperial Prelate and ruler of far-flung territories, was pushing the wheelchair of his lame monk.

The contrast was great between the abbot, who remained a giant even in his old age, and the slight figure of the monk in the fragile vehicle. The prior wrinkled his brow in irritation. Did not this Hermann play much too great a role on Reichenau?

The wheels of the vehicle imprinted a double gray track on the carpet. The inhabitants of the island came from all sides to greet the abbot. They did not find it so strange that he was driving the lame man. The Lord Berno thanked each one, even the little fisherman's child who was putting a few flowers on a garland. But otherwise, the abbot was very taciturn on this walk, and he nowhere made any comment on the preparations that had been made. A nod of approval had to suffice for even the most zealous workers. He never asked the lame man for his opinion. Why had he brought him along? In order not to be alone? Hermann did not ask. It was enough for him to know that the Father needed him.

When they came back to the monastery church, the servants were just removing the last part of the wooden framework. A white dove flew around the crest of the bell tower. Was it the same dove? "She does not want to go away from your tower, Father Abbot!"

The Lord Berno drove him through the twilit narthex into the house of God. Here too, no words were necessary, since they both loved the generous width of the arches in the west-work and the simple, relaxed austerity of the building as a whole, which united width, a buoyancy that was a source of inspiration, a noble harmony, a directness, and solidity. The ambulatories beside the imperial loge were modest additions, too modest to turn the church into something bright and playful.

This west-work, Abbot Berno's building, had a strong symbolic power. Its builder had been like a firmly established, absolutely solid, and yet generous and bold "building of God" for the past four decades, both for his own monks and for many people outside, including popes, princes, and emperors. They often looked to him as a man completely united to this earth, yet pointing to heaven. His clarity, directness, and simplicity attracted people more than his considerable achievements in the fields of poetry and music. His artistic works decorated his life in the same way as the arcades, friezes, and pilaster strips decorated his west-work: they did not disrupt the direction his life took, nor were they a displeasing interruption of its consistency. The imperial loge above the west apse, with its modest furnishings, corresponded to the political attitude of the Lord Berno. He had served his emperors faithfully, whether they honored him (like Henry II) or despised him (like Conrad the Salian). But the kingdom of God mattered more to him than the kingdom of the emperor. On its deepest level, his service of the emperor was a service of God.

"

The abbot pushed the wheelchair into the narthex. Did he intend to bring the lame man into his cell? A white dove sat on the square before the church, as if she was waiting for them; but when the men came nearer, she flew away. The Lord Berno drove the wheelchair past the monastery gate and turned into a bumpy cart track. He steered it carefully by a circuitous route through green meadows and flowers, back to the Gnadensee. Bushes and willows protected them from inquisitive eyes on the "Emperor's Path." The spring day was exhilarating, and the Gnadensee smiled up at the bright sky. Abbot Berno turned the wheelchair to face the lake, and sat down beside it in the young grass on the shore.

Externally, everything was as it had been on that day, some time ago, when Hermann's words about ruling and serving had led to a calamitous misunderstanding—

which in turn, thanks to each man's acknowledgment of his guilt, had brought about a mutual understanding and a friendship in the Lord that had not existed before.

"Was it a coincidence that Berthold caught a white dove for you, Hermann, and that a white dove met us a second time?" the abbot asked, pensively.

"Do coincidences exist, Father Abbot? Does not everything, no matter how tiny it may be, belong somehow or other to the great plan of God's love?"

"A white dove?"

"Even a white dove!"

"Good." The Lord Berno's ring almost slipped off his finger, and he pushed it higher up. "Everything has its meaning in the plan of God's love. Then let me meditate a little on the white dove ..." Hermann, Hermann (he reflected), there were no coincidences—and the ring, the sign of his abbatial dignity had become much too wide for him. There were no coincidences.

But the abbot did not mention the ring. He said:

"The white dove over the dark parapets could be seen as a metaphor for a human being who rises up above the dark parapets of physical distress and afflictions, because his desiring and his loving have remained pure in the grace of the Holy Spirit. He can fly. And he ascends higher and higher in order to bring back home a blessing from the light, the love, and the peace.

"When you were a young man, Hermann, you wanted to fly away like a little bird. And now you are charged to spread out your wings. Listen to me, my dear son in Christ: You must ascend higher and higher out of the depths. No matter what may happen on Reichenau, you must not be content to remain in the depths and complain. You must ascend, you must rise above the dark parapets and bring back home a blessing for the abbey of Saint Mary on Reichenau, which needs blessing ... needs it, for otherwise, the rich meadow[4] will turn into a barren wilderness in which the life of grace can no longer grow."

The lame man was shocked by the urgency of this interpretation, which sounded like a testament.

He asked, while his whole being trembled, "Father, can a dove fly if its wings are fettered?"

"Your fetters fell off a long time ago, Hermann. You are free. You must fly, and you can fly."

Once again, the abbot found it difficult to keep hold of his ring, which threatened to slip off his finger. That is how your entire life's work is, Berno (he told himself). It is slipping away from you. And what remains? What remains of your forty years of working, praying, and making sacrifices on Reichenau? Have I not become poorer than the young monk Berno in Pruem? Am I poor enough to be permitted to hope in God's mercy?

The lame man looked down at the Father, at the figure that huddled in the grass, at the stooped shoulders that were almost like his own, at the white hair. What ought he to say? The Father knew that Hermann would entrust himself wholly to the will of God as long as he lived. The dove would fly, when the grace of God bore it upward.

The Lord Berno began to speak again: "You once spoke to me at a grave moment, not far from here. Only a few months have passed since then, but I have traveled a long way in that time, my son. We stood by the Gnadensee,

---

4. [The name "Reichenau" means "rich meadow."]

which belongs to you in such a way that I am inclined to call you 'Hermann of the Gnadensee.' And you reminded me of the real task of an abbot, which is not to rule, but to serve, to serve for His sake, to serve Him in those who are His. Tomorrow, a man is coming who has been given power, and who is therefore exposed to the same temptation, the great and dangerous temptation to forget the charge he has received, the mission with which God has entrusted him.

"To rule by serving, to serve by ruling.—The proud human mind does not find it easy to get the balance right. Those who have power succumb again and again to the temptation to claim for themselves the honor that belongs only to the Most High. There is no ordination and no high office that can protect them from that temptation, not even the highest ministry in the Church of Christ, that of Peter's successor.

It is necessary to pray, to pray a great deal, especially for those who represent Our Lord on earth and who are exposed to the temptation of power. Must they not give a very strict account of themselves? Is it not terrible that they must give an account, before the eternal Judge, of every soul that is entrusted to their care?

"I am grateful to you for having the love and the courage to speak so openly to me, Hermann! I was taking a dangerous path. I wanted to consolidate my office with harshness and force, rather than with humility and love."

"Father Abbot, you have made up a hundredfold to the brethren whatever your excessive strictness may have failed to give them in the past. The brethren of good will are devoted to you in reverence and in grateful love, and in you they honor Our Lord."

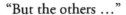
"But the others …"

"No abbot will ever have the good fortune to win the hearts of all the monks. There will always be some who insist on hardening their hearts against him."

"Is not even one monk … too many? It is of course true that they all bow down before the one to whom the external authority, the office, has been given. But are their souls bowing down before Christ, when he, in the person of the abbot, demands obedience from them? Are they serving Christ? Or are they merely motivated by human prudence when they adapt to the wishes of the powerful man—for that is all they see in the abbot—without thinking of Christ? Are they opening up to the Lord in humility and love? I see that you do not dare to tell me that the answer is 'yes'!

"Hermann, how powerful the human will is! I would like to go down on my knees before those brethren and beg them: 'Open up to God!' But all I can do is to weep before the closed doors of their hearts, because their hardness and their pride degrade God to a powerless beggar …

"And then I am afraid that I may not have made use of all the possibilities I had to help them."

"Father, God does not ask anything impossible of you. It is only human beings who do that. God wants us to do what we are capable of doing."

The Lord Berno had closed his eyes, and he did not notice that his ring had slipped down onto the grass.

"But … who can give us the certainty that we have truly done what we are capable of doing?"

"We are not given certainty. We are permitted to hope and to trust. God is mercy …"

The abbot now felt that his right hand had become

lighter. He opened his eyes in surprise, saw his empty ring-finger, and began to look for the ring in the grass on the shore. There it lay, the shining little piece of metal, decorated with a sparkling gem, the sign of his abbatial dignity. He still had his pectoral cross. He nodded.

"Yes, Hermann, we must entrust our humanity to the Lord, to his cross, to his love, and to his ... mercy. Everything else ..."

He lifted the ring and weighed it in the hollow of his hand, as if he wanted to estimate its weight. "Everything else that sometimes seems important to us must pass away, must be taken away from us, in order that we may experience the full truth of what I once wrote: 'I am made for God, and God is love.'"

Slowly, the Lord Berno put the ring back on his finger and stood up, supporting himself on the wheelchair.

"There is one other thing I wish to say to you in this hour, my dear son in Christ ... When one is surrounded by people who have drawn narrow boundaries for the Lord, it is good to encounter someone who has stopped drawing boundaries, and who hands himself over to God without reserve. One can entrust one's tiredness and one's poverty to him, so that he can bring all the distress to the Lord. Hermann, I have often thanked him for you."

In silence, the abbot steered the wheelchair back to the abbey. The sick man felt strangely empty and exhausted. Had he not thrown his entire being onto the scales, in order that the Father might find peace? What was he required to give now?

The monastery porter was watching impatiently for their arrival. He spoke agitatedly: "The Lord and Father Abbot of Einsiedeln has just arrived."

"Thank you, Brother. I shall go to him at once," replied Abbot Berno calmly. Then he bent down once more to the lame man: "Are you my praying Moses in the monastery church tomorrow, while I receive the emperor at the Herrenbruck harbor, my son?" he asked quietly.

The tall figure straightened. The Lord Father Abbot and Imperial Prelate, the master of Reichenau, strode with dignity to the guesthouse.

Hermann did not follow him with his eyes. He was looking at a white dove that tirelessly circled the tower. Her plumage shimmered in the sun, and the sky above her was bright and clear, like a promise that brought consolation.

When a heart loves, everything speaks to it of God. He sensed the great coherence, the unity of all that existed.

"Without the Word came nothing that came to be." Berthold read this sentence on the wax tablet after he had put Hermann to bed for the night and tidied up the cell. A second sentence was written below it: "In him, everything becomes so simple."

"In him, everything becomes so simple." The Brother would have asked for an explanation, but the great silence had already begun ... In him, everything becomes so simple.

"

The island monastery awoke to the new day earlier than usual. Everyone who lived there, from the prior to the youngest scholar, was excited, with the exception of two persons. Abbot Berno and the lame man prayed and sang with complete composure, as if the emperor were not at

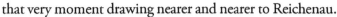

that very moment drawing nearer and nearer to Reichenau.

A smiling spring morning shone over the blessed island when the splendid ship of the emperor approached from Constance.

The Lord Berno was pale after a sleepless night, but his voice sounded firm, and he strode rather than walked. He was almost a head taller than his monks and his guests. His right hand clutched the golden pectoral cross. His furrowed face was serene and relaxed; weariness and fear had given way to a warm joy. The one who was coming was his friend, and he would spend his monastery's festival day with him. There were no longer any somber and heavy thoughts to oppress his soul. It sang a secret *Te Deum*.

The bells of the island churches began their resonant song. A mighty hymn surged up in praise of the Lord.

The solitary adorer, the sick man in his choir stall in the monastery church, felt as if the song of the bells was taking hold of him and lifting him out of the distress and narrowness of earthly existence.

The dove was flying, the white dove with the fettered wings, the dove that nevertheless was free. She was flying. Far below her were the dark parapets of physical distress and afflictions. They sank down. The darkness sank down and became an unsubstantial depth.

The light increased and became ever brighter. The dove ascended higher, until its white plumage was immersed in the dazzling light of the Godhead.

Hermann had lost all awareness of his own self. His prayer was a pure devotion to the eternal love, freed from the fetters of earthly demands, words, thoughts … light, flame. And his self-forgetfulness became a power. His self-surrender became an invitation to God's love, and the utter powerlessness of the gift he made of himself became a penetration into the freedom and the richness of the divine grace.

"

Abbot Berno wanted to fall to his knees before the emperor, but he bent down and clasped him in his arms. "My friend!" said the Lord Henry.

And the bells of Reichenau sang their sacred song.

The Miraculum[5]

Bishop Theoderich of Constance consecrated the church of Saint Mark, and Abbot Berno celebrated the holy Eucharist. The emperor assisted with devotion at the celebration. He was visibly moved by the generous width and the austere dignity of the new church, and impressed by the sublime ceremonies of the consecration.

The choir of monks sang the chants of the Mass. All at once, everyone pricked up their ears, and even the less pious abandoned their vain thoughts.

"*Credo in unum Deum ...*"[6]

One single male voice sang the principal parts of the creed, and the choir responded. The voice came from a distance that was not spatial. It ascended from a faith that was very ardent and profound.

A believer was adoring here, venerating the mystery of the Incarnation of God from Mary the Virgin:

5. ["miracle."]
6. ["I believe in one God ..."]

"*Et incarnatus est de Spiritu sancto ex Maria Virgine et homo factus est ...*"[7]

The lame man's head was raised and his eyes shone as he sang these words.

Perhaps because the singers were too deeply moved by the exultation that was so clearly perceptible in this voice, the choir failed to come in at the proper time. The singer repeated the same words. Then he sang them a third time, and finally Gunter gave the choir the signal that they were to sing:

"*Crucifixus etiam pro nobis sub Pontio Pilato ...*"[8]

The soloist fell silent, and the choir of monks finished the creed.

At the words "*Crucifixus etiam pro nobis,*" the sick man suddenly collapsed, although Berthold was holding him. He slumped forward in the choir stall like a dead man.

"*Crucifixus etiam ...*"

With the unconscious man in his arms, Berthold made his way through the staring crowd. He would have liked to cry out: "Let me through!" The crowd was inquisitive; they huddled together and were unwilling to make way for him.

"*Crucifixus etiam pro nobis ...*"

That was surely how they had stared at the Lord as he died on the cross.

"

7. ["And he was made incarnate by the Holy Spirit of the Virgin Mary, and became man ..."]

8. ["And he was crucified for us under Pontius Pilate ..."]

Once he was out in the courtyard, Berthold stopped with his burden. Was the Father still alive? His head was slack and hung backward. His face was deathly pale, and the closed eyelids had a bluish color. His mouth was half-open, his lips were drained of blood. The Brother laid the lame man softly down on the flagstones, put his ear to his breast, and listened anxiously for the beating of Hermann's heart. The heart was beating weakly and irregularly. His breath was very thin.

With some effort, Berthold lifted the unconscious man and carried him into his cell, where he laid him on his hard bed and massaged his brow with a strong-smelling essence. Many anxious minutes passed before Hermann opened his eyes. Memory returned to his eyes, and he murmured something.

Berthold bent down to him. "Do you want something, Father?"

"Poor Berthold, I have deprived you of a wonderful celebration," whispered the monk.

Berthold was so moved and embarrassed that he moved hastily backward and overturned the little jug with the essence. A pungent smell at once filled the cell, causing them to cough and sneeze. The Brother was more strongly affected than the sick man. While he rubbed his watery eyes, he heard the sick man's quiet whisper: "You are indeed a powerful healer, Berthold."

Coughing and snorting, Berthold wiped up the pool of fluid and opened the door wide to let fresh air in. The *Salve Regina,* the closing canticle of the liturgy in the church, could be heard from the monastery church across the inner courtyard.

Despite his weakness, the lame man listened, as happy

as a child that has just received a present. Then he told the Brother to go quickly to the community of monks.

"I shall recover on my own in this fresh and spicy air. Close the door of the cell, so that I may have what remains of it."

He was joking—and that meant that the worst was over. Berthold obeyed at once. He wanted to see the emperor making his entrance into the chapter room.

It was only when Berthold had left that the sick man permitted himself a sighing groan. He had successfully deceived the Brother, who could thus take part at least in the general joy of the celebration. In reality, however, Hermann did not feel like making jokes. Once again, the waves of the Gnadensee rolled over him. The quick sequence of jolts of pain, the whirlwind of his pains that knocked the breath out of him, sent him through heights and depths. But he hoped that the Father Abbot would be joyful and strong on his great day. That would be enough, that would be enough …

He did not even wonder whether the assembled company would miss him. The breakneck journey through the waves of his Gnadensee did not allow him much time for thinking.

All he could do was to endure, to hold out, to emerge for a moment from a trough in the pains, to breathe again, and then to be submerged anew.

The pains gradually subsided, the attack lessened. Abbot Berno arrived.

"Hermann?"

"Father?" The labored answer was itself a question.

"The emperor wishes to see you and to speak with you."

"Tomorrow … please … tomorrow. Today, I belong

to the Gnadensee," replied Hermann languidly. He attempted to smile, as if he were asking for pardon for his inability to come.

The Lord Berno felt helpless. What could he do for the sufferer? He could dry his moist brow, give him a little wine, or make his bed more comfortable.

"You have undertaken too much, my dear son," said the abbot quietly.

"God knows his donkey, Father," joked the sick man. "He knows how much he can and must load onto me."

"

Abbot Berno informed the emperor that Hermann of Altshausen was unable to receive him, since he was having an audience at that moment with a much higher Lord. He had to suffer much. He asked the Lord Henry to graciously be patient until the following day.

With the secret displeasure of one who never needed to wait, Henry III furrowed his dark brows. "It is a very fragile *miraculum* that you have on your Reichenau, Lord Berno."

The abbot looked musingly at the determined face of the monarch, who knew how to guide the destinies of the peoples—and, at the appropriate time, the destiny of the Church too—with such a firm hand. It was a face that spoke of the power the emperor had amassed and of his decisiveness in action. Abbot Berno addressed this face with a wise gentleness: "Are not God's miracles greatest when they are made known in human weakness?"

The Emperor Henry shrugged uneasily. "That may be the case, Lord Berno. But do not lead me onto the field of theology, for a warrior and ruler always feels uncertain there. That is when I need my court chaplain. I am now all the more eager to see your *miraculum*."

Bishop Theoderich of Constance, who had formerly been the emperor's chancellor and confidant, felt obliged to warn him: "You will be shocked by his appearance, my Lord Emperor. Hermann is a poor wretch, crook-limbed and sick, and almost completely lame."

Can a weak cripple be in any way congenial to the nature of a master? Does not the Lord Henry love only the strong and the healthy?

But the emperor rejected the objection. "I have already heard that. And that is precisely why I admire his great achievements in the sciences."

The Abbot of Saint Gallen remarked casually: "Not everyone agrees that Hermann is the greatest scholar of our age." Some names from his own monastery lay on the tip of his tongue.

Abbot Berno smiled a scarcely perceptible smile, and turned to his guest. "Is Hermann the greatest scholar of our age? Reverend Lord and Brother, that is a question I have never asked myself, because I regard it as of secondary importance. He has made the best use of his rich talents in every field. But he has never striven for greatness and fame. He studied and wrote, composed and drew, constructed his apparatuses and his musical instruments, his clocks and his astrolabe, with the joy and the self-forgetfulness of a child ... and with the glowing zeal of a lover, who aims at God and seeks him through all that he does. He knows nothing at all of his greatness in the world of the intellect. That is why I do not see the *miraculum* in his scholarship, my Lord Emperor ..."

The emperor looked at him questioningly, without attempting to conceal his expectancy. What else could the *miraculum* be?

"… but rather in the glorious inner freedom that allows him to triumph over the terrible fetters of his sickness. He presents a picture of bodily weakness, of helplessness, of powerlessness, of one abandoned. His appearance may at first sight be shocking, but one who truly gets to know him and who sees deeper, knows that the one who meets Hermann is receiving a gift."

"And therefore: a *miraculum*, Lord Berno," observed the Abbot of Einsiedeln.

"Your judgment amounts to a canonization," added Bishop Theoderich.

"Yes, a *miraculum*, my Lord Emperor and Reverend Lord Brothers, but a *miraculum* of the love of God, which led him to this inner freedom—and which at the same time *is* this freedom. Hermann of Altshausen's life displays to us the meaning of some words that I once wrote: 'I am made for God, and God is love.'"

"Would it be possible for Hermann to write a world chronicle for us, a book that contains all the great events since the birth of the Lord, Abbot Berno?" asked the emperor. "The events in time are also a path from God and to God."

"He has already begun such a work, my Lord Emperor. He has done much preliminary work, and he attempted to compose an initial chronicle. But he was not content with it, because there were difficulties in the computation of time. In order to exclude inaccuracies, he drew up for his own use tables with the events in the computation of time of the Romans, the Greeks, the Jews, the Arabs, and the Christians. I too learned a great deal from his first chronicle. He never takes sides. Where there are bad things, he calls a spade a spade, even in the Church. In the form of his expression, he makes no borrowings from the writers of classical antiquity. He has a style of his own, allowing him to make essential points in few words."

"My Lord Abbots, your conversation about Hermann of Altshausen has made me even more eager to meet the *miraculum*," said the Lord Henry. "And I shall not permit you to deprive me of that, my former Lord Chancellor Theoderich. That was surely not your intention? Well, that was how your words sounded. Lord Berno, you were the only one who let the *miraculum* be a *miraculum*." The emperor looked at them with a slight smile, but Abbot Berno was the only one who returned his gaze without embarrassment. "Forgive me, my Lords, I am no theologian, but I do believe that one should keep one's eyes and one's heart open for the miracles of God, wherever and however he may wish to perform them."

The emperor rose and asked Abbot Berno to accompany him. The other Lords bowed deeply before the monarch. When they reached the inner courtyard, Henry III breathed more freely. "Now we will have a good talk, my dear friend. I am convinced that I have left the spiritual Lords with enough topics of conversation." He laughed.

"You have certainly succeeded in doing so, my Lord Emperor," said Abbot Berno, with a slight note of reproof in his voice.

"Do not hold it against me! I was tired of hearing their objections to your *miraculum*."

The emperor and the abbot spent a long time walking up and down in the inner courtyard. When the emperor noticed that the abbot was growing tired, he offered him his arm. They did not speak about military campaigns and conquests; they spoke about eternal matters. At one point, the emperor asked the abbot: "Whom do you consider worthy to be the next to sit on the throne of Peter? Could you give me a name?"

"That is a weighty question, my Lord Emperor. But I have reflected in silence, and prayed ..." The Lord Berno hesitated.

"And which name did you discover in the presence of God?"

"The name of a young bishop. I have met him only once, and yet I know him ... Bishop Bruno of Toul."

"The son of the count of Egisheim? That is strange, Lord Berno. I too have thought of him. Bishop Bruno is pious, prudent, and energetic."

"And he is an adherent of the reforms of Cluny."

The emperor said, calmly: "If you were younger, Lord Berno, I would have thought of you."

The abbot blushed and shook his head in confusion. "How absurd, my Lord Emperor ... Forgive me for using that word. But such a choice would be a disaster for the entire Church of Christ."

"I have the impression that you know your spiritual son Hermann better than you know your own self, my friend. You underestimate yourself."

The abbot attempted to put an end to this embarrassing conversation: "Thank God I am an old man, my Lord Emperor."

"But I hope that you have many years left for Reichenau and for me, Lord Berno. An emperor has few genuine friends."

The abbot looked the emperor directly in the eye. "God has allowed me to exercise my ministry on Reichenau for forty years, my Lord Emperor. Today, my dearest work, the building of the monastery church, was consecrated. Have I not fulfilled what the Lord charged me to do? I almost think that the time has come … Please remain the kindly patron of our abbey, even when another abbot is in office."

"No!" the emperor cried vehemently, taking the abbot's two hands in his own. "Lord Berno, it is too soon for you to leave us!"

"When God calls one, one must bow to his will, no matter who one is …"

The Lord Henry fell silent and looked down at the ground. Then he said: "Yes, no matter who one is, he must leave everything and follow the call of God … even the emperor."

"He will find in God what he leaves here."

"

Berthold carried as many books and parchment rolls into the lame man's cell as his arms would bear.

"What are you doing?" asked Hermann, who was at his work desk.

The Brother carefully lowered the mountain of books onto the sick man's bed.

"The emperor is on his way to you …"

"Yes, I am aware of that. But that does not explain why you are so busy."

The young monk was surprised. "Ought not the Lord Henry to get to know your works, Father?"

"If that is his wish, Father Abbot will show him them in the library. Do you believe that our Lord the Emperor is interested in all these writings?"

"The emperor ought to see how much you have written and to admire you ..." Berthold faltered. The master's eloquent look confused him.

"And admire me? No, that is not what he ought to do. Bring the books quickly back to the place where they belong!"

Hermann gave the order in a strict tone of voice, and the Brother hurried away with his burden, disappointed and crushed. He did not see the friendly smile on the Father's face. "Berthold is really a big child, a good big child ..."

"

Shortly after this, the emperor stood on the threshold and looked around. He was visibly moved as he noted the clean, austere poverty of the room. Abbot Berno then accompanied him to the lame man's work desk. Like every visitor, the emperor had to move into Hermann's field of vision, so that the lame man could see him.

The abbot had forewarned him, while they were still in the cloister: "Hermann cannot turn round to greet you, my Lord Emperor. Would you go up to him?"

The Lord Henry gave the sick man his hand, but did not allow him to kiss it. Accordingly, Hermann only bent down, and his ingenuous blue eyes, shining with reverence and gentleness, met Henry III, the *Imperator mundi.*[9] The brilliant face almost made the emperor forget the crooked figure. The emperor thought back to the abbot's words. He had not said too much about this Hermann. His face spoke of an inner freedom, an assured serenity and cheerfulness. This man must be sheltered in the love of God, where he was at home and free—free in spite of his suffering.

"What are you working on at the moment, Father Hermann?"

"On a Sequence for Easter, my Lord Emperor. I already have the words, but now I am working on the melody. I believe that it ought to move forward joyfully, increasing in volume and in speed. For what could give us more reason to rejoice than the fulfillment of our redemption through the resurrection of Our Lord Jesus Christ?"

The emperor read aloud: "*Rex Regum Dei Agne, Leo Juda magne ...*"[10] When he came to the words: "Make us worthy of this mystery ...," he interrupted his reading and looked up. "The real reason for my being here, Hermann of Altshausen, is that I wanted to thank you ..."

The sick man was astonished. "You want to thank me? My Lord Emperor, what reason could you have to thank me?"

"Through your chants at the holy sacrifice of the Mass, Brother, you have given a child of the world a notion of what heaven is, above all through your Credo ... and through your marvelous canticle about the Mother of mercy. Do you have a copy for me?"

Hermann looked questioningly at the abbot, who gave

9. ["Ruler of the world."]
10. ["King of kings, Lamb of God, great Lion of Judah ..."]

him permission with a sign. The crooked hands found a parchment among the various writings on the work desk and gave it to the Emperor. Henry III took it from him and handled it with care.

"*Salve Regina, Mater misericordiae ...,*"[11] he read aloud. "The words and the melody inspire the heart with confidence ..."

Abbot Berno felt glad. Had he not understood the emperor better than the other prelates? For all his thirst for power, Henry was a man of deep faith.

"Are you not entitled to have an especially intimate confidence in the Mother, my Lord Emperor? It is her Son that you are serving in your high office. And that," the lame man said simply, "is why Our Lady loves you from the heart."

The emperor brushed his dark hair from his angular brow and hid his face in his brown hand. He seemed sunk in thought. The abbot and his lame monk prayed for him. In the poor cell, Henry examined in the presence of God what he did and what he was.

"Do I serve the Son of the most blessed Virgin Mary?" The emperor's dark eyes looked directly at the cripple. "Hermann, you see things too simply, and you see me as nobler than I am. I had three Popes deposed in Sutri, and I appointed Clement on the basis of my own absolute power."

"What you did was right. You wanted to save the Church from her threefold fragmentation, and you gave us a Pope of high morals and piety."

"And I will give her a new Pope once again. I want

---

11. ["Hail, O Queen, Mother of mercy ..."]

what is good. The highest office in the Church ought not to be bartered for money, and the Pope ought not to be a plaything of the Roman aristocracy. But am I not acting in a very violent manner?"

The monk looked at his emperor as if he wished to console him. "You must act in this way, my Lord Emperor, since it is impossible for the Church of Christ at present to confer this office freely on a worthy man. This means that you are the arm of God. Since you want what is good, what you do will endure before God."

"It is true that I want what is good … but is my intention selfless and pure?"

"Our knowledge and our action always have defects, my Lord Emperor. Often, it is only our longing that is pure. And is not our longing the only real action we human beings perform? It opens the door through which God can enter. One who wants to be good, one who wants to love, will be loved by him."

The emperor addressed the cripple with a confidentiality that he never otherwise displayed: "Now, I must thank you once again, Brother Hermann. You have given me more in this brief hour than you can imagine … Do not forget me and the empire in your prayers. Pray for a good Pope, and ask that I may receive something of your freedom.

"Let me entrust one more request to you. Your Father Abbot has told me that you have already done much of the preliminary work for a world chronicle. Write it, Hermann, write it soon at my request and on my commission. You have already written an exquisite little book about my father, the Lord Conrad. Do you know what I most admired in that book?"

The sick man looked at him helplessly. How could he know the answer to this question? He himself did not find his little book admirable at all.

"In this account of life of the Emperor Conrad II, you did not pay him back for what he did to Reichenau and its abbot. In that respect too, you were free!"

Henry III gave the lame man his hand as he turned to leave. Then he hesitated. "You are a priest, are you not?"

Abbot Berno replied for him: "Hermann is a priest, my Lord Emperor."

"Then give me your priestly blessing!"

The Emperor Henry III knelt down on the stone floor of the poor cell, while the sick man spoke the words of blessing and traced the sacred sign of the cross over the head that wore the imperial crown.

"

In the cloister, the abbot walked in silence beside the emperor, who likewise said nothing. When they were approaching the library, he asked: "May I show you Hermann's works?"

"No, Lord Berno, I have seen and heard enough to know him and to agree wholeheartedly with your judgment. He is a *miraculum*. I felt just now that he was looking through me, down into the depths of my soul."

"He saw you in the love of God."

"And that is precisely why I felt small before him. The criteria of human greatness disappear in the love of God. All that remains is a human being stripped of all his earthly dignity, a human being in the presence of God."

The emperor looked absently at the sunny inner courtyard and the columns that gave shade in the cloister.

"Your spiritual son, this poor, distorted man, possesses the gift of bringing out the best in us. The pure longing for God is awakened. With his gentleness, he overwhelms the rigid rules that our self-seeking employs to keep the door anxiously closed against the Lord."

The Emperor Henry III walked toward the monastery church. Before they entered the west wing through the side entrance, he turned once more to the abbot.

"Lord Berno, I thank you for bringing me to him! This meeting was both painful and joyful. It embarrassed me, and it consoled me. I will never forget it In my good hours, when I am close to God, it will be present to me, and I will compare the fetters on my existence with the freedom of your son."

"

The sick man laid the Easter Sequence aside. He had to yield to the urgent pleading of his heart, and sing a new canticle to his Mother Mary. It was she who opened in human hearts the doors that were closed to the Lord. For the Lord, she was the gate that opened onto the earth. For human beings, she was the *porta caeli,* the gate of heaven.

The canticle was also meant as a gift for Father Abbot, who had stood behind the young emperor like a silent shadow ...

"

The Brother waited expectantly for his Master to tell him about the emperor's visit. Instead, he heard the request: "Could you write down a canticle for me, my son? I will dictate it to you first for the wax tablet, but then you must write it very beautifully and decorate it with an elaborate initial. Take the best parchment for it!"

Berthold thought: "No doubt, the canticle is for the emperor."

With lengthy pauses, Hermann dictated a new Marian canticle to him.

"*Alma Redemptoris Mater, quae pervia caeli porta manes et stella maris ...* Loving Mother of the Redeemer, you who remain the gate that gives access to heaven, and the star of the sea, help the people that falls down and tries to rise up again."

This petition was followed by a praise of Mary's dignity as the inviolate and virgin Mother of God, who had once been greeted by Gabriel in Nazareth and the request that she might now obtain mercy for the sinners ...

While Berthold transferred the canticle onto the parchment, Hermann gave the words a tenderly wafting melody.

"The melody is virginal, like the words," said Berthold admiringly.

"Thank you for your help, my son. Now please bring the canticle to ..."

The Brother's enthusiasm led him to interrupt too hastily: "To the emperor!"

Hermann corrected him calmly: "To Father Abbot."

The young monk departed shamefacedly. The Lord Bruno was in his apartment. The emperor had already gone to bed, and the abbot wanted to make use of the long evening for study. But he showed no displeasure when Hermann's messenger entered.

"Do you bring me news from your Master, Brother?"

"Master Hermann sends you this canticle, Father

Abbot," replied Berthold respectfully, as he handed him the parchment.

The old man's eyes looked kindly at the young man. How faithfully and selflessly Berthold served the lame man! A faithfulness of that kind was not an everyday virtue, even in a monastery. When Hermann's attacks became frequent, the Brother was often obliged to stay away from the fellowship of the brethren for days on end, and to devote himself exclusively to the care of the sick man.

Abbot Berno looked steadily at Berthold, until the young monk felt uncomfortable. The abbot's eyes tested him and weighed him up, as if he was pondering some grave matter.

"You have an excellent teacher in theology, do you not?"

"Lord and Father Abbot, the Master continually showers gifts on me out of the rich treasury of his knowledge. I must, of course, add that I am not always as good at receiving as he would wish me to be."

"That is not how I see it, Brother. You have done your honest best, and you are certainly not poor in knowledge. That is why I believe that the time has come to confer the sacred ordination to the priesthood on the professed monk Berthold."

Berthold could hardly believe his ears. "Father Abbot, I ... I ..." he stammered. "I thank you with all my heart, and I am ready with all my joyful heart."

"Good, then hurry to tell your Master."

Berthold had seldom carried out a command so literally. He hurried: he ran through the cloister and only just avoided bumping into an older monk.

"Excuse me, Father ...," he gasped, and ran on. The old monk shook his head as he looked after him. These young monks nowadays ...

"

Without knocking, Berthold rushed into the corner cell.

"What a hurry you are in ...!"

"Father, Father, I am to be ordained," he cried, breathless and overjoyed. "And I am to be allowed to take my vows!"

"Sit down beside me first, and then tell me everything."

Berthold obeyed, and told him what the abbot had said. He also mentioned his discomfort under the abbot's scrutinizing look. Hermann listened attentively. Berthold seemed unaware that he had spoken to the abbot on his behalf: he wanted his most faithful pupil to be ordained.

"I look forward to ... your first priestly blessing, my dear son."

"You want *me* to bless *you*? But that is impossible!" stuttered the Brother.

The lame man laughed heartily at the confusion of his companion. "Why should that be impossible? Ah, I know! You have just realized that I am too much of a sinner. Before you bless me, I would like you to hear my confession."

"Never!" cried Berthold, with unusual vehemence.

"Let me stop joking ... Berthold, you will soon be a priest, and then you will be allowed to perform a different service. A priest should not be a nurse who carries out the most menial services for a lame man. Be quiet, my son.

You will obey. You will do what the abbot charges you to do—and you will do it with at least a *super*natural joy."

"You want to have another helper, Father," muttered Berthold darkly.

"You foolish young man, if only you knew ..." Hermann pretended to be angry as he berated him. "What you do know is that it would be a great sacrifice for me, if I had to do without you!"

The Brother's face lit up. "And do you truly suppose that our good Father Abbot would demand such a sacrifice of you? No, I am convinced that he will not ask it of you, if I tell him what you have just said."

"You are too clever for your own good!" The sick man laughed as he shook his finger at Berthold. "Woe betide you, if you say one single word of this to the abbot! And a willful young man like this wants to become a priest soon!"

Berthold nodded pensively. "Yes ... And strangely enough, Father, I ask myself all the time who suggested to Father Abbot that I should be ordained now. Do you know anything about this?"

The lame man did not reply. The two monks smiled at each other, each knowing that the other knew.

"

In the meantime, Abbot Berno had read the lame man's canticle to the sublime Mother of the Lord. He understood what Hermann had meant by giving him this gift. He was pointing the abbot to Mary and telling him to entrust himself completely to her "before the ending of the light," *lucis ante terminum ...*

"

When the monks sang these words at Compline, the aged abbot lifted his head and looked for the little figure in the choir stall on the other side.

"Your evening prayer to Our Lady came just at the right time. The light of my day will soon be over, Hermann. I can feel it ... the shadows are growing longer."

* * *

CHAPTER 8

THE ETERNAL CITY

The Harp Falls Silent

"RICH WAS THE ISLAND, when Pirmin the Bishop brought it the sacred grace of Christ ..."

With many hesitations and falterings, Randolf read out the Latin hymn that he had written in honor of Saint Pirmin. It was the outcome of many hours of hard work, and he presented it timorously to the utterly honest verdict of the lame scholar. Hermann listened attentively. Taken as a whole, the verses had an excellent form.

After praising him sincerely, he added: "But there is one reservation I must mention, dear Brother. Have you not made Saint Pirmin too much a man of action, rather than a man of contemplation?"

"But, Master Hermann, was not Saint Pirmin a restless worker for the kingdom of God? Just think how many monasteries he founded!"

"Yes and no, dear Brother. Pirmin was able to do so much for the kingdom of God because he was a man of silence, of contemplation. Great things grow in silence … Is that not what you read in the book that has come down to us, his *Dicta Abbatis Pirminii*?[1] Believe me, it was from his intimate conversation with God that he drew the strength for his apostolic activity. And that must be so. We give what we receive. Look at our Father Abbot. He was very much a man of silence; and he was very much a man of action for four decades, here on Reichenau."

Hermann suddenly fell silent. He looked down at his trembling hands, which were attempting in vain to stretch a string on a harp. The string escaped from his hands and sprang back into place.

"Abbot Berno was a man of silence, and that is why he was a man of action. Now, he is permitted to rest and to dedicate himself more and more to the silence that he has always sought and loved."

Hermann spoke of the abbot as of one who was dead. "He *was* a man of silence."

He took a deep breath and fastened the string on the harp. He touched it lightly, producing a bright tone. When he touched the other strings, they gave out a melody.

"Brother Randolf, I wonder whether Our Lord is answered by such tender sounds when he touches souls with the gentle breath of his Holy Spirit? Often, a heavy

---

1. [Title: "The Sayings of Abbot Pirmin."]

gale is needed, before we give him any answer at all. And is our answer then a harmonious melody? Far from it … discords, the braying of asses! Dear Brother, if only we were more sensitive and receptive to the light breathing of the Spirit!"

Randolf felt confused. If the sick man had such a low opinion of his own response to the call of God, what then was Randolf to think of his own efforts?

"Yes, are we not slower and more obstinate than snails and donkeys when God comes, Brother Randolf?"

The lame man did not wait for an answer. The harp resounded under his hands, which were very skillful, despite their lameness. It sang a melody that recalled the rushing of water, the murmuring of the wind, a kindly voice.

Then the melody changed. It became deeper, sadder … pouring rain, falling leaves, mist, loneliness. It was only now and again that a little ray of light pierced the gray clouds.

The music ended abruptly. While the last dark note died away, Brother Berthold said: "Father Abbot asks you to bring him your notes for the world chronicle."

Hermann at once laid down the harp and reached for a bundle of parchment sheets. Berthold lifted him into his wheelchair.

Randolf opened the cell door for the vehicle. "May I come another time with the hymn, when I have altered it in accordance with your suggestions, Brother?"

"You are always welcome, Randolf." The lame man smiled at him, but the soil from which his smile blossomed forth was a profound sadness.

Randolf took his parchment sheet despondently. Before

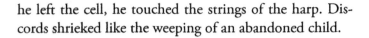

he left the cell, he touched the strings of the harp. Discords shrieked like the weeping of an abandoned child.

"

The old linden tree in the inner courtyard was in bloom, and its sweet fragrance wafted into the cloister, but Hermann did not notice it. He asked his companion almost timidly, in a subdued voice: "Berthold, how … did you find Father Abbot?"

The Brother reflected carefully on how he should reply. What was the point of Father's question, when he himself would shortly be meeting the abbot? And how was he to clothe his impression in words?

"Father, our Father Abbot is far away, somehow. I felt that he was still living in this world, and at the same time, that he was at home in the other world."

Hermann pressed the bundle of parchment sheets to his breast. "You too had the feeling that …"

He did not continue, because the Lord Berno was approaching them in the cloister. In the interplay between light and shade, he seemed almost unearthly. His tall figure stooped forward. His eyes sought the ground. For some days now, his steps had changed their quality. They were more cautious, almost gingerly, as if he had first to test the surface to see whether it would support his feet.

The faithful worker in the Lord's vineyard was tired. He had borne the burden and the heat of the day of Christ for far too long. He stood still and looked with a benevolent kindliness at the lame man and his young companion. Berthold would soon be a priest of the Lord … He would take up the chalice that Abbot Berno's weary hands would no longer be able to hold. The one sacrifice of Christ would continue on Reichenau. It was good to bear that in mind, when one was tired …

The abbot's faded hand pointed to the inner courtyard. "Has our linden tree ever bloomed as it does this year, Hermann? Come, we will look at your notes in its shade."

The Lord Berno sat down, somewhat laboriously, on the round bench. Its wood was gray and brittle after many summers and winters. "I had it made in *Anno Domini* 1030."[2] He brushed the cracked wood with his fingers. "*Anno Domini* 1030 …" Memories overwhelmed him, until Hermann broke the silence by clearing his throat.

"Father Abbot, did you not want to look through the notes?"

"Forgive me, my son. I had forgotten that. Many things are slipping away from me these days, not only my ring." The abbot took the sheets and read some passages at random. The plan Hermann had drawn up said a great deal about the future work.

"Despite all my efforts, some inaccuracies have escaped my notice …"

"That may be, Hermann. But do we not always leave material for those who come after us, so that they can continue the work and improve the building? Those who are reverent will gratefully receive every gift from the past, and those who are not reverent will laugh at such gifts as obsolete things. They are so poor that they do not grasp that while they are sneering, they themselves are becoming the past for others."

The past …

2. ["The Year of the Lord."]

Berno found great and resonant names in the notes; battles and glorious deeds; emperor, kings, wise men, and saints.

The past ...

"*Anno Domini* 1008: the monk Berno from Pruem becomes Abbot of Reichenau."

"Forty years on Reichenau," he murmured, "forty long years! How quickly they have passed!"

"Forty years of blessing for our abbey, an important and significant epoch for our island monastery, a new golden age of scholarship, of art, and of piety, to match the period when Walafried Strabo was abbot."

Abbot Berno laid the sheets down. They rustled like dry leaves.

"Important and significant, Hermann? No, my son." He shook his head gently, but deliberately. "Only one of the events that you will list in your world chronicle, when it is finished, is important and significant: *Qui propter nos homines et propter nostrum salutem descendit de caelis et incarnatus est de Spiritu Sancto ex Maria Virgine et homo factus est.*[3] That is what you must tell people loudly and clearly, because most of them think that they themselves are important and significant ... And the coming of God is *the* event for all of us. It was toward that event that the millennia were hastening until the turn of the ages, and since that event, we walk in the power of his love until his second coming ... the coming that we experience in the process our personal perfect-

3. ["Who, for us human beings and for our salvation, came down from heaven and was made incarnate by the Holy Spirit of the Virgin Mary, and became man."]

ing, and the coming that everyone will see at the end of the ages.

"*Et iterum venturus est cum gloria.*[4]

"Christ alone is important and significant. And it is important and significant that we belong to him, so that he can walk in us through the present age, through this short span of world time.

"The morning light of eternity already shines for the believing heart, which sees in the distance the New Jerusalem, the Eternal City of God.

"Faith, hope, and love are of God—so much so, that they make it impossible for any time to retain its 'today,' or any place its 'here.' The more we belong to the Lord, the more will we be persons who live close to eternity. Indeed, I might almost say that we will be persons who see eternity.

"The things of this time and this world, which can shackle those of an earthly disposition, become transparent to us. We can look through them and see eternity. It is not necessary to grow old, in order to experience this. But it is necessary to love."

Berthold had been right. Abbot Berno was living in other spheres, nourished by a different view of things. In reality, he had already taken his departure.

Hermann did not let the stooped figure of the aged Father under the blossoming linden tree out of his sight. It was as if he was seeing him for the last time. He wanted to ask Berno to remain with him, but he knew that such a request was foolishness. The Lord Berno had already moved on. Might he ask God to be allowed to follow him

---

4. ["And he will come again in glory."]

soon? Or was this a selfish request on the part of a lame cripple?

"You are aware that most of the journeys I undertook were on the emperor's business. Sometimes, I was permitted to accompany the Emperor Henry II to Rome. I was in the city that they call the 'Eternal City,' and I told you about it. The Eternal City ... It is rightly given this name. Rome will pass away, like all the cities on this earth. But it is in Rome that the heart of the Church beats. What is the Church, if not Christ on earth, the love of the Lord, transmitted through those who are his, and in those who are his?

"While I was in Rome I met the Holy Father, the Pope. And I saw in him more than the Vicar of Christ, as canon law understands that term. For me, he is the heartbeat of the Church, throbbing life, a gift of the Holy Spirit. Even the unworthy men who have seized the Chair of Peter from time to time had to serve one and the same faith, without falsifying it ...

"But who is worthy of such an office? Who could claim to be worthy? Indeed, which of us is in any way worthy of the grace of God, and, still less, of a special vocation? None of us, Hermann. None of us. To be called is always, always an unmerited grace of the Lord. It is nothing other than compassion on his part. It is pure mercy.

"In spite of all the human failings, I experienced in Rome how truly the Lord is with us. His love sustains the Church. He who is eternal is more clearly at work in Rome, and that is why it is the Eternal City for me.

"I spent many happy hours in Saint Peter's at the tomb of Peter the Rock, hours that were radiant with joy and ardor in the faith!

"And I also saw the Romans' love for Mary! They taught me what Mary's sacred motherhood can mean for people. Mary, the Mother of the Church, the Mother of the Christ who is on our altars and in our souls, became my Mother in Rome, more than she had been before. Before I visited Rome, she had been too much the Queen. The heart plays a central role in the external form of the homage that her children in southern lands pay her. And we can certainly learn from them how to love Mary in a more childlike manner. You called her '*vita, dulcedo, et spes*'[5] in your Marian canticle, and your love of Mary has much in common with the Romans, although you have a mind that imposes order on things and appears so unemotional."

"Oh, Father Abbot, you know that when I impose order on things, when I try to identify a plan and a system, that is only a way of praising the One who has bestowed order, plan, and system on everything that exists. His law, which he has placed in all things, is love. And even the driest of the formulas that I use in my attempt to give an account of that law does not seek to be anything other than love. I impose order, so that others may be able to love better."

"I know, my son. But you are happy when you have the chance to sing, to play, and to gather colored stones together like a carefree child who has no fixed plans. I wonder if I made you do too much serious work in imposing order on things, when you yourself wanted to create something freely. How many of your songs remained unsung?"

"Not every song got finished, Father Abbot. But I was

---

5. ["life, sweetness, and hope."]

more cunning than you think. I have made colored stones out of my serious and important activity. Whatever I did, I did it only with a view to the big picture. And my mosaic depicts the same face as in Aachen: Christ."

"Christ. He lives. Everything finds its unity in him. The colored stones that we bring to him are the hours of our life, and the apparent variety becomes unity in him, becomes God's own simplicity. We have often spoken about this, Hermann. We believe that all the moments of our life flow into his heart, into his love. Is that not a wonderful consolation at the end of one's way? How great and sublime is the simplicity of God ..."

After these words, the Lord Bruno rose abruptly, lifted his hand as if in blessing, and departed through the sunny inner courtyard. He walked laboriously, a stooped old man, through the superabundance of life.

Hermann, driven by a secret concern about the Father, had himself brought to the monastery church, where he found the abbot kneeling on the ground before the high altar. Abbot Berno's face was peaceful as he prayed. Had he wanted to have a conversation just now, or did he only want Hermann to have a glimpse of his inner world?

"

At the monk Berthold's ordination to the priesthood and his profession, Abbot Berno sat on a throne before the altar, in a dignity that was not of this world, but belonged to a higher sphere. The stiff ceremonial garments, embroidered with gold thread, emphasized the transparency of his figure, which had become smaller; but his voice was strong and vigorous. He preached like one who had power; like one who was permitted to see further than the others; like one who stood on the threshold and knew what would come after this life.

His old eyes lit up in his furrowed, pallid face, as he spoke about the New Jerusalem that was to descend from heaven like a bride.

"Rejoice in the truly 'Eternal City,' in which God himself will be the light. Let all that we do on earth be only a preparation for our homecoming into eternity."

He described the New Jerusalem with warmth and youthful enthusiasm. Suddenly, in the midst of the sublime gravity of his sermon, he paused and smiled. The smile made his old face young and full of life. With a simple, profound gratitude, his eyes sought out the crippled monk in the first choir stall on the left-hand side.

"The Eternal City will nevertheless have its stars, my beloved sons in Christ. Naturally, those stars receive their light from the one light of God. Does not sacred Scripture say: 'Starry-bright forever their glory, who have taught many the right way'? Accordingly, Our Lord Jesus Christ will give his light to those who have taught his son, the priest and monk Berthold, the right way."

"What light will be yours, then, Father?" thought Hermann. "You have led many people to Christ for forty years. I am one of them."

The closing words of the sermon made the entire monastic community shudder. The Lord Berno called out the well-known words of the Apocalypse of John in the monastery church: "*Maran atha!* Come, Lord Jesus, come soon!"

This was no pious formula. This was a prayer both personal and urgent.

"

In the meantime, however, the abbot went about his daily duties. His voice became steadily weaker, and his steps dragged more heavily. He forgot things. But his mind retained its freshness. He could still see and evaluate situations and persons clearly. He noted that some monks were huddling together; and it was not the best monks who were having weighty discussions and whispering secretly. They were discussing his successor. It did not take long for him to discover this, and that was painful enough; but what caused him great concern was that they were thinking of Udualrich in this context. Udualrich as Abbot of Reichenau?

Udualrich had the arrogant harshness of a self-righteous man, and quite apart from his intellectual capacities, he was a crude hedonist. Not even the studies that Abbot Berno had strictly imposed on him had helped to make him a man of the spirit. He treated the sciences as he handled his spoon at mealtimes. In his eyes, whatever promoted his well-being was good.

The Lord Berno had struggled for many years with this difficult character, without succeeding in changing him. Udualrich had indeed submitted to the abbot, but what motivated his submission? The abbot tried in vain to recall one single gesture of warm-hearted and self-forgetful brotherliness, or any indication of a deep religious emotion. Did Udualrich actually give God a place in his life?

One last great anxiety led the tired man to take up his pen. He wrote to the emperor, to the Pope, and to the bishop of Constance with the urgent request that they should do their utmost, for the love of Christ, to see that the abbey would once again receive a true father.

"... an abbot who carries out his office as a father, but in the spirit of the reform of Cluny ..." He himself would soon have to leave his monks. He asked them humbly to forgive all the mistakes that he had made in his long period as abbot. He dispatched express couriers, but no answer came.

This was the final sacrifice that God demanded of him. He had to abandon all his anxiety about the future of Reichenau. It was no longer his task to form and to direct. All he had to do now was to go to God. Silence cloaked him. He understood the Lord, and he submitted willingly. He handed himself over to silence, even before he was welcomed into the silence of eternity. But as long as his heart continued to beat, his silence was a power in the abbey. And when that heart beat for the last time one June day, grief for the Father purged everything that was bad in the community of brethren. They wept for their Father like children; even Udualrich wept.

"

The lame man's grief was so deep that he had no tears. Had the dead man bequeathed him his silence? A feeling of emptiness penetrated him and surrounded him. It was as if he hovered in an infinite space that had no boundaries, no light or darkness, no sound ...

It seemed that he had lost the place that had been his. He leveled no accusation against God, nor did he rebel or protest in his mind. He knew that the Father was at home and safe. Was it for this that he had had to sacrifice his own security? He continued to believe with a childlike naturalness. But where were the hands of God that held him? He believed, but he felt nothing at all that could have made this act of faith light and joyful.

He felt as if he was penetrating further and further into this region of unlimited solitude, into a silence that was immense and impenetrable. It was as if he was falling, like a meteor in outer space. People and things fled from him and became strangely insubstantial. They faded into specters that could not alleviate his inner loneliness.

His hair turned white in these days. He was thirty-five years old.

He crouched without tears in his wheelchair beside the abbot's bier. He spent many hours in the monastery church, looking steadily at the face of his dead abbot. His crooked hands were folded; his prayer repeated the words: "Lord, I thank you that you have given him peace."

But his soul did not ascend with these words. He was recollected, but his recollection resembled the rigidity of a dead man's face.

Were the strings of his harp torn out when the Lord Berno died? Had something in him died when the Father died?

He made no objection when Berthold brought him into his cell. He spoke and ate and worked. He was kindly and willing to help. But the young priest-monk listened attentively to the sound of Hermann's voice, which seemed different.

Berthold could not understand why Hermann did not weep for a man whom everyone mourned—even those who had been his adversaries. Why had he let another monk compose the obituary notice for the Lord Berno that was to be sent to the other monasteries in the fraternal union of prayer? His words were logical enough, but did not Hermann speak like one who did not know what he was saying and doing?

Hermann revealed absolutely nothing of his inner experience to his companion. He found no words for it. How could he explain solitude and emptiness? How could he describe something that did not exist?

Was he really so little interested in what was going on in the abbey? Delegates from many monasteries were expected to attend the solemn funeral ceremonies. When Berthold told him about this, he listened with polite attention, without making any comment. The young monk was bewildered. "It is as if it had nothing to do with him," he thought.

He merely noted down a few neutral sentences for his world chronicle about the long period of government of Abbot Berno, "who was distinguished for his great scholarship and piety."

"

Hermann broke through the wall of his inner silence only once. The assembled brethren were discussing where the body of the departed abbot was to find its last resting place.

Brother Norbert, the abbot's confessor, related the explicit wish of the dying man to be buried in the westwork of the monastery church: "I would like to rest where I spent such a long time, so many years of my life, building."

Many monks murmured their approval, but Father Prior had serious doubts.

"My lords and Brothers, if we grant this wish, we must take up the new flagstones and destroy what has just been finished. The building activity lasted far too long as it is, and it has imposed heavy burdens on our abbey."

The excitement ran like a flame across the gaunt face of the sick man. He straightened himself as far as was possible, put up his trembling right hand, and asked for permission to speak. His voice reached the furthest corners of the chapter room.

"Dear Brothers, ought not the last wish of our Father in Christ to be a sacred obligation?"

Udualrich spoke up. "The costs, Brother," he pointed out. "You are a man who belongs to the other world. Is it necessary to remind you that it is rather unimportant where precisely the earthly body falls into dust?"

With the death of the Lord Berno, the time of Hermann of Altshausen was definitively past, and this celebrated man, this "favorite son" of Reichenau, was to get a taste of the new order of things without delay. Udualrich looked at him with undisguised antipathy, but the sick man's blue eyes met his gaze without resentment or guile.

"You may be right, Brother, as far as the location of *our* last resting place is concerned. But ought we to refuse the tomb in the west-work to our Father Abbot Berno, who gave Reichenau for four decades his heart's blood, his labors and cares, his suffering and loving, his prayer and his sacrifice? Nothing that he could do for us was ever too much for him. Would it not be a special grace if we were to be given a place of remembrance and of meditation there, a place where we can examine in future years whether we are still walking in the spirit of the great reform of Cluny, in the spirit of the Lord Berno, in the spirit of the Lord

Jesus Christ, which is the spirit of love? And precisely in this spirit, is it not essential for the grateful spiritual sons of such a Father to lay him to rest where he asked to rest?

"In order that this may not impose excessive costs on the abbey, Lord Prior, I should like to request your permission to ask the Lady Hiltrud at Altshausen to cover the costs. My lady mother always revered our Father Abbot."

The prior looked in shock at the lame monk. His words had been bold, but they had been spoken in a modest tone. For the first time, he and the brethren in the chapter room noticed the cripple's white hair.

Udualrich looked around uncertainly. He read assent on the faces of the monks. Hermann had won, and the dead man was still a power to be reckoned with.

The prior granted the lame man's wish.

"

"How disgraceful, Father, that our rich abbey lets the burial crypt of its abbot be paid for by your lady mother!" said Berthold, once they were in Hermann's cell.

The sick man silenced him with a weary gesture. "That will do, Berthold. Do not mention this again. Our Father Abbot will receive a worthy resting place. Many things will happen now, and we shall have to accept them."

And Hermann let things take their course. He fell back into his inner detachment from the affairs of the abbey, and he did not display the slightest sign of unease when Udualrich was elected abbot.

When the monks formally promised him obedience, Hermann bowed in homage over the broad hand of the new abbot, which did not move one inch in his direction.

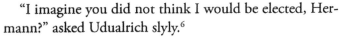

"I imagine you did not think I would be elected, Hermann?" asked Udualrich slyly.[6]

"I expected that you would be elected," replied Hermann calmly.

His voice betrayed no fear, but only a quiet certainty, a great distance.

"Well," said the abbot, with a rush of anger, "we will not hear much about you now. You will play no role, as far as I am concerned. And that means that you will play no role in the abbey."

The blue eyes looked guilelessly up at him, and simultaneously past him. Hermann smiled a quiet, knowing smile that was free of bitterness.

"Thanks be to God, Father Abbot. I have always wished to be in reality what I in fact am, because of my sickness—the last of the poor ones of Christ."

The abbot's brows drew together, and his powerful chin jutted forward. "So ... that is what you have wanted? What if I now take from you your Berthold, who is far too faithful? It is an indignity for a gifted priest to perform the most menial duties for a cripple."

"Yes," Hermann agreed, "that is what I told your predecessor many times. I asked him to give Berthold a more worthy task."

A sound was heard from somewhere in the community of monks, the sound of barely suppressed anger. Berthold?

6. [From this point on in the German text, Abbot Udualrich employs the "du" form when he speaks to Hermann. In other contexts, this form implies friendship, but here it is an expression of contempt.]

"And your loneliness?" Udualrich could scarcely conceal the tension he felt as he waited for the answer.

"Can my loneliness be increased?" asked the lame man. "Lord and Father Abbot, there is a loneliness that not even the most faithful person can banish."

The monks stared at the little, white-haired brother with the shining blue eyes. They perceived that this poor handicapped man dwelt in an unattainable solitude and freedom.

Abbot Udualrich passed the tip of his tongue over his dry lips and murmured: "Prepare the writing of the world chronicle, Brother, as has been arranged. You have done excellent preparatory work for it."

Without noticing what he was doing, he had once again addressed the lame man with the honorific "Ihr" form. He had no desire to humiliate someone who was invulnerable to him. Accordingly, he left the priest-monk Berthold with him.

Where Are We at Home?

The new abbot never took the path to the lame man's corner cell. He never spoke to him when they met. He overlooked him just as deliberately as he overlooked the burial crypt in the west-work, where most of the monks prayed zealously. Reports were brought to him of prayers at the tomb that were heard, and he consciously failed to hear them. The spirit of Abbot Berno was not to have any dwelling place on Reichenau.

Slowly and with great caution, Abbot Udualrich

altered here and there a little of the inheritance of the Lord Berno. He warily loosened the reins of the monastic discipline. In the chapter meeting, he issued warnings against excessive asceticism. When no stimulus is offered, people sooner or later slacken. Abbot Udualrich counted on this, and time worked in his favor. The monks lacked the great model they had had in Abbot Berno, who exemplified the spirit of Cluny.

The new abbot now showed them how, with a certain amount of prudence, it was possible to organize religious life more comfortably, although he kept initially within the framework of the existing regulations. The human reason finds many grounds, apparently objective and just, for avoiding things that are laborious or unpleasant.

The softening began slowly, but it gathered speed and had a profound effect.

The liturgy lost its splendor. The meals of the monks were more ample. Gossiping and laughing monks often stood idly around in the corridors. Their work was not done, or else it was carried out quickly and superficially. The feudal subjects of Reichenau groaned under their increased burdens, and some estates in distant regions were mortgaged in order to cover the increased expenditure. Pilgrims brought the Cluniac Pope Leo in Rome news of the changes on Reichenau.

After one chapter meeting at which Hermann could not take part, Berthold came to him full of consternation. He performed the necessary services for the Father without saying anything, put him in his bed, and gave him something to eat. But the hand that moved the spoon was unsteady.

"Be careful, my son," the sick man warned him in a friendly tone, "or you will spill the soup."

Berthold could no longer contain himself. He threw the spoon down into the bowl so vigorously that the soup splashed.

"I cannot do it! I cannot do it!" he groaned.

The lame man, whose head rested on Berthold's shoulder, as always when he had to feed him, asked tranquilly: "Tell me what is oppressing you. That may make it easier for you to bear."

"He called your book about music bad and inadequate … I did not want to tell you, Father, but if I do not do so, others will take pleasure in telling you."

Hermann's face did not move. "Who is 'he'?" he asked, although he could guess the answer.

"Udualrich … in the chapter meeting just now. And he is the last one who can judge your book!"

"Berthold, no matter what the case may be, you must not withhold the reverent form of address from our Lord and Father Abbot."

The younger monk flared up suddenly: "And he, who himself lacks all reverence, is allowed to call you a superficial writer and a man who thinks he knows a lot? He said that since no one can be at home in every field of knowledge, anyone—like you—who tries to do so will not do justice to any one single field."

The lame man pressed his lips together.

"Be quiet, Berthold, be quiet! Even if the consecrated one of the Lord has committed a fault, you must not speak thus. For us, he is still the one who bears God's commission, the one to whom we owe reverence. God permits much that is all too human in those who are his representatives. We do not hold the office of judge.'"

Berthold was embarrassed, and picked up the spoon again. But he muttered, in one last attempt at self-defense: "There are so many bad things that have happened in our abbey recently, things that are certainly not in accordance with the Lord Berno."

"But they have a bad effect on us only when we refuse to give God what is God's."

The sick man finished his meal. Before Berthold laid him back to rest in the cushions, he had one final question:

"Father, what will happen if a yawning abyss of lovelessness opens up?"

"In that case, my son, you should trust in God and spring into that abyss. You should have the courage to go on loving.—We must pass through immeasurable abysses and endure endless nights, without experiencing with our senses that God is with us. But our trust ..."

A short, hard knock on the cell door startled them. Abbot Udualrich entered the room. Berthold could not rise to his feet, because he was supporting the sick man.

"Are you better, Hermann?" asked the abbot diffidently.

"Thank you, Father Abbot. I am still somewhat weak, but my strength is gradually returning."

The abbot was visibly embarrassed. Did the sick man know what he had just said in the chapter meeting about him and his book? When he had uttered those words, he did not yet realize that he would need this lame man.

"I have just received news that will bring you joy, Hermann, since you love holy Church." He put on a winning smile. "Pope Leo IX has surprised me by accepting the invitation to come in person and consecrate the church on Ergat, which my blessed predecessor began to build. He will then spend some days on Reichenau. That is a great honor for our abbey, is it not?"

"Yes, Father Abbot," replied Hermann briefly.

Udualrich rubbed his broad hands uncertainly. Could not this lame man come to his aid? He surely grasped what the abbot wanted. For if he had not needed him …

"It has occurred to me that you would want to use your talent, and that it would bring joy to your heart, to honor the Holy Father with little masterpieces of poetry and music. Pope Leo IX prizes the fine arts. When he was bishop of Toul, he wrote poems and composed music, in order to enrich the liturgy."

"I did not know that, Father Abbot. I only heard that he was a Cluniac."

Udualrich shot him a piercing glance. Did the lame man say this without any ulterior motive? Or did he sense that this fact diminished all the joy that a visit by the Pope should bring? A Cluniac Pope was coming to Reichenau. Abbot Udualrich shivered secretly.

"Draw up the program for the feast as you think right, Hermann. I trust your wisdom and your skill, and I rely wholly on your mastery. You will hit the right note that satisfies the Pope. What would you say to a *Vita Sancti Adalberti*?[7] Saint Adalbert is the patron of the new church."

"Saint Adalbert of Prague is a great figure, Lord and Father Abbot. There is a lot to be said about him."

---

7. [Title: "Life of Saint Adalbert."]

"Well, then ... get to work, Master Hermann!" The Lord Udualrich sketched a sign of the cross and left the cell.

"Saint Adalbert of Prague ..." The lame man spoke meditatively, as if the first images were already taking shape in his mind.

Berthold had followed the conversation with astonishment and irritation. Now he spoke out: "Father, do not let yourself be exploited. Think of what the abbot said in the chapter meeting. You are a 'superficial writer and a man who thinks he knows a lot,' and now you are to help him out of a difficulty. Surely you see that the task he has given you was not suggested by any kind of positive feelings toward you on his part?"

"My dear son, we must accept the demands of God without making any distinctions, and we must let ourselves be consumed in his service. Why should we reflect on the motivations of those who issue commands? We know the motivation of God in everything that happens—namely, love."

Hermann was startled by his own words, and he paused, as if he had just discovered that he had done something wrong.

The motivation of God was always love ... In that case, the tremendous loneliness in which he lived did not denote a lack of security. God's motivation was always love.

Even in the unfathomable silence that had enfolded him since the death of Abbot Berno, there was a song that sang: "I am made for God, and God is love." He was safe. The song of his life resounded, even if he did not hear it—or at least, not yet.

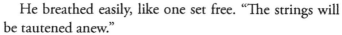
He breathed easily, like one set free. "The strings will be tautened anew."

"What do you mean, Father?"

"The strings of my harp, my son. I will be able to sing again."

"You must sing, because the Pope is coming."

"I can sing because God is coming; because he is here."

Berthold did not understand him. He did not know about the deepest loneliness, about the harp whose strings had split when the Lord Berno died.

"

The sick man worked for weeks on end, until he was utterly exhausted. Berthold brought the abbot in good time the address of welcome and the address of homage that he had requested. Hermann's Latin was mellifluous and easy to understand. The choir studied his canticles, and the *Vita Sancti Adalberti* was copied by several scribes onto fine parchment. Reichenau made ready to welcome the Pope, who was reputed to be a saint.

And then Pope Leo IX came, bringing rich blessings to Reichenau. He finally broke the spell of grief that had lain on the soul of the lame man and showed him the great breadth and holiness of his *oblatio* for the *Missa orbis,* the *consecratio mundi.*[8] Hermann responded to him with the powerful faith and love of a man who had passed through silence and solitude to become more mature, emptier for God and for his grace. The real reason why Pope Leo IX had come to Reichenau was to

8. ["oblation"; "the Mass of the world"; "the consecration of the world."]

meet the lame man, and he asked Berthold to write an account of his life for him.

"

By the time that Hermann had told his companion the story of his life up to the visit of the Pope, the world chronicle that he had written at Leo's request had reached the year 1050. The account had been delayed again and again by other writings, and by illness and weakness.

"Now we have come full-circle. Once again, we are in early spring, dear son, just as in the year 1030, when the lame little bird flew away from Reichenau."

Berthold had brought him to the Gnadensee, to help him recover from the long winter, which had caused him more pain. The waterfowl in the reeds were noisy, but the Gnadensee itself was at rest, silver and smooth with a blue sheen, under the delicate white and blue of the sky. Nature was starting afresh …

"And there is spring in the holy Church too," said the lame man, happily. "Our Holy Father is like a Pentecostal storm that awakens new life everywhere."

"The pilgrims from Rome related yesterday that the Eternal City is able only seldom to keep him inside its walls. He turns up all over the place and checks whether everything is in order."

"He extends the walls of the Eternal City," replied Hermann, "for wherever he is, the heart of the Church beats there."

At the same time, he recalled Leo's request, which went in the opposite direction: "Widen the walls of your cell, until it encompasses Rome."—"Holy Father," he thought, "what are your plans for a poor little monk like me? But

I will love and suffer as best I may, without trying to see the significance of what I can contribute. I will dedicate myself without reserve to the Lord and to his Church. One who gives himself to God must no longer measure and weigh ... with the secret desire of ensuring that he gets his own share."

After the Pope's visit, the monks on Reichenau had begun once more to live in this spirit. The Crucified Lord received incense and chants. All went with him as far as the breaking of bread, but only a few followed him as far as Golgotha. Were there blossoming thorn bushes on Reichenau? Many preferred to uproot the thorns, because sacrifices hurt.

"

In summer of 1030, the Lord Udualrich granted the sick man a favor for which he had not asked.

"Hermann, go with Berthold for some weeks to Altshausen. We wish to give your lady mother this pleasure, which she had in the days of Abbot Berno."

The abbot basked in his own generosity. But inwardly, he was relieved to be rid for a time of the tiresome admonitions of a monk who reminded him constantly of Abbot Berno and of Pope Leo IX. The Lord Udualrich took no pleasure in remembering the serious exhortations of the Pope. In a letter to the Holy Father, he mentioned casually the permission he had given the man from Altshausen. The lame man enjoyed high prestige in Rome ... But when he spoke with his counselors, the abbot groaned that he was obliged to yield to pressure from Hermann's aristocratic family.

"It is very difficult in the long term for a community to have a sick man in its midst. One has to keep on granting him exemption from the Rule."

Randolf objected, courageously: "Hermann is given only a few exemptions from our Rule, Father Abbot, only those forced on him by his illness."

The abbot looked at him with displeasure. "No doubt you are right," he said in a surly voice, "but they are more than enough."

Must this Hermann continue to enjoy such prestige in the abbey? And this ungainly cripple was supposed to be great, free, and rich? The idea was intolerable!

"

"Eight years ago, we went together on our pilgrimage across Reichenau," Hermann reminded his companion, when they sat in the wagon that traveled slowly northward. "It is summer once again, and the farmers are once again making hay ..."

Berthold sighed loudly. "Oh, Father, how much has happened since those carefree days! If Saint Pirmin came out of his crypt in the imperial cathedral in Speyer, he would have to drive out the poisonous serpents from Reichenau all over again."

The sick man laid a warning finger on his lips. He did not know the driver.

"Sometimes, I wonder why the Lord tolerates abuses in his sanctuary," said Berthold quietly.

"God respects our free will. He wants the free gift of a free heart. Even those whom he has called retain the possibility of choice, and one who is bound with the fetters of the religious vows is free to say 'no' to God."

"

They continued their conversation during a rest by the forest edge, where they need not fear that the driver would overhear them. They were alone. Hermann leant his painful back against the barky, gray-brown trunk of an old fir tree with broad branches, and rested. His eyes rested too, as they contemplated the bright and dark green of the meadows and trees.

Berthold crouched in the grass at his feet and looked up at his Master. The pallid face under the white hair looked as if it had been formed from finely chiseled marble. It made a striking contrast to the gray-brown of the trunk. In the aftermath of the visit of Pope Leo IX, this face displayed a lively interplay of emotions. It now looked directly at other human beings.

"Father, how can you see the abuses on Reichenau without being tormented and exhausted? Do they not cause you suffering? After all, you love Reichenau."

The Master felt that he ought to ask his disciple if he did not yet know him.

"Berthold, one who loves must suffer. One who loves Christ, or who at least wants to love him, must suffer when he is so little loved by those who have consecrated themselves to him. One who does not suffer does not love either. Nevertheless, our suffering must bear the sign of peace and ... of joy."

Berthold plucked a long blade of grass and wound it artistically around his fingers.

"Joy, Father?" he asked, reflectively. "I have often pondered how it is possible for suffering and joy to coexist in a human heart. Saint Paul writes that he rejoices in tribulation. How can he do that? If I suffer, I suffer."

Instead of replying, the lame man pointed to the twig of a wild rosebush. "Would you break that twig off for me?"

The young monk got up willingly, but it was not so easy to do what the Father had asked. He had to twist and tug, to break and to pull, until he held the twig in his hands.

"And I have pricked my hand too," he noted, when he gave the sick man the prize of his endeavors.

"Blossoms between the thorns—you have felt the tips of those thorns—wild roses between the thorns. Does not that tell you something, my son?"

"Your prayer, Father? 'Let blossoms bud on the dry branch of my thorns'?"

"Just as these thorns and these blossoms grow on one and the same branch, Berthold, suffering and rejoicing can coexist in a heart. Our Lord did not love suffering for its own sake. He loved suffering for the sake of love and of mercy, and of our redemption. He loved the thorns for the sake of the blossoms. That is why he was under constraint until it was accomplished. The joy that we can experience in suffering ... it may be different in a saint ..."

Hermann fell silent, and shook his head. A small smile played around his mouth, a smile that was very playful.

"You know, Berthold, a poor little monk like me can scarcely grasp what a saint thinks. I can never under any circumstances take delight in suffering, nor will I ever rejoice to suffer. Because of my limitations, I see no meaning in suffering. I rejoice in the love of God, which comes to meet me in his cross and also makes it possible for me to say 'yes' to the cross and to bear it. I trust that my suffering can become mercy for others. We will one day experience the full meaning in heaven; but I believe that there is such a thing as vicarious expiation, acting as the advocate of others, fetching other people back home through the oblation of a suffering that one accepts. Our 'yes' to the cross can bring help in situations where no word can help ... and it can benefit those who are apparently beyond the reach of the grace of God."

Hermann's right hand lightly brushed the thorns of the wild rose twig. "Berthold, you must not misunderstand me. What I have just said to you is not about me, about my suffering. Our Holy Father exalted to the rank of an apostolic activity something that is in reality an act of accepting and enduring. I told you what he said to me. The one who loves, the one who loves while he suffers, is bread in the hands of the Lord, bread for the world."

The priest-monk Berthold looked at the cripple, the poor, stunted man whose face was marked by suffering. How great must his faith and his love be, if he willingly entrusted himself to the Lord's hands as bread and rejoiced that the Lord was permitted to distribute him—without ever receiving any confirmation of that in this life!

A squirrel darted down the neighboring tree, took its place on the carpet of fir needles not far from the lame man, and looked inquisitively at the monks.

"Father, there is a squirrel ... right beside you!" Berthold, who was sometimes a very young man, cried out. The animal flinched at the sound of the loud human voice and scampered back up the tree trunk. Hermann had not altered his position; he could not look so far to the side.

"Forgive me, Father, I forgot ..." murmured Berthold in confusion. But the lame man looked at him kindly, and

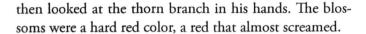

then looked at the thorn branch in his hands. The blossoms were a hard red color, a red that almost screamed.

"

The people in the small villages in the hilly landscape welcomed the two monks cordially. Hermann avoided the castles and manors of his fellow aristocrats. He preferred the hospitality of the farmers. They displayed neither curiosity nor an exaggerated sympathy, and they shared the little that they had with the travelers.

In one larger village, with its own parish church, the priest caught sight of them and invited them to spend the night in his imposing house. Hermann accepted the invitation, because he was tired.

"You must feel at home in my house, reverend Brother," said the country priest, when they were sitting in his parlor. "You come from Reichenau?"

He had doubtless learned this from the driver, so Hermann saw no point in not admitting it: "Yes, we are monks of Reichenau, and we want to go to Altshausen."

"To Altshausen?" The parish priest shot the lame man a penetrating look. "Are you then the son of our gracious Lord Count Wolfrad, whom he brought to the island monastery as a small child?"

"You have guessed correctly," replied the sick man, suppressing a sigh. That was precisely what he had wanted to keep secret.

"Our rooms are too modest for such an exalted guest, my Lord Count," confessed the parish priest. His brown brow broke out into a sweat. Ought he now to stand up in the presence of a count, or might he remain seated?

"Sir Priest, pray do not forget that we are simple monks who have vowed poverty. Do not be concerned in any way. You will surely find a bed for my lame limbs somewhere or other ..."

The parish priest sprang up in alarm. "You must go to bed after the long journey. Forgive me, forgive me, that I have been so thoughtless. My sister will get a chamber ready for you at once, my Lord ..."

The lame man corrected him gently: "Brother ..."

The priest rushed off, not without attempting a bow as he stood in the door frame. He crashed into the door frame.

"The poor man," said Hermann, feeling sorry for him. "If I had suspected that our coming would put him out to such an extent, we would have continued on our way despite the invitation."

"I wonder if your name is known here, your name as a scholar, Father? That may be why the parish priest was so impressed."

"My father's name is well known here, my son. As you have just heard, we are in the territory ruled by Altshausen. The honor that is shown to us is honor shown to him," said the lame man soberly.

The parish priest's sister, a maid, and an elderly female relative bustled in and out of the room, casting astonished glances at the lame monk while they worked. Finally, the oldest man in the parish arrived, an emaciated and deeply tanned figure with no teeth in his mouth. He greeted Hermann in a quavering voice as "the celebrated scholar from Reichenau, who is at the same time a son of our gracious Lord Wolfrad."

Berthold was careful not to show the triumph he felt,

since he saw how exhausted the Father was. The pains of his body and the attention that was paid to him meant that the sick man had only one wish: to go to rest soon.

Just as the parish priest was bringing the welcome news that the chamber was ready, the parlor door opened, and a young woman in a frilly dress entered.

The parish priest addressed her in a harsh tone: "Magdalen, what do you want here?"

She tossed her strawberry blond hair back. Her green eyes blazed maliciously, and her big red mouth smiled bitterly. "How very kind you are to your parishioner, Sir Priest. Is that Christian conduct?"

"How dare *you* talk about what is Christian?" The priest took a threatening step toward her, but she avoided him with a supple movement.

"Do not lose your temper. All I wanted to do was to greet the son of our most gracious Lord Count. I am surely allowed to do that?"

A strange danger vibrated in the woman's voice. Her sparkling eyes fell on the young Berthold.

"Gracious Lord …," she began in a cooing voice, and the priest-monk automatically recoiled.

"Madam, you are mistaken. I am Hermann of Altshausen," said Hermann quickly. He guessed what would now happen: when the woman had spoken his Father's name, her voice had been filled with hatred.

She stared at him, inspecting his poor crippled figure in breathless amazement and a curiosity that took no account of what he might be feelng. Then she flung her hair back with the same wild movement as before. "You …? You …? A cripple!" she laughed scornfully. But her contempt was accompanied by a visible satisfaction, and she went on: "Oh, I am very happy that the proud count has such a son! I am delighted for him!"

The parish priest tried to intervene: "Magdalen, be reasonable."

She hissed like a cat. "Be quiet!" She stood directly before the sick man, and her green eyes stared at him.

"I would like you to know why I am so glad you are a cripple. Your father took my husband from me."

"Your Bruno was a thief," objected the priest. "He received his just penalty."

"Just?" She pursued her big lips. "Just?" Her green eyes remained fixed on the lame man's face. "Is that what you call justice, Sir Priest? I hope that your Lord God uses other measures when he judges. Listen, my Lord Count: my Bruno was a thief. He killed the boars, the wild boars of the count that ruined his fields, and he brought back the cow—the last cow that the henchmen of the Lord Count had taken out of his shed. He was desperate, because his wife was about to give birth to a child at home. So he took a sack full of corn, in order to bake bread for the other four persons, and two loaves. He gave the children milk from his own cow, and he gave them the bread as well. That is why he was hanged."

"My God ..." said Hermann quietly.

"At the very hour when my husband died on the gallows, I bore him his fifth child. And do you think that the noble Lord cared what happened to the wife and the children of the man who was hanged? Not in the slightest, my Lord. After all, they could surely go to the workhouse. Or else ..."

For the first time, she lowered her eyes.

"So now you can despise me, if you want to. I have told what I wanted to tell you."

"No, Mistress Magdalen, why should I despise you? I very much regret what has happened to you."

She looked at him in surprise. This cripple had compassion on her, genuine human compassion. All she ever met in other persons was contempt ...

"We all need much mercy from God, Mistress Magdalen. We are all sinners. I cannot undo what has been done. But you may be sure that you and your children will find help—I promise you! You will see that these are not empty words. Trust me, and try to overcome hatred and evil. God is waiting for you, Mistress Magdalen. He wants you to come back home."

She would have liked to sneer and rebel once more, but his kindness had disarmed her, since she felt the truth in his words. She bowed her head deeply, and the strawberry blond covered her face. It seemed as if she wanted to kneel.

"My Lord, forgive what I said, and forget my words!" she pleaded in the thin voice of a child. Her endeavor to suppress her tears was audible.

"You have been forgiven long ago. But I will not forget you, nor your situation. May I bless you, in order that God may help you to continue on your path in goodness?"

As soon as the woman had left the parlor, the parish priest burst out:

"My Lord, you have converted this woman. How often have I tried in vain to do so ..."

"With kindness?" asked the sick man calmly. "With harshness, all you do is to club people's souls to death."

The priest defended himself: "She was so obstinate ..."

"Let him who is without sin throw the first stone at a woman like that."

"

Berthold carefully got the Father ready for the night. The bed was hard, and the chamber had a low ceiling with heavy beams. All at once, Hermann felt the overexertion of the day, and the agitation caused by the conversation with the wife of the man who had been hanged, where he had needed all his strength in order to remain master of the situation. Ought he perhaps to ask his companion to spend the night in the room? But it was too narrow for a second bed, and it was important that Berthold should sleep. Accordingly, he said nothing about his distress, and dismissed him with his customary evening blessing.

When he closed his eyes, a slow sequence passed before his inner eye: the woods and fields, the mountains and hills that he had seen in the course of his journey that day. When he opened his eyes, he saw the little square of the open window. In the cold light of the moon, he saw a bare branch.

"Like a gallows," he thought with a shudder. He prayed for Mistress Magdalen, for her husband, and above all for his father. That verdict could never be confirmed in God's eyes. To hang a man for poaching and for stealing a little corn in his great need ... the man went to the gallows, the woman to a life of disrepute. He had seen how the gaudily dressed woman earned the bread for herself and her children.

"Father, is that your fault? What have you done?" he thought, appalled. No man of his father's rank would have dealt differently with the poacher and thief Bruno. But did that justify what he had done? What was the value of a human life in God's eyes? The answer was: the blood of his Son, who had forgiven even a Mary Magdalene.

"Much is forgiven her, because she has loved much." God would forgive Mistress Magdalen. He would do so! The parish priest was shocked that he had blessed her. God would forgive her ...

The old floorboards creaked. Mice scampered up and down the beams. A cow mooed somewhere, long and miserably. A dog howled. Were the creatures singing a lament because there was so much hardness of heart in human beings?

"Lord, have mercy on us."

The sick man was very tired, and he wanted to sleep. But he felt that this was one of those nights he would have to endure until the dawn came. He would not be allowed to rest and to forget the existence of his pains. His crooked breast rose and sank again in heavy, laborious breaths. His back hurt from sitting upright for such a long period. If only he could lie a little differently in bed!

"Tomorrow, I shall be in Altshausen," he told himself. He attempted to think of the village, of the castle, and of his mother. But he could not prevent his thoughts from focusing immediately on the imminent conversation with his father.

The dry branch swayed, black in the moonlight ... like a gallows.

He heard the woman's shrill voice: "You? A cripple! I am delighted for him."

He would have liked to cry out: "Father, what have you done?" But no words came from his mouth. The lameness once again took hold of his poor body, slowly and inexorably, but he still wanted to use the power of his will to get the mastery over what now awaited him.

"*Ave praeclara maris stella / In lucem gentium Maria ...*"[9] He prayed the first verses of his long Sequence in honor of the Most Blessed Virgin. But he got hopelessly lost in the multitude of words, and could not go on.

He experienced in the narrow chamber something that he had hitherto been spared in his attacks. A terrible fear seized him. He was completely unable to move, and stared with wide-open eyes at the black branch in the cold moonlight, the swaying "gallows," while the fear made his heart beat very quickly.

He would have liked to cry out and call for help, but no sound came from his throat. His teeth were clenched, and the fear of death befell him in the prison of his silence. He felt as if a hand were clutching at his throat to strangle him. Was that the hand of Bruno, or of his wife?

Outside, the "gallows" swayed in the moonlight.

"I am delighted for him!" laughed the young woman with the red hair and the green eyes filled with hate.

A terrible burden lay on his breast, and pain hammered away in his head. He was being crushed in a vise. This was no longer his "Gnadensee," the familiar ups and downs of the pains.

His mind was so clear that he could follow every phase of his state of health. He prayed silently the psalm that

---

9. ["Hail, most celebrated star of the sea, / Mary, (you have become visible) in order to be the light of the nations."]

the brethren prayed by the bedside of a dying monk: "*De profundis clamavi ad te, Domine ...*"[10]

He then prayed the *Miserere,* the psalm of repentance,[11] and his own *Salve Regina,* and waited, waited for the Lord to set him free by saying to him: "Come!" He waited for the summons to come home.

But the Adversary too knew that this hour was propitious for him. Ugly thoughts made their appearance, and buzzed around the sufferer's mind like nasty flies.

"What a glorious end for the learned Master of Reichenau! Alone and abandoned by all, dying without receiving the sacraments, reviled by a woman whose husband ended on the gallows ...

"You blessed the witch, thereby putting your own father in the wrong. You blessed the woman who rejoiced to see your wretched existence. Is that love?

"Love! What good did love ever do you in your life, Hermann of Altshausen? Where is the One to whom you gave everything? Where is he now? And are you really sure of his love? For what has it brought you? Sickness, distress, pains, contempt, loneliness. What a truly *kind* love!

"And your works—your writings, your inventions? All your activity was nothing. It is nothing, nothing. Future generations will forget you as quickly as a leaf that falls from the tree. You have lived and loved in vain. There are some on Reichenau who will be happy if do you not come back."

The night prayer of the monks included this passage of

---

10. ["Out of the depths I cry to thee, O Lord."]
11. [Psalm 51 in the Hebrew Bible (Psalm 50 in the Vulgate): "Have mercy on me, O God."]

Scripture: "Brethren, be sober, and watch well; the devil, who is your enemy, goes about roaring like a lion, to find his prey."

Hermann felt that he could almost feel the lion, his ferocious and seductive proximity. His mind was dull, benumbed. Logical thought was no longer possible.

"Your life is nothing, Hermann of Altshausen, nothing …"

Outside, the black branch swayed in the moonlight.

The lame man dredged up a thought to the surface: "If I am nothing, then I am God's nothing."

The words of the Lord Berno occurred to him, and he repeated them with a sense of liberation: "I am made for God, and God is love."

The whispering of the ugly thoughts died down. When a person entrusted himself unconditionally to that love, evil had neither power nor space to act.

But his bodily distress increased. His head and his body jerked convulsively, as if invisible fists were tugging the sick man to and fro. Then the muscles contracted again. He could not close his mouth. Spittle ran down over his chin and onto his garment.

In the morning, Berthold found his Master in a state of complete exhaustion. His face was disfigured by struggle, pain, and distress, and bore witness to a terrible night. Berthold knew how embarrassing it was for the Father when he was powerless to wipe away the external traces of an attack. He washed and dressed him, and put him to bed again.

Hermann said nothing until Berthold lifted his head to pour a little wine into his mouth. Then the torments of the night found release in an unrestrained weeping. The priest-monk held the sick man's body, which was shaken by violent sobs. This was the first time that the Father's lamentation had revealed how painful an attack had been. Now, tears were coursing down his hollow cheeks, and the half-open mouth stammered a few fragments of words:

"Lord, Lord ... why do you not come to fetch me? It ... was ... terrible ... Lord ... have mercy ... and come!"

Berthold prayed in silence. What could he say or do in face of such distress? It took a long time for the sobbing to ebb away. Hermann's eyes, red with weeping, looked at his companion.

"Please forgive me!"

"What do I need to forgive, Father?"

"My lack of self-control. I ought not to whine like this."

"Father, I am happy that this has shown me for once your real condition. You know that I want to help you, and you must allow me to do so. Let me remain with you in the evening, if you feel that your condition is worsening."

"I would like to ask you do that, Berthold. It is then that I need a hand that holds me and a heart that prays for me. Let me tell the priest Berthold about this last night ..." The lame man told his priest friend about the inner distress he had experienced.

They could not continue their journey that day. Hermann was still tired and weak, and Berthold was afraid that he would have another attack that night. He refused to be dismissed that evening; Hermann tried in vain to assure him that he would probably be able to sleep. This time, Berthold won the day.

The hours crept slowly by. The moon hid behind a wall

of clouds. It was dark in the chamber. Berthold stretched himself cautiously on his uncomfortable stool.

"Please go to your bed, my son. The attack will not return tonight …"

"No, Father, I shall remain with you. Otherwise I will have no rest."

The young monk hid a yawn with his hand. A screech owl hooted somewhere: "Tu-whit! Tu-whoo!" He yawned more copiously. A night like this was long and quiet. He rubbed his tired eyes.

After some time, deep and regular breaths could be heard from the bed. Thanks be to God, the Father had fallen asleep, and now Berthold too could go to his own chamber and rest. But what if there was a sudden repeat of the attack, and the Father was alone? He manfully resisted the temptation to go, but he did cross his arms on his knees and lay his brow on them. He would just rest a little, just close his eyes for a moment. Like this …

He woke up in the bright light of morning and saw the lame man's eyes looking directly at him.

"So, did you sleep well, Berthold?"

"Sleep? Me? I did not intend to sleep at all." He moved his cramped limbs cautiously. "I really did not want to sleep."

"I believe you, my son. And that is why you slept twice as soundly as usual."

"Did you not sleep, Father?"

"Yes, indeed … long and deeply, by my standards. And that is why I feel much better. I suppose that a monk who can sleep as well as you can drive out the devil thereby."

"One can drive out the devil by sleeping? That is a thesis I have never heard."

"You will not find it in any of the doctors of the Church, but I propose this thesis. You have assuredly driven out the devil by the way in which you slept, for you gasped and snored so furiously that even a spirit from hell could be stricken by fear."

Berthold breathed a sigh of relief. The Father was his old self again. Despite his misery, he could make jokes.

"Just one little suggestion. When you are fully awake, Berthold, remember that I am hungry after yesterday's fasting."

Berthold stretched his stiff neck awkwardly and uncomfortably. His face, with his eyes full of sleep, did not seem particularly intelligent; the small eyes announced that he was still in need of sleep.

"That is the outcome, my son, of insisting on doing something other than what the Father thinks right," said Hermann mischievously.

The young monk left the chamber quickly, before Hermann could say anything more. It was good that there was a well with clear, cold water in the courtyard of the priest's house! Berthold let the bucket down, and wound it up on the long rope.

"How many hands have had to help me up to now," thought Hermann, while his companion attended to him, careful as always. "Mostly, they were good and gentle hands. But how humiliating it was when the hands helped only reluctantly. Every touch that lacked reverence and mercy meant an inner torment."

When Berthold had laid him down anew on his bed, he held him fast by the arm of his habit.

"Do you still lack something, Father?"

"No, my son, I only wanted to thank you!"

"You must not do that, Father. I am, and remain, in your debt. After God, it is to you that I owe the grace of my ordination to the priesthood. Tomorrow is the second anniversary of my ordination. That gives me a reason for gratitude."

The lame man fell silent. When Berthold gave him his morning meal, he said: "We would give my lady mother a great joy, if you celebrated the holy sacrifice in our castle chapel on the anniversary of your priestly ordination. She regards you as one of her sons. And there is another reason why I am anxious to get to Altshausen. I must speak with my lord father."

"About the thief Bruno?"

"About the thief Bruno, about his wife Magdalen, and about his children; and about the injustice and inadequacy of the human administration of justice."

"You have a difficult task ahead of you, Father."

"When my conscience makes demands of me as clearly as it does here, I must accept the difficulties. The uncomfortable situation makes it possible to accomplish the mercy of God, even for Count Wolfrad II of Altshausen. He needs that mercy more than does Mistress Magdalen. There will be no lack of human charity in Altshausen, because my lady mother will be glad to help the poor people and to do what she can to heal the wounds."

"

On the evening of that day, the wagon from the monastery of Reichenau drew near to Altshausen Castle. The peace of evening lay over the green hill-country. The evening sun shone on the walls and roofs of the castle. The village huts crouched at its feet, like chickens under the wings of a hen.

Berthold had noted apprehensively the increasing pallor of the sick man. The journey had been too tiring. "You will soon be home now, Father," he said, to console him.

"Home?" asked Hermann in surprise. "Home? Do you think that I regard Altshausen as my home? Even Reichenau seems far off, unreal like a mirage. Home? Berthold, we are wanderers who are not allowed to settle anywhere. We must take down our tents again and again, until we reach our home at last."

"But where are we at home, Father, if not on Reichenau?"

"The Lord Berno is at home, my son."

Altshausen stood under a thundercloud, a glorious white cloud shot through by the sun, grandiose and spreading wide. There was nothing threatening in its brightness.

Berthold cried out: "Father, look ... the cloud is like a city ... towers, domes, walls ..."

They looked at the clouds, shot through by the sun.

"Do you remember the Lord Berno's sermon at your ordination, Berthold? He spoke about the city that would come down from heaven, the Eternal City, the New Jerusalem ..."

The monks saw the flagpole on the castle tower. The flag with the three red stag's antlers on a gold ground flapped in the evening wind.

The shining cloud-city seemed to be descending, as it moved northward. Its radiant whiteness haloed first the flag on its own, then the tower, the roof of the private quarters, and finally the whole of Altshausen Castle.

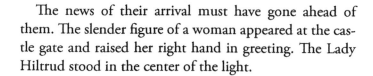

The news of their arrival must have gone ahead of them. The slender figure of a woman appeared at the castle gate and raised her right hand in greeting. The Lady Hiltrud stood in the center of the light.

CHAPTER 9

* * *

FROM THE OTHER SHORE

Winter

ON JANUARY 13, 1052, Hermann of Altshausen sat by flickering candlelight, poring over a book that he was analyzing for his world chronicle. But that day, the strange visions of the monk Wetti of Saint Gallen failed to hold his interest. It was extraordinarily cold in the cell. Berthold had covered the two windows with leather hides and woolen coverings, and had kindled a good log fire, but an icy draft kept blowing through the room.

The Master had dismissed the students after a brief lesson. "Go and run about outside, so that you may get warmer. Remain in the inner courtyard or in the abbey garden!" He could no longer bear to see their blue, frozen young faces. Once again, his kindness had gotten the better of him.

From time to time, his numb fingers wrote a word on his wax tablet. Then he pricked up his ears. He had heard voices in the cloister outside his cell. He heard the dark tones of Berthold and the quick tenor of his brother Werinher.

"No, I cannot tell him! I simply cannot!" Werinher lamented. "If you tell him, it will be easier for him to bear ..."

"But you alone are the proper person to do so, Werinher," replied Berthold with great seriousness. "In this case, I am only an outsider. But ... perhaps it is really better ... Yes. I will do it, no matter how difficult I find it."

"May God bless you for this, Berthold! There is no greater service of love that you could ever do for me, Brother."

Berthold fended off his thanks: "I am doing it for the Father."

It was only at this point that Hermann noticed that his stylus had etched deep, meaningless runes on the wax. He slowly smoothed the writing surface, without realizing what he was doing. Was it him they were discussing outside the cell door? What was Werinher not able to tell him? Bad news? Well, Berthold would come in now ...

The door opened. The sick man waited, motionless, for the first word from his companion.

"Father ..." Berthold began, and cleared his throat. He remained in the shadow, and Hermann could not see his face.

"Father, would you like to go to the Gnadensee?"

The Gnadensee—on this icy January morning? The lame man reflected: Does he want to tell me outside? I expect that he wants to go to the lake because he knows that I love it. Well, if that helps him …

"Good, Berthold," he said aloud. "We will go to the Gnadensee."

The young monk wrapped up the Father carefully in his coat, in cloths and coverings, and lifted him into the wheelchair, spreading a sheep's skin over his knees. He anxiously avoided meeting the sick man's eyes while he was going about these preparations. His hands, otherwise so nimble, were nervous and clumsy.

The monastery porter opened the gate for them with a reluctant grumble. "I have never seen anything so ridiculous. You want to go out in weather like this? If you get ill …"

The icy wind attacked the two monks savagely. Berthold's wide black coat flapped like a flag at half-mast. Unkempt ravens flew off with ugly screeches. No white dove circled around the crest of Abbot Berno's tower.

Without a covering of snow to protect it, the landscape seemed rigid and dead. The filigree of branches rose up to meet the monotonous gray of the low sky. The land on the other shore had withdrawn into a gray mist. It was a dreary, lifeless picture.

Would this landscape turn green and blossom in a few weeks? Could the warmth of the sun give this dead land a garment of mild and lovely colors, and make the lake shine?

Berthold steered the wheelchair to the Herrenbruck harbor, where an emperor and a Pope had once walked with all the splendor and pageantry of their courts. Now, a couple of gray planks lay over the gray water. The frozen ground crunched under Berthold's feet, and the wheelchair creaked. The wind howled painfully, as shrill as a professional mourning woman. The brown reeds rustled and crackled as the wind took hold of them, and the pale grass by the wayside shivered.

Like a shadow, the church of Saints Peter and Paul emerged out of the gray mist. Berthold had still not spoken.

"Can I help you in any way, my son? You are bearing a burden of some kind."

Every word of the sick man took the form of a cloud of breath that hung before his stiff lips.

"You want to help me, Father? I ... it is I who want to help you," replied Berthold, hesitantly. "Father, you ..." He still hesitated, then he asked: "May I bring you back?"

The sick man had an uneasy premonition. It ascended threateningly from his subconscious mind: if Berthold had to struggle so hard to bring him the news, it must be terrible indeed. And it was in fact Werinher who ought to have brought it to him. Werinher, his brother ... was the news about his family?

No, no! Let it be anything else ... anything else than that! His mother? No, nothing must have happened to her. Had she not been transparently pale, the last time he had seen her? Pale and weary, although she had tried to hide it? "Dear Lord, anything else ... but not that. Lord, have mercy on me ... not my mother ..."

Berthold brought him quickly to the abbey. The wind had dropped, and it began to snow. At first, fine little flakes fell, but they became bigger and more numerous, as the snow fell thickly. Soon, the frozen ground had a white covering. The white flakes slid over the lame man's face like tears running down. He did not even know that it was snowing. Not his mother ... not his mother ...

In the narthex of the monastery church, Berthold shook the snow from the cloths and coverings and dried the Father's face. Hermann freed his right hand from the layers of fabric and took his companion's hand.

"Tell me, Berthold!" he asked, while he thought all the time: Not my mother ... not my mother ...

Berthold crouched down, so that the Master could see his face. The young priest still shrank from the task that lay before him.

"Father, the Lord asks you to make the greatest sacrifice of all ..." he gasped. He did not finish the sentence, but Hermann knew everything.

"My lady mother?"

"Your lady mother, the noble Countess Hiltrud of Altshausen, fell asleep peacefully in the Lord on January 9, in the presence of your lord father and her children."

The sick man stared at him. In his mind, he saw the narrow, still face of his mother, as he had seen her when he left Altshausen. His mother had passed away; did not that mean that the last remnant of warmth had departed from his wretched existence?

The tears ran down over the sunken cheeks of the lame monk, silently and ceaselessly.

"My lady mother," his trembling lips murmured, "now heaven has found you. You are at home. I am sure that we must not mourn too much for you, since you are certainly with God. You spent your life doing good to others ... and to me, the last of the poor ones of Christ."

Berthold knew where he must bring the Father. He

steered the wheelchair into the monastery church and took it to the altar of Our Lady, the Mother of all mothers. He knelt for a long time on the cold stone floor beside the vehicle and prayed the *Salve Regina* for the deceased and for her lame son.

"Mother of mercy, show the Lady Hiltrud your Son, just as I hope that you will one day show him to my beloved Master. Ask your Son to be consolation and strength for him. Dear Mother of God, be to him a Mother, more than ever before."

A little while later, he took the lame man to the crypt of Abbot Berno, which had been erect four years previously with money donated by the Lady Hiltrud.

Hermann felt the loss of his mother deeply and painfully, but he never for one moment had the feelings of insecurity, of loneliness, and of abandonment that had tormented him after the Lord Berno's death. The strings of his harp were not torn out. For were not the two departed ones very close to him?

"The curtain has become very thin, my lady mother, the curtain between time and eternity. Your son is even more keenly on the lookout for heaven now. You promised to help him find it."

The two departed ones also knew about him. Their love and their care had made a rich and meaningful life out of his wretched existence as a cripple, and they would also guide his homeward path. Would his pilgrim journey be long?

"

Werinher was waiting for his brother in the corner cell. He was speechless, and Hermann had to console him.

"You will bring our dear lady mother the last greetings I give her as her son, Werinher."

"What? You are not going with me to Altshausen, Hermann?"

"No, brother, I shall pray here for our lady mother."

"Why do you not want to come with me?" Werinher's incomprehension was giving way to an angry impatience.

"I would not survive the journey at this time of year, Werinher."

The younger brother was unconvinced. "But do you not owe our lady mother the journey? Think of all she did for you! You were her favorite son."

The sick man's face reddened with anger, and his eyes blazed. It was only with an effort that he suppressed a heated answer.

"Brother, your pain is robbing you of the ability to think clearly. I cannot travel. Would it please our lady mother, if the journey meant my death? Would she not rather wish that I remained on Reichenau and thought of her here? It would have been a consolation for me too, if I had been permitted to pray at her grave." Hermann hid his face in his hands.

Werinher was deeply moved. "Forgive me!"

Hermann immediately looked up. "But of course. All that matters is that you understand me, brother."

"

Their conversation was interrupted by the entrance of the monk Dietbert.

"Hermann, Father Abbot wishes to see you."

"And why does not the abbot come here, on this occasion?" grumbled Werinher. "Now my sick brother has to go through the winter cold again."

"I have no idea," shrugged Dietbert.

"Father Abbot did once come to us," said Berthold furiously. "On that occasion, he needed texts for the Pope."

"He should have done the same today," said Werinher harshly.

"What a fuss you are all making," said the lame man in surprise. "I am supposed to be able to travel to Altshausen, but I cannot cover the little distance to the abbot's quarters?"

"In this case, it is not a question of the shortness of the distance," said Berthold darkly. Then he fell silent, and Hermann took care not to ask any questions. He had understood Berthold and Werinher perfectly well.

The cloister was bitterly cold and draughty, but a boy stood there in a light garment, a boy with strawberry blond hair and green eyes.

"Bruno!" Hermann called out in surprise to the fifth child of Mistress Magdalen, who had been born on the very day on which his father died on the gallows. "How did you get in here?"

"The side door in the monastery church is usually open," smiled the boy. Then his bright young face turned serious. "I ... I just wanted to tell you that I was sorry to hear the news ... and to give you this."

He quickly pressed a little wooden figure into the sick man's hand and ran with light and nimble steps into the inner courtyard. The driving snow swallowed him up as rapidly as if he had been an apparition from the other world.

What present could Mistress Magdalen's son have given

the Father? Berthold was curious, and bent forward. He saw a little wooden figure, obviously meant to be Our Lady. Hermann's crooked fingers caressed the little statue.

"It is still very much the work of a child ... and yet there is more to it than that. Just see, Berthold, how slender and fine the face is. The figure is delicate, the figure of a young girl, and yet the posture is that of a queen."

"The boy knew your lady mother well," said Berthold in a quiet voice.

"You too saw the resemblance? He probably thought of her while he was carving the statue. After all, he knew that it was thanks to her request that my father permitted him to leave the county, so that he could learn an honest trade here on Reichenau."

"And he had seen, even before that permission came, how your lady mother cared for his family, how she healed the wounds that had been inflicted by a harsh law. It was the most moving experience during our time in Altshausen to see how Mistress Magdalen found herself again and began a new life, thanks to your lady mother."

"Berthold, she was only one of the many who were restored to health by the kindness of my dear lady mother."

"

The Lord Udualrich opened the doors of his chamber to the lame man. He praised in eloquent words the noble benefactress of Reichenau, who had now departed from this life.

"I shall offer the holy sacrifice for your lady mother tomorrow."

"My Lord and Father Abbot, I thank you for this gift,

which is the greatest of all gifts. Would you permit me on this occasion to celebrate the sacrifice of the Mass, for the third time since my ordination? If Brother Berthold stands beside me and supports me with his help at every point, I will be able to do so, by the grace of God."

"I am happy to grant your request, Hermann."

"May I also compose an epitaph for my lady mother? Werinher could take it with him."

"But surely you will go to Altshausen yourself?"

"I would almost give in to the temptation, my Lord and Father Abbot, if you were to offer me the journey. But ... I may not do so."

The Lord Udualrich was perplexed. "Do you feel worse, Hermann?"

"If I were to go to Altshausen, Father Abbot, I would expend my last strength on the journey. But my last strength must belong to Reichenau."

The abbot's visible astonishment at this reply gave way to a feeling of kindness toward the sick monk. The old antipathy, which had existed so long, disappeared.

"Would you please look at this carving, Father Abbot? A child made it and gave it to me." He handed the abbot the little figure of Our Lady.

The Lord Udualrich studied the carving intently.

"Doubtless you too think that the boy is gifted."

"Certainly, Hermann. This child's statue bears the promise that he will one day be a great artist. He must be given help and encouragement."

Abbot Udualrich smiled at Hermann.

"And that was what you wanted to suggest to me, was it not?"

"Yes, Father Abbot," said the sick man candidly. "I secretly hoped that you would guess that."

"And that is what I did," said the Lord Udualrich cheerfully. "We agree, then."

"The little master carver is Bruno, whom you entrusted to our Brother carpenter as an apprentice, Father Abbot, because ... the Lady Hiltrud asked you to do so."

"Take the carving with you as a greeting to your lady mother. I shall not forget Bruno. What else can I give you ... my son?"

"Your blessing, Father Abbot."

For the first time, Abbot Udualrich's blessing was no mere formula. He had a genuine desire to give it.

Berthold's amazement had increased, as he followed the conversation. Could one believe the Abbot? His conduct hitherto had not been such as to inspire confidence.

"

The little statue of Mary stood before the lame man when he dictated the epitaph for his mother's tomb. It began: "*Mater egenorum, spes auxiliumque suorum* ...Hiltrud, mother of the needy, the hope and help of those who were hers, gives back to the earth here in this mound what she owes to the earth. Hiltrud ennobled her most noble parents, from a noble lineage, through the brilliant splendor of her striving for perfection. She entered only once, in chastity, into the sacred covenant of marriage. She devoted her mind and her heart to the divine service. Martha's modest portion appeared to her to be worth striving for. What she taught others, she herself exemplified faithfully.

"She gave joy, richly and piously, to the poor with clothing, with food, and with consolation. She went wherever distress commanded. She was submissive and mild. She was meek and patient, and avoided strife. She was loved by all, and we hope that she found favor with Our Lord ...

"Believe me, this is not a poet's nonsense. Nor am I a son who heaps excessive praise upon his mother. Ask the voice of the people in the meadows of our homeland, and it will be clear to you that I have said only a little ..."

Berthold too found that the verses contained no exaggeration of any kind. He too had seen how the "good Martha" looked after those who were in need, including the family of the hanged thief Bruno. Thanks to her intervention, the clash between Count Wolfrad and Hermann, initially so harsh, had been resolved in the lame man's favor. Without his noticing it, she had mollified her husband's roughness. And how kindly she had welcomed her son's young companion! Berthold, who had been an orphan since the age of nine, had felt once more like a child sheltered in the love of a mother.

But she had not only looked after her children and her household. The people of Eritgau also belonged to her great family.

Even in her old age, she had remained maidenly, this wise, well educated, and cheerful woman who lived in the splendor of marital chastity. Her family could always rely on her for help, and she won over people's hearts and minds to goodness. The true source of her strength was her deep interior life, which prompted her to trust steadfastly in God. In this trust, she had accepted the death of her eight children, and had endured every suffering.

"

While Werinher was making his way through the wintry Swabia to Altshausen, Hermann offered the holy sacrifice of the Mass for his deceased mother. Abbot Udualrich and the monks were present, praying in their choir stalls. Berthold had prepared everything, down to the smallest detail, in order to make it possible for the sick man to celebrate the sacred liturgy, and he stood at his side.

None of those present could tear his eyes away from the extraordinary and moving impression made by the picture: the lame man sat in an armchair behind an improvised altar. The high altar, with the great cross above it, soared up like a mountain behind him. In the center of the wide room, the sick man seemed even more sunken, more stooped, and more fragile than usual.

The light of the candles fell on the furrowed, shrunken face and the crooked hands, which moved in slow and laborious gestures. It was still early in the morning, and the monastery church lay in a gray twilight. The only pool of light was on the sacrificial altar of Hermann of Altshausen.

Berthold gave him all the support he needed, without drawing attention to himself. It was as if he had rehearsed every movement carefully.

Hermann had lost his awareness of the community. He scarcely felt the supportive hands of his companion. He was completely recollected. He had entered into the sacred action, and was filled with a marvelous peace. He believed firmly that his lady mother was at home.

At the offertory, the *oblatio,* he once again laid the sacrifice of his own life alongside the bread on the paten, so that he too might become bread, bread for the hands of the Lord. He felt a new love growing in him while he celebrated the sacrifice of Christ, a gentle and compassionate love for those who were far from the Lord, and a kindly mercy. It was as if he had to fetch those persons home into the communion. He knew that his sacrifice had been accepted anew.

Just at the moment when he bowed his head to give thanks after the sacred celebration of the Eucharist, the sun rose. Its rays fell through the windows in the eastern choir, lit up the cross and the high altar, and wrapped the lame man too in their splendor.

The Sequence of the Cross

In the year of grace 1052, highly disturbing things happened behind the stout walls of the abbey. The monastic life ran, to all appearances, within its pre-ordained framework, which was laid down by the Rule. The bells rang at the appointed times, calling to prayer and to work, to meals, to recreation, and to the chapter meeting.

The monks of Reichenau got through their day as they had always done. But only a very superficial observer would have thought that nothing had changed.

A pressing unease had grown in the hearts and minds of most of the monks. Perplexity, indignation, and hurt pride smoldered there, and awaited their hour. The Lord Udualrich had dismissed the prior, and other monks of proven quality, from their offices, without consulting the community of the brethren. He had then appointed men who were sympathetic to him. His wasteful and imprudent administration imposed ever new burdens on the abbey. He separated himself haughtily from the monks. He never took one step in their direction; they had to come to him. He did not serve; rather, all had to serve him.

Hitherto, the disquieting talk that was buzzing through the monastery had stopped at the cell of the lame man. It had not dared to cross the threshold. Would not the internal mutiny break down before his clear eyes and the objective reasons he would put forward? Had not a wave of indignation ebbed away before him, once in the past? Some monks remembered all too well the pitiful attempt to act against Abbot Berno.

Berthold seemed to have changed: he had avoided Hermann's piercing eyes for some days now. What was he hiding from him?

The sick man was working on a new Marian antiphon.

"O blossoming rose, Mother of the divine light. Virgin chaste and pure, fruitful branch of the vine, brighter than the dawn, pray for us in our needs, so that we may be worthy of the home of the eternal light on the day of the strict judgment ..."

The door slammed shut and put an end to his prayerful meditation. Berthold came up to his work desk. His face was somber.

"Since when have you made such a din?" Hermann rebuked him indignantly. His train of thought had been interrupted.

Berthold did not excuse himself. He stretched out his finger and knocked the little statue of Mary once or twice on its head.

The sick man was puzzled. "What is that supposed to mean?"

"I thought at the time that it was nothing but hypoc-risy."

"What are you talking about?"

"About the terribly generous decision of our Lord and Father Abbot Udualrich to let young Bruno be appren-ticed to a master carver," replied the young monk, with caustic bitterness. "Do you know where Bruno is now?"

"No, but ..."

"Please, Father, do not react by defending the abbot because he is the abbot. I could not stand that! Injustice is injustice. A broken promise is a very great injustice, and that has been done both to you and to the boy. Bruno is working as a groom in the stables on the estate. What do you say now?"

After a pause, Hermann replied, composedly: "I shall speak to Father Abbot."

"And you think there is any point in doing so? He will probably make you another fine promise, and he will be even more ready to forget what he has promised."

"Berthold, I forbid you to speak like that! How do you know that Bruno was assigned to serve with the prior knowledge of Father Abbot?"

"Well, I have no evidence of that. But I am convinced that the words he spoke to you then were empty. He did it only to please you."

"My poor friend," said the lame man compassionately, "has your aversion to the Lord Udualrich so completely overwhelmed your ability to think in supernatural terms?"

Negative reports about the abbot were brought to Ber-thold from all quarters, and he found this question more than he could bear. He turned abruptly and left the room.

Hermann had to wait for a long time, far too long,

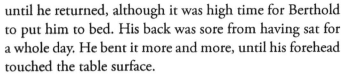

until he returned, although it was high time for Berthold to put him to bed. His back was sore from having sat for a whole day. He bent it more and more, until his forehead touched the table surface.

Where was Berthold?

Berthold had to trust Hermann to investigate the matter of Bruno. He had to struggle to adopt the correct attitude to the Lord Udualrich.

Where was Berthold?

The sick man's pains intensified, and his impatience increased and made him bitter. "He knows how tired and exhausted I am, when I have been sitting all day. Does he want to punish me for rebuking him?"

Darkness fell, and the lame man's forehead was still on the table surface, supported by his trembling right hand. Hermann had never before found his dependence on the help of the young monk a source of humiliation, but now he felt degraded and abandoned.

When steps approached, he straightened up with a great effort. There were red imprints on his brow and his hand.

"Forgive me for not coming before now," murmured Berthold. Hermann had the impression that he spoke hastily; but it did not occur to him that the brevity might have been the fruit of uncertainty and embarrassment.

"He does not even tell me why he has neglected me. Well, he does not have to give an account of himself to me," thought the lame man, wearily and bitterly. Without a word, he let himself be helped onto his bed; without a word, he shook his head at the question whether he had any wishes for the coming night; without a word, he gave the blessing. He himself had secretly hoped for a good word.

"

Next morning, another monk entered his cell, Gerfried of Augsburg. Had Berthold asked the abbot to discharge him from his service? Gerfried remained standing at the foot of his bed, without offering to help him.

"Forgive me, dear Brother, for coming to you so early in the morning, but I am charged with a commission that brooks no delay. The brethren have sent me to you, who are the faithful son of our revered and blessed Abbot Berno."

The sick man had the feeling that a great and imminent danger threatened. Had not Gerfried been one of the most zealous adversaries of Abbot Berno in the past? And was he not still one of those who spread rumors and stirred up strife? Hermann's shining eyes looked directly at the unctuous monk. He said nothing. Whom did this stocky man with the brown skin remind him of? Was it Cheirisophos?

The smooth voice of Brother Gerfried sought to woo him with flattery: "We attach great value to your prudent counsel and your utterly honest judgment, Master Hermann."

Yes, this reminded him of Cheirisophos.

"We intend to present a petition to the emperor."

The lame man asked, calmly: "Who are 'we'? And why do you want to present a petition to the emperor?"

This objectivity confused Gerfried. "We ... well ... most of the members of the community of Reichenau, or a good number of them, at any rate. You yourself can surely identify without any difficulty the reason for our petition, Hermann. We want to complain about the way in which Abbot Udualrich governs our abbey. Just think: he has sold off works by you that ought to have remained in the monastery library! You surely do not want the inheritance of the Lord Berno—especially his spiritual inheritance—to be reduced any further. It is vital for you, just as it is for us, that the spirit of Cluny should be preserved intact here."

Hermann lifted his head as far as he could. He breathed more quickly, but his words betrayed nothing of the agitation that had befallen him.

"So," he said, to all appearances serene and uninvolved, "you want to present a petition to preserve the religious spirit in the abbey? Dear Brother, I know of a simpler way to attain that goal. Live the spirit of Cluny, all of you, and then the inheritance of the Lord Berno will not be diminished. Why do you not speak openly with Father Abbot about your difficulties?"

"With Udualrich?" cried Gerfried, shocked. "Speak openly with Udualrich?"

"In my opinion, that is the only path you can take with a good conscience. If you have complaints about essential matters, it is your sacred duty to present them to Father Abbot in reverence and openness, instead of intervening secretly with the emperor. Every secret of this kind is a conspiracy against the spirit of the religious life. Let me add one thing: never again mention where my writings are to be found. What I have written belongs to the Lord. I have neither the right nor the wish to make any objections on that score."

The visitor smiled scornfully. "I see. That tells me a lot! And we thought that you were an honest disciple of the

Lord Berno and that it mattered to you whether his work was preserved. You adapt to whichever abbot is in office, don't you, Hermann?"

"The abbot who is in office is God's representative for us," said the lame man, with a certain severity.

Gerfried waved his hand dismissively. "I do not believe in your theological motivations. It is a human and a very ... natural prudence that makes you take Udualrich's side and refuse to support us."

Without greeting him, the monk left the cell, and at once Berthold entered.

"Are you too one of them?" shouted the sick man.

"One of whom, Father? I do not understand you. Gerfried asked me to wait outside, because he had something important to say to you."

"Forgive me, Berthold! I have done you an injustice."

"You ... to me?" stammered the young monk in confusion. "And *I* wanted to ask *you* for forgiveness. I have behaved toward you like a little boy."

"Does the little boy see that his attitude toward Abbot Udualrich is mistaken?"

"Father ... I have tried to see that, but I cannot. You ought to hear what the monks in the abbey are saying. You ought to hear the bitterness that is spreading everywhere!"

"Do you make your own attitude dependent on what other people are saying, my son? We must continue on our own path, without being disturbed by other people's attitudes, if that path proves to be path indicated by God." The lame man's eyes were sad. His words had not convinced his companion.

"How can we be certain that it is God's path?"

"Berthold, I could give you many reasons, but all I ask for is your trust. Go with me, even if that runs counter to what you think and feel at present. Do not leave me alone now!"

"Father, I have no intention of leaving you! What makes you think that?"

"Berthold, I am asking much of you. The disciple must not leave the master alone, even when he would prefer to flee," replied the lame man. He added, quietly: "He must not abandon him, even when that seems to him to be the better and more prudent thing to do. Faithfulness is rare. I know that your faithfulness will be put to a hard test in the coming time."

"Why do you doubt me?" cried Berthold, almost indignantly. "I will stay by you, no matter what happens."

"Simon Peter once promised the Lord Jesus Christ that he would remain faithful, even if all the others abandoned him … Let us not make presumptuous promises. Let us rather pray that the Lord may give us the strength to remain faithful."

"

In the next weeks, many attempts were made to win over the lame man, who had experienced much injustice and many slights from Abbot Udualrich, to join in presenting the petition. His name was well known, and carried weight with the emperor and the Pope.

Neither requests nor threats had any power to influence Hermann. When monks visited him, he did his best to set out the religious reasons for his refusal, and he succeeded in convincing Dietbert, Fridebolt, Randolf,

Tradolf, Eginhard, and several other monks of the folly and injustice of such an intervention.

"Why do they want to present a petition? Is this not, in reality, prompted by jealousy? No one would think of doing such a thing, if he himself was one of those to whom the abbot has entrusted offices in the monastery. That is why this intervention is contrary to the will of God. The Lord Udualrich is our legitimately elected superior. God gives every community the superior whom it deserves. Let us pray much for our monastic family. Let us pray much for our Father Abbot Udualrich. Let us observe our Rule with great faithfulness."

Hermann did not realize that he was the heart of Reichenau at this critical time. He often had himself brought to the tomb of Abbot Berno, where he prayed for the Holy Spirit for the abbot and the brethren. His love for Reichenau had become a painful and selfless love.

One day, Abbot Udualrich sought him, and found him alone at the tomb of the Lord Berno.

"Hermann," he whispered, "may I ask you for a favor? I should like to enclose a prayer or a hymn from your hand, as a special greeting, in a letter to the Holy Father. You know our Holy Father, and you know what would bring him joy."

The sick man looked without suspicion at the broad face of the abbot. Were not his eyes full of uncertainty? Did he not truly need help?

The Lord Udualrich, who otherwise paid little attention to the sick man, now steered his wheelchair through the cloister to the corner cell. Some of the eyes that observed this unusual scene darkened with malice. The man from Altshausen was ingratiating himself with Udualrich.

"

When Berthold went to fetch him from the monastery church, Gerfried beckoned him. "Save yourself the trouble of looking for your Master in the church. Someone else has taken excellent care of him. You should have seen how carefully our Lord and Father Abbot Udualrich personally steered the wheelchair. A truly touching picture! It reminded one of another abbot who steered his wheelchair once."

Gerfried was delighted with the effect his allusion to Abbot Berno made. Berthold's shoulders twitched uncomfortably. Was the Father seeking the abbot's favor? That was unthinkable, even if the lame man spoke out against an intervention and was indefatigable in his defense of the Lord Udualrich.

Hermann was already sitting at the work desk when Berthold entered the cell. The Lord Udualrich had lifted him onto the armchair, and that too displeased the young monk. He studied the face of the sick man attentively, and with a distrust that he did not admit to himself. Was not his face more cheerful than it had been recently? If Berthold had come a moment earlier, he would have seen the bird that had hopped through the open window onto the work desk—a man of childlike purity could find pleasure in something like that. But Berthold supposed that the smile meant that Hermann was pleased with the service the abbot had rendered him.

Hermann pondered aloud: "I wonder whether the Holy

Father would like it if I wrote again about the thorns? Or should I sing the praise of the holy cross, which is laid so very much on his shoulders?"

"You ... you are writing to the Pope, after all?" cried Berthold in agitation. The most recent wish of the discontented monks was that not only the emperor, but also the Pope should be informed about what was happening on Reichenau.

Hermann looked at him darkly, and his brows met in the middle of his forehead. "Are you too starting to talk like the others? Do you think that I would now, after all this time, take part in the disobedient petition?"

Berthold was so confused that he stated, honestly: "Without you, there will be no petition."

"Thanks be to God! I will never ever support this plan. Ruodhard is going to Abbot Udualrich, and he will tell him openly why there is discontent in the abbey. We can safely entrust the further course of events to the Lord. I have just mentioned a poem. Father Abbot wants to enclose it in a letter to the Holy Father."

"So that is why he took care of you. After all that he already knows, he probably wants to cover his back with the Pope. And to that end, he is misusing your name and your influence with the Pope. You cannot and you must not write for him."

"Berthold, I hope you are not conscious of what you have said."

"I said it very consciously, Father. And I shall say it once again: You cannot and you must not write for him, because otherwise, the brethren will believe that you are courting the abbot's favor."

"Let them believe what they like. I obey."

"In this case, you do not need to obey!" cried Berthold, passionately and loudly. "In Rome, you are a protective shield for the abbot. He is exploiting you, and later on, he will despise you all the more. Do not write!"

"Have you forgotten that we are to obey our superior as we obey God himself?" asked Hermann, in a serious tone.

"God cannot want you to be exploited and abused in this way. He cannot want you to attract the hostility of many persons." Berthold flew into a rage. "This command is not from God!"

All at once, Hermann of Altshausen was only the theologian and older confrère whose words were uttered with dignity, from a position of distance and superiority.

"Brother, you are a professed monk and a priest, and yet you do not know that the commands of the superiors are to be regarded as coming from God, even when the one who issues the commands does not possess the degree of perfection that we would like to see in him? God speaks through the mouth of the superior—of every superior, Brother. And we must accept the commands of our Lord and Abbot Udualrich as if Our Lord Jesus Christ were issuing them to us. You may, and you must, say 'no' only in the case of an instruction that is contrary to the honest decision of your conscience, an instruction that enjoins a sin upon you.

"Let me give you one piece of advice: Do not allow yourself so easily to pronounce a destructive judgment on the behavior and the state of soul of another person. That is unchristian and Pharisaic. Each person is guilty only to the extent that he possesses knowledge of what he is doing. Only God knows when and where his guilt begins. We are sinners, and that is always something we share with those whom we judge or condemn ...

"It would be too much to ask of you, if I were to dictate the verses to you. So go, and take your writing implements with you!"

"Father ... I ..."

"That is enough, Berthold. I can manage on my own."

The priest-monk turned brusquely on his heel and left the room. His rapid, angry steps echoed in the cloister.

For a long time, the lame man sat before his work desk, as if he had been turned to stone. So Berthold too was one of them. He felt no indignation. What was he to do? How could he help? As he pondered, he folded his trembling hands.

"Lord, do not allow Berthold to become an adversary of the abbot. Do not allow him to stray from the path of obedience in his youthful impetuousness, for there is no other path for one whom you call to serve you. Lord, have mercy on him and grant him understanding. Do not permit him to run away from you by refusing to obey the Lord Udualrich.

"Let my other brethren too learn that you are to be found only along the path of obedience.

"Our community is at risk: have mercy on it. Discord, hatred, jealousy, mistrust, and coldness have made their way into the abbey. Do not allow your work to perish through our guilt.

"Grant us love for one another and reverence for our superiors! If there is anything that I can give you, take it, O Lord. Give us only your mercy, and we will be saved!"

"

The lame man wrestled with the Lord in prayer, over and over again. Then he forced his weak fingers to take up the goose quill. He laid his left hand heavily on the parchment. In shaky letters and at the cost of great exertion, he wrote for Leo IX a hymn in praise of the Crucified Lord, *Grates, honos* ...[1] He knew in advance that the unclear letters he wrote would not meet with the Lord Udualrich's approval. This time, the verses did not flow (as they usually did) from the free and effortless stream of his thoughts. They were wrested from his tormented and struggling spirit. They had neither facility nor a self-contained conceptual meaning. His inner distress cried out from the words. The hymn in praise of the cross and the Crucified Lord was the lament stammered by the soul of a crucified man.

Once again, Berthold was late. He brought the evening meal with a feigned tranquility. They were polite to each other, but precisely this politeness denoted a distance between them.

"Would you be so kind as to bring this parchment to our Lord and Father Abbot, Brother?"

Berthold bowed and left. Hermann sat before his meal. He knew that he could not eat anything. Nor was that all: he knew that, when Berthold came, he would have to ask him to spend the night in his cell. The day's exertions were wreaking their revenge on the lame man. His hands trembled continually after the excessive strain of writing, and unusually strong headaches told him to expect

---

1. [First line of the Sequence: "May thanksgiving and honor (be to you) ..."]

another of the terrible attacks that he had known and feared since the journey to Altshausen.

He breathed in relief when a knock came. But instead of Berthold, it was his brother Werinher who entered.

"You are at your supper. Am I disturbing you?"

"No, come in. I am not eating."

Werinher sat down opposite him. Lost in thought, he contemplated his older brother, the most beloved and the most hated monk of Reichenau.

"Hermann, do you know what they are saying about you? I have told them clearly that their conjectures are complete nonsense. Even if the abbot pushes your wheelchair on one occasion, that means nothing at all. But life here is getting more and more intolerable. People talk all the time. They whisper and criticize. I cannot endure it any longer. I want to go."

Despite the growing dusk, Hermann tried to catch his brother's eyes. "Do not talk like that, Werinher. You had similar plans once in the past."

"And now I am going to put them into action. I will go on a pilgrimage to the Holy Land. Abbot Berno held me back that time. I felt so secure with him that Reichenau became my home. But I am not going to remain here now. I must go to the places where Our Lord lived and suffered. It is there that my earthly journey will end. No, brother, do not contradict me. I know your objections. You will tell me that one can become holy anywhere, and under any abbot. You will tell me that going away, even on a pilgrimage to the Holy Land, is a cowardly flight ..."

"Yes," Hermann broke in quickly, "going away is a

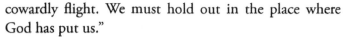

cowardly flight. We must hold out in the place where God has put us."

"And what if he calls us to the Holy Land?"

"If he wants to have you in the Holy Land, the abbot will not refuse you permission for the pilgrimage. Take that as a touchstone that shows whether or not your plans come from God. Have the courage to present your wish to Abbot Udualrich."

Werinher cried out indignantly. "What are you asking of me? I am to tell a man like Udualrich …?"

The lame man could no longer control the jerky twitching of his hands. The attack would come any minute now. This made him interrupt his brother.

"Werinher, brother, dear brother, for the sake of Christ …" His words became indistinct, as a spasm seized his facial muscles. "The Lord Udualrich is the abbot appointed for you by God," he babbled imploringly, "appointed by God. Promise me …"

"What am I to promise you?" asked Werinher sharply.

"To … say … it … to … him!" gasped Hermann with the last reserves of his strength. After this, only inarticulate sounds came from his mouth.

"What is wrong with you, Hermann? Is it your sickness? Did I excite you so much?"

He lifted his brother, who was rigid from the spasm, from the armchair and laid him carefully on his bed. He looked helplessly at Hermann as he groaned. "I will fetch Berthold!"

Hermann of Altshausen lay there, fettered by his lameness and dependent on the services of the companion who was his Good Samaritan—and who had just gone from him in rancor and bitterness. The last of the poor ones of Christ ...

When Berthold came running into the cell, the attack had reached the same level of vehemence as in the night in the parish priest's house near Altshausen.

The sick man's illness was now writing a new and more impressive Sequence in honor of the holy cross than he himself could ever have composed.

For hours on end, Berthold supported Hermann as he fought for breath or was shaken by spasms. He wiped sweat, tears, and spittle from his face, made him poultices with the herbal essence, and gave him small quantities of spiced wine.

Slowly, the sick man slid into a sensation of soothing languor and detachment. Everything became distant and unreal. The pains fell silent. He slept. The presence of his companion had spared him the worst—the dreadful inner distress.

Berthold carefully renewed the poultice on his forehead and listened to his weak but peaceful breaths. In the light of the candles, he looked at the emaciated face with its hollow cheeks, the deep furrows excavated by pain, the dark rims under his eyes, and the eyelids that were bluish and transparent.

"Have I caused him concern?" He could no longer understand himself or his conduct.

At one point, he left the cell and returned with his writing implements and the parchment that Hermann had given him that evening. He wrote all night long. He had never made such a beautiful and smooth copy.

When morning came, he brought the Abbot Hermann of Altshausen's hymn in praise of the cross.

"Finished already? That is good." The abbot's self-assured smile daunted Berthold, but he had taken his decision, and he was not content with half-measures.

"The Father finished the hymn yesterday evening, but I ... I ..."

"Well, of course, you wanted to copy it out first. That was very sensible on your part. No one can read the shaky scribblings of the lame man."

The abbot's superficial manner sorely tempted the young monk not to expose himself to humiliation, but he remained on his knees.

"Do you have a wish, Berthold?"

"Yes, Father Abbot, I want to tell you something. There was another reason why I did not want to bring you the parchment yesterday evening, although the Father had instructed me to do so."

The Lord Udualrich looked at him in astonishment. "I see. And why did you not want to obey, Berthold?"

"Because ... because I did not believe in the legitimacy of the commission that was entrusted to him. I thought that it would damage the Father, if he carried it out, and I had already attempted to persuade the Father that he should not write."

The abbot's broad face was hard at work as he registered this. Was he about to explode in fury?

"And why was it so important to you to prevent my commission from being carried out?"

"Because ..." Berthold faltered. His face was bathed in perspiration, and in his distress he pressed his damp hands together in the arms of his habit. "Because the brethren believe in any case that the Father is trying to ingratiate himself with you."

The abbot looked at him with an expression of utter amazement. Then he laughed a booming laugh. "Hermann? What are you saying? Hermann is ingratiating himself with me? Is that what they think?"

The laughter ceased abruptly, and his brows came together.

"What happened then? You tried hard to prevent Hermann from writing … and what did he do?"

"The Father became very angry at my behavior. He rebuked me severely and sent me away. He wrote down the Sequence without my help. I ought to have brought it to you yesterday evening, but I was disobedient."

"And why are you now bringing me the parchment that you have copied out, Berthold? Did he convince you?"

"Yes, Father Abbot, he convinced me. He had a new and particularly grave attack. It was terrible to have to see how he was tormented. But he sent me a look from time to time that showed me that he was consciously enduring his distress in expiation of my attitude and my conduct. When the attack wore off, my mind had changed. I wrote down the hymn for you, and I now ask you for forgiveness and for a penance."

Had the abbot heard the last words? He was looking down at the parchment with the Sequence of the cross.

"A strange man, this Hermann, a strange man. Powerlessness and power. He does not hate me, he sees through me. He sees through you, Berthold. He conquers you, as he did this night."

Berthold ventured to interpose: "He conquers the evil in me, Father Abbot."

The Lord Udualrich bowed. "The evil in us. If he were healthy, he would have to be the Abbot of Reichenau."

He straightened himself. "You know that, despite your openness, you have merited a penance, Brother. I charge you ... to offer the holy sacrifice of the Mass in the cell of Hermann of Altshausen."

"Oh, Father Abbot, thank you for this penance!"

"Berthold, even a man who never became father can act like a father, if there is someone to speak to the good that is in him; someone who respects him when others despise him."

Flight

Dawn was just beginning to creep over the mountains by the lake, when Hermann woke from a light slumber. In the semidarkness, he recognized the outlines of a man.

"What is it, Berthold?" he asked in a low voice.

The monk came closer and bent over him.

"It is not Berthold, Hermann. It is me—Werinher."

"Werinher?" What brought his brother to him at this time of day? "Has something happened, brother?"

"No, nothing has happened. But something is about to happen, Hermann. Luither and I are beginning our pilgrimage to the Holy Land," whispered Werinher.

Hermann took hold of his brother's habit with both hands, as if he wanted to hold him fast.

"You are going on pilgrimage? Are you leaving Reichenau in secret?"

His hands clutched the black woolen cloth.

"Yes, Hermann, we are going away in secret. Is there anyone here who would have any sympathy with our wish? Do you? So we are going on pilgrimage to the

Holy Land without telling the abbot and hearing him say 'no.'"

"Werinher, you cannot do that! You must not! You would be deserters, absconders, excommunicated … Werinher, think about what you are doing." Hermann gasped as he implored his brother. In this emergency, his hands, which were otherwise so weak, held the cloth in an iron grip.

"We have thought of everything, brother. There is no turning back now. A fisher boat is waiting not far from the Herrenbruck harbor. I just wanted to bid you fare-well. I expect that you will refuse me your blessing …"

"Werinher, my brother, by the memory of our lady mother, remain here! I ask you!"

The lame man tugged frantically at his brother's habit.

"Hermann, I have to go. Pray for me." He noticed that the sick man was holding him fast. "Let go of me!" he demanded impatiently.

"Werinher! Remain here!" Hermann groaned.

"Let go of me! I do not want to hurt you."

"You are doing that in any case. Remain here!"

The lame man held his brother's habit so firmly that Werinher had to use force to get it out of his hands. An unequal struggle began.

"Let go of me!"

"Remain here!"

When Werinher finally freed himself forcibly, the sick man's hands still held a piece of cloth. Hermann fell back on his bed, exhausted.

"I must … report your … flight …"

"Follow your conscience, Hermann. I am following mine."

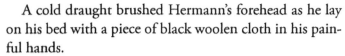
A cold draught brushed Hermann's forehead as he lay on his bed with a piece of black woolen cloth in his painful hands.

"Werinher?"

The door closed quietly, and Werinher crept away through the cloister.

"I must inform the abbot. I must report my own brother," thought Hermann despondently. A little bell stood on a stool beside his bed. After several vain attempts, he had it in his hand, and then he rang it. It sounded loud in the silence of the cloister, and he hoped that Berthold would hear it. The bell cried out its desperate plea for help, until it slipped from his hand and rolled over the stone floor with a noisy clang.

Berthold rushed in, out of breath and agitated. "What is wrong, Father?"

"Help me! I must get to Father Abbot as quickly as possible!"

The lame man's voice held such distress that his companion did not ask any questions. A short time later, the wheelchair was creaking on its way through the cloister. Berthold knocked at the door of the abbot's quarters. A somewhat reluctant voice asked from within the room what important matter was at stake.

"Hermann of Altshausen asks urgently to speak to you at once, Father Abbot."

The door opened at once.

"Hermann, what has happened? You look like a ghost," said the Lord Udualrich, blinking and still half asleep.

The sick man's hands tensed up. He felt like shouting.

"Father Abbot, I have something important to tell you … My brother, the monk Werinher of Altshausen and the

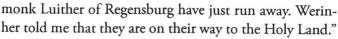

monk Luither of Regensburg have just run away. Werinher told me that they are on their way to the Holy Land."

The lame man bowed his head low. It was hard to denounce his own brother ...

The abbot did not reply. Had he not grasped the significance of Hermann's words? Berthold pressed his right hand to his lips in horror. Poor Father Hermann! He was not to be spared anything.

Finally, the Lord Udualrich spoke in a cracked voice: "You yourself are telling me that your brother has absconded, Hermann? Why did you not give him the chance to get away first? You could have covered his flight for long enough."

"No, Father Abbot, I could not do that. I told Werinher that I would tell you about his flight. They are rowing over the Gnadensee."

Once again the abbot, who was visibly shaken, hesitated before he took the grave decision: "Then we must pursue them."

"That is what I would ask you to do, Father Abbot!"

The two monks stared at the sick man, almost in shock.

"You ask me to do so, Hermann? But Werinher is your brother."

"Werinher is my brother—my brother who is running away from God."

Abbot Udualrich sent monastery servants after the runaways, but they came back without results. Hermann sat for hours on end at the window. Before him lay a piece of black woolen cloth, torn from a monastic habit.

He saw many a boot crossing the Gnadensee, but none of them brought the two monks Werinher and Luither back to Reichenau. In his presence, no one spoke about what had happened. The sick man's pain at his brother's infidelity was too great.

"

One day, a messenger from Italy came to Abbot Udualrich. The man, a pilgrim on his return journey from Rome, gave the abbot a letter that the two monks had written somewhere in Italy. Had the unceasing prayer of the sick man reached them and moved their hearts to repentance and conversion?

They implored the abbot to forgive them for acting without his authorization. They asked for the retroactive permission to go on pilgrimage to the Holy Land.

"If you do not permit us to travel farther, Lord and Father Abbot, we shall return by the quickest route to Reichenau. We shall cast ourselves before your feet as penitents and ask for the grace to be readmitted to the community of the brethren. If you are so generous as to grant us retroactively the unmerited permission to go on pilgrimage, we shall not cease to pray for you, our Lord and Father Abbot, in reverence, gratefulness, and penitence, at those sacred places that were sanctified by Our Lord Jesus Christ. We will faithfully take with us all the concerns of our beloved Reichenau to the Holy Land ..."

Initially, the Lord Udualrich was little inclined to grant the wish of the two absconders. They were to take the quickest route home and receive their punishment and penance. Was he to give a retroactive permission that approved of the way they had behaved? That was too much to ask.

Abbot Udualrich needed the celebration of Vespers,

during which he saw the grief-stricken face of the sick man in the choir stall opposite him, in order to change his mind.

He forgave the two absconding monks and gave them retroactively the permission to go on pilgrimage. He wanted to see a smile on the lame man's face again, and he felt very richly rewarded when Hermann thanked him.

A change had taken place in the Lord Udualrich. Once he had understood who the lame man was, and once he had lost his old aversion, he automatically took his cue from Hermann's every word and wish. Without any presumption on his part, it was Hermann who guided the abbot, and thus the abbey too. The lame man served by means of his counsel, unreservedly and unassumingly. Udualrich sought his advice ever more frequently before taking any decision. The complaints of the monks diminished, until they finally disappeared. The spirit of Cluny had imperceptibly reconquered Reichenau. And the abbot was now seen in prayer at the tomb of his predecessor.

"

Months passed. The year 1054 was noted in Hermann's world chronicle before Reichenau received any further news of the pilgrims. The monk Luither had written a letter. He began by describing their happy arrival in Jerusalem, after they had overcome many obstacles and dangers.

Then he went on: "And now I must give very sad news to you, Lord and Father Abbot, and to the dear brethren on Reichenau: our Brother Werinher of Altshausen is dead.

"He was at the very grave of Our Lord Jesus Christ when he first began to feel seriously unwell. He rejoiced at this: 'Brother, my wish will be fulfilled! I shall find my last resting place in the Holy Land.'

"But he soon recovered, and we went on pilgrimage to the Jordan, where Our Lord was baptized by John. The long, hot, and stony way was doubtless too much for Werinher. He bent down over the water that was sanctified by the Lord, dipped his hand in it, and blessed himself. Suddenly, he stood up and asked me: 'Luither, do you hear a call from the other shore?' I listened, but all I heard was the rushing of the water.

"'I have been called!' he insisted, obstinately. 'I must go over to the other shore!'

"It was then that I noticed that he had fever again. It was only with the aid of another pilgrim that I brought him back to the hospice in Jerusalem, where I found a doctor, a Greek. He was celebrated for his skill in healing, and he had lived for more than a decade in the Holy City. But the doctor could do nothing for this sickness. The body of our Brother Werner deteriorated, and he had great pains. He suffered with patience, indeed with joy. His last words were: 'I am coming to the other shore!'

"He died on December 25, *Anno Domini* 1053,[2] the feast of the Nativity of Our Lord.

"Pray for the soul of our departed brother. After such suffering and such a death, we may surely believe that he will enter into the peace of God.

"The Greek doctor, Master Theophilos Cheirisophos, sends special greetings to the monk Hermann of Altshau-

---

2. ["In the year of the Lord."]

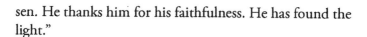

sen. He thanks him for his faithfulness. He has found the light."

"

This time, the monks of Reichenau were afraid to encounter the lame man. How could a man bear such blows of fate? His behavior made them uneasy, because his face, which was becoming ever more transparent, bore an expression of peace.

"Werinher followed the call of God. He more than atoned through his suffering and dying for what he had done wrong by acting secretly. Thanks be to God!" said the sick man to Berthold when he assured him gently of his sympathy. "And Master Theophilos Cheirisophos ... Do you still remember him? He was my doctor in Aachen. Now he lives in the Holy City. He calls himself 'Theophilos' once more, and he has found the light. A home has been given to the homeless wanderer. Berthold, God is infinitely good!"

He intoned the Magnificat. The young monk responded only hesitantly. At this moment, there was something almost uncanny about the Father, who behaved so little like one who belonged to this world.

"

Berthold wrote down the news of the death in the world chronicle. As was the custom, Abbot Udualrich decreed the celebration of a Requiem Mass, followed by a funeral banquet, on the next day. The news of the death of the monk Werinher of Altshausen made its way slowly to more than one hundred abbeys with which Reichenau was linked through the fraternity of prayer. Many prayers for the dead man were sent after him into eternity in each abbey. Even in death, the brethren did not abandon him.

Tomorrow, there would be a candle at Brother Werinher's empty place in the refectory, burning as a symbol of his entry into the light of eternity.

"

That night, Brother Hermann had a strange dream. Berthold brought him to the Gnadensee, which lay in the gleam of the springtime sun like a vessel full of light. At Herrenbruck harbor, a well-known shining figure awaited them—Pope Leo IX. He greeted the sick man with great cordiality.

"Would you like to cross the Gnadensee, Hermann? I must go over to the other shore. You have accompanied me so faithfully all these years, and I do not wish to do without your companionship now."

"May Berthold travel with us, Holy Father?"

"No, not yet. He must stay behind. He will follow us later."

The lame man was sad that he had to leave his faithful companion behind—all the more so, since he was pleading: "Father, remain here!"

"I leave you my thorns, my son."

Then he was on the white ship, which slid calmly over the tranquil Gnadensee. The abbey became gray and shadowy, until it dropped out of sight.

"The star is going out," said the Lord Leo in a serious voice.

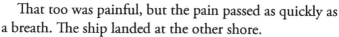
That too was painful, but the pain passed as quickly as a breath. The ship landed at the other shore.

"Hermann, we are at home."

The lame man looked into a brightness, shining and sparkling. With some difficulty, he could make out in this light the outlines of huge buildings, domes, roofs, and gates.

"The New Jerusalem, the Eternal City," called the Holy Father joyfully.

Then one of the gates opened, and they came out, shining and bright, youthful and healthy, those whom he loved, his lady mother, his brother Werinher, and Abbot Berno.

"Do you know now why all suffering must be, Hermann?" Abbot Berno asked him.

"In order that Christ may be glorified, for his sake."

"For his sake!" The words rang out like a bell. "For his sake! For his sake ..."

Abbot Berno bent down to him. Hermann looked into the joyful, kindly eyes of his father in Christ, and felt clearly the sign of the cross that the abbot slowly traced on his forehead.

"You are still sick, Hermann, my son. Do not be afraid. Soon, you will be healthy ... like us."

And Abbot Berno turned to Pope Leo IX. With a grave and solemn voice he asked him: "Are you ready? Then come with us, Holy Father. The gates of the Eternal City are opening wide to welcome you. The Father, the Son, and the Holy Spirit are waiting for you."

Pope Leo IX went into the midst of the radiant light.

CHAPTER 10

* * *

LIGHT

Until We Meet Again—Hermann

A MILD SUNSHINE lay over the island in Lake Constance. There were only some light clouds in the sky, the friendly accompaniment of good weather. The woods on the Swabian mountains on the other shore sent a tender green greeting.

At his open window, Hermann absorbed the picture of the springtime landscape. His face was terribly gaunt. The pale yellow skin stretched over his cheekbones like a parchment that had been scraped thin, so that his eyes appeared all the bigger and more dominant in his narrow face. His back was even more bent than before.

But his character displayed no unease. His lively temperament had given way to a mellow poise, and kindness and serenity were his constant expression. In earlier years, he had often rebuked the students harshly and strictly, and he had been impatient when they were slow to understand or to follow his train of thought. Now, he only helped them with an utterly inexhaustible patience.

He had not noticed Berthold's entrance, and he continued to look at the peaceful picture. His stooped figure was immobile by the window. Did his faithful companion sense that the time had come for his life to undergo its final maturing?

"Father?"

"Berthold, how good that you have come! Would you please take me outside? There is one omission that I must make good for you."

"What do you mean, Father?"

"Guess!" said Hermann in a kindly tone.

"Riddles of that kind are too difficult for me ..."

"The words of a mentally lazy man who did not want to make the effort in the first place," chuckled the lame man. "Come now. The difficult riddle will be solved at once."

What did the Father intend? The young monk felt a certain excitement as he lifted the sick man into the wheelchair—and noticed how much lighter his body had become.

They passed through the monastery gate. A tall young man approached them. A tangle of blond and strawberry blond locks framed a face with well-proportioned features, and his green eyes lit up when he saw the lame man.

Hermann stretched out his hand to the young man.

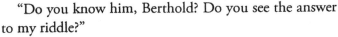
"Do you know him, Berthold? Do you see the answer to my riddle?"

"Bruno?" asked Berthold, after an initial hesitation.

"Yes, our Bruno, the son of Mistress Magdalen. Do you know where he landed, thanks to the help of our Abbot Udualrich? Bruno, tell your story!"

"I am apprenticed to the woodcarver George in Constance, and I enjoy my work very much. Master George thinks that I have already learned a great deal," said the young man, unselfconsciously. "I came here today because I have brought Father Abbot a statue for the church of Saint George, and I did not want to miss the opportunity to thank you once again, Father Hermann."

"Have you now found the solution to the riddle?" the sick man asked his companion. "Our Father Abbot kept his promise. Bruno was only helping out for a couple of days on the monastery estate. I did not even need to remind the Lord Udualrich of the situation. It was he who saw to it that Master George took the boy into his workshop very shortly afterward. Now let us go to the lake together."

Berthold steered the wheelchair to the Gnadensee. He had understood what the Father wanted to teach him. The tall, slim young man ran cheerfully beside them, finding his path adroitly and gracefully. How much he resembled his mother, Mistress Magdalen!

"Bruno, how are your lady mother and your brothers and sisters?"

"They are all well. Gertrude got married last year, and now she has a little son, who has the same name as you, Father."

"Well, well," smiled the sick man, "so there is a little

Hermann once again in Altshausen. I wonder if he too will go out to look for heaven? Do I know your sister's husband?"

"You know him well, Father. It is your servant, Walter."

"The good Walter ..." Hermann nodded. "So everything turns out for the best."

"No, not everything," said the young man somberly.

"What is wrong? Is Count Wolfrad causing difficulties for your family again?" asked the sick man, who had always been afraid that that might happen.

"No, Father, he is particularly kind toward us since the Lady Hiltrud's death. The problem is ... about me." The boy sighed.

"Have you done something wrong? Can I help you?"

They had now reached the Gnadensee. The lake had an almost unearthly beauty that afternoon. There was a golden light in the air over the clear and tranquil water; it seemed to announce its presence in the depths of the lake and to be reflected by these depths. The light fell on the pointed stalks of the reeds, and on the willows and the bushes on the shore, and clothed them in a warm glow. The low ranges of hills on the other shore looked like mysterious mountains, full of promise. There lay a peace over all this beauty and radiance, a peace that was both calm and joyful. The Gnadensee ... the "lake of grace."

Berthold brought the wheelchair to a halt. He sensed now, more than ever before, what the lake meant to the Father. It symbolized both the divine grace and that which the divine grace can give the human person.

"Now, Bruno, tell me what is worrying you," said Hermann.

"Why can I not become a monk, a monk on

Reichenau?" cried the young man, while the fine skin of his face flushed a deep red. "You need master painters here. Could you not also use a carver who was a monk, and who plied his trade for the glory of God?"

Before the lame man could answer, the young man went on: "I know what you will say ... Reichenau admits only sons of the aristocracy. Do you believe, Father, that God calls only noblemen? Our Lord Jesus Christ was born in a stable and died on the gallows of the cross. His foster father was a carpenter in Nazareth, not a king or a count ..."

Berthold wanted to cut him short: "Bruno, you must not ..."

A gesture from the sick man silenced him.

"Let him tell the truth, Berthold. Bruno, say without fear what you are thinking."

"Yes," cried the young man, turning his green eyes with an expression of joy and trust on the man in the wheel-chair. "You too are an aristocrat, but I can tell you everything. You are not desperate at all costs to maintain your distance from us common people."

Once again, Berthold wanted to object. He felt that Bruno was going too far. But a sign from his Master's hand told him to be silent, and the boy continued:

"Look at the life of Our Lord here on earth. He was poor, completely poor. He called fishermen, tax collectors, and sinners to be his apostles. He did not call people from the upper classes. He ate with those who were despised by the rich.

"Are we to believe that this God has changed, and that he wants to be served only by those who were born in a noble house? Are the sons of the common people allowed to serve him only as servants of the aristocrats? Can that be the will of God, Father? Do you not agree with me that young people from farmers' cottages or fishermen's huts can be called by God?"

"Where do you get these ideas, Bruno?" asked Berthold, shaking his head. "Who put them into your head?"

"I have reflected on this all by myself, after a priest in Constance told me that men like myself could at best be a village curate, but never a monk of Reichenau."

The young man's complaint concerned a problem that Hermann had often pondered in his mind. The noblemen who had laid down such regulations were depriving the monasteries of great powers of the mind and the heart!

"I am aware of my own rank in society, but is it more valuable in the eyes of God than a lower rank? Does not a higher rank entail a greater measure of responsibility? Many aristocrats see only the rights of their rank; they overlook its stricter obligations. In the long term, our monasteries—and Reichenau among them—will become poor and desolate if they admit only members of the aristocracy. Is that always the best and purest source of new monks? Is every aristocratic monk truly called by God? Or was it not merely the desire of his parents to secure a respected state in life for their younger sons? Why do we not admit men from the common people to our monastic community, if God grants them the grace of a vocation? Will he not punish us bitterly for our arrogance?"

Hermann turned to his companion with a gesture that was almost a challenge.

"Tell me, why should not Bruno be admitted to Reichenau, initially as a student? He has a clever mind and a special talent. He is pious and healthy ..."

Berthold was almost horrified. "Father, you must bear in mind ..." He said no more, but Hermann knew in any case what he had meant to say: "Bear in mind how his father ended!"

"The noble lord of the manor committed an injustice. Is this injustice to continue to exist? I am his son, and it is therefore my duty to make amends."

"You have done so over a long period, and more than sufficiently."

"Is there a statute of limitations in this case? Can one fully make good the wrong that has been done? No! It is God alone who can bring that about, and now he shows me a new possibility.—Bruno, I shall speak with Father Abbot and ask him to admit you as one of the students of the school inside the monastery."

To his surprise, the young man's face remained somber.

"For the rest of my life, I would merely be someone who was tolerated."

"Yes, you will feel that painfully, just as everyone does who takes—or must take—a special path. You will probably succeed to my office, and you will carry it out in a different way."

"Your office?" Bruno was astonished, and his eyes widened.

"My office is to be the last of the poor ones of Christ. If you live for God on Reichenau, you will gladly assume even that office. My sickness imposed it on me. It is not an easy office ... and yet I have been happy, young man." The sick man plucked at his companion's sleeve. "Berthold, there is something I must say to you alone."

The young man at once moved a few steps away from them.

"Father?"

"Like me, you loved our great and holy Abbot Berno, did you not?"

"Yes, Father," answered Berthold quickly, without knowing what Hermann was getting at.

"Well, then, tell me the noble family from which he was descended!"

"The Lord Berno's family? I do not know, Father ..." admitted the young monk awkwardly. "You told me about the noble Arnulph of Rahnwyl in Aachen, who was a relative of our Lord Berno."

"But you will search in vain for his family name, my son. The father of our beloved and noble abbot was a farmer with a smallholding, and his mother was a simple miller's daughter from the Eifel mountains. The great Abbot of Reichenau was born in a farmhouse. But the Abbot of Pruem was too wise—and also too pious—to reject the boy Berno when he asked for admittance to the abbey. The Lord Arnulph himself told me that story. He was not ashamed of his poor relative."

A large boat with three men in it was approaching the shore. They waved and called out incomprehensible words to the three men on the shore. What news were these people from the other shore bringing? They hoped for good news, and Bruno was so curious that he at once went closer to the Herrenbruck harbor. Berthold would have liked to do the same.

When the boat was almost ashore, one man leaped out. He wore the colorful jerkin of a messenger from the city council in Constance, and he waved a letter with the imposing seal of the Lord of Constance, Bishop Theoderich. He hurried to the shore. As he rushed past them, he called out to the monks: "Our Holy Father, Pope Leo IX, died on April 19 in Rome!"

The monks stayed rooted to the spot while the men hastened to the monastery.

Pope Leo IX was dead.

That radiant man, that inspiring personality was no longer among those living here on earth.

"Pope Leo is on the other shore," said the lame man quietly. He thought of his dream, where the Pope had invited him to cross with him …

This great Pope had had only a short reign. After becoming Pope when he was nearly fifty, he had consumed all his energies for the sake of Christ's kingdom in scarcely more than five years. Here he had stood on the Herrenbruck harbor in 1049, a powerful and vigorous figure against the cloudy gray autumnal sky.

Today, the sky was high, bright, and shining, and the Pope was dead—or rather, he had returned home.

The lame man looked at the sunshine over the lake. Did not the jetty simply end in the midst of the light? The Lord Leo was on the other shore. Soon, he too would be invited to cross over, to return home. He shuddered.

Berthold was concerned, and bent over him. "Father?"

"Let us go back to the abbey. They will miss us. Bring Bruno to the guest master and see that he is looked after until I can speak with Father Abbot."

They left the shining lake and turned in the direction of the abbey, where the black shadows of evening were already falling. The bell that tolled to announce a death was ringing dully from the tower of Abbot Berno's monastery church.

Hermann dictated the following text, which Berthold

copied out carefully for the world chronicle: "Our Lord Pope Leo, the ninth of that name, was at Benevento for a long time, intent upon the service of God. When he fell sick, he returned to Rome shortly before the Easter feast. His weakness increased, until finally he died. His death was glorious. When he was departing, he blessed everyone. He confessed his sins to Saint Peter and recommended himself humbly to his intercession. He was buried in Saint Peter's church on April 26, alongside Pope Gregory the Saint. It is said that miracles have already occurred in testimony to his holiness."

Then he asked him: "Give me parchment, the ink, and the goose quill." He wrote a few words under the text he had dictated—a few words in his shaky handwriting under the even letters of his pupil. Then he drew a line under them and gave the sheet of parchment back to Berthold, who was astonished and deeply concerned to read the words: "Until we meet again—Hermann." What was that supposed to mean? He did not dare to ask, because he guessed the meaning of these concluding words and of the line drawn under them.

"Until we meet again—Hermann."

"

"We must in fact praise Our Lord for calling Pope Leo IX to himself. In that way, this great and holy life remained a pure flame, a Pentecostal storm, without losing any of its strength and its blaze because the path was too long. This Pentecostal storm did not fall in vain on the holy Church. It set fire to many souls, and they will bear its blaze to others. The light of Christ will grow and shine. We may know much that is great, magnificent, and moving about the Lord Leo; but he was at his greatest when he opened up in simplicity to receive the Holy Spirit ..."

Berthold looked down at the words that Hermann had written with his own hand, and he could not concentrate on what the Master was saying. He would have liked to ask him, but he was afraid that the answer would only confirm what he guessed at.

"Would you go to the young man Bruno and tell him that he may come? Abbot Udualrich has not closed his ears to the call of God to the boy, and to the abbey itself. This call is also addressed to you, Berthold. Look after him with particular care. Promise me, my son!"

"Do you not want to look after the boy yourself, Father?"

"I would like to do that, Berthold, but Our Lord has other plans for me. Lead him to God."

"Who am I, that I should be able to bring someone closer to God?"

"On your own, you are nothing, nothing at all. But with God, you are able to do everything that he charges you to do. He gives us what we need, when he sends us out. I have experienced again and again in my life that God is infinitely good!"

Berthold looked at the lame man's cheerful face. The blue eyes shone in grateful joy, as he remembered the good things God had given him. The crooked hands were crossed over and rested on his lap. They too had become thinner and more transparent.

"Father, you have experienced many hard things in your life. God took from you the people who enriched your existence."

"He takes only in order to give, my son. My experience has been that his blows are the blows of a loving Father ... and every fetter is a grace. The Lord is infinitely good!"

The priest-monk then did something he had never done before. He took hold of the poor hands of his teacher.

"If it is your lips that proffer such a testimony, I must believe it, Father. Your suffering sets the seal upon what you say. And yet ... I would wish that you had experienced more security and human warmth. Am I to see it as signs of the love and kindness of God, when all who were close to you had to leave you ... our Father Abbot Berno, your lady mother, your brother Werinher, and now Pope Leo IX, who was your kindred spirit? Is not your suffering so hard on its own that you need no further torment?"

Hermann knew the purity of Berthold's good will, and he smiled up at him. He cautiously withdrew his hands.

"My friend, we must not yield to the temptation to tell the Lord how far he may go. If we have said 'yes' to the oblation of ourselves and have declared our willingness to be bread in his hands, we must not set any conditions. It is difficult, very difficult, to make the gift of oneself without any limitations, Berthold. But the Lord takes our sacrificial will seriously. He comes and helps us to become a sacrificial gift. If we have once prayed honestly for thorns, because suffering love is a prolongation and a perfection of our redemption, the Lord gives us the thorns. He is faithful, and he answers our deepest prayers."

"He gave you an abundance of thorns. If only you had seen something more of their blossoms!"

"I must contradict your words. My thorn branches blossomed, and they are still blossoming. God has given me many joys: my Gnadensee, the creation with its flowers and trees, its stars and clouds; music and the sciences; people who are dear to me, industrious pupils, confrères, and you, my faithful companion and friend. I will not tell you everything that has been given me in the natural and the supernatural spheres, for I would never come to an end. Berthold, my soul is continually aware of the kindness of the heavenly Father."

The young monk made no more protests. After a pause, Hermann went on: "We are allowed to penetrate the mystery of a life—even the mystery of our own life—only up to a point. But there is a sphere of the innermost grace in a soul where God responds, if we allow his will to be done in us. If one's only desire is to be bread in his hands, one feels the Lord breaking the bread. But one also experiences, precisely in that breaking, that God is not destroying him, but is admitting him more and more into his love."

Christus—Vita Mea[1]

The lame man's bodily weakness increased. It was only seldom now that he could sit at his desk, working or looking out at the Gnadensee. One day in June, after a sleepless night, he sat in his armchair. He was on the point of asking Berthold to put him to bed, when the monk entered with a message from the abbot: "Father Abbot requests you to come to an extraordinary meeting. Can you do that?"

"Very well, Berthold," said the sick man quietly, "take me to the chapter room."

Hermann crouched in his wheelchair, small and

---

1. ["Christ—my life."]

sunken, frighteningly pale, with red-rimmed eyes that sat far back in his head. He felt cold even in the warm summer weather, and he was wrapped in several coverings. But he smiled at the brethren, who scarcely managed to conceal their shock when they saw him.

The Lord Udualrich stopped at his wheelchair and asked anxiously: "Have I asked too much of you, Hermann? Should Berthold bring you back to your cell?"

The sick man would have liked to assent to this suggestion, but he had seen the grief in the abbot's eyes. He had to remain.

"No, Father Abbot, it will not be too much for me." But he was very cold …

With a faltering voice, the abbot announced to the community, who listened in horror, that the separation between the Church of the East and the Church in Rome had become a reality. The Roman legate, Cardinal Humbert, laid the bull of excommunication against Patriarch Michael Caerularius on the altar of the Greek church of Hagia Sophia in Byzantium.

"And that, at a time when the Church in Rome has no head. This schism may well have terrible consequences for the Church, even if we cannot yet see them fully!"

Abbot Udualrich uttered no rebukes when an excited chattering broke out in the chapter room. A wave of grief flowed over the sick man. The catastrophe of which Pope Leo IX had been afraid had now come about. The Pope himself had not lived to see it. He was at rest in the peace of God and saw the great patterns in all that happened on earth.

Was the separation between East and West only a catastrophe for the Church? Was it not also a powerful warning and appeal on the part of God? Must not each one ask whether he bore a part of the blame?

The abbot requested the sick man to say a few words to the brethren about this news. "You knew Pope Leo better than any of us, and so you are better informed."

Berthold brought the wheelchair into the middle of the room, where the brethren could see him—as on that day when he had accused himself in front of Abbot Berno. The lame monk looked decrepit, but his voice was surprisingly clear and vigorous.

"Lord and Father Abbot, dear brethren in Christ, have we not all contributed our share to what has happened in Byzantium? Every 'no' to the love of God made us gravediggers of unity. All false pride, every lack of consideration, of patience, and of kindness has widened the rift, because it is only love that creates unity and peace. Have we not all too often left our Holy Father alone in his endeavor to preserve the unity with Byzantium?

"Now the great schism, and the great suffering, is here. But all suffering means grace, if one accepts it. In this painful hour, all we can do is to face up to the cross and take our position under the cross. We must pour ourselves out in a love that serves, and we must hope in faith that the love of us all will one day be so great—perhaps only after centuries of separation—that God will say: 'My will is that they should once again be one!'

"What then can we do to counter the separation? Beloved brethren, let us aim to be one among ourselves in our monastic community, even if the price is hard sacrifices, even if that means renunciation, silence, and putting up with difficulties!

"Often, we have not borne this in mind. Nor have we

acted accordingly. And so we bear our share of the blame for what has happened in Byzantium.

"Without prayer, however, our sacrifices would lack something essential. Let us pray with especial intensity to Our Lady of Reichenau. Our separated brethren in Byzantium also venerate her with all their hearts."

The Lord Udualrich took up this last suggestion.

"Let us sing one of the canticles to Mary that Brother Hermann has given us, especially his *Salve Regina,* in this intention every day. Let us ask Our Lady, the Mother of mercy, to spread out her hands over Reichenau. May she obtain for us the grace to be one among ourselves in the love of Christ."

"

The month of August brought hot days of harvesting and heavy thunderstorms. The heat tormented the lame man. The afflictions of his poor body increased day by day; his body was visibly waning. The brief periods in which he could do something were like a sigh of relief between the long phases of his lameness.

When Berthold asked him to dictate a text for the chronicle about the events in Byzantium, he refused.

"My son, have you not read what I wrote under the last entry: 'Until we meet again—Hermann.' Now it is you who will continue the chronicle."

Abbot Udualrich accepted his request to be relieved of the duty of teaching the students, and freed him from every other obligation. Berthold was beside him day and night. He prayed with him and celebrated the holy sacrifice in his cell. The days of pain, on which Hermann did not have the strength to move his head, but only saw the whitewashed ceiling above him, were very long. He was intimately acquainted now with the fissures and spots on the ceiling. His weary mind never tried to make sense of this strange map.

Sometimes, he asked his companion to lay him down in such a way that he could see the cross. He then spoke with the Lord who hung there. He had much to thank him for, especially for the gift of grace that preserved his inner peace. He prayed for those who must still stay on this shore. He read in the eyes of his faithful Berthold an increasing distress, the fear of being alone. He often prayed for the abbey, for the abbot, the brethren, and the holy Church. He had not forgotten the commission that Pope Leo had given him.

September brought the thirty-fifth anniversary of the day on which Count Wolfrad and his wife Hiltrud had brought their son Hermann to Reichenau in order to consecrate the crippled child at the altar as an oblation to the Lord.

The lame man asked his companion: "Would you remember that and give thanks to God in the Mass that day?"

The young monk told the abbot that Hermann's anniversary was drawing near.

"How could we give him pleasure on that day?" said the abbot at once. "What if our monastic choir sang one of his canticles before his cell?"

"That would give him very great pleasure, Father Abbot."

"Then discuss the details with the choirmaster."

Gunter decided on the Magnificat from the first period after Hermann's return to Reichenau.

"Before that, we will sing one of his favorite songs ... '*Christus—vita mea.*'"

"

On the morning of September 15, after the Mass, Berthold stealthily opened the door to the cloister. The monks had already gathered there, and now their well-trained voices rang out.

They sang the canticle about the Lord Jesus Christ, who is life. Then the solemn tones of the Magnificat resounded joyfully through the cloister.

Hermann listened with his eyes shut and his hands folded, and he remained thus after the door closed quietly.

After some time, the abbot came. "Hermann, you know why we have sung these canticles for you today?"

"Yes, Father Abbot, and I thank you for sharing in my anniversary. How have I deserved such a gift?"

"In my person, Reichenau thanks you, Hermann, for your loving, your suffering, and your serving."

The Lord Udualrich laid his right hand gently on the white head, and then departed with surprising haste. He felt a great distress at the thought that this heart would soon stop beating; this great heart of a little cripple, that had space even for him and had so often helped him to take the path of conversion.

"What will Reichenau be without him?"

Abbot Udualrich was afraid of his own weakness. He knew how easy it was for him to succumb to temptation. On his own, he was at the mercy of his vacillating nature; and he would be alone when Hermann died.

"

Christmas, the coming of the Lord, was approaching in the Advent of that year. The lame man was tormented by pains, fever, and weakness.

"I have been glad to be alive, despite my sickness. The world told me about God. It was beautiful to exist in his presence and to live for him. But now I only long for the other shore. Nothing detains me here any longer."

Berthold was not ashamed of his tears.

"Do not weep, dear friend," said Hermann in a weak voice. "Do not weep. Rejoice with me and wish me happiness, because at last I can go home. Take everything away with you, including my chronicles, and continue them faithfully. I entrust them to you with full confidence. You will do the work correctly, and complete conscientiously what now falls from my weak hand."

Berthold obeyed and took the books and writing implements, the musical instruments, the sundial, and the astrolabe out of the cell. Some projects remained incomplete, but did that matter? What did a dying man need, other than the cross?

When Berthold returned, Hermann made a sign to him and took his hand.

"My friend, you must be ready at any moment to follow me on this path. You have followed me faithfully here on earth. Whatever was not done for God, whatever is outside of love, loses its value ...

"I should like to thank you sincerely, my beloved son, for your faithfulness. God will reward you for everything, for every delicate action in your humble service of a poor cripple. If I am permitted to do so, I shall be your intercessor in the presence of God.

"Forgive me for making things difficult for you so often, through my moods and my other defects.

"Forgive me for giving you scandal when I was remiss in the observance of the Rule. Do not judge me in accordance with my bad example."

"Father, you must not speak like that!" protested the young monk, with tears in his eyes. "For me, you were the model of a monk."

"Well then, my friend in Christ, let us hand over to the Lord both what we have to thank each other for, and what we have to forgive each other ..."

Suddenly, his face turned even paler and he whispered urgently: "Call Father Abbot to me."

Berthold came back with the news that the abbot had gone to Hegne for a few hours.

"Across the Gnadensee," murmured Hermann with a smile.

"May I bring the Lord to you, Father?" asked Berthold.

"Yes," breathed Hermann laboriously, "everything ... you ..."

And the young priest-monk gave the consolations of Mother Church to his dying teacher, who had once prepared him for the priesthood.

The physical distress of the sick man grew hourly. By the time the abbot hastened to him that evening, Hermann could no longer ask for pardon. He could no longer give thanks.

The Lord Udualrich was sensitive enough to grasp what Hermann wanted, and to respond. He bent down to him and said in a cordial tone: "My dear son, I know about everything that you would like to say to me. You need no longer do so. If human frailty led you to sin now and again, you have long since atoned for it.

"Hermann, I thank you for all the good you have done for Reichenau through your heroic life for Our Lord Jesus Christ.

"And I thank you for all you have done for me. May it be a consolation to you to know that your life has left its traces on me.

"It was through you that I learned the power a humble heart possesses. You are the heart of the Abbey of Our Lady on Reichenau. Do not forget us here in our distress when you are with her and she shows you her Son."

The abbot bent down even further and whispered, as if he had an inner vision: "*Ite missa est.*"

The dying man's lips breathed, scarcely audibly: "*Deo gratias!*"[2]

And Abbot Udualrich gave him his blessing, slowly and solemnly.

"

The bell was calling the monks to Compline. Some brethren remained in Hermann's cell. The lame man's breathing became ever heavier; he gasped as his poor breast rose and sank again. Berthold took him in his arms and let his head, wet with perspiration, rest on his shoulder. The dying man's breathing became even more labored. What mountain of pain must he still cross? His compan-

2. [The words of dismissal at the end of the liturgy: "Go, the Mass is ended," and the people's response: "Thanks be to God!"]

ion moistened his chapped lips with a wet cloth. Then he heard a familiar word between the whistling and wheezing breaths. The word was only a breath, but he understood it perfectly: "Christopher!"

The blue eyes looked at him. There was no more distress in their clear gaze, but only kindness and thanks.

The monk wanted to cry out: "Father, remain here! Do not go!" But he kept silent and prayed.

One of the brethren opened the door, so that fresh air might flow into the cell and make it easier for the dying man to breathe.

"

A south wind blew, carrying the chanting of the choir of monks into the corner cell:

"*Te lucis ante terminum ...*"[3]

Hermann became quiet, and listened. It was clear that he was following the prayers of Compline. His eyes were turned in the direction of the green dusk of the inner courtyard.

"*In manus tuas, Domine, commendo spiritum meum ...* Into your hands, O Lord, I commend my spirit ..." He nodded his assent.

Compline continued: "*Nunc dimittis servum tuum, Domine, secundum verbum tuum ...* Now you let your servant depart, O Lord, in accordance with your word ..."

When Abbot Udualrich blessed the brethren in the monastery church, the trembling right hand of Hermann of Altshausen made the sign of the cross in the air. Whom was he blessing? Himself? Berthold? The abbey?

---

3. ["(We beseech) you before the ending of the light."]

He now breathed calmly and lightly. There was no sign of fear on his face. A child was going home. As a child, he had left Altshausen to look for heaven. Now he was given the joy of seeing the curtain lift—the curtain that separated heaven and earth.

Berthold wanted to lay him down. He was afraid that the sitting posture might hasten the end. Then the monks began the *Salve Regina,* which they sang every evening after Compline.

"*Salve Regina ... Mater misericordiae ...*"[4]

The lame man's lips moved soundlessly. His eyes lit up. Was he joining in his spirit, in his heart, in singing the canticle in honor of his beloved heavenly Mother? Soon, he would see her, and she would show him her Son.

The choir finished the canticle: "*Et Jesum benedictum fructum ventris tui nobis post hoc exsilium ostende ...*"[5]

All at once, Berthold felt that the dying man was being taken out of his hands. The head rose from the shoulder that supported it; the crooked upper body straightened up; the trembling hands stretched out like a vessel, wide open and demanding to be filled.

"Father?" stammered Berthold in his alarm. He knelt down, without knowing what he was doing.

The dying man remained in the same posture. He smiled. A radiant shining transfigured his face, and his eyes reflected an unfathomable bliss.

And the monks in the corner cell clearly heard two words that erupted victoriously and exultantly from his mouth: "Light! Light!"

---

4. ["Hail, O Queen ... Mother of mercy."]

5. ["And show us Jesus, the blessed fruit of your womb, after this exile."]

And after a short pause, Hermann of Altshausen said in an astonished voice: "Lord?"

He drew a trembling breath that resembled a sob of joy, and his body fell back onto the bed.

His friend's hand gently moved over the dead man's eyelids and closed them. Had his eyes seen the Lord?

"

Once again, the bell that announced deaths tolled its solitary song through the starry September night. Berthold walked slowly over the inner courtyard.

He lifted his eyes to the tower of the monastery church, the tower of the Lord Berno. He saw the sky, the innumerable stars that Hermann had loved because they proclaimed the greatness and glory of God. Three or four shooting stars were just falling along their golden path, as had often happened on September nights when the sick man sat awake at his window.

Berthold went on with dragging steps, overwhelmed by tiredness and grief. The empty place that the Father's death had made in his life would never be filled again.

Such a friendship in the Lord is a very rare and incomparable gift. "How good, that I did not understand the mechanism of the water clock that time," he thought, and could not suppress a smile. God often links his gifts to strange things …

Alongside the grief, there was also joy in his heart. The Father no longer had to bear the unrelenting pains of his sickness. Now he could live at last, he could be completely alive in Jesus Christ.

The young monk shrank from the thought of being

alone for a long time, of inner solitude, and of a path that would be difficult without his spiritual guide. He had been his bridge to God. Would he continue in that role?

"Father, you must help me! You know me. You know all my foolish impetuosity ..."

Berthold stopped once more. A bundle of sheets, closely covered in writing, rustled in his hand. He would do what the abbot had just given him permission to do. The abbot had made no objection. The Lord Udualrich grieved sincerely and deeply for the Father, and the entire community of Reichenau grieved with him. "They loved him, even if they did not always understand him. And did I always understand him? How often he had to wait patiently until I grasped what he meant. But he always conquered through his selfless love. He loved us, and that is why he remained the conqueror ... Father, do not forget Reichenau!"

Berthold recalled what he proposed to do. The Pope who had given him the commission to write down the life of Hermann of Altshausen was now dead. Should he expose the Father's life to every inquisitive eye, to anyone who lacked reverence and might pluck it to pieces, or even laugh at it?

"I will write down the most important things about the Father. I will sketch a portrait of his life. Anyone who wants to get to know him better and in a spiritual way, anyone who wants to experience him, so to speak, ought to do it in Hermann's own way. He must take the path that the Father took. He can find him in Jesus Christ, if he loves and suffers and serves. Yes, then he will meet him in the Lord, he will learn to understand him and love him. The Father will come close to those who try to forget themselves, and whose life becomes more and more like his own, a life that bears another name ... *Christus—vita mea ...*"

"

Berthold made up his mind, and went into the kitchen. The brethren looked at him in astonishment, but he said nothing as he went through the big sooty room. The open hearth painted wild pictures of flame on the low ceiling. For one instant, he stopped and looked at the flickering tongues of fire. Then he made a sign of the cross and flung the sheets into the flames with a quick movement. The fire crouched down, as if it wanted to go out. It became almost dark in the room.

But the red-yellow flames, like shining arms, reached out for the parchments, and then everything was a flame, a bright, high, and pure flame ... and Berthold stood in the midst of the light.

THE AUTHOR

Sister Maria Calasanz Ziesche was born on April 29, 1923, in Düren in the Rhineland. She joined the Congregation of the Sisters of Our Lady in Mühlhausen on the Lower Rhine in 1951, and made her religious profession there on August 12, 1953. After studies at the Pedagogical Academy, she worked as a teacher and head of the boarding house at St. Joseph's High School in Rheinbach near Bonn until her retirement. Her unforgettable historical novels and other works were written during this period. They feature the great figures of Reichenau: the itinerant Bishop Pirmin (*Stab und Quelle*), Abbot Berno (*Die leeren Hände*), and Hermann the Lame (*Die letzte Freiheit*, which has also been translated into Croatian, Czech, and Slovakian). She died on July 31, 2001, while she was on holiday in Allensbach-Hegne on Lake Geneva. Her secret wish had been to give her life back into the hands of God at Lake Constance, looking out toward the island of Reichenau, and this wish was granted.

You May Also Like

Asta Scheib

Katharina and Martin Luther
The Scandalous Love Story at the Heart of the Reformation

Illustrious German novelist Asta Scheib
offers a remarkable window into the intensity
and depth of one of history's most notable
marriages, told from Katharina's viewpoint.
Starting from the dramatic night that Katharina
and her fellow nuns were smuggled out of
the convent, to the decisive moments of the
Reformation itself, this novel is sure to
provide suspense, inspiration, and delight.

Paperback, 268 pages,
978-0-8245-2366-4

*Support your local bookstore or order
directly from the publisher at
www.crossroadpublishing.com.*

*To request a catalog or inquire about
quantity orders,
e-mail sales@crossroadpublishing.com.*

The Crossroad Publishing Company